STEVE BRICKMAN – SUPERCHARGED FIGHTING MACHINE

Everything came into extra-sharp focus. Steve saw, with dreadful clarity, the samurai raise and draw the bow; saw the faint glint of light on the wide-bladed, razor-sharp steel point, felt his heart miss a beat as his chest tensed in anticipation of the fearful, piercing blow.

Steve was less than ten yards from the archer, but as the bow-string was released and the arrow sped towards his chest, he advanced the curving blade of the quarterstaff and swung his body to the left.

The steel-tipped point struck the angled bl‍ and was deflected upwards. Steve saw i‍ moving streak of light as it flashed ‍ shoulder, then heard a strangle‍ back, he saw that the arrow‍ in the throat of the ride‍

Also by Patrick Tilley:

PATRICK TILLEY

The Amtrak Wars
Book 3: Iron Master

ORBIT

For Sophie, Mike and Adrienne

An *Orbit* Book

First published in Great Britain by Sphere Books Ltd 1987
Reprinted 1987, 1988, 1989, 1990, 1991
Reprinted by Warner Books 1993
Reprinted 1993, 1995
Reprinted by Orbit 1998

ISBN 1 85723 537 1

Printed in England by Clays Ltd, St Ives plc

Orbit
A Division of
Little, Brown and Company (UK)
Brettenham House
Lancaster Place
London WC2E 7EN

THE AMTRAK FEDERATION & ITS ENEMIES · 2990 AD

Northern Limit of Mute Territory not yet established

OVERGROUND TERRITORY
CLAIMED BY FEDERATION

Total Control

Mutes killed or enslaved

Partial Control

Marauding Mute clans

Disputed Territory

Way-stations established

IRON MASTERS

PLAINFOLK MUTES

SOUTHERN MUTES

OUTER STATES

NEW TERRITORIES

OUTER STATES

INNERSTATE

SOUTHERN MUTES

The following list is a guide to the names given by the Iron Masters to major towns and locations in Book 3.

Ari-bani	Albany, NY	Kei-pakoda	Cape-Cod, Mass
Ari-dina	Reading, Pa	Konei-tika	Connecticutt River
Ari-geni	Allegheny River	Mana-tana	Manhattan I, NY
Ari-saba	Harrisburg, Pa	Mah-ina	Maine
Aron-giren	Long Island, NY	Mara-bara	Marlboro, Mass
Atiran-tikkasita	Atlantic City, NJ	Masa-chusa	Massachusetts
Awashi-tana	Washington, DC	Mei-suri	Missouri River
Awiri-kasaba	Wilkes Barre, Penn	Midiri-tana	Middletown, Penn
Awirimasa-poro	Williamsport, Penn	Mira-woki	Milwaukee, Minn
Awo-seisa	Worcester, Mass	Mi-shiga	Lake Michigan
Baru-karina	Brooklyn, NY	Nofo-skosha	Nova Scotia
Bari-timoro	Baltimore, Md	Nya-gara	Niagara Falls
Basa-tana	Boston, Mass	Nyo-jasai	New Jersey
Bei-sita	Bay City, Mi	Nyo-poro	Newport, RI
Bu-faro	Buffalo, NY	Nyo-yoko	New York City, NY
Du-aruta	Duluth, Minn	Ori-enita	Orient Pt, LI
Eri-siren	Ellis Island	O-hiyo	Ohio River
Firi	Philadelphia, Penn	Porofi-danisa	Providence, RI
Fyah-jina	Virginia	Pi-saba	Pittsburgh, Penn
Gofo-nasa	Governor's I, NY	Ro-diren	Rhode Island
Hui-niso	Windsor, Ontario	Sa-piryo	Lake Superior
Iri	Lake Erie	Sara-kusa	Syracuse, NY
Iyuni-steisa	United States	Skara-tana	Scranton, Penn
	(of America)	Sta-tana	Staten I, NY
Kara-li	Carlisle, Penn	Taro-ya	Troy, NY
Kari-faran	Cleveland, Ohio	Uda-sona	Hudson River
Karo-rina	Carolina	Uti-ka	Utica, NY

THE SEVENTEEN DOMAINS
OF NE-ISSAN 2990 AD

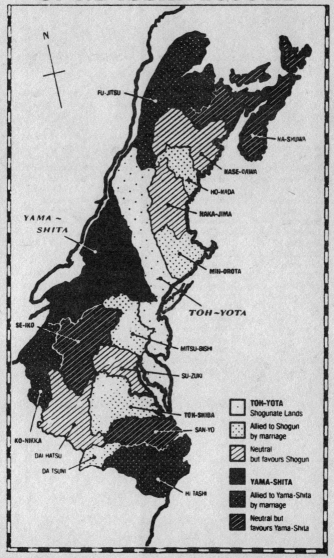

N

FU-JITSU

NA-SHUWA

NASE-GAWA

HO-NADA

NAKA-JIMA

YAMA ~
SHITA

MIN-OROTA

TOH ~ YOTA

SE-IKO

MITSU-BISHI

SU-ZUKI

TOH-SHIBA

KO-NIKKA

SAN-YO

DAI HATSU

DA TSUNI

HI TASHI

TOH-YOTA
Shogunate Lands

Allied to Shogun
by marriage

Neutral
but favours Shogun

YAMA-SHITA

Allied to Yama-Shita
by marriage

Neutral but
favours Yama-Shita

*The following extract is drawn from
the First Family's private archives
stored within
COLUMBUS,
the guiding intelligence of the Federation.*

RELEASE LEVEL: FF–1 thru 5 ONLY

IRON MASTER/S (*generic noun of Mute origin*)

A race of clear-skinned hairless anthropoids inhabiting the eastern coastal strip of America from Maine to North Carolina. The overground area under their control (known as Ne-Issan) includes the western flank of the Appalachian mountain range and extends across the Ohio state line as far as Cleveland, a navref point on the shores of Lake Erie.

Iron Masters have their roots in illegal immigrant communities of various asiatic sub-types that managed to infiltrate the major north-eastern urban centres during the pre-Holocaust era. Between AD 2300 and 2400, there was a small but significant influx of 'boat-people'; asiatics who spoke a language known as 'Japanese'. Allying themselves with the resident groups of similar origin, the boat-people rapidly seized power and have remained the dominant racial group ever since.

On the evolutionary scale, Iron Masters are positioned halfway between the Trackers and the Mutes, who are inferior to both. Officially categorised as a sub-human species, Iron Masters are, nevertheless, literate, numerate individuals with a high degree of manipulative skills, proficient in agriculture, fishing, wood- and metal-working (esp: weapons), weaving and building with dressed stone.

Through a process of genetic mutation common to all sub-human species and the lower animal orders, Iron

Masters have become immune to atmospheric radiation but, once again, acquisition of immunity has had a negative impact on other vital functions. In the case of the Iron Masters, the most obvious side-effects are their diminutive stature, yellow-tinted skin, and total lack of body hair, but the greatest damage has been to the circulatory system. This manifests itself in a high incidence of haemophilia, and weak-walled blood vessels which can rupture under stress, bringing about a fatal haemorrhage.

Through *bushido* (see following reference) these inherent defects have acquired positive values, engendering a calm, disciplined approach to life and an unquestioning acceptance of death.

Iron Master society is a pyramidal class structure based on a 17th-century model ruled by warriors (*samurai*). Below them, in descending order, are – administrators and scribes, craftmasters, merchants, farmers. The base of this pyramid is underpinned by a large reservoir of slave labour; Mutes obtained through barter deals. At all levels of society, women are allocated a secondary, subservient role as consorts, housekeepers and child-bearers.

Supreme power is vested in the *shogun*, head of the leading samurai family and titular head of the government (*bakufu*). The *shogun* is, in theory, supported by the heads of the other *samurai* families who hold the title of domain-lords.

As their title suggests, these individuals derive their power and wealth from their territorial possessions and the population under their direct control. They also lead and maintain private armies pledged (again in theory) to the service of the *shogun* and the maintenance of law and order.

As expected, the main features of such a society are (*a*) its martial character and (*b*) its respect for authority and tradition. Over the years, these attitudes have been codified into a belief-system (*bushido*) which lays great emphasis on duty/obligation to one's superiors (*giri*), to which any human feeling (*ninjo*) takes second place. The result is unquestioning obedience and loyalty, first to one's own domain-lord and through him to the *shogun*.

Succession is through the male line, and some shogunates hold sway for several generations before being displaced by a stronger rival. As the leadership of the First Family is unchallenged and inviolate, this systematised impermanence requires clarification. For Iron Masters, the *shogun* is regarded as 'first among equals'; a domain-lord whose family has won pre-eminence by the consent of his peers or by force of arms. As a result, the power of the shogunate ultimately depends on, and is maintained by, alliances with other domain-lords whose loyalty is spiced with a large measure of self-interest – a pernicious by-product of all 'open' systems.

Although ruled by a warrior caste, the Iron Master's principal activity is internal trade. Mineral resources, agricultural produce and manufactured items are shipped on a supply-and-demand basis from one area to another. All domain-lords are required to make annual support payments (taxes) to the shogunate. The amount paid by each represents a percentage of the assets of their domain. Since the valuation is carried out by government agents, this has, in the past, proved to be a potent source of disaffection.

These payments, together with the sale of trading licences and manufacturing monopolies, provide the revenue needed by the bakufu to carry out the various functions of government.

All surplus goods are bought and sold via a pre-H

medium of exchange known as 'money'. This takes the form of small, thin, rectangular sheets of compressed wood pulp (dollars) and small metal discs (yen), each representing a given number of exchange units (currency) which confers an equivalent purchasing power upon the holder and gives rise to the curious notion of personal 'wealth' – an outmoded concept that the Federation has wisely dispensed with.

EXTRACT ENDS

See related entries: CHINKS, DINKS, GOOKS, JAPS, MEAT-BALLS, NIPS, SLANTS, V–C, YELLOW PERIL.

PROLOGUE

Cadillac handed his bathrobe to his servant, stepped into the deep tub and sank down until the steaming water lapped his chin. Two more female dead-faces, naked except for their white cotton headscarves, stood in the water on either side of him, waiting to cleanse and massage his bronzed body. He motioned them to begin, then closed his eyes and reflected, once again, on his good fortune. Even though he was able to read the future in the seeing-stones, they had not revealed that, in a few short months after leaving the Plainfolk, everything he had ever wished for would be within his grasp. Power, responsibility, a task worthy of his talents, and – most important of all – standing.

His life had been utterly transformed and, for the first time, he felt truly content. The warmth of the water pervaded his body, gently dissolving the flesh and bone. With his eyes still closed against the flickering yellow light of the lanterns he had the sensation of floating, formless, like a spirit-being poured by Mo-Town into the womb of its earth mother.

He cast his mind adrift . . .

*

Shortly after Steve Brickman had soared into the dawn sky, pursued by several posses of Bears, Cadillac began the construction of a second arrowhead from the parts which the clan had kept hidden from the cloud warrior. Armed with the skills and the knowledge he had drawn from Steve's mind, he found it proved a relatively simple task. It was also immensely satisfying, for *his* arrowhead was sleeker and stronger than Bluebird, the ramshackle

5

rig he had helped Steve to build and on which he had been taught how to fly.

Cadillac smiled as he remembered how careful he had been not to learn too quickly. Brickman had gone back to the dark world of the sand-burrowers without realising he had given away the key to a treasure house of information. Using the power granted by Talisman, he had made a mental carbon copy of everything the cloud warrior knew; every fact he had acquired, every learning experience since birth. The entire range of Brickman's talents, skills and knowledge were now his to command.

Yes . . . the loss of Clearwater's soul was a small price to pay for such gifts.

*

The craft was powered by an electric motor culled from one of the Skyhawks that had fallen in the battle with the iron snake. It was the same motor that Brickman had fitted to Bluebird and then discarded just before his escape because he could not make it work properly. Cadillac did what Steve, in his haste, could not be bothered to do; he took it to pieces, checked every part, rebuilt it with loving care, and then continued to work on it until it functioned perfectly.

Now the equal of Brickman in the air, he took off from the bluff above the settlement, skimming with the same lack of fear over the edge of the steep escarpment into the void. He felt the wind embrace him, felt its cool sweet breath upon his face; was overcome by a rapturous sense of freedom as he was borne upwards in great sweeping spirals like the golden eagles who nested on the nearby mountain peaks.

Higher and higher he went, into the sky-world with its ever-changing sunlit terrain, climbing and diving between the towering walls of the cloud canyons. From afar, they looked like vast impregnable wind-carved snowdrifts, but the curving terraces and lofty pinnacles

6

that cried out to be explored melted away as he approached, dissolving into a soft formless veil that enveloped his craft and swallowed the sun – like the dawn mists that shrouded the earth at the Yellowing. For this was the domain of the Sky Voices; a magical landscape that existed only in the mind's eye – serene, awe-inspiring, majestic; endowed with the same fugitive beauty as a rainbow – forever beyond the grasp of mortal man.

Looking down, everything seemed so small. The problems that were so burdensome on the ground shrank into insignificance. The sense of release was so overwhelming, he stayed aloft for two whole hours. Even after landing, he was on such an emotional high, his feet hardly seemed to be touching the ground.

Mr Snow, in his characteristically sly way, let him wallow in the glow of self-adoration for a few days then brought him down to earth with a bump by telling him about the bargain he had struck with the Iron Masters. He made it sound so simple: an arrowhead complete and undamaged plus a cloud warrior in similar condition in exchange for new, long, powerful sharp iron. Rifles . . .

Cadillac responded with a baffled stare. There *was* no arrowhead. The wrecks of the craft launched from the iron snake had been picked to pieces. And the cloud warrior was long gone.

Mr Snow, seated on the other end of the talking mat, read his thoughts and answered with a glum nod. 'You're right. I guess that means it's down to you.'

Sweet Sky Mother. Cadillac went cold at the thought. For no Mute had ever returned from the Fire Pits of Beth-Lem.

Mr Snow brushed aside his objections. Such ingratitude. Was this how he rewarded Talisman – who had made him a wordsmith and seer, and had now made him the equal of any cloud warrior? Gifts such as these were given to be used on behalf of the Plainfolk. 'Don't ever forget what I'm about to tell you,' he said, solemnly wagging his finger. 'There is no such thing as a free lunch.'

'Free lunch . . .?'

Mr Snow brushed aside the question and proceeded to explain the plan in greater detail. Cadillac was to fly north to the Yellow Stone river, then turn east towards the trading post in the lands of the San'Paul. From there he was to follow the shoreline of the great river, the first of several. The last, which ran north to south, was called Iri. Beyond its eastern shore lay the land of the Iron Masters and the domain of Yama-Shita, lord of the wheelboats. To reach the trading post would mean a perilous journey across hostile turf held by the D'Troit and the C'Natti, but by flying high he could evade the bolts from their crossbows. And although it was asking a great deal, it would be safer still if he was prepared to fly when the world slept under Mo-Town's starry cloak. By leaving at sunset before the next full moon he would – if all went well – reach his destination sometime during the following day.

At this point, Mr Snow broke off and rummaged through his untidy pile of possessions. After much cursing he eventually unearthed two folded pieces of cloth which, when opened out, proved to be rectangular banners made of fine white fabric.

In the centre of each was a blood-red disc – the mark of the Iron Masters. The banners – which had been brought from Beth-Lem aboard one of Yama-Shita's wheelboats – were to be fixed beneath the wings of the arrowhead where they could be seen by people on the ground. To ensure its safe reception, the craft was also required to give off a trail of white smoke as soon as it reached Iron Master territory. Green rockets – which Cadillac had seen fired into the sky on his last visit to the trading post – would signal where he was to land.

So far so good. The Iron Masters appeared to have covered all the angles. All except one – the possibility that Mr Snow might proceed to embellish the agreed plan with a few details of his own. Cadillac was to shed his body-paint and go disguised as a Tracker, wearing the clothes of one of the fallen cloud warriors whose head was now staked outside Clearwater's hut. With his clear skin, his newly acquired knowledge and a short haircut, no one would suspect he was not a Federation wingman. But there was more. The ribbon sewn above the right-hand pocket of his tunic would identify him as '8902 BRICKMAN S.R.'

The irony of the situation triggered a burst of shared laughter, obliterating all thoughts of danger – and the equally daunting prospect of losing his long black hair.

While Cadillac tried to strike a mental balance between the risks and the benefits that might flow from accomplishing such a challenging task, Mr Snow unveiled his final surprise. The craft Cadillac had built would need an extra seat for his armed escort.

Clearwater.

Dressed as a She-Wolf, with her unblemished olive skin hidden under swirling patterns of black and brown, Clearwater would pose as an emissary from the clan M'Call. Her real task was to provide moral support and – if the need arose – use her formidable powers as a summoner to protect him and ensure their safe return.

Cadillac bit his lip, choosing not to speak of what he had seen in the stones – that the bond between Clearwater and himself had been broken. Despite the outward pretence, she was no longer his soul-mate. Her thoughts and earth-longings were now centred on the cloud warrior; the Death-Bringer who was fated to return and carry her away on a river of blood.

The blood of the Plainfolk.

At the time when Cadillac had drawn this knowledge from the stones, he had also seen the place where Mr Snow would give up his life so that he, Cadillac, might be saved. In his grief he had shed bitter tears, cursing the gift of seership, and he had silently vowed never to pick up a seeing-stone again. The Wheel turned, the Path was drawn. If nothing could be changed then it was better not to lift the Veil. Let the future hold its secret sorrows; the pain of the present was burden enough.

In the days that followed, as he lengthened the slim fuselage pod and fitted a second seat behind his own, Cadillac tried to come to terms with what had happened. Standing on the bluff with Clearwater and Mr Snow, watching the cloud warrior rise on the freshening wind and turn over the hills towards the south, he had decided there would be no accusations, no recriminations. The true warrior did not allow himself to be deflected by such unworthy emotions as envy or jealousy. But Cadillac had only just begun to take the first few faltering steps along The Way and had not yet attained the necessary degree of philosophical detachment.

Clearwater's infatuation with the cloud warrior had hurt him deeply. Already persuaded by his own inner demons that he lacked standing, he could not bear the idea of being second-best. Had he wished to avenge his honour, he could have denounced her in front of the assembled clan and demanded her death. By the laws of the Plainfolk, her trial would have been a mere formality.

But that route was not open to him. Even now, Cadillac would have gladly given up his own life to save hers. The bonds of friendship, rooted in the shared pain and joy of their childhood and nurtured by their special 'otherness', could never be broken until Mo-Town called their spirits back into the luminous crystal waters that filled the great Cup of Life. Moreover, he had no proof Clearwater had betrayed him. She had not confessed her guilt. Indeed, her manner towards him had hardly changed. But he knew! He knew! Her clouded blue eyes told him that her mind and heart had parted company with his.

He also knew that, as a fellow-summoner, Mr Snow was bound to leap to her defence, leaving him completely tongue-tied. The degree of respect and obedience demanded by the ancient code of the wordsmiths made it impossible for an apprentice to contradict his master publicly. To do so would have been an unforgivable breach of etiquette. But even if he had been foolish enough to try, he could never have won an argument with Mr Snow. Far from gaining any sympathy, he would find himself being mocked by those who envied him and sought to bar him from the ranks of the Bears.

The simplest solution was to drop out of the contest; give up all claim to Clearwater. But even this had its dangers. If she ceased to visit his hut, eyebrows would be raised, tongues would start to wag. And if, as he suspected, she and the cloud warrior had laid between the fox and the wolf, it would not remain secret from her clan sisters for long. Women had a way of knowing these things. They were also unable to keep a secret. Once the news spread it would not be long before both of them were called to account before the clan elders.

No. Regardless of his feelings, the most sensible course of action was to take her with him to Beth-Lem. By so doing the truth could be concealed from the clan until their return – perhaps for ever. Given time, a reconciliation was not impossible. His pride had been hurt but he was not too proud to admit that her presence on such a perilous journey would still be welcome.

What had happened was the will of Talisman. So be it . . .

But understanding had not dulled the pain. Even now, almost nine months later, when his mind and his days were happily filled with the myriad problems that arose from his new responsibilities, the invisible wound would occasionally open, spoiling his newfound contentment. Fortunately, the Iron Masters had a potent cure for this type of affliction – a fiery liquid called 'sake' that gave him a new, reckless courage, gave his tongue a new edge, and awakened desires that his body-slaves eagerly satisfied. And when all passion was spent, and the bittersweet pain had been numbed . . .

Oblivion.

CHAPTER ONE

The summer palace of Yoritomo Toh-Yota was situated at Yedo, on Aron-giren, a huge tract of land that he had christened his 'floating domain'. Yedo was a place-name plucked from the distant past of his own race; Aron-giren was the name given by the people of a long-dead nation which had once inhabited the land on which his palace stood – a fish-shaped island with a ragged forked tail reaching out into the Eastern Sea. A hand-painted silk map on the wall of his book-lined study showed its great shark head lying close to the mainland, with several smaller islands trapped like tiny minnows in its gaping jaw. Long slender reefs of sand hugged the line of its belly like pilot fish hoping for scraps from the feast.

Several other islands lay between Aron-Giren and the mainland; Sta-tana and Mana-tana were the largest; others, like Govo-nasa and Eris-iren, were very small. These too formed part of Yoritomo's domain and, depending on their size, had one fortified harbour or more, garrisoned by sea-soldiers. Day or night, no vessel, be it sea-going junk or one-oared dory, escaped inspection by the everpresent watchboats that patrolled the surrounding waterways, and no one was allowed to dock on Aron-giren when Yoritomo was in residence without a special pass. The vigilance of the sea-soldiers prevented his island retreat from being invaded by what were politely termed 'foreign bodies', and ensured safe passage for Yoritomo, his family and their high-ranking entourage on their journeys to and from his vast estates on the mainland.

The Toh-Yota, who had emerged as one of the leading samurai families in the previous century, had held the

13

reins of power for the last eighty-two years. Yoritomo, its present head, was the sixth successive member of the family to assume the title of Shogun, supreme ruler of Ne-Issan, Land of the Rising Sun. The Toh-Yota had gained their pre-eminence by the matchless skill of their warriors and with the help of their allies – other domain-lords who had risked the heads of their entire families by placing their banners alongside those of Yoritomo's great-great-grandfather.

In the old days, the task of ruling Ne-Issan had been easier. In that first period of rapid conquest, after the landing of the boat-people – the historic 'Seventh Wave' – there had only been a handful of domain-lords but, over the succeeding centuries, new warrior families had emerged in the border regions, planting their banners on the Western Hills and in lands to the south of Awashi-tana. Now, there were seventeen powerful domain-lords; seventeen warrior families backed by their own armies of samurai, each one bound to him by sacred oaths of fealty; some bound closer still by ties of blood.

Since the basic structure remained unchanged, the governing of Ne-Issan should, in theory, have presented no problem. As Shogun, Yoritomo could command the instant obedience of his subjects, from the most powerful domain-lord to the lowest peasant farmer or fisherman. He held the power of life and death, and his decisions in such matters were unchallenged. With a simple, dismissive gesture, and without any explanation, he could order a samurai to commit *seppuku*, ritual disembowelling – an appallingly painful self-inflicted death reserved exclusively for samurai and to which they readily submitted with the most admirable fortitude.

In practice, things were not that simple. If they were, the Shogunate would have no hidden enemies and the shores of Aron-Giren would not need to be guarded against 'foreign bodies'. The one-great Da-Tsuni would still be in power, and the Toh-Yota would still be hewing timber amid the lake-strewn hills on the northern marches. The supreme authority of the Shogun could only be maintained if the holder of that office displayed resolute, forceful leadership combined with an unswerving regard for tradition and an iron will. But it was equally true that those who did not pause to consider the possible consequences of an irreversible decision did not, as a rule, remain in power for long. Action begat reaction. It was a fundamental law. The stone in the water. The Shogun might be revered as a figurehead by the mass of his lower-ranking subjects but to his fellow domain-lords he was first among equals, not an untouchable god-emperor. Despotic behaviour was no longer tolerated. Nowadays, the art of government consisted in striking the right balance. And despite the stark philosophy of *bushido*, the choice, more often than not, was no longer simply between right and wrong, but between the lesser of two evils.

As Shogun, Yoritomo's decisions were influenced by an unceasing flow of information brought to his trusted advisers by a large network of government spies. He knew that the outward calm imposed by the code of *bushido*, the formal etiquette of court procedures and the restrictive ordinances issued by the governing council of ministers formed a screen that concealed a brooding pit of vipers, restless with dreams of power, their forked tongues charged with venomous rumours, forever hatching murderous conspiracies.

Once, loyalty had been given unstintingly, without question. But those were the lean, hard days, when the survival of Ne-Issan was at stake. The establishment of the first Shogunate by the Da-Tsuni, the leaders of the 'Seventh Wave', was a model of purity. Their overthrow had been followed by two centuries of turbulence; periods of uneasy peace interspersed with bloody civil wars. The rise to power of the Toh-Yota had restored the previous authority of the Shogunate, bringing firm government and more than three-quarters of a century of relative peace and prosperity.

But even peace had its dangers. It had enabled the

domain-lords to grow richer and ever more powerful. The annual taxes they were required to pay into the coffers of the Shogunate had also increased the already considerable wealth of the Toh-Yota family, but now loyalty, like everything else, had its price. For prosperity brought not only a change in a society's material wealth, it also changed its values. It awakened the desire for progress, and progress was a two-edged sword that, in the wrong hands, could destroy Ne-Issan just as the world of their ancestors had been destroyed.

Yes, reflected Yoritomo, these were troubled times. Absolute power was a dangerously seductive brew that had to be handled with caution – even more so when it was absolute in name only. There were moments when the task of governing became a crushing burden. On the nights when he lay awake, trying to decide on the correct course of action, Yoritomo often found himself wishing he could exchange his life for the quieter and more rewarding existence of a saddle-maker, an armourer, or a swordsmith. Being Shogun was an awesome responsibility – especially when you were only twenty-eight years old.

*

It was towards the Shogun's summer palace at Yedo that Toshiro Hase-Gawa now journeyed aboard a ferry-boat from Nyo-poro, a fishing village on the cost of Ro-diren. The boat – a wide-hulled barge with steam-powered paddles – steered a westerly course close to the shore, then headed out across the channel following the line of islands that led to the north-eastern tip of Aron-giren.

Despite the fact that the ferry was flying his two personal banners which identified him as a government official, they were intercepted within sight of land by a watchboat, and boarded by a detachment of sea-soldiers. Once a gangway had been secured between the two vessels, the watch-captain hurried aboard the ferry where, after a deferential exchange of greetings, he

16

courteously asked for further proof of Toshiro's identity. When Toshiro's papers bearing the Shogun's personal seals had been reverentially examined, and the ferry thoroughly searched, the watch-captain withdrew his men and offered his profuse apologies for the inexcusable delay. Toshiro responded in similar vein. Had the watch-captain been less zealous, and the search less thorough, he would have had cause to be angry. The sea-soldiers were only carrying out orders and their exemplary bearing brought honour to their regiment and, above all, to their commander. Et cetera, et cetera.

An hour later, the flat, drawbridge bow of the ferry was lowered on to the slipway at Ori-enita, whose only virtue lay in the fact that it was situated at the point where the northern road met the sea. Alerted by the banners carried above the ferry's small wheelhouse, the lowly harbour officials and the few fisherfolk who happened to be ashore gathered expectantly on either side of the road leading away from the beach. The atmosphere of expectancy increased as two sailors carefully removed the banners from the roof of the wheelhouse and took them below. Shortly afterwards, the crew of the ferry assembled on the foredeck and sank to their knees as Toshiro Hase-Gawa appeared in full ceremonial armour astride a proud, stout-legged pony.

They were an imposing sight. Toshiro's body-armour was made up of black lacquered plates edged with gold and fastened together with cords of crimson silk; on his head, a matching helmet with a wide, flaring brim. On the front of the helmet, cut from a circle of polished bronze, was the emblem of the present Shogun – the raised wings, breast and crested head of a long-necked wading bird.

The pony's trappings were of the same stamp and splendour. Its dappled body was caparisoned in black and gold; its mane and tail braided with crimson cords and tassels. The bamboo poles carrying Toshiro's personal banners were now mounted in leather sockets attached to the backplate of his body-armour, the tall narrow bands of silk fluttering and snapping in the sea-breeze.

The spectators on shore fell to their knees as Toshiro directed his steed down the ramp, then pressed their foreheads to the ground as he passed by. Their obeisance was a sign of the reverence accorded to the Shogun and the government officials who, under his guidance, ordered the affairs of their nation. A reverence accorded but also demanded. Had Toshiro been ill received, he could have called for the immediate execution of anyone deemed guilty of insolent behaviour and indeed, as he had demonstrated in the past, was quite capable of carrying out the sentence himself.

Toshiro let the pony take him slowly through the village at a pace known among samurai horsemen as the 'parade trot' – a jaunty, high-stepping walk. The laws that obliged the lower ranks to push their noses into the dirt also obliged their superiors to conduct themselves with a certain style. When he had passed the last prostrate inhabitant, he spurred the pony into a canter along the winding road that led to Yedo.

The road swung from side to side of a narrow, ragged peninsula which, in the mind of the Shogun, formed the upper half of his fish-island's forked tail. To Toshiro's right, waves from the Eastern Sea broke gently on the smoothly curving shore. To his left, the land was eaten away by backwaters and bays, some of which had joined to form islands linked at low tide by threads of rock and sand. Ahead lay a forty-mile stretch of open road. The pony, responding to his urging, lengthened its stride. Behind him, the tall slender poles arched gracefully, their narrow banners with their word-signs and emblems ironed flat by the wind.

*

Toshiro Hase-Gawa was a Herald of the Inner Court, one of a small, select band of samurai who received their instructions from and reported directly to the Shogun.

18

Although such messengers were not of exalted rank, this privileged access to the summit of power meant that Toshiro and his colleagues enjoyed the favour of senior – and sometimes envious – court officials. It also meant they were accorded similar treatment in the houses of the powerful domain-lords, whose hospitality was often designed to loosen tongues.

Heralds of the Inner Court were the Shogun's eyes and ears and spoke with his voice, carrying his innermost thoughts to the furthest corners of his realm. Because of their highly public role they were not officially viewed as being part of the Shogun's network of spies and informers but, amongst the schemers and the power-hungry, they were known to act as a conduit for sensitive information gleaned by important government agents; men (and women) who played many roles and assumed many guises.

*

If an imaginary line were to be drawn through the Shogun's fish-island from tip to tail and the island then divided into three equal parts along the line, Yedo would be found close to the line dividing the second section of the body from the tail. Situated on high ground, almost equidistant from both shores, the multistoreyed summer palace stood aloof from the neat clusters of low-lying dwellings that had been built near by. Under an edict issued by the *bakufu*, no dwelling place could be erected within a league of its walls, and no home within ten leagues could be inhabited by any family unless one or more member of the household was in the direct employ of the Shogun or his court officials.

Built from mortared blocks of stone from the quarries of Baru-karina, the sloping walls of the Yedo palace rose from a huge square moat. Perched atop the walls, fifty feet above the surface of the water, was the first layer of its wood, stone and tile-roofed superstructure. The towers at each corner rose another sixty feet into the air and these were joined together by an intricate maze of screened galleries, with ornate cross-beams and curving rooflines. The feeling it conveyed to an approaching visitor was one of wealth, solidity and power; the precise qualities that its first owner – Yoritomo's grandfather – had demanded of his architects.

The entrance, with its wide, gently arched bridge, was guarded by two keeps; one at the end of the approach road, the other set on a stone island halfway across the moat. This palace, with its pleasure gardens and artfully sculptured rock pools and waterfalls, was also a fortress with secret stairways, exits and entrances.

*

Toshiro had no need to show his papers at the outer keep. The guard-captain, alerted by a keen-eyed sentinel, recognised him with the aid of a spyglass and rode out with two other samurai to meet him. Captain Kamakura and Toshiro exchanged the usual saluta-tions, but their voices lent a warmth to the formal exchanges. They were old friends despite the difference in their ages. Kamakura, the senior by some fifteen years, had helped Toshiro to perfect his swordmanship and would practise with him, or counsel him, whenever asked.

Over the last two years, Toshiro had been constantly on the move, arriving with eagerly awaited information only to find himself dispatched on some new errand with barely time to catch his breath. As a consequence, the two men had seen less of each other than they would have liked but their friendship remained undimmed.

Kamakura, a samurai cursed with five daughters, treated him like a surrogate son. Whenever Toshiro came to Aron-giren, the captain and his wife Yukio received him into their household with the utmost warmth and generosity. Although Toshiro had never doubted his mentor's sincerity, it was only natural to assume that at the back of this charming couple's mind was the hope that one of their daughters might find favour in his eyes. It was evidently a hope shared by their offspring because, over the years, all but the youngest, who was not yet thirteen, had taken it in turns to favour him with a more intimate form of hospitality.

Their nocturnal visits which, by custom, one was not expected to refuse, had been executed with an admirable discretion equal to that practised by the ladies of the court. And their subsequent behaviour gave not the slightest hint of what had occurred. Each one had remained as courteous and respectful as before. Toshiro had said nothing to their father. He preferred to think that the good captain had no idea what was going on. However, the expertise his daughters had displayed could not have been achieved without *some* degree of parental guidance. Although it was something that he and Kamakura had never discussed, Toshiro knew that their mother had once been a courtesan. It was a well-known fact that the warmth of their embrace was often fuelled by a burning ambition.

The two horsemen who had ridden out with Kamakura dismounted and rejoined the guard as Kamakura and Toshiro trotted their ponies through the arches of the outer and inner keeps and went on into the main courtyard of the palace. Civilians – mainly tradesmen of low rank – who found themselves on the bridge fell to their knees and pressed their faces to the close-fitting planks. The iron-shod feet of the ponies sent thunderous echoes through their heads as the riders passed by.

As a member of the house of Hase-Gawa, Toshiro had his family home on the seaward edge of the northern marches. Only two domains were equally remote – the Fu-Ji and the Na-Shuwa, whose lands lay to the north-west and north-east of the Hase-Gawa. Beyond them lay the Fog People. Kamakura, on the other hand, resided on Aron-giren. As a close friend and his swordmaster it was only natural to offer his house to the younger man, even though accommodation was always available for Heralds whenever they arrived and wherever the court happened to be. The Shogun had four other palatial fortresses on the mainland and numerous other residences on the Toh-Yota family estates.

Toshiro thanked Kamakura for the invitation and promised to dine with him at the earliest opportunity. Unfortunately, he could make no plans until he had reported to the Shogun. Only then would he know whether he would have time to sample the delectable joys of family life in the Kamakura household before being dispatched on some new errand. In the meantime, he begged the good captain to convey his respectful yet tender greetings to Yukio, his wife, and her five daughters whose peerless beauty, selfless devotion and pristine decorum reflected nothing but credit upon their parents. Et cetera, et cetera.

Kamakura wheeled away and headed back across the bridge, his honour satisfied. Since his respect and friendship for the young man pre-dated Toshiro's elevation to the rank of Herald he knew that his offer of hospitality would not be construed as an attempt to curry favour. Nevertheless, as his wife constantly reminded him, any one of their eligible daughters would make an ideal match for Toshiro. And with a Herald for a son-in-law, the marriage prospects for the remaining girls would be immeasurably increased. One noble scion was the least they could expect. Maybe two!

Women! Despite their supposedly submissive, secondary status, it was rare to find one able to resist the lure of social advancement. It was just as well they had a multitude of domestic tasks to attend to: otherwise their days would be filled with all manner of vainglorious dreams. In his years of service with the Shogunate, Kamakura had seen enough to know that, unless governed by an acute and disciplined intellect, bodies freed from the daily grind of physical labour or the demands of soldiering soon became breeding grounds for discontent. Idleness led first to the unbridled pursuit of pleasure, then, when jaded appetites could no longer be whetted by the most deviant perversions, the ladies of the court turned into malicious gossips and schemers. Having destroyed their own sense of moral worth, they set out to destroy those around them. There were men of privilege who fell into this category too – and it had led to the collapse of more than one Shogunate.

Nobility, reflected Kamakura, was not all it was trumped up to be. It was the samurai ethic that was the bulwark against mental and physical corruption, and he was thankful that the new Shogun was the embodiment of all he held dear. Unfortunately, Yukio, his wife who, as a young concubine, had pleasured the present Shogun's father did not share this jaundiced view of the nobility – even though her lord and master, in a fit of generosity, had presented her to Kamakura in return for services rendered. Yukio, then a slim girl with a flawless, resilient body, had submitted dutifully as her status demanded but, like all women, she had found ways to convey her resentment.

That was in the beginning. Their relationship had improved in the intervening years for, with time, he had proved a reasonable catch, especially when Yoritomo, on his accession to power, had promoted him to the rank of guard-captain and, at the same time, had swept the remaining sybarites out of his father's 'pleasure dome'. But the gilded life of the Inner Court leaves an indelible mark. Kamakura knew that, in her heart of hearts, Yukio wished she could have married into the nobility which, for a daughter of a well-to-do merchant family, had not been beyond the bounds of possibility. There were times when even Kamakura wished he could have been born with a silver cup to his lips. But he was old enough and wise enough to know that the fledgling heirs to wealth, power and privilege often found themselves holding a poisoned chalice.

*

Entering the palace, Toshiro presented himself to Ieyasu, the Court Chamberlain, and learned that word of his arrival had already reached the Shogun. The Herald was to join him in the pebble garden as soon as he had cleansed his travel-stained body.

Ieyasu, a tall angular man with a lined, cadaverous face, prided himself on his efficiency. How it was achieved was something of a mystery to Toshiro. Ieyasu never seemed to *do* anything and on the rare occasions. Toshiro had seen him in motion, each gesture, like his speech, was slow, deliberate and precise. He exuded a quality of stillness – and a disquieting degree of menace – like a female spider poised at the centre an invisible web of power.

Toshiro thanked the Chamberlain in the customary manner and exited backwards from his presence.

Ieyasu made his way to the window and watched Toshiro swagger across the small courtyard below followed by the two pages who carried his travelling bags. Such energy! Such muscular dedication! Where would it all end? Under the previous Shogun, Ieyasu had acted as a filter for the information that the Heralds had carried to and from court. But Yoritomo had changed all that. Nowadays, this new band of jumped-up jack-a-knaves reported to the Shogun in person – and in private! An unheard-of and most unwelcome break with ancient tradition which opened the way to a further dilution of the powers held by the office of the Chamberlain.

Ieyasu was one of the 'old school'. He had held the same post under Yoritomo's father and, barring some unforeseen disaster, was widely expected to remain in office until he became senile; a state which some of his critics felt he had reached already. On his accession, Yoritomo had pensioned off many of his father's staff, along with the inhabitants of the 'pleasure dome'. The sybarites and the obsequious self-serving leeches that somehow always manage to gravitate towards the centre of power had gone. But Ieyasu had remained. A new

24

broom can never sweep entirely clean. And contrary to accepted wisdom, some old dogs are remarkably adept at learning new tricks.

In a nation built upon ancient traditions and held together by the rigid observance of age-old customs and protocols, changes are seen as a threat to the fabric of society – to be resisted at all cost. They can only be introduced gradually, if at all, and when making them, the wise leader does so whilst maintaining a strong sense of continuity with the past. Ieyasu was not the person Yoritomo would have liked as his Chamberlain but he was, without doubt, the best man for the job. The sly old fox knew everything and everybody and Yoritomo – then only twenty-three – was quick to see that he had to ally himself with Ieyasu until he had made his own position more secure. As a result, his cleansing operation had removed the froth and the scum but, when calm returned, the basic mixture was very much as before. Apart from the new status of the Heralds – a point which the old fox had deemed advantageous to concede – Ieyasu's power and influence remained unchanged, and most of the key positions were still occupied by like-minded place-men.

Yoritomo was aware of the situation, and although there were other means by which Ieyasu could have been removed he was content to leave things as they were. Palace revolutions were destabilising events, which sent shock-waves through the country and gave people ideas. Besides which, he enjoyed pitting his wits against the wily old campaigner. Time was on his side, and it was precisely this – his extreme youthfulness – that was the root of the problem. The Chamberlain, with his wealth of experience, honestly believed that someone as young as Yoritomo should not make any decisions without first seeking his advice and approval. He was, after all, his grand-uncle.

As one of the family, Ieyasu's loyalty to the Shogunate was beyond question but he was, above all, an influence-pedlar who knew every step of the way along the corridors of power; a man who could dispense sought-after privileges and preferments – and was not averse to enriching himself in the process. In so doing, the Chamberlain embraced an earthier tradition which pre-dated the rise of the samurai ethic by many thousands of years and which, given time, Ieyasu felt that Yoritomo would come to recognise as the only one worth preserving: the exercise and maintenance of power in a world of increasing complexity.

A problem that was as old as Time itself.

It was laudable of the young man to seek a return to the purer forms of conduct as prescribed by *bushido*: it was right that he should place new emphasis on its central tenet, *giri* – the sense of duty and obligation. Without it there would be anarchy! But the drive to impose a stricter morality was counter-productive. Human beings were flawed creatures that could never attain the perfection of the higher *kami*. Their inherent venality always surfaced sooner or later and, deplorable though it might be, it was through their weaknesses that they could be more effectively controlled.

Sinners were easier to do business with. And also much better company. Despite his advanced years, Ieyasu had not forgotten how to enjoy himself. And in his case, it was not only the spirit that was willing.

*

The pebble garden was made up of a subtle arrangement of rocks set amid an undulating sea of fine gravel which had been raked into a seamless pattern of lines and whorls. Each morning at first light, and at various times throughout the day, leaves, twigs and all other extraneous matter were assiduously removed by a team of light-footed gardeners who raked the gravel back into place as they made their exit. When the Shogun came, the garden was always magically restored to pristine condition. It was a landscape frozen in time, an exquisitely harmonious arrangement of line and tone, texture and mass which, like all great masterworks, constantly revealed new depths to the eye of the beholder. It induced serenity and invited profound contemplation, rewarding and restoring those whose minds were able to achieve the necessary degree of stillness.

Yoritomo was one of those who drew strength from the garden – a treasured re-creation of a fragment of a past life in a place known to the chroniclers as The World Before. Yoritomo had fallen under its magic spell at the age of nine, and from then on had made daily visits to the same spot on the top step of the veranda whenever his branch of the family had been in residence at Yedo. His feelings toward it had not changed – only now, no one else was allowed to sit in his chosen place which, upon his accession, had assumed the status of a shrine.

Although austere by nature, Yoritomo was not, and had no wish to become, an ascetic saint-like figure. During his adolescence, his periods of contemplation had been sandwiched in between the normal activities and youthful excesses one would expect a young nobleman to indulge in. Sensual delights, while not encouraged, were not forbidden and although young samurai were taught that the companionship of other warriors was preferable to that of women, they were not always able to resist the lure of a sentimental – and sometimes illicit – relationship. And neither could the new Shogun.

Toshiro, now clad in a broad-shouldered kimono of dark-toned brocaded silk, approached the guard-captain whose men were posted round the perimeter of the pebble garden. Both samurai wore white headbands fastened at the nape of the neck over wigs made of Mute hair, swept upwards to form the traditional top-knot. The guard-captain's headband bore the usual blood-red disc flanked by two word-signs denoting his rank and function. On Toshiro's headband, the Shogun's bird emblem took the place of the red disc. A long and short sword, housed in gently curving scabbards, were thrust through the sash around his waist.

Had he been anyone else, he would have been obliged

to remove them but, as a Herald of the Inner Court, he had the right to bear arms in the presence of the Shogun. It was a sign of the extraordinary trust Yoritomo had in this band of young men. It was not entirely by chance that Toshiro happened to be the same age as the Shogun. None of the new Heralds chosen by Yoritomo was over thirty; the youngest was twenty-five.

The guard-captain led Toshiro along the path towards the open-sided summerhouse where Yoritomo sat cross-legged, lost in contemplation of the stone landscape. The five samurai seated behind him in a semicircle sprang silently to their feet, then relaxed their grip on the handles of their long-swords when they saw who it was. These men, like the guard around the garden, had been raised from birth in the Toh-Yota family household and were totally dedicated to the protection of the Shogun. The guard-captain bowed low and backed away as Toshiro mounted the wide lower step of the veranda and knelt down in line with the Shogun's left shoulder. Yoritomo continued to stare straight ahead at the garden. Toshiro placed his forehead on the straw matting covering the top step and waited.

'What kept you?' said the Shogun, in perfect American-English. It was a language he and his Heralds were able to speak fluently – although they were not encouraged to use the same colloquial mode of address. The five guards, now ranged on the far side of Yoritomo, spoke only Japanese.

Toshiro assumed a cross-legged position. 'There were certain aspects of the situation that needed further investigation, sire. It wasn't easy. They're playing the cards close to their chest.'

'Are they holding many aces?'

'I'm not sure, but . . . there's a joker in the pack.'

Yoritomo dragged his eyes reluctantly from the pebble garden and let them rest briefly on Toshiro. The Shogun also wore a wig made from Mute hair but it was a more imposing arrangement made of coiled plaits combined with a small, flat pill-box hat and lacquered wooden combs – a design exclusive to his rank as the overlord of Ne-Issan. 'Is this going to be as bad as I think it is?'

Toshiro bowed low. 'It's not good.'

Yoritomo sighed and returned to his contemplation of the stone landscape. 'Okay, let's have it . . .'

CHAPTER TWO

During the past six months, Toshiro's principal task had been to monitor the work being carried out at the Heron Pool – a new craft centre that had been set up to the west of Ba-satana. At the beginning of the previous year Lord Yama-Shita, who held the licence to trade with the Northern Mutes, had persuaded Yoritomo of the need to rediscover the secrets of powered flight. His plan had been to seek the aid of the Mutes in obtaining a flying-horse and its rider. Much could be learned from a close examination of both, saving months, perhaps even years, of fruitless experimentation.

In pressing his case, Yama-Shita had emphasised that there was little time to lose. The desert warriors of the south – called lone-dogs because of their height and their angular, bony features – were poised to move north into the lands of the Plainfolk. In a few short years, their powerful weaponry might be turned against Ne-Issan. Through his contacts with the Mutes, Yama-Shita knew that the flying-horses were an important element in the long-dogs' military strategy. Ne-Issan must equip itself with its own airborne cavalry in order to meet the threat when it eventually came.

Yoritomo promised to think the matter over. It all made sense, of course. Lord Hiro Yama-Shita – who, with the merger between the Yama-Ha and the Matsu-Shita families, had become the single most powerful domain-lord in Ne-Issan – was a hard-headed realist. Any proposal put forward by him merited serious consideration.

It had been the Yama-Ha and the Matsu-Shita, builders of the first wheelboats, who had opened up the lucrative western trading routes and had tapped into the

30

seemingly exhaustible supply of Mutes – the strangely marked half-humans that made up the bulk of Ne-Issan's labour force. The licences, which gave them a virtual monopoly on trade with the west, had been granted by Yoritomo's grandfather. The Yama-Ha and Matsu-Shita had long been allies of the Toh-Yota and had supported them in their bid for the Shogunate. But the unprecedented marriage between the two houses had resulted in an unwelcome concentration of power and, if one looked at the map with the eye of a military commander, their combined domains were poised like a dagger at the heart of the Toh-Yota.

Fortunately, the forty-year-old Yama-Shita seemed to be more interested in trade deals than political alliances, but it was a situation that had to be kept constantly under review. The country had been riven more than once by factional disputes, and despite the era of firm central government instituted by the Toh-Yota, the domain-lords had kept a jealously guarded measure of independence. While all had sworn oaths of fealty to the Shogunate, there were some whose word could not be taken entirely at its face value. As a result, Yoritomo, like the previous holders of high office, kept two lists in his head – one headed *fudai*, those considered loyal and trustworthy; the other, *tozama*, unreliable.

Hiro Yama-Shita, despite his family's links with the Toh-Yota, occupied a grey area in between.

After consulting Ieyasu (the Chamberlain had known Hiro since he was a boy), Yoritomo agreed to the acquisition of a flying-horse and its rider. Through Yama-Shita's trading activities, a number of long-dogs had fallen into their hands. Their interrogation had enabled the Shogun to build up a partial picture of the strange underground domain known as the Federation. But their testimony was flawed. These captive long-dogs were criminals, renegades – like the small bands of rootless *ronin* that lurked in dark recesses of the forests blanketing the slopes of the western hills. The pale warriors of this underground world could also be disloyal

31

to their masters. Even so, the threat from the south could not be ignored. Hence the chosen strategy, put into effect through Yama-Shita, to arm the Mutes, who were numerically superior to both sides.

Because of their alien culture and backwardness, the Mutes could never be considered as allies, but their concept of warrior-hood was worthy of respect. The years of trading had brought about a state of friendly neutrality. No pledges had been exchanged, no plans were ever discussed but, over the last few years, Plainfolk territory had become a buffer zone protecting the frontiers of Ne-Issan. The warrior clans were now armed auxiliaries who, if everything went according to plan, would wear the long-dogs down in a slow war of attrition.

On Ieyasu's advice, Yoritomo had awarded the manufacturing licence for the flying-horses to Kiyomori Min-Orota, whose lands, bordering the Eastern Sea, lay just across the water to the north of Aron-giren. Kiyomori's father had married one of Yoritomo's aunts and the Min-Orota were on the list marked *fudai*.

As the snows deepened, burying the old year, Toshiro had returned with his first dispatch: a flying-horse had landed near Bu-faro, a harbour on Lake Iri on the western border of Lord Yama-Shita's domain. It carried two riders: a long-dog called Brickman and his escort, a female Mute warrior from the clan M'Call, who were the donors of this long-awaited object.

Without more ado, the craft and its riders had been shipped via the canal and river system to Ro-diren and from there by road to the aptly named Heron Pool, the site chosen for this new enterprise. The workshops had not yet been constructed at the time of Toshiro's first visit, but he had brought back sketches of the alien craft together with verbal portraits of Brickman, the brown-skinned long-dog, and Clearwater, his blue-eyed Mute escort.

After an initial hesitation, Brickman had proved remarkably co-operative and eager to please. The Mute, on the other hand, had informed Yama-Shita – with all due deference and through the usual intermediaries – that the clan M'Call had delivered the flying-horse on the understanding that she and the long-dog were to be shipped back to her homeland when the wheelboats made their next voyage across the great lakes.

But there had been no such understanding. The eventual fate of those delivering the craft had never been raised by the white-haired leader of the M'Call's trade council. And Yama-Shita had no intention of renegotiating the agreement with a female Mute. Once they set foot in Ne-Issan, Mutes were slaves; non-persons with no rights whatsoever. But even if this had been the case, by the very nature of the enterprise, Clearwater's request was bound to fall on deaf ears. It was vital that the Federation should remain unaware of what was afoot for as long as possible. If she and the long-dog were to return to the Plainfolk and subsequently fall into enemy hands, it would be a secret no longer.

As the Mute had no further part to play, she had been placed in the custody of Consul-General Nakane Toh-Shiba, nephew to the domain-lord of that name. Nakane was the permanent representative of the Shogun to the House of Min-Orota. Military men, appointed by Yoritomo, held similar posts in all subject domains. They occupied imposing residences on private estates maintained by the Shogunate and which also served as a base for a team of provincial administrators, tax inspectors, and a regiment of government soldiers.

At the Heron Pool, the necessary buildings were completed and a team of long-dogs, recruited from mines and quarries, was set to work under the supervision of local craftsmen. The dark-haired, brown-skinned Brickman quickly revealed himself to be an ideal overseer, totally dedicated to the task he had been assigned. He was, moreover, endowed with a formidable intellect and displayed a keen interest in, and appreciation of, every aspect of Iron Master society; its art, culture, custom and tradition, its spiritual ethos. His grasp of these matters was so instinctive, Min-Orota was moved to seek permission to allow him to be taught Japanese.

Ieyasu had passed his written request to the Shogun with an appended note recommending its rejection. For once, Yoritomo and his Chamberlain found themselves in agreement. Despite his willingness to share his skills and knowledge, the long-dog was an alien, a renegade, and was thus without honour. The language of Ne-Issan was a sacred relic from The World Before that had to be zealously protected. Never again was it to be debased by foreign influences and, above all, it must never be allowed to issue from the mouths of the unworthy. Yoritomo, like his Heralds, might speak what the long-dogs called 'Basic' but that was merely a means by which they could discuss confidential matters in the presence of others.

Brickman, unaware of the representation made on his behalf, continued to work like a man possessed, and by early March, a much-improved version of the craft he had delivered was ready to take to the air. It was to be launched from high ground, gliding like a sea-bird from its clifftop nest. Preparations had also been made to produce several more but, before they could be completed, a suitable mechanism had to be found to move them through the air. Steam was a possibility, but none of the existing engines was small enough, and the craft could not be fuelled by logs or coal whilst in the air! If steam *was* the answer, then a special lightweight engine using entirely new principles would have to be created. Undaunted by the problems, Brickman set to work.

Lord Kiyo Min-Orota, impressed by Brickman's energy and his impeccable demeanour, which was the equal of a samurai's in every respect, sought some way to reward him for the host of useful devices created by his restless pen. This was a goose driven by some inner compulsion to lay golden eggs. The bird must be kept well-fed and given a comfortable nest until it was time to wring its neck.

Like Mutes, long-dogs had traditionally been accorded

slave status, but Min-Orota felt that Brickman was a special case meriting more favourable treatment. And so it was, as if by magic, that Brickman was installed in a small but elegant dwelling-house, staffed by Korean female body-slaves. Lord Min-Orota accepted his effusive thanks without telling him that Koreans, along with Thais and Vietnamese, were one of the 'unpure' breeds who inhabited the lower strata of Iron Master society. To a true Son of Ne-Issan – a samurai from a noble family – the provision of such inferior servants would have been a mortal insult; to the long-dog, unaware of such subtleties, it was an undreamt-of luxury.

During an earlier visit, Toshiro had tactfully conveyed to the domain-lord the Shogun's feeling that Brickman's unprecedented elevation from slave status was both unnecessary and inappropriate. Lord Min-Orota had been at pains to reassure him that it was purely a temporary arrangement which could bring important material benefits not only to his house but to the Shogun himself. And the long-dog's eventual fall from grace would provide an amusing diversion.

But there were other aspects of the present situation which were less amusing and it was upon these that Toshiro proceeded to report. The female Mute who had been taken into protective custody by Consul-General Nakane Toh-Shiba had mysteriously dropped out of circulation. By diligent detective work and with the help of the local network of agents and informers, Toshiro had uncovered an illicit sexual liaison which, although disturbing in itself, had turned out to have far more sinister ramifications.

Toshiro reported on Brickman's latest work, then made a casual reference to the fate of his Mute escort. 'I regret to tell you I have received information from an unimpeachable source that the Consul-General of Masachusa and Ro-diren has given a new meaning to the phrase "protective custody".'

The Shogun reacted with a sharp-eyed glance. 'Are you sure of this?'

'Absolutely. By all accounts he has been gripped by a grand passion. The, ah . . . "lady" in question has been set up in some style with her own body-slaves. Picked from the gutter, of course.'

The Shogun's face showed no sign of the wave of revulsion that swept through him. His eyes remained fixed on the garden. 'Where?'

'His estate includes a lake with a small island in the middle. Apparently there is a house on it. The trees which surround it make it difficult to see from the shore. I believe it has been put to similar use before.'

The Shogun nodded. His face remained impassive but Toshiro knew the mental anguish his news had created. Consul-General Nakane Toh-Shiba was married to one of Yoritomo's sisters. To visit her bedchamber after coupling with a Mute slave was an affront to her honour – and one which, at the appropriate moment, would have to be avenged.

'It's not quite as bad as it seems,' said Toshiro.

'You mean . . . that's the *good* news?'

'Yes, sire. The bad news is . . . she's not a Mute.'

The Shogun closed his eyes and breathed deeply. 'How come you didn't notice when she arrived?'

'I had no reason to suspect anything. We had been told the long-dog would have a Mute warrior escort. Who could have figured she was decked out in body-paint? I don't know what prompted her to remove her disguise, but she's clear-skinned – just like Brickman. They're two of a kind.'

'Both long-dogs . . .'

Toshiro watched the Shogun as he weighed up the implications. Their eyes met. 'Why the deception?'

Toshiro chose his words carefully. 'Perhaps the deal that Lord Yama-Shita claimed to have set up with the Mutes was a . . . cover for a more direct arrangement with the manufacturers.'

'The Federation . . .?'

Toshiro bowed under the Shogun's piercing gaze. 'It's the only explanation that makes sense, sire. On the other hand, you may know something I don't.'

'I wish I did.'

'Lord Yama-Shita is a man who likes to make deals.'

'And he's also ambitious. But to suggest he may be in business with the Federation . . .' Yoritomo left the sentence hanging in the air.

'I am aware it's a serious charge.'

'The worst kind of treason. Death for him and his immediate family, plus the confiscation of his entire domain. But before I put Ieyasu on the case I'm going to need more than inspired guesswork.'

'Given time, I think I can get proof. But that doesn't solve the problem of how to put the collar on him.'

'Exactly. Is Kiyo Min-Orota involved?'

'Let me put it this way. I find it hard to believe he doesn't know who the Consul-General is spending most of his afternoons with. Even if the family weren't in on the deal with the long-dogs, they must have put two and two together by now.'

The Shogun sighed regretfully. 'That's all I need.' His mouth tightened. 'How long has my dear brother-in-law been . . .?'

'Since early January.'

'And you've only just found out . . .?'

Toshiro bowed. This was not the moment to make excuses.

'I just don't understand,' mused Yoritomo. 'My sister and her children were here just a few weeks ago. She never gave the slightest hint that anything like this was going on.'

'She may not know, sire. The reason it took me so long to get on to this was that certain people have gone to great lengths to keep the whole thing under wraps.'

Yoritomo breathed out sharply through his nose. 'If he wasn't part of the family he'd be on the mat tomorrow morning. How could he do this to me? It's unforgivable.' He regained his calm and a measure of rueful good humour. 'On the other hand, I can't say it's all that surprising. I've known for some time that he has somewhat eccentric tastes in that department.'

A silence descended as Yoritomo considered the moves that were open to him.

'I suppose we could always put a stop to it by putting something in her rice bowl. Or maybe catch them both together. Make it look like a suicide pact.'

Toshiro answered with a shake of the head. 'Bad move, sire . . .'

'Are you suggesting it can't be done?'

'Not at all. Compared to Lord Yama-Shita, the Consul-General is a reasonably soft target. I just don't think that killing any of the players at this stage of the game would be to our advantage. If the hit was traced back to you . . .'

'Ye-ess.' The corners of the Shogun's mouth went down as his face darkened. 'What a mess. We've always known that Yama-Shita's family would be the focal point of any move against the Shogunate. And it was clear that my brother-in-law was the kind of idiot who would eventually self-destruct, but . . .' He sighed, then said, 'The person I feel most let down by is Kiyo. Are you absolutely sure he's in on this?'

'I'll stake my life on it, sire.'

Yoritomo shut his eyes tightly as if trying to ward off this revelation. In a slow, deliberate movement he drew both hands down over his face, wiping it clear of all emotion, then placed them palm down on his splayed knees. 'So . . . we may have lost the Min-Orota. And one of my Consul-Generals is in their pocket too.'

'Not totally. I don't believe he knows what they're planning. He may not have been minding the store properly but he's still on your payroll, and he *is* family.'

'Don't remind me . . .'

'Lord Yama-Shita's prepared to take chances but he's no fool. Can you honestly see him conspiring with a man who's prepared to lay everything on the line in order to hump a long-dog?'

'No, I guess not. So how does it play?'

'If Yama-Shita *is* in bed with the Federation then he must have known who was delivering the winged pony.'

'So it was a set-up.'

'It has to be. But whichever way you slice it, the Consul-General had a chance to blow the whistle when he found out what was under the body-paint. He didn't take it. From there on in he was on the hook. What can Lord Min-Orota tell you? I'm sure he and Lord Yama-Shita can produce a string of witnesses to swear they handed over a female Mute. And we can't check out the Plainfolk clan that Yama-Shita claims to have done a deal with because –'

'He's our only contact.'

'End of story. Toh-Shiba's the one in the hot-seat. He's been caught with his stick out and they're aiming to use it to gain some leverage.'

'Like persuading him to order his garrison to look the other way if and when the Min-Orota decide to move against me . . .'

Toshiro shook his head. 'There's a long way to go before we reach that bend in the road. They haven't even begun to consider the military options yet. Even with the help of the Min-Orota, Yama-Shita and his friends are not strong enough to topple the Shogunate with one, swift, bloody stroke.'

'They might if Toh-Shiba's family was to change sides.'

'We must make sure they don't.'

'So, in other words, I must let sleeping dogs lie.'

'I'm sure we can come up with some ploys that'll give them a few restless nights. But even if the Toh-Shiba went over, it still wouldn't guarantee Lord Yama-Shita a clean hit. Neither side wants to get bogged down in another long-running civil war. We've all got too much to lose. No – what we've got on our hands right now is a battle for hearts and minds.'

'The most difficult kind of battle to win.'

Toshiro bowed. 'Sire, with you at the helm . . .'

'Is that all?'

'Not quite.'

Yoritomo sighed again. This time, the air of regret had

been replaced by a note of weary exasperation. 'Tread carefully, my friend. You're beginning to spoil the view.'

Toshiro accepted this philosophically. The risk of incurring the Shogun's wrath by being the bearer of bad tidings went with the territory. 'A rumour, sire, nothing more. I just thought you ought to know about it.'

'I'm waiting.'

Toshiro steeled himself. Rumour it might be but it was still dynamite. 'The flying-horse was driven through the air by an engine whose workings could not be fathomed.'

'I know. Yama-Shita ordered it to be destroyed.'

'It wasn't.'

The news raised the Shogun's painted eyebrows.

'Nothing's happened yet, but the word is our friends in the north have decided to ask their tame long-dog to reveal its secrets and help them devise ways to –'

'To what . . .?'

'To recapture the . . .' Toshiro's throat dried.

'. . . The Dark Light.' The words conjured up a chill spectre of death and disaster.

The five samurai guarding the Shogun did not understand what he was saying, but they sensed the feeling of dread in his voice and looked at each other uneasily.

Toshiro averted his eyes as Yoritomo willed himself to remain calm. In this situation, the laws of etiquette forbade him to look at the Shogun. He had to kneel with his head bowed until Yoritomo addressed him.

As the present holder of the supreme office and guardian of the sacred principles and traditions that governed the world of the samurai, the Dark Light was the thing Yoritomo feared most. It was the evil force that had led to the destruction of The World Before; the power that must never again be allowed to fall into the hands of men. Its secrets had become hidden knowledge, shunned and feared like the magic spells cast by the wizards and witches of ancient times.

The long-dogs were masters of the Dark Light and also its slaves. It gave strength to their awesome weapons and controlled their thoughts. It was the lifeblood of their underground world; its beating heart. But it was a diseased organ; within it were the seeds of a plague that weakened the body, paralysed the brain and destroyed the soul. In time, the Sons of Ne-Issan would find a way to tear that heart from its earthly body. And once it was stilled, the long-dogs would be trapped like maggots in a buried corpse, forced to feed on each other in the darkness until the last were overcome by suffocation and the stench of decay.

But first, their advance had to be halted with the aid of the Plainfolk. Only then, when a way had been found to overcome their war machines, could they be driven back into their desert lair and sealed off for ever from the rest of mankind.

The Dark Light was both beautiful and terrible. It seduced and corrupted, and made prisoners of all who tried to master it. The fools who now sought to resurrect it would first be driven mad, then be utterly destroyed by the demons that dwelt within it. From the moment the warriors of the Seventh Wave had stormed ashore, those demons had been banished from the lands bordering the Eastern Sea, and those that haunted the minds of the long-dogs had been kept at bay far beyond the Western Hills. But now, moved by blind ambition, a cabal of domain-lords was planning to let them loose again! It was insane! Yoritomo felt himself gripped by a deepening despair. Was history forever bound to repeat itself?

Like all true Sons of Ne-Issan, Yoritomo knew the story well. It was a cautionary tale that had been handed down through the ages; a lesson to which, from early childhood to his accession, his parents, teachers and advisers had constantly returned.

Ne-Issan, the Land of the Rising Sun, lay on the eastern shore of a vast continent that, in The World Before, had been called Iyuni-steisa. In those far-off days, the warriors whose descendants had given birth to the Sons of Ne-Issan had lived in a distant place that had also been called the Land of the Rising Sun. A land of

41

great beauty, whose people had risen to great wealth and power and had then lost their souls to the spinners and the weavers of the Dark Light.

The Dark Light was the earth-bound brother of the white sky-fire that split the heavens when the evil *kami* of the cloud-world tried to storm the castle of Ameratsu, God of All. The blinding flash was made up of the chain of sparks that flew from his sword as he struck down 10,000 of his foes with one fearful blow. And the fire that fell to earth and flowed through the world was filled with his divine power.

The spinners found secret ways to draw this power from the forests and rivers, the stones and the grass, and from the air men breathed. They captured it on magic wheels and bound it fast with metal threads as fine as silk. The weavers took these threads and wove them into thin ropes from which they made a giant net which, in time, encircled the globe. No one resisted because, in the beginning, they were entranced by its magical power. At the snap of a finger, the ropes brought light where there had been darkness, provided warmth for cold bones, and filled the air with music.

These were good things, but it did not stop there. New ways were found to throw the Dark Light through the air. A second net was woven across the sky using invisible threads. The world was made prisoner by stealth but once again no one resisted, for the spinners had built ever more powerful magic wheels and the weavers had devised ways to release men from his labours. The Dark Light turned drills, drove saws, raised hammers, forged iron and joined metals with a single spark of fire.

For the dull-brained layabouts and ne'er-do-wells this, too, was a good thing. Idleness became a virtue. But the craft-masters soon found no market for their skills. Their nimble fingers were replaced by the metal talons of headless slaves with tireless arms of steel. Fed by the Dark Light, oblivious of the seasons or whether it was night or day, they fashioned objects in the twinkling of an eye out of materials which had not sprung from the natural world. Such objects, fashioned without love, had no soul. They were worthless baubles, passing fancies for people who would pay any price to cloak the growing emptiness of their lives.

It was the weavers who had created the emptiness and now they worked ceaselessly to fill it. The world of nature was replaced by a world of illusion: a world of false hopes and hollow dreams which grew ever stronger as it fed on the energy stolen from the old.

Within less than a century, the earth was turned into a giant pleasure dome filled with magic windows that seduced the eye and siren sounds that lured all but the strongest from the Way of the Warrior. Fantasy became the new reality. Men lost all sense of honour as sensation replaced sensibility. The principles which underpinned the samurai's code of ethics were discarded; the fruits of ancient wisdom withered untended on the vine. Wives neglected their family duties; husbands abandoned their trades and professions and all sense of honour to take part in absurd games and trivial pursuits, eagerly submitting themselves to public ridicule and humiliation in the vain hope of winning worthless prizes. Fool's gold.

The spinners and weavers grew richer and ever more powerful. Anyone who resisted was pilloried and crucified. Rulers played host to them and sought their favours; governments acquiesced or fell.

Given the example of their parents, it was inevitable that the children born into the Age of the Dark Light would reject the moral and spiritual traditions of the past. As for the future, it did not exist. They lived in a lurid world which offered instant, mindless gratification and where Time was eternally present. They became shadow-people, rising with the moon to roam the streets, gathering together in their thousands when offered some new sensation.

Pain or pleasure, it mattered little. Jammed back and front and shoulder to shoulder in the gaudy temples of the dream-makers, they swayed like river-weeds in the grip of a flood tide of sound, their arms and eyes raised in adoration to the images created by the light. They were in the power of the weavers and their dress reflected their condition. Their bodies were strapped and chained, they had rings through their ears and noses, and needles stuck in their arms. Their hair stood up on end like the quills of demented porcupines and their faces were striped like rainbow-coloured Mutes. In a world without meaning, style was all. Like strutting peacocks, outward display was their only concern; eccentricity the ultimate goal.

Freed from the restraints imposed by moral and spiritual laws, men and women became prey to criminal elements which pandered to their worst instincts, drawing them down into a morass of licentiousness and corruption. Terror ruled the cities, cowards attacked the weak and defenceless, armies lost the will to fight, government became a meaningless ritual, kings and their ministers were publicly mocked and scorned by scribes and merchants and the lowest rapscallions.

Ameratsu-Omikami, the great sky-spirit, sickened by the evil in the world below, hurled the sun into the sea where it exploded with a mighty roar, setting the oceans aflame. Those who dared to look upon the scene were struck dead with terror. The waves bubbled and boiled like molten gold. Driven by a twisting wind with the voice of a thousand storms, they rose high in the air, clawed at the layered clouds with glowing fingers, then crashed down upon the shore, consuming everything in their path. No one was spared, not even those who had fled to the summit of the sacred Mount Fuji.

Only the boat-people survived, hidden behind the iron walls of their floating villages among the snow mountains beyond the Southern Seas. They saw the fire in the sky but the flames did not reach them, for Ameratsu, who wished to spare them, summoned cold white winds to draw the heat from the waves. For these were the chosen ones. Within their souls dwelt a spark that would become a flame. The flame that would one day temper the steel in the heart and mind of a new nation of samurai.

Time stood still. The sun had vanished, swallowed up by the oceans leaving a fugitive after-image in the sky; a dull red ball which occasionally pierced the leaden gloom that had descended like a funeral shroud.

As they drifted silently amid the pillars of grey ice, the boat-people slowly became aware that the world they had known had vanished. The earth had been turned into a charred wasteland where nothing moved and nothing grew. The clouds sucked up the death-laden dust and cast it down upon the sea as poisonous rain. Since their only source of food was the fruits of the ocean, the boat-people reaped a deadly harvest. Many perished, but not all. Some, blessed by Ameratsu, fell sick then recovered a measure of their former strength. Their numbers dwindled, but a nucleus survived and were joined by other ocean-wanderers who spoke their tongue and shared their dreams.

The odyssey lasted for more than two centuries. Generation after generation was born and buried at sea, but the descendants of the chosen ones never lost hope, and gradually they grew stronger. They kept the memory of their once-glorious past alive in the minds of their children, made eyes dulled with hunger, sickness and resignation sparkle with tales of heroic deeds by bold, fearless samurai for whom the thought of death was 'as light as a feather'.

They also handed down precious knowledge of the world that had been, and the skills that would be needed to build a new one when the earth had begun to heal. Above all, they passed on the code of *bushido*; the spiritual laws which governed the thoughts and actions of the Warrior and set him apart from ordinary humankind. And they entrusted to them a sacred task: to root out and destroy the Dark Light and banish it from the world for ever.

It was a task that the Sons of Ne-Issan had never abandoned. On the establishment of the first Shogunate, it had assumed the form of an edict. The Dark Light was the greatest enemy of mankind; to seek to recapture it was the greatest crime. Successive rulers of Ne-Issan had carried on the fight with crusading fervour and the present Shogun was no exception.

Yoritomo knew that if the rumour proved to be true, then those involved would have to be ruthlessly eliminated. But how widespread was the conspiracy? Prior to Toshiro's return, the Min-Orota had been regarded as *fudai* – loyal allies of the Toh-Yota. It was an extremely delicate situation. With the forces in the opposing camps so finely balanced, the Shogunate could not risk making any overt moves against the conspirators – if that was what they were. Even if he ordered his brother-in-law, the Consul-General, to commit *seppuku* – as family honour demanded – it could, given the present climate of intrigue, have unforeseen consequences.

No . . , The insult to his sister and his own house would be avenged – but at a time of his own choosing. For the moment, it was wiser to let the pot simmer.

CHAPTER THREE

Once again, Toshiro Hase-Gawa had demonstrated his remarkable flair for information-gathering, drawing together the loose strands from his network of agents and informers: eyewitness reports, tell-tale documents, pillow talk, drinking-den gossip and bath-house rumour. But the picture the herald had woven for the shogun was seriously flawed. Domain-lords Yama-Shita and Min-Orota *had* entered into a covert alliance, they *were* contemplating the construction of devices to recapture the Dark Light, and Consul-General Nakane Toh-Shiba *was* involved in an illicit sexual liaison. But Yama-Shita was *not* in league with the Federation or its agents. Toshiro had drawn the wrong conclusion from the information presented to him. The scenario he had constructed was based on one fundamental error: his assumption that the love-object – Clearwater – was a long-dog.

It was a mistake which Toshiro could not be blamed for making. Like most Iron Masters, his knowledge of Mutes was limited to those he had encountered in Ne-Issan; dull-eyed slaves who were fed and watered like cattle and who worked better under the whip. They were primitive outlanders whose place in Iron Master society was on a par with field-oxen and, at times, they were accorded even less consideration.

As a samurai and Herald of the Inner Court, Toshiro was bound by strict social conventions. It was unfitting for him to converse with such individuals, he could only give orders. And, had he owned slaves, those orders would have been transmitted through an intermediary. As a result, he knew next to nothing about their customs and traditions or their unfettered mode of existence in the vastness that lay beyond the waters of the O-hiyo and Mei-suri. In particular, he was unaware of the existence of 'super-straights'; Mutes whose bodies were not only straight-boned and smooth-skinned but who were also *clear-skinned* – like long-dogs and the Sons of Ne-Issan.

He was not alone.

Lord Hiro Yama-Shita had made exactly the same mistake some months before – despite the fact he knew more about the Plainfolk than anyone else in Ne-Issan.

Over the years, Yama-Shita had amassed a considerable body of information about the nomadic Mutes, but only senior members of his own family had access to it. The annual expedition by the wheelboats across the Great Lakes was one of the many enterprises that had made the Yama-Shita rich and powerful. The Mutes were not only a source of cheap labour; the goods they supplied helped to feed and clothe their captive brethren. The facts at his command were trade secrets; knowing his clients' strengths and weaknesses enabled Yama-Shita to extract the most favourable rates of exchange, and the rivalry between the various clans usually meant his trade-captains got the best of the bargain.

Unlike the majority of Iron Masters, Yama-Shita did not despise the Mutes, even though he personally found their disfigured bodies somewhat repugnant – in particular, their hairy armpits and bushy sexual organs. But, despite their bizarre appearance and their lackadaisical approach to hygiene, they possessed a certain nobility and, in their natural state, were strong, fearless individuals with their own code of honour which, in many ways, paralleled that of the samurai. They also had sufficient good grace to recognise and defer to a higher authority – namely himself and his entourage – and the wit to realise that the continuing exchange of goods and people for arms and artefacts was a profitable enterprise for both parties.

The picture they presented to outsiders was that of a largely untutored race endowed with a certain low cunning, but with more brawn than brains. However, there were some Mutes – notably the wordsmiths – who displayed a keen intelligence and an unexpected degree of subtlety. The individual named Mr Snow, the wordsmith of the clan M'Call, was one of them, and it was to him that Yama-Shita had turned for help in acquiring a flying-horse.

The domain-lord was also familiar with the unsubstantiated claims that certain Mutes possessed supernatural powers: mysterious gifted individuals known as summoners and seers. The Iron Masters, who worshipped at shrines dedicated to Ameratsu-Omikami, believed that the world of nature was permeated by the spirit-world – the realm of the *kami* – but Yama-Shita treated the stories of Mute magic with derision. In his view, the Mutes posed no danger to the Iron Master. Despite their vast numbers, the fragmentary nature of the clan system and the traditional hostility with which the rival factions viewed each other made it impossible for them to mount a large-scale military action against their benefactors in the east or their enemy in the south. The Plainfolk were fiercely territorial but they were not empire-builders. That was why it was safe to supply them with arms. Their implacable hatred for the long-dogs, and the guerrilla tactics they employed, were ideally suited to counter the probing advances of the Federation's overground war machines.

Yama-Shita sometimes wondered if the Plainfolk realised they were being manipulated, but it never occurred to him that they might also be inspired by a sense of destiny. He had never heard of the Talisman Prophecy but, had it been brought to his notice, he would have given it short shrift. His curiosity about the Mutes was blinkered by the innate belief in his own superiority and that of the system he represented. In his view – which was shared by all Iron Masters from the Shogun downwards – there was nothing to be learned *from* the Mutes, one could only learn about them. Yama-Shita was not an anthropologist, nor was he a student of comparative religion; he was engaged in resource-management.

This selective garnering of information meant that Yama-Shita, like the Herald, was completely unaware of the existence of 'super-straight' Mutes. He was thus fated to draw the same wrong conclusion and, when the news of Clearwater's unexpected transformation from multicoloured Mute warrior to unblemished long-dog reached him at the end of January, he had shared the Shogun's present sense of betrayal.

In the case of Yama-Shita, his anger had been directed against two targets: Mr Snow, for attempting to deceive him, and the Consul-General for his weakness and stupidity. When Kiyo Min-Orota had informed him of what had taken place, his first impulse had been to have Clearwater dispatched by an assassin, but Kiyo had reassured him that, when all the circumstances were taken into account, neither of them could be accused of complicity.

On reflection, Yama-Shita had agreed but, like the Shogun, he now found himself on the horns of a dilemma. The concealed presence of the female long-dog was simultaneously an unwelcome embarrassment and a heaven-sent gift. The Consul's inexplicable desire to tup females from the lower social orders had finally rendered him vulnerable to blackmail. The man was a degenerate clown but his high-level connections, through his marriage to one of the Shogun's sisters, made him a valuable pawn in the dangerous game that was now afoot.

Mr Snow, the obliging wordsmith, was another problem entirely. What game was the sly old lump-head playing? Since it was he who had undertaken to deliver a flying-horse in exchange for a shipment of rifles, it followed that he must be party to the deception. Did that mean he was in league with the Federation? If he was, the request by the disguised female long-dog to be returned to the M'Calls with the cloud warrior when he had accomplished his task now made sense. She and her partner were obviously expected to report on all they had seen: the craft skills of the Iron Masters and their ability to adopt new techniques, the methods by which they would power the flying-horses, and their mastery over them in the air. No wonder the cloud warrior had requested that he and his escort be allowed to remain together. It was a clever ruse, but no Mute or renegade Tracker who had entered Ne-Issan had even emerged to tell the tale – and this impudent pair would share the same fate.

But one important question remained unanswered: why would the Federation voluntarily hand over the secrets of flight to a potential enemy? The gift had, admittedly, been delivered in the guise of damaged goods, but that merely lent plausibility to Brickman's claim to have built it from salvaged bits and pieces while held captive by the Mutes. Despite its somewhat battered appearance, the craft was still capable of carrying two people through the air, and it had arrived bearing two objects of immense value: a rider who was eager to explain in detail the function of every part and the theory behind its design, and a working example of an engine powered by the Dark Light.

To Yama-Shita – a born entrepreneur – this had proved too good an opportunity to miss. After hiding it away, he had used considerable ingenuity to fake its destruction under the watchful gaze of the Shogun's representative in a spectacular bonfire containing crackerjacks and several concealed charges of gunpowder.

The mistake over Clearwater's true identity – which was later to lead the Herald, Toshiro, into believing that Yama-Shita might be in league with the Federation – prompted the domain-lord to evolve his own elaborate scenario around Mr Snow. In Ne-Issan, no one attained the position of power that Yama-Shita enjoyed without being ruthless and cunning – and he was no exception. Like most domain-lords, he had a naturally suspicious mind and a penchant for labyrinthine conspiracies. He was certain that Mr Snow had not expected the female long-dog to reveal her true colours. And there was no way the wordsmith could have known she would be placed in the custody of Nakane Toh-Shiba, nor could he have foreseen what was to follow.

So what had been intended? Was the delivery of the craft with its intriguing engine and its obliging rider an attempt to solicit further interest as to what other items might be on offer? After years of trading with the Mutes, Yama-Shita was clearly a person one could do business with. And his wheelboats offered a secure delivery system for goods *and* people. Was it possible that the Federation was seeking to make contact with him via Mr Snow?

To respond to such a move would be high treason. It was also high treason to flout the sacred edict concerning the Dark Light. But Yama-Shita did not see himself as a traitor. He wished to preserve Ne-Issan – but not necessarily in its present form. Peace and prosperity were not enough. Yama-Shita wanted progress. To achieve it, he would have to become Shogun. That meant displacing the Toh-Yota. If the knowledge that lay behind the Federation's war machines could help him do that, then, under the right conditions, he might come to an arrangement. And when he had achieved absolute power, he would use that same knowledge to defeat the long-dogs, destroy their underground kingdom and remove all trace of their presence from the face of the earth.

Yama-Shita knew that any kind of deal with the Federation was fraught with danger, but he was already running an immense risk in contemplating the capture of the Dark Light. He was not even sure if he had the courage to translate such thoughts into action. Were he to do so, he would be forced to obtain the devices used by the spinners and weavers. These forbidden objects, and the materials from which they were made, could only be brought into Ne-Issan when his position was unassailable.

In the meantime, there was no harm in keeping his options open. He would keep his word and deliver the promised shipment of rifles to the M'Calls. He would not seek to punish Mr Snow or his clan for attempting to deceive him; he would not seek to reproach him or even ask for an explanation. He would simply bring the old fox and the female long-dog face to face and watch what happened when he saw the change in her dress and appearance and heard, from her own lips, that she and the cloud warrior were being well treated and that neither yet wished to return to the Plainfolk.

From the moment he set eyes on her, Mr Snow would be left in no doubt that he, Yama-Shita, the most powerful domain-lord in Ne-Issan, knew everything. But the wordsmith would be able to read nothing from his face, for that would be hidden behind a black and gold mask. He would address his visitor with the same elaborate degree of courtesy he would offer to a fellow-samurai; his voice and demeanour conveying no hint of approval, or disapproval. It would be up to Mr Snow and his unknown associates to interpret his silence on the subject, and make their next move accordingly.

*

Nakane Toh-Shiba, the Consul-General, had been under strict instructions to say nothing to the long-dog apart from disclosing that she was to be transported to another location, but it was all to no avail. Plunged into despair at the thought of their coming separation, he had been hopelessly indiscreet. Knowing that the man's tongue was as restless as his dong, Lord Min-Orota had taken care not to tell him the whole story, but the moment Clearwater knew she was to meet Yama-Shita at Kari-faran, she had guessed that the domain-lord must be taking her to see Mr Snow. April was the month when the Plainfolk began to prepare for the 'walk on the water' – the name they gave to the brief period of peace when the rival clans gathered at the trading post at the edge of the Great River.

Since Cadillac was, apparently, quite content to remain at the Heron Pool, Clearwater knew she would have to return to Ne-Issan. In fact, she had no choice in the matter. When she had turned on the tears at the news of their forthcoming separation, the Consul-General had been quick to console her. He had, he assured her, extracted solemn guarantees from Yama-Shita that she would be provided with every comfort and returned to him unharmed.

Clearwater knew there was no time to lose. She begged to be allowed to take a small token of his affections with her. Something she could caress in the hours, the days, the weeks they would be apart. A small lacquered box, perhaps, decorated with images of her own choosing . . .? And once again she had fixed him with that look. So appealing, so ardent, so full of promise.

Toh-Shiba had been unable to refuse. Those eyes, ah! Her eyes were like shimmering jewels. At one moment, they were sharp-edged emeralds, filled with blue fire, and in the next, they softened, melting into liquid azure pools. Had he been a stone, he would have plunged willingly into their mysterious depths. He had lost count of the number of women whose sexual favours he had enjoyed – or made use of – but none had ever satisfied his physical desires or darkest fantasies in the way this long-dog had. She was, quite simply, the most skilled practitioner he had had the good fortune to encounter. But she was more than just beautiful, her whole being exuded a mysterious, vibrant sexuality. She was the embodiment of carnal desire. And Toh-Shiba was so besotted with her, he was prepared to do almost anything she asked.

Within reason, of course.

The truth was somewhat different. The Consul-General had, without any shadow of doubt, penetrated Clearwater's body, but every time he did so, she penetrated his mind, imposing her will upon the fevered images within. Fantasy became reality. Toh-Shiba's wildest imaginings took on physical form as she became whatever he desired; yielding and submissive at one moment, ravishing and devouring him the next. His nerve-endings went into overdrive. Sight, sound, touch, smell – every sensation was magnified, then moulded to marry with his deepest needs. His weapon, already nobly proportioned by nature, was expanded by his mind's eye into an awesome ivory shaft which he wielded with the thrust and vigour of a stallion and the stamina of a pack-mule. Time became distorted so that when the climax came the delicious jolt that filled every fibre of his being was transformed into a flood-tide of exquisite satisfaction on which his mind and body seemed to float for a joyous eternity.

In sum, the Consul-General *thought* he was enjoying himself a great deal more than he actually was. Clearwater drew no pleasure from their encounters, but she was obliged to use her body in order to maintain her hold over his mind. The Consul-General was totally unaware that, whenever he lay with her, his eyes, his ears, his tongue, his fingers and his indefatigable dong were sending back signals that had been generated by his own lascivious brain.

The power Clearwater had used was the same power that Mr Snow had employed to cloud the brain of Hartmann, the commander of the first wagon-train to enter Plainfolk territory. But Mr Snow had no need to encounter the sand-burrower in person. As a Storm-Bringer he held the Seventh Ring of Power and this enabled him to make contact through the mental image of Hartmann that Cadillac had drawn from the seeing-stone. Clearwater's abilities were formidable, but they were far below those of Mr Snow. The powers that flowed through her did so by the will of Talisman; they were not hers to command. That was why she knew her present actions had his blessing. She had been driven into the liaison with the Consul-General by the need to stay close to Cadillac. Toh-Shiba's estate was not far from the Heron Pool. If Cadillac had a change of heart and turned his mind back to her and to thoughts of escape, she would be in a position to help.

The Sky Voices had told her the wrath of the Iron Masters must fall on the sand-burrowers, not the Plainfolk. That was why her power – if it had to be used openly – must appear to be that of the Federation. She had been distressed by Cadillac's apparent indifference to their separation, but she quickly realised she had been fated to fall into the hands of the Consul-General. She had also seen enough to know that, as a Mute, she was beneath consideration and that, despite her well-formed body, her multi-coloured skin would condemn her to a harsh, degrading existence as a beast of burden, staggering under the weight of baskets filled with stones and earth, hauling cartloads of excrement to the paddy fields, or yoked to an irrigation wheel.

Clearwater did not despise the condition to which her kinfolk had been reduced, she deplored it, and had shed many bitter tears since her arrival in Ne-Issan. But she could not improve their situation by sharing it, and she had no need to share it to understand what they were going through. Her task was equally arduous, and her humiliation at the hands of the Consul-General was no less than theirs despite the relative luxury with which she had been surrounded. If what Mr Snow had said was true, 'The Lost Ones' – the Mutes held by the Iron Masters – would be freed when Talisman entered the world. Mr Snow had also said that Cadillac and she were the sword and shield of the Thrice-Gifted One. He had not explained what that meant , but he had stressed that the prophecy which spoke of his coming and of the victory of the Plainfolk over their oppressors would only be fulfilled if they followed the path that had been drawn for them.

Part of her task was the protection of Cadillac, mainly from himself, for dark forces were at work within him. And so, when she had been briefly paraded before Nakane Toh-Shiba, she had realised what was required of her. Their eyes met only for a few fleeting moments but it was all she needed. Her mind pierced his, uncovering his unfulfilled desires to possess the body of a long-dog. She also sensed an element of lustful curiosity in his cursory appraisal of her, but even the Consul-General had his limits. Mutes were beyond the pale. Despite this, she was able to plant in his mind the idea of placing her in solitary confinement with a supply of running water and the small bag of possessions she brought with her. Toh-Shiba obliged her by giving the necessary orders, but did so with the slightly hesitant air of a man who was not quite sure if he was doing the right thing.

Each evening, when the guards grew lax and ceased their prowling and peeping through the barred spyhole in the door, Clearwater used her supply of pink leaves to remove the patterning on her body, starting with the parts hidden by her walking skins. On the fourth day of her confinement, the transformation was complete. The guard who brought her meagre breakfast was so startled he almost dropped the tray. After bringing his immediate superior to confirm the evidence of his own eyes, the news was quickly relayed up the chain of command and, within the hour, the Consul-General himself had entered her cell and ordered her to be stripped naked.

Clearwater offered no resistance, standing with downcast eyes as Toh-Shiba slowly circled her, drinking in every detail of her body. Finally, he had ordered one of the guards who was standing behind her to pull back the long dark hair that was shrouding her face. As the white-stripe drew it over her shoulders and twisted it roughly together on the nape of the neck, her chin came up and her eyes met the Consul-General's. Toh-Shiba had expected to see the cringing look of an inferior creature filled with fear or apprehension; what he saw were two lightning bolts of blue fire that skewered his soul like a fish on a spear.

And from that moment onwards he was held in thrall by the power given to her by Talisman.

57

Despite Toh-Shiba's previously insatiable appetite for women, Clearwater was confident she would not be replaced in her absence. His illicit desires were now totally centred on her and would remain so even though they were to be parted for several weeks. However, there was no point in taking chances. On the eve of her departure, while Toh-Shiba lay in her embrace, trembling with ecstasy as he ran through his latest round of imaginary sexual gymnastics, she directed his thought back to the marriage-bed by overlaying her own image with one of his wife. It was, therefore, not surprising that the Shogun's sister had little to complain about during her visit to the Summer Palace at Yedo.

The power Clearwater had used to manipulate the Consul-General also enabled her to direct the hands of the craft-master who had prepared the lacquered box. Without knowing, he had decorated the tops and sides of the box with pictures that would speak to those who were to receive it: Mr Snow and the golden-haired cloud warrior, whose destiny was inextricably entwined with hers.

To the Iron Masters, who remained in total ignorance of her powers, it was nothing more than an empty box. An object of some worth and beauty, but nothing to compare with the exquisite works of art that adorned the great houses of the domain-lords and the palaces of the Shogun. But the wood of the box was filled with her being and the pictures were cunningly disguised maps which could direct Steve to the Heron Pool and to the concealed lake-house where she was held by Nakane Toh-Shiba. When it was placed in Mr Snow's hands he would feel her presence, her voice would enter his mind, and the images would reveal their secrets.

*

In the middle of May, a flotilla of giant wheelboats, led by Yama-Shita's own gilded vessel, had sailed from their home port of Bu-faro, by the thundering waters of

Nya-gara. They ran south-west along the shoreline to the port of Kari-faran in the neighbouring domain of the Ko-Nikka – close allies of Lord Yama-Shita. The wheelboats anchored offshore at sunset and then, when darkness masked all movement from prying eyes, a dory brought the female long-dog out to Yama-Shita's vessel in a sealed carriage-box.

At dawn, the wheelboats resumed their westward journey. The trip had been uneventful. As they crossed Lake Huron, Yama-Shita dispatched a vessel to Bei-sita, and another to Mira-woki, to trade with minor gatherings of Mute clans who trekked up annually from the southlands. On the tenth day of their outward journey, they sighted the usual vast crowds of Mutes camped around the trading post at Du-ruta, at the western tip of the Inland Sea.

During the week of brisk trading that ensued, Mr Snow, the M'Call's wordsmith, had made several attempts to raise the subject of the cloud warrior and his escort, but Yama-Shita had kept him on tenterhooks until the eve of their departure. Only then did he take the unprecedented step of inviting the wordsmith and two clan elders on board his own vessel. The Mutes were, of course, obliged to submit to a thorough cleansing before being allowed into his presence and had to relinquish their foul-smelling animal skins and furs in favour of cotton smocks and trousers. By all accounts, they had not found it too great an ordeal, and Yama-Shita was gratified to observe that Mr Snow, when properly clad and with neatly dressed hair, carried himself with a certain dignity. Indeed, had it not been for the lumps on his forehead, the bark-like skin on his forearms and the irregular pattern of black and brown that covered him from head to toe, one might have said he looked and behaved like a real human being.

As planned, Yama-Shita had confronted him with Clearwater – now richly dressed in clothes provided by her ignoble benefactor. She had been warned what not to say under pain of instant death, and two hidden archers were poised to carry out the sentence the instant he gave the command. They had only been allowed a brief audience, but it had been most revealing. Yama-Shita could tell that Mr Snow was clearly taken aback by her changed appearance, but his expression was one of surprise, not astonishment: the uneasy surprise of someone who knows he has been found out, not the genuine astonishment of someone presented with a totally unexpected transformation. From that moment on, the Mute wordsmith had proceeded gingerly, choosing his words with the utmost care. Their guarded conversation contained phrases whose meaning escaped Yama-Shita, but he was not perturbed. Mr Snow, on the other hand, never recovered his initial composure.

Yes, thought Yama-Shita. Let that be a lesson. I am a man who keeps his word but I am not easily deceived. Your move, my lump-faced friend . . .

*

Besides delivering the box, Clearwater had another reason to look forward to the journey. Having left the Consul-General squirming with anticipation at the end of a psychic fishing line, she was now hoping for an opportunity to sink her hooks into the man at the centre of this affair. Yama-Shita – who, with the snap of a finger, could order their return to the Plainfolk. But she quickly discovered that the domain-lord was no easy catch. Throughout the journey she saw virtually no one, apart from the two house-women who had been appointed as servant-guardians. The carriage box which had carried her from Bo-sana to Kari-faran had been sealed while on the road, and the only thing she had been able to see through the ventilation holes were small slivers of sky. At night, when the road convoy stopped to rest at inns – known as post-houses – she emerged from the carriage box to find herself in a room which offered no view of the outside world.

She had been similarly confined on the wheelboat and,

as a result, did not set eyes on Yama-Shita until the screens were drawn back to reveal Mr Snow, Rolling-Stone and Mack-Truck, kneeling on coloured straw mats and dressed up like low-ranking Iron Masters in dark cotton smocks and trousers. His directions on how she was to behave and what she was to say had been relayed by his samurai interpreter, a supremely cold fish whose voice and manner made it perfectly clear he would not have chosen to speak to her unless ordered to do so. It was almost as if, by conversing with her, he felt he was exposing himself to some dreadful airborne infection.

The samurai's attitude was understandable. The ordered world of the Iron Masters was based on the concept of superior and inferior beings whose status was decreed by the circumstances of their birth. It took the form of a multilayered pyramid with a few fortunate individuals at the top and a great many less-fortunate bimbos at the bottom. But while people could descend through the ranks, there was very little movement in the opposite direction. Rank, function and the attendant privileges depended on the degree of racial purity and nobility of your parents. Your career possibilities were defined at birth. Only top people got the top jobs. If your folks were at the bottom of the heap then, in most cases, that was where you stayed. Like all aliens, Clearwater was excluded. She was not only a social outcast, her liaison with Nakane Toh-Shiba had made her a social leper. She was a danger to all who came into contact with her.

The few other Iron Masters she came face to face with on the outward journey were not privy to the secret, but they all reacted in the same way. Her eyes rarely met theirs and when they did it was by accident. But even then, Clearwater could not force an entry into their minds. There had to be a way in. A half-open door, an unbarred window. Toh-Shiba's undisguised lust had made it easy to penetrate his defences; likewise the craft-master who, following the instructions from his patron, had been eager to please. But Yama-Shita's entourage looked upon her with contempt. To them she was a pawn that would be discarded when her usefulness came to an end. And she sensed that the Consul-General was viewed as an errant knight who would also be sacrificed when the time came.

As for Yama-Shita, he was the ice-king himself. Cold, calculating, implacable. The image that came into her mind when in his presence was that of a steel-jawed pike drifting imperturbably among the minnows, manoeuvring into position with barely visible movements of fin and tail, then striking with electrifying speed. Yama-Shita could not be lured into the same trap as the sex-crazed Consul-General. The walls around his mind could be breached – but only by blowing them apart. And this was not the moment to strike.

With Yama-Shita and his samurai listening to every word, she had been unable to explain why she had removed her body-paint or why she was now clothed in richly coloured silks. She could only say what she had been told to say, and hope that her few brief words would speak volumes. It was clear that Mr Snow was under similar constraints, but she had understood the veiled references to what had been seen in the stones and to the seed which had been carried away on the wind and which had now sprung again from the earth.

The cloud warrior had returned and would be sent to rescue her. It was the news she had been waiting for and it meant the gift she had been allowed to offer Mr Snow would not be wasted.

*

On the return journey, as on the outward leg, Clearwater was kept incommunicado, attended only by the Vietnamese house-women. From time to time, Yama-Shita observed her with cold-eyed detachment through a secret panel, usually when she was taking a bath. The sight of her naked body did not arouse anything other than curiosity. Yama-Shita had never been overly fond of the female sex even though he had a wife, and two daughters amongst his five children. Marriage, for him, was a domestic necessity; a strategic alliance of interests. Women were merely a means to an end. And an inferior one at that, for in Ne-Issan even high-born ladies took second place to males of equal rank. The noble, comradely love of one warrior for another was laudable, but to allow your thoughts and actions to be dominated by a physical desire for an inferior person – and that included your own wife – was utterly demeaning.

Love and the delights of the flesh were temptations the true samurai constantly strove to master. Given his natural inclinations and the fact that, since early adulthood, his mind had been entirely occupied with the expansion of his family's wealth and power base, Yama-Shita's warrior psyche was untainted by such weaknesses. The long-dog was tall, straight-boned and well-proportioned but, on Yama-Shita's scorecard, she had three strikes against her: she was female, she was an alien non-person, whose place lay below the bottom rung of the social ladder, and she had repellent, hairy loins like a Mute. And in all probability carried the same infestations.

Hhhhawww!

The thought of dallying in such an unwholesome environment never failed to raise a shudder. If Nakane Toh-Shiba felt the need to couple with this gutter-animal the least he could have done was to have her body shaved but, even then, what on earth had driven him to possess her in the first place?

Good question. Unfortunately, having derided the stories of Mute magic, Lord Yama-Shita had blinded himself to the answer: the Consul-General had not possessed Clearwater; it was she who had possessed him.

*

When the three wheelboats passed back through the

narrows at Hui-niso and were heading eastwards across Lake Iri towards Kari-faran, Yama-Shita ordered the vessels to heave to. Eight Mutes – four males and four females – were ferried over from the flank boats and lined up on the stern with their backs to the long, iron-strapped blades of the immobile paddle wheel. Following the example of their escort, they bowed their heads to Yama-Shita, who sat facing them on a raised section of decking.

Clearwater was brought out on to the deck by two red-stripes – sword-bearing functionaries who ranked below samurai. Clearwater's face was concealed behind the traditional rouged and chalk-white mask of a courtesan. Her head was shadowed by the cowl of a long, closed cape, and her hands were covered by long gloves. She bowed low as soon as she saw Yama-Shita, then knelt on a mat to his left, between her escorts. Facing her across the deck were six more red-stripes, their left hands resting on the hilts of their gently curving swords. Twelve white-stripes armed with whipping canes stood guard over the prisoners; Lord Yama-Shita was accompanied by his usual guard of high-ranking samurai – all wearing the ferocious metal masks that had caused the Mutes to christen them 'dead-faces'. Those worn by the reds and whites were more modest affairs made of lacquered papier mâché, like Clearwater's, the sole decoration being a band of colour running down the middle from forehead to chin.

On Yama-Shita's command, his interpreter turned to Clearwater. 'My lord wishes you to choose a male and female from among these slaves.'

After several painful lessons, Clearwater knew better than to ask why. The interpreter waved her to her feet and, after she had bowed once again to Yama-Shita, directed her over to the line-up.

All eight Mutes looked utterly wretched. They had already been afloat for nine days and, like most of their kin-folk, had been suffering from motion-sickness. Clearwater had been sick several times during the first half of the outward journey, but since then had only experienced bouts of queasiness. It was a very different feeling that gripped her now; a feeling that something awful was going to happen. She selected a young man and woman at random, then returned to her place on the mat as the couple were brought out and made to kneel before the raised decking. They were both strangers: their clothes, which would have identified their clan group – She-Kargo, D'Troit, San'Paul, M'Waukee – had been replaced by a cotton loincloth. Neither looked as if they gave much for their chances of surviving beyond the next few minutes, but they faced the prospect with the stoicism that was the hallmark of the Plainfolk.

Through his interpreter, Yama-Shita asked, 'Are you satisfied you have picked the strongest?'

Clearwater bowed humbly. 'I believe so, sire.'

'Lord Yama-Shita wishes to make certain,' said the samurai interpreter. 'A person of your importance deserves only the best.' He barked out a brief, unintelligible command.

With terrifying suddenness, the red-stripes facing Clearwater burst into action, hurling the chosen couple back into line. The red and the lower-ranking whites then waded into the shackled Mutes, flailing away with their whips, brandishing their swords, and screaming Iron Master gobbledygook. They were like a frenzied pack of coyotes yapping and snarling at a group of cornered fast-foot. The pointing swords and canes made it clear what they wanted, but several of the masked guards spelt it out in fractured Basic.

'Up! Up!' – 'On wheel!' – 'Now! Now' – 'Monkey go for ride on merry go-roun'!'

The eight Mutes were forced up on to the paddle wheel and were made to stand in a line along the blade that had stopped in a horizontal position: women on the left, men on the right, with an arm's length between them, faces to the wheel. The paddle blade was broad, but their foothold was precarious. The wood was dripping wet and their movements were hampered by the chains around their wrists and the heavy metal collar around their right ankles. Those who glanced nervously over their shoulder to see what was going to happen next received several whip lashes on the backs of their thighs.

Clearwater's feeling of dread deepened as she realised what Yama-Shita was proposing to do. The domain-lord waved brusquely to a subordinate, who shouted to another minion standing by an open hatch. The order was promptly relayed below. There was a loud hiss of escaping steam, then the deck trembled as the two huge wooden beams which drove the paddle wheel took up the strain, one pushing as the other pulled the wheel over and down towards the watching Iron Masters.

Guh-CHOONG-goin, guh-CHOONG-goin, guh-CHOONG-goin . . .

The paddle wheel had turned into a giant treadmill, forcing the eight Mutes to climb up the descending blades in order to escape the whips and jabbing sword points of the Iron Masters below. But an even worse fate awaited them. If, through error or exhaustion, they missed their footing, they would be carried down by the blades and crushed in the narrow space between wheel and the surrounding deck.

Guh-choongah-join,   guh-choongah-join,   guh-choongah-join . . .

The laboured ascent of the wheel turned into a mad scramble as it began to move faster. When it had achieved a relentless but not impossible rate, another order was relayed to the engineers in the bowels of the boat – presumably an instruction to keep the boat at the same speed. Yama-Shita was running a sadistic endurance race; a race which only the fittest and most agile could hope to survive.

Clearwater agonised over what to do. The Sky Voices had told her that she must not reveal her gift to the Iron Masters, but had they foreseen a situation like this? Should she ignore their warning and try to summon up the earth forces? Would they respond? The wheelboats were now out of sight of land, and a fathomless ocean lay beneath them. If Talisman did give her the strength to wreck havoc on her tormentors and tear their ship asunder, what then? It would not save the Mutes on the wheel and would also bring certain death to any other Plainfolk held in chains below. Her heart sank. She could do nothing. Her first duty was to Mr Snow, to honour her vow to do all in her power to protect Cadillac and bring him safely back to the clan.

The first to fall was a man.

The white-stripes shouted excitedly as the Mute lost his footing and made the fatal mistake of throwing himself lengthways along the descending paddle blade in a desperate effort to climb back up, instead of throwing himself clear. His scream of terror and pain was cut short as the massive blade scythed downwards, severing his right arm and leg as it drove his mangled body into the sea below. Amid roars of laughter, two white-stripes picked up the limbs, waved them mockingly at the Mutes on the wheel, then threw them over the side.

Rather than share the same horrific fate, two of the three remaining men decided to throw themselves overboard. The first – the nearest to the right-hand rim of the wheel – scrambled over the top, ran with amazing sure-footedness over the rising blades and leapt into the sea. He bobbed to the surface, floundered briefly, then sank beneath the weight of his chains. The second, following hard on the heels of the first, reached the top of the wheel, then slipped and fell between the blades into the maze of supporting timbers inside. Trapped helplessly in the narrow V formed by the junction of two beams and the huge axle, he was plunged into the seething cauldron below. When the same beams rose out of the water, he was seen clinging to one of the paddles like a waterlogged hamster. Unable to get through to the sea beyond and fearful of being carried higher, he fell back into the swirling water. At some point death overtook him, but the wheel continued to dredge up his limp body. Each time, it tumbled back down the rising blades or slid down the dripping spoke beams towards the axle – which tipped him forwards into the water – and the whole grisly cycle began again.

The women were not slow to follow. As the men made their leap for the sea, the woman placed nearest the left-hand rim of the wheel tried the same escape route. Just as she was about to jump off, she also lost her balance. Arms flailing, she toppled sideways on to the deck, landing back-first across the huge iron-strapped and bolted beam that drove the left-hand side of the paddle wheel. Her spine snapped with an audible crack that sent an electrifying quiver through Clearwater's body. The woman she had chosen began to lose ground. She cried out despairingly, begging for someone to help her. She was close to the middle of the wheel but the sole surviving man on her right was too far away. Oblivious of the danger, her nearest companion reached out towards her. Their hands closed round each other's wrists. Clearwater willed them to succeed. To find the strength to climb over the top and make that final leap into the sea beyond. It was not to be. Within seconds, the woman was clinging with both hands to the arm of her helper as she made one last frantic attempt to get her feet back into step with the moving blades. It was hopeless but she refused to let go and, an instant later, they both tumbled to their death beneath the wheel.

A new command from Yama-Shita was relayed to the engine room. The wheel slowed rapidly and, when it came to rest, the white-stripes ordered the two weary survivors to climb down, laughing and patting them on the back. The young man was the one Clearwater had chosen. The sudden switch from sadistic brutality to apparent sympathy at having survived the terrible ordeal had left him and the remaining woman confused and close to tears. The six armed red-stripes moved in and hustled them towards Yama-Shita.

On the order of the samurai-interpreter they turned the pair towards Clearwater and forced them to their knees.

'Lord Yama-Shita wishes to know if you are happy to

accept the gift of these two individuals now that they have given proof of their fitness.'

Clearwater bowed in the direction of the domain-lord. 'I am deeply honoured to receive any token – be it great or small – from the hands of the most high lord, and will do all within my power to make my undeserving self worthy of his unparalleled generosity.'

The samurai interpreter turned back to Yama-Shita expectantly. The domain-lord nodded. The samurai bowed, then spun on his heel. 'They will be brought before you shortly.' He barked out another unintelligible order to the red-stripes and waved Clearwater to her feet. She paid the usual courtesies to Yama-Shita and was escorted back to her cramped quarters.

That evening, at the time the two house-women usually brought her something to eat, the door was unlocked by the usual red-stripe but instead of the two small dark-eyed women, Su-Shan and Nan-Khe, the samurai interpreter entered followed by two white-stripes carrying two circular dishes covered with domed lids. Clearwater knelt as she was required to do when in the presence of a samurai. The whites placed the dishes on the low table in front of her and withdrew.

The samurai motioned to her to lift the lids from the dishes. Clearwater did so and found herself confronted by the severed heads of the two Mutes who had survived the ordeal on the paddle wheel. That, in itself, was bad enough, but they had not simply been beheaded, they had been savagely mutilated as well.

Clearwater was no stranger to either death or violence, but the cruelty that had been inflicted on this luckless pair made her senses reel.

The samurai bowed. 'Lord Yama-Shita wishes you to reflect on the fate of your Mute friends.' He placed a subtle emphasis on the word 'friends'. 'If such things can happen to those who did nothing to incur my lord's displeasure, then the fate of those who betray him will be terrible indeed.' So saying, he picked up the domed lids and brought them together sharply, smashing them to pieces.

Clearwater flinched as the fragments of porcelain showered over her.

'You will never speak of this journey to anyone. Nor will you ever reveal what you have seen or who you have spoken to since you left the presence of Consul-General Nakane Toh-Shiba. In particular you will never confess to having been in the presence of Lord Yama-Shita. Is that understood?'

Clearwater nodded meekly, and tried to avoid looking at the charred sockets that had once framed the eyes of the two young Mutes. 'Yes, sire . . .'

The samurai gestured to the severed heads. 'Neither you or your house-women are to touch these. They will remain here, uncovered, on this table, until you are ordered to leave this vessel. Is that also understood, long-dog bitch?'

'Yes, sire.' Clearwater remained with her head bowed until the samurai left the room.

And I also swear by Mo-Town, the great Sky Mother, and by the might of Talisman, the Thrice-Gifted One, that the deaths of my brothers and sisters will be avenged a thousand times over . . .

CHAPTER FOUR

At the beginning of June, Toshiro Hase-Gawa returned from yet another fact-finding mission. The Shogun received him, as before, in the pebble garden. Toshiro began with a progress report on the work at the Heron Pool, and the problems encountered in trying to find a suitable propulsion unit for the flying-horses now under construction.

The Shogun listened with his usual attentiveness, but it was obvious he was more interested in getting an update on the affair between his brother-in-law and the latest resident of his notorious lake-house – the female long-dog.

'She is no longer there, sire.'

'No longer there . . .?'

Toshiro bowed under the Shogun's impassive stare. 'According to the information I have, she disappeared from the Consul-General's estate towards the end of April –'

'So in other words, you've caused me considerable anguish over the plight of my sister without providing one tangible piece of evidence, and you are *now* telling me it's over and done with,' said Yoritomo brusquely.

'Uhh . . . not quite.'

Yoritomo's mouth tightened. 'What do I have to do to get the rest of this story – drag it out of you with red-hot pincers?'

Toshiro bowed again. 'Towards the end of April, a sealed carriage-box carrying an unidentified female personage of high rank joined a road convoy at Nyo-poro. That, at least, was the impression formed by the few people who managed to catch a glimpse of her. My informant was the wife of the convoy-master.

According to her, the lady in question also bore the mask of a courtesan.'

'Go on . . .'

'The name on the travel documents was given as Yoko Mi-Shima, the portage fees were paid by a merchant known to have connections with the Consul-General, and her final destination was Kari-faran.'

'One of the ports of call for Yama-Shita's wheelboats. And you think this woman was . . .?'

'It works for me.'

'Incredible . . . Did you check the local registers to see if there is such a person, or was this name pulled out of a hat?'

'Well, *I've* never heard of her – but that doesn't mean very much. And I couldn't bandy her name around in case I gave the game away. Your grand-uncle, Ieyasu, might know. It is said that the Lord High Chamberlain –'

'Ye-esss . . .' Yoritomo turned his eyes back to the garden. 'Where is the monkey man right now?'

'Out west.' In the Iron Master's native language, the Mutes were often referred to as *saru* – grass-monkeys – and it had become the Shogun's nickname for Yama-Shita.

'Do we have a return date?'

'Not a firm one,' replied Toshiro. 'But the ferry-captain did tell me that a vessel was being readied at Nyo-poro to take one of Lord Min-Orota's house-captains down to Firi. The town is hosting a slave auction in about a month from now.'

'Which means the wheelboats should be docking at Kari-faran in the next few days . . .'

'Kari-faran first, then Pi-saba. That's the main unloading for the goods to be sold on the open market.'

'And you think this female will be on one of the boats?'

'Yes, sire. No one else has been moved into the lake-house. That in itself is not significant but, if he was not expecting to see her again, why would the

Consul-General send her gift-wrapped to Kari-faran at his own expense? If he wanted to get rid of her, he could have had her buried under the nearest dung-heap – or chopped up and fed to the pigs.'

'You're right. But if, as you suggest, Yama-Shita has taken great care to stand well back from all this – I mean, the way you tell it, he and Min-Orota are practically fireproof – right?'

'It certainly looks that way . . .'

'So why would the monkey man compromise himself by taking the long-dog for a boat-ride?'

'Good question, sire. It depends what the initial deal was. She may have to report back – or maybe she's taken a shopping list of things that they need at the Heron Pool. There could be all kinds of reasons. Let's face it – the risks are minimal. You've given me to understand that what happens aboard his wheelboats is a closed book –'

'It's true that, up to now, we have never been able to get any of our people on board.'

'Then provided no one catches the lady actually getting on or off the boat, he's in the clear. Once she's back in the box, the only person she can be linked to is to the Consul-General.'

'Mmmmmm. . .' Yoritomo pulled slowly at his bottom lip. 'It's a neat theory but – let's face it, my friend – it's pure supposition. Don't get me wrong. I'm not trying to wish this conspiracy away, but, so far, you haven't presented me with one shred of hard evidence. You haven't even come up with any first-hand information – it's all hearsay.'

It was a harsh judgement, but Toshiro was obliged to take it on the chin. He bowed. 'That's the way the system works, sire. I am only a conduit for information – not a government spy.'

'I know, I know. I'm not questioning your competence. And I have every faith in the people we have out there in the field, but . . . I'm not entirely convinced you've interpreted the information correctly.'

73

'I share your concern, sire. But I *can* name names. Three, to be precise. If you were to bring them to the boil I'm sure they would only be too happy to confirm that the female in the Consul-General's lake-house is a long-dog. With dark hair and blue eyes.'

'Is there any other way we can get at the truth? Something a little more devious, perhaps?'

'I can think of one way. But it will take some organising and we would have to move fast.'

'Shoot.'

'Our people at Kari-faran and Pi-saba will have to be alerted to maintain a day and night watch on the wheelboats bringing in the new shipment of Mutes. They'll have to keep tabs on everybody who comes ashore from those boats – and that includes any captured long-dogs. We also need to know in advance who is booked to travel on any of the eastbound road convoys.'

'That's a tall order.'

'It is, sire. But I do not believe it is beyond the power of the Shogunate. Our chief agents can be alerted by pigeon post.'

'Okay. Let's assume we do all that and find that some generous soul has paid the portage fees for a certain "Yoko Mi-Shima" – or whoever. What then?'

'Somewhere between Pi-saba and Bo-sona the road convoy has the misfortune to be waylaid by lawless elements and –' Toshiro spread his hands – 'the lady is kidnapped. It's deplorable but, even under your firm leadership, a certain level of criminality persists.'

Yoritomo's eyes hardened. 'Do you realise what you're asking?'

'Yes, sir. People are liable to get themselves killed. But those who lose their lives will die in the service of the Shogun.'

'And if it turns out you're wrong about this woman?'

Toshiro inclined his head meekly. 'Then, no doubt, I shall also have the honour to make the same sacrifice . . .'

'I may take you up on that,' said Yoritomo as the

74

Herald's eyes rose to meet his. 'But let's suppose you're right. What happens next?'

'Nothing, sire. Once we have proof that she is a long-dog, we arrange to have her put back into circulation without delay.'

Yoritomo frowned. 'Wait a minute. Aren't you going to question her?'

'No, sire. That would be fatal. I am assuming that the, uhh – outlaws, if captured, will not confess they were in your employ.'

'No chance . . .'

'Then it will work. It is common knowledge that lawless bands of *ronin* often attack road convoys in search of plunder, sometimes carrying off high-born travellers to hold them for ransom. On this occasion they will find their prize is worthless – and they will turn her loose.'

'Go on . . .'

'When the lady is recovered by her present owner and his patrons, they will ask her what happened, and she will tell them what little she can. Since they are all party to the deception – and to a larger conspiracy – they are bound to be suspicious about the real motive for the kidnapping. They're not going to be happy with her story. They may not even believe it. They'll begin looking for evidence that points to you but, if we don't ask her any questions, they've got nothing to go on. They'll be left wondering if they've been rumbled, how much you know, who blew the whistle, and – best of all – whether we are now running the Consul-General's lady friend.'

'I like it,' said Yoritomo. 'You'd better get moving.'

'Uhh – me, sire?' Toshiro was unable to hide his confusion. 'This kind of operation is way out of my league. The hit on the road convoy would probably have to be made in Lord Se-Iko's domain. That's not my territory. And besides, I don't have the authority.'

'You do now.'

Toshiro bowed low and tried to sound sincere. 'I'm

honoured, sire. But I beg you to reconsider your decision. I am already known to be your eyes and ears in the lands of Lord Min-Orota. If, by some mischance, he and his associates came to hear of my involvement in the kidnapping of the long-dog, it –'

'– would blow the whole deal . . . Yes, okay, we'll talk about it later.'

*

At Kari-faran, the three wheelboats dropped anchor briefly before making the run through the canal system to Pi-saba. While stores were being taken aboard and a certain amount of cargo was unloaded, Yama-Shita was invited ashore to a lavish reception laid on by members of the Ko-Nikka family. During the meal, a senior lieutenant of the absent domain-lord advised Yama-Shita that the known agents of the Shogun were displaying a greater interest than usual in the movements of goods and people in and out of the docks.

Yama-Shita thanked him and altered his plans accordingly as the wheelboats proceeded on their way.

Most of the spies working for the *bakufu* were employed by the Shogun's tax collectors; their task was to keep tabs on the volume of trade, who was selling what to whom, and into whose pockets the money was going, so that the usual swingeing demands could be made twice a year. But one could never be too careful. There were other government agents looking for different fish to fry. Yama-Shita had received word that the Shogun's Herald to the house of Min-Orota had been trawling the sinks and stews around Ba-satana and the newly built Heron Pool at Mara-bara. Could a whiff of what was afoot – or rather abed – in the Consul-General's lake-house have reached the nose of this tiresome bloodhound? Only time would tell. Meanwhile, he and Min-Orota must do everything they could to distance themselves in the public and private eye from Toh-Shiba and his hairy gutter-animal.

From Pi-saba, Yama-Shita had been planning to make his usual ceremonial progress along the Great East Road, the highway that, in the dim distant past, had been known as the Pennsylvania Turnpike. This was the route that Side-Winder had recommended Steve to follow in the belief that – by tailing Yama-Shita's party – he would eventually find his way to the Heron Pool. But Steve was to be left high and dry for, by the time the wheelboats arrived at Pi-saba, the canny domain-lord had decided to take evasive action. Only the long-dog and her fellow renegades destined for the Heron Pool would return along the Great East Road; he and his massive entourage would take the northern route (the pre-Holocaust Highway 80) to Wirimasaporo before turning north into his own domain – and he would leave a week before they did. It would mean missing the planned reception at the house of his southern neighbours, the Se-Iko, but he had no doubt he would be royally entertained on the way.

Reasoning that any government spies would redouble their surveillance as darkness fell, Yama-Shita decided that Clearwater should be put ashore in broad daylight. Better still, she would be the first item to be unloaded. He ordered her to be bound with strips of cloth into a foetal position, then hidden inside a bundle of furs. Concealed behind a pierced screen on the uppermost deck, he watched as, amidst the usual feverish activity, it was carried down the gangway on the shoulders of a sturdy Mute and dumped into a handcart. Those following him threw their loads on top then, when the cart was full, it was hauled away into one of the warehouses.

After a bone-shaking ride, the crushing weight that had threatened to suffocate Clearwater was removed. Several more stops and starts followed. Voices and footsteps came and went. Clearwater felt the cart move off again. It rattled over cobbled streets, then the bundle of furs in which she lay hidden was hoisted on to another strong back. She felt herself being carried up a flight of stairs and was once again dumped unceremoniously, this time on to a floor. Despite the thick cocoon of furs, the impact drove the breath from her body. Doors slid shut and were barred, making it clear that her period of incarceration was not yet over. Even so, she was relieved to be back on dry land.

Eventually the door opened again and she heard the familiar sing-song voices of Su-Shan and Nan-Khe. They untied the bundle of furs and Clearwater emerged to find herself in another windowless room. It was, however, larger and better furnished than the cabin which she had occupied on the wheelboat and which, for the last three days, she had shared with two severed heads. She had tried to avoid looking at them but the room was so small, they hovered constantly at the edge of her vision. At mealtimes there was no escape: the house-women had been instructed to place her meals on the table between the heads and wait until she had eaten every last scrap.

It was not the heads that upset Clearwater. Headpoles were a common sight in any Mute settlement and were the visible proof of a warrior's prowess. The heads of two cloud warriors had been placed on poles outside her own hut in recognition of the part she had played in their downfall. What she found hard to stomach was the hideous way in which the two victims had been mutilated. And that, in turn, reminded her of how the other six had died on the great waterwheel, and the cruel laughter their deaths had provoked.

The Plainfolk did not kill in cold blood, nor did they attack the weak, or defenceless. Where was the honour in that? Warriors of both sexes fought only to defend their turf against rival clans. When it came to killing, the dead-faces were as ruthless as the sand-burrowers. They were two of a kind and both would suffer the same fate when Talisman entered the world like an avenging angel.

And that day would come. Towards the end of the voyage and even now, as she sat imprisoned in another gilded cage, Clearwater sensed that the cloud warrior was already in Ne-Issan. The golden one who had captured her soul was here! Close by to where she now lay! Her mind had picked up the faint vibrations that emanated from his presence – reflections of the power she had poured into his bladed quarterstaff to help protect him from the dangers that lay ahead. The stones had not lied. He had returned with death hiding in his shadow and would carry her away on a river of blood.

What had been foretold would come to pass: the Plainfolk *would* become a bright sword in the hands of Talisman their Saviour. And that sword would reap a grim harvest under a blood-moon. The weeds and thorns that threatened to choke the seed of the Plainfolk would be cut down. Their roots would be torn from the earth and consigned to the fire; their ashes would be ground to dust. And from that dust a new generation of Plainfolk would rise, straight and strong as the Heroes of the Old Time. The world would be made whole, the blood would drain from the earth and the land would be green again.

*

For Jodi Kazan and Dave Kelso, who, along with thirty other renegades, had been captured and traded by the clan M'Call, the relief at being back on terra firma more than outweighed the harsh treatment meted out by their guards. Like all Trackers, Jodi had been trained to cope with physical violence, constraints and abuse, but an extended sea-journey and the debilitating effects of prolonged motion-sickness had been a nightmare trip into a totally new dimension. For ten days and nights she and the others had sat huddled together on the quivering through-deck of the wheelboat, listening to the rumbling thunder of the paddle wheel and taking turns to be sick in a wooden bucket. Whenever it had fallen to Jodi to empty it into the endless, undulating grey-blue wastes that surrounded them, she had been sorely tempted to follow its contents over the side.

During the voyage, the relatively small number of renegades travelling with the Mute journeymen had been taken away in turn for interrogation. The questions had been detailed and far-ranging, covering everything from their name, rank, number and technical qualifications to the operational capabilities of wagon-trains and the conditions inside way-stations and the underground divisional base that had been their home-station.

The fact-finding sessions were conducted with the same thoroughness as any of the operational debriefings that Jodi had attended, but the Iron Masters' information-storage methods were right out of the Stone Age. Each of the chief interrogator's questions were translated into Basic for the benefit of the renegades; their replies were then translated *back* into gobbledy-gook and meticulously noted down by a wizened clerk on sheets of yellowish material resembling plasfilm using a brush and a pot of black liquid. The signs the dinks made were as incomprehensible as the sounds they uttered, but Jodi found the whole process fascinating to watch. It might be a crazy way to do things, but the old guy was certainly a whizz with a paintbrush.

At the end of the session a short length of coloured tape had been threaded through a slot in the metal I-D plaque that she, and everyone else, now wore fastened round their right arm. When all the renegades on their boat had been processed, Jodi and Kelso found they were the only ones with blue tapes. As wingmen, they had always considered themselves something special, but the thought that they had now been singled out from their fellow-breakers made them feel distinctly uneasy about their future prospects.

*

The port of Kari-faran had marked the beginning of the scenic route that took them across country through a system of locks and canals. It also marked the end of their period of enforced idleness. Mutes and Trackers were formed into work-parties and herded down gangplanks to help open the lock gates and haul the huge wheelboats through the sections where the gates were bunched close together. Jodi had a hunch the vessels could have manoeuvred under their own steam, but doing it the hard way gave the Iron Masters an opportunity to knock the new batch of 'guest-workers' into shape.

Those who weren't hauling ropes or heaving open lock gates were divided into small groups and made to jog up and down from bow to stern until they had completed ten circuits of the deck. Jodi and the others did this fun-run twelve times in the two and a half days it took to get from Kari-faran to the inland port of Pi-saba. Their wrist shackles and the drag-weight clamped round their right ankle did not make it easy or enjoyable but it did at least give them a chance to get a breath of much-needed fresh air and take a look at the brave new world they were soon to be part of.

The trio of wheelboats reached Pi-saba about four hours before sunset. There was a lot of traffic on the river. Besides several smaller steam-driven wheelboats, Jodi glimpsed square-sailed barges, shallow-draft ferries and small, one-oared dorys going up and down and back and forth across the waterway. Columns of dark grey smoke drifted up into the sky from an area where there seemed to be several large fires. Finally, the paddles slowed, stopped, then went into reverse. Ropes were thrown ashore and anchored round bollards by teams of waiting men and, after much heaving and shouting, the wheelboats drifted gently into contact with the woven rope bumpers hanging from the wooden jetty.

It was the signal for a mini-horde of white-stripes and boot-licking Mute overseers to go on the rampage. They ran through the closed deck, cracking their whipping-canes across the shoulders of their human cargo, yelling at them to get to their feet and form up in the groups to which they had been allocated.

Having helped to pull the huge wheelboats through the canal system, the Mutes and Trackers were now given the privilege of unloading their cargoes. But first, their wrist shackles were removed. Every item carried aboard at the trading post had been checked, labelled and listed by tally-masters, and now the whole laborious process went into reverse as the bales and bundles were carried down the gangways to be carted away and piled neatly in stone-walled storage units that had curious sloping roofs.

The only overground constructions Jodi had seen before coming to Ne-Issan were the almost featureless way-station bunkers, the forbidding work camps with their towers, traps, and wire cages, and the fortress-like access ramps at places like Nixon/Fort Worth. She had never seen any buildings whose design pre-dated the Holocaust – in this case by several hundred years – and the video archives she could access with her ID card contained no record of them.

The unloading was completed as darkness fell, the final checks and tallies being made by the light of lanterns while the newly arrived additions to the labour force devoured a generous ration of steaming rice, shredded vegetables and meat balls, washed down with a draught of hot, pale green liquid.

It didn't taste anywhere near as good as java but what the hell, thought Jodi, it's no good pining for the tastes of yesteryear. We ain't ever gonna get our lips round a cup of that again.

As she watched the tallymasters and their clerks comparing their stock lists with the bills of lading, Jodi found herself wondering why some bright spark hadn't gotten around to generating electricity. After all, they had steam power, everything she had seen so far had been beautifully made, and the way the clerk had keyed all that data on to the page was proof of their amazing dexterity.

It was really strange. They had all the skills and the tools they needed, and it wasn't as if they didn't know it existed. The present batch of renegades were not the first to be interrogated, and the questions she and the others had been asked showed that they were anxious to discover what made the Federation tick.

So how come they were still in the dark ages?

When the brief meal-break came to an end, Mutes and Trackers were ordered to wash their thin metal cups and bowls in big wooden tubs before putting them away in the small cotton bags that had been distributed with the eating utensils. The bags had ties so they could be fastened around the waist. There were no knives, forks or spoons. You ate with your fingers and licked or drank whatever was left.

The next thing on the schedule was a clothing issue. The Mutes had been stripped down to a cotton loincloth and their moccasins; the Trackers had been allowed to keep their T-shirts – if they had them – and their camouflage trousers and boots. The night of 10 June 2990 was mild and dry, but they were all issued with ponchos woven from coarse strands of jute, wide cone-shaped straw hats, and a thin cotton quilt. As with everything the Iron Masters did, the distribution was smoothly organised, the strange sign and number on their armplate being quickly stencilled on their poncho, hat and quilt as they waited in line to pick them up.

Once they had been kitted out they were ordered to reassemble in their respective colour groups. Being the only blues, Jodi and Kelso decided to stay well behind everybody else. As people milled around in an effort to find their place, they managed to catch sight of Medicine-Hat and several other breakers from Malone's outfit. They exchanged silent but expressive farewells, then stood up straight and tried to fade into the background as the white-stripes began chivvying people into neat lines with their whipping-canes. The canes were made from several thin sharp-sided strips of bamboo bound together to form a flexible rod not much thicker than your little finger. When it landed, it married itself to the curve of your back, transmitting its force along its full length. The edges cut deep into naked skin and it hurt, man, it really hurt.

Encouraged by a chorus of screams, shouts and a flurry of blows, the luckless Mute journeymen and women were formed into a long column and then marched off to whatever fate awaited them. Jodi watched them trudge past but was unable to feel any sympathy for their plight. The lumpheads had been sold down the river by their own kinfolk; the same four-eyed bastards who had traded her and the other breakers for a few pots and pans. She had had no choice in the matter, but these guys . . . hell, you had to be pretty stupid to let someone swing a number like this on you. Serve 'em right.

A masked samurai and four red-stripes approached the goon in charge of the assembled renegades. Since docking at Pi-saba, the lower echelons of Iron Masters had dropped the Phantom of the Opera routine, exposing their flat-featured, yellowish faces and their curiously shaped eyes. At first Jodi couldn't figure out why they looked so odd, and then the penny dropped: they had no eyebrows – and the hair the samurai wore wasn't their own.

In the ten miserable days spent at sea, Jodi and the other breakers had learned the basic rules of Iron Master etiquette the hard way. You went down on your hands and knees whenever a samurai came by and you put your nose to the floor and kept it there till he left town. Above all, you never looked 'em right in the eye.

It wasn't exactly a new situation. The Deputy Provos back home regularly roughed up defaulters who came on strong in the eyeball department, but with these high-flyers it was fatal. Federation justice was thought to be swift and tough but it was a slow-motion replay compared to what happened when these dinks got on your case. If you stepped out of line that was it, you got it right there and then. Jodi had seen a breaker and three Mutes get their cards cancelled and, from the few words they had managed to exchange with guys from the other flank boat during the meal-break, it was clear they weren't the only ones. Whatever the treatment being handed out, the dinks allowed no protests. They expected total submission, and the best way to stay out of trouble was to walk around with your head permanently bowed. So far it had worked. There had been a few occasions when Jodi had toyed with the suicidal idea of sinking her teeth into the cotton-clad tootsies of the pugnacious pygmy that towered over her, but she had wisely kept her mouth shut.

The red-stripes set down a stepped box in the middle of the assembly area. The samurai mounted it, surveyed the kneeling renegades, then addressed them in Basic. 'Now you a-SITA!'

Everybody sank back on their heels and placed their hands on their thighs. Most kept their eyes down, chins on their chest. Those that didn't got a whip laid across their neck.

'Arr those wiv baroo arma-ribbon wee-rah now stair fo'wah!'

Baroo . . .? Jodi and Kelso exchanged hesitant glances, then leapt to their feet as they saw several white-stripes converging on them with raised canes. They ran through to the front and knelt, as directed, before the samurai.

'Ah-raise ah-rye han' i-fuh you know how fly-uh sky ma-shin.'

Kelso extended a clenched fist. With a sinking heart, Jodi did the same. A similar procedure was employed during training in the Federation to recruit 'volunteers' for shitty details like swabbing down the john.

The samurai switched into Japanese and issued a string of instructions to his sidekicks. Jodi and Kelso were hauled to their feet and hustled away.

Jodi cursed inwardly. Oh, Dave, you meathead! Fancy telling those dinks on the boat you were a wingman! And persuading me to do the same! They'd never have known if you hadn't gone and opened your big mouth. What a dumb thing to do . . .

The red-stripes ran them at the double down a confusing maze of alleyways, some lit by solitary lanterns, others in darkness. They stopped before a stout door. It was quickly unlocked and they were pushed inside. As they ducked their heads, wooden-soled feet slammed painfully into their backsides, propelling them headfirst on to a pile of straw. The door closed with a bang. A key turned in the lock, bolts slammed home.

Jodi and Kelso dragged themselves into a sitting position against the wall and listened as the jabber of voices faded away. It was too dark to see one another but she could hear Kelso gulping down air as he tried to recover his breath. When he finally lapsed into silence, Jodi heard her own heart pounding.

'At least we're still in one piece,' she murmured.

'For the moment,' grunted Kelso. 'Fucking Brickman . . .' He spat into the darkness. 'If you hadn't gone back for him, we wouldn't *be* here! I must have been crazy to let you talk me into it.'

It was a familiar refrain. 'It wasn't just you and me, Dave.'

'Damn right! You dropped Medicine-Hat and Jinx in it too!'

'Gimme a break. There were plenty of other guys who got picked up – and they were miles away.'

'Yeah, and we could have been miles away too! If we'd stuck with Malone, we might still be out there! Instead of which we walk right into it! Christo! That fucking Brickman was waiting to *meet* those lumps!' He laughed bitterly. 'I heard of guys bouncin' beaver but, boy – I never thought I'd live to see a true blue dolled up the way he was!'

'Yeah, I know,' said Jodi tiredly. 'I asked him about that. He said it was all in a good cause.'

'Yeah, well, friend or no friend –'

'Dave, how many times do I have to tell you? He's no friend of mine.'

'So you say. But if our paths ever cross again I swear I'm gonna kill that lump-sucking sonofabitch stone dead.'

'I hope it's soon, Dave, I really do.' Jodi wriggled deep into the straw. *Maybe then you'll quit bellyaching* . . .

*

A carrier pigeon, landing in the loft atop the western tower of the Shogun's summer palace at Yedo, brought news of Lord Yama-Shita's arrival at Kari-faran. A second confirmed his docking at Pi-saba; a third announced his departure for Wirimasa-poro. None of them made mention of any untoward activity. Using the abbreviated secret code, the third message also reported that two long-dogs had been selected for dispatch by road convoy to Lord Min-Orota. One red-haired male, one female, her face and neck disfigured by pink scar tissue. There was no mention of the mysterious Yoko Mi-Shima, or any other unidentified voyager.

Toshiro began to feel uneasy, and took to pacing the upper stone terrace along the outer wall, scanning the sky for the next arrival. Since carrier pigeons were arriving at frequent intervals from all parts of Ne-Issan, his hopes were first raised and then dashed as the incoming birds failed to deliver the news which could make or break his career.

It was that crucial. He had laid accusations of treachery on two counts against the most powerful domain-lord in the country, had accused a second, a close ally of the Toh-Yota, of disloyalty and conspiracy with the first, and had accused the Shogun's brother-in-law of dishonouring his wife by coupling with a long-dog. If he now failed to substantiate any or all of these claims he could – to use a phrase from the ancient language of Iyuni-steisa – find himself well and truly up Shit Creek without a paddle.

Six agonising days after Yama-Shita's reported departure for Wirimasa-poro by the northern road, a courier pigeon finally winged its way out of the west and brought a glimmer of light to the end of Toshiro's tunnel. The message came from Pi-saba. The carriage-box transporting a certain Yoko Mi-Shima had been booked into a road convoy travelling along the Great East Road. Ox-cartage had also been reserved for her two Vietnamese house-women. The carriage fees had been paid by a merchant connected by marriage to the

Ko-Nikka family. The given destination was Firi, but travelling with the same convoy were two long-dogs bound for the Heron Pool at Mara-bara.

The Shogun passed Toshiro the tiny slip of rice paper without comment and watched with an expressionless face as his Herald's eyes hungrily devoured the almost microscopic text.

Toshiro was swept by an overwhelming sense of relief. He was not out of the woods yet but he sensed it was all coming together.

'What do you think?'

'I think we've got 'em, sire.' A quick laugh broke from his lips. 'Can you imagine – I mean, using the same name both ways? Unbelievable . . .'

'So . . . what now?'

'We have to lift her and the two servants while the convoy's passing through Lord Se-Iko's domain. As I understand it, you have him down as, uh – neutral.'

'Not exactly. If the balloon went up, Se-Iko would probably wait to see how things were going then come down on Yama-Shita's side of the fence.'

'Then it's the best place. It would be safer once they cross over into Mitsu-Bishi territory, but they're one of the pillars of the Shogunate. It would look too much like a set-up.'

'True. But how about this? Take them out of the convoy while it's travelling through Se-Iko's patch, hold them overnight, then cross over the border and release them on the other side. That way we can stage-manage whatever . . . judicial response is required.'

'Meaning?'

'My dear Toshiro, we cannot allow such lawlessness to go unpunished. I'll ask Mitsu-Bishi to gather up thirty or more common criminals, dress them up as *ronin*, chop their heads off to exhibit by the roadside, and have him claim his men caught the people involved. Before anybody gets to question them, of course.'

'Who is going to make the raid on the convoy?'

'A very reliable group led by a man who answers to the

name of Noburo Naka-Jima. A real pro.'

'May I ask, sire, if he knows what is expected of him?'

'Not yet. I'll set up a meeting. The most convenient place is the post-house at Midiri-tana. Just south of Ari-saba. You'll need a disguise, of course. Ieyasu will provide you with false papers and give you all the details.'

Toshiro sat back on his heels, his mouth opening and shutting like a stranded carp. 'M-me, sire? B-but –'

'Yes, I know what you said, but I've decided it's better not to have too many people involved. That's why I want you to handle this personally. After all, it *is* your conspiracy. And if anything goes wrong, I'll know who to blame.'

'B-but sire. Ari-saba is –'

'– miles away. That's right,' said Yoritomo. 'You'd better get moving.'

Toshiro placed his forehead on the top step of the veranda, then rose, backed down the path for the required ten paces and turned and hurried away.

Yoritomo watched him until he disappeared behind the neatly trimmed shrubbery. He knew that when the Herald had recovered his composure, he would tackle this assignment with his usual vigour and dedication. His hunch about Yoko Mi-Shima, the itinerant courtesan, was probably correct. Toshiro had a flair for sensing the ins and outs of this kind of situation. Even so, success was not guaranteed. The risks were considerable but it was worth the gamble. If the Herald had proved to be right, Yama-Shita and his friends would be severely, perhaps fatally, compromised and his dear brother-in-law, Nakane, the Consul-General, of whom he had never been particularly fond, would finally get his well-deserved come-uppance.

And it was not that much of a gamble. Yoritomo had taken steps to limit the risks. Noburo's '*ronin*' could be relied upon to die without revealing their connection with the Shogunate. Indeed, not all of them were aware they were in Yoritomo's employ. His Herald was

89

another problem. If things did not go as planned and Toshiro was caught in the subsequent fiasco, he could be recognised and the Shogun's hand would be revealed. It was for this reason that Yoritomo had made separate arrangements with the head of his own very private team of assassins for Toshiro to disappear without trace if circumstances required it. Yoritomo might, in Ieyasu's eyes, still be wet behind the ears, but no one ever became Shogun without first learning to cover his ass.

It was not the way Yoritomo would have liked to conduct the business of government, but his scope for action was limited. The Yama-Shita could not be brought to heel by direct confrontation. They were too powerful, their influence too widespread. Yoritomo could not afford to have the authority of the Shogunate openly rebuffed and the alternative – armed conflict – was out of the question. The years of peace under the Toh-Yota had sapped the desire for large-scale conflicts. But it had not stilled ambition. The struggle for power continued, and the secret weapon Hiro Yama-Shita had turned against the Shogunate was far more destructive than the greatest army ever raised. It was called progress.

Yama-Shita was a cunning, ruthless individual. He was also highly intelligent and capable of great subtlety. Given the present situation, his plans had to be countered by equally devious means. The unsuspecting Herald who would soon be galloping westwards, changing horses at the post-houses on the way, had likened it to a poker hand. It was an apt comparison. Yoritomo weighed up the odds and concluded that the only way he could win this particular game was to play a wild card.

*

As he came to that decision, the young Shogun had no inkling that the wild card he sought lay hidden in a forest on the western flank of the Ari-geni Mountains, above a road that had once been known as the Pennsylvania Turnpike.

It took the shape of a hungry, dirt-stained fugitive armed with a knife and a primitive halberd. His body bore the swirling patterns that identified him as a Plainfolk Mute. But he was no ordinary lumphead. His bones were well formed, the skin covering his young hard body was as smooth as saddle leather and he had not been ringed or branded. The hard blue eyes were those of a warrior at bay, not a hunted slave, and a keen observer would have noticed that his dark brown hair had turned blond at the roots to match the growth around his mouth and along the line of his jaw.

His name was Steve Brickman but, unlike the industrious long-dog at the Heron Pool who answered to the same name, he was the genuine article: 2102–8902 Brickman, S.R. from Roosevelt/Santa Fe, New Mexico: graduate of Lindbergh Field Air Force Academy, Class of 2989.

Trained as a wingman, Steve was now a 'mexican', one of a select group of undercover agents controlled by AMEXICO, an ultra-top-secret unit working directly for the President-General of the Amtrak Federation. Officially he was dead, killed in action over Wyoming Territory. The fiction was not all that far removed from the truth. He *had* been shot down during a combat mission over Wyoming and, since hitting the ground, had come close to death on more than one occasion. In an action-packed year, Steve had found himself in some tight corners and, once again, he was in all kinds of trouble.

CHAPTER FIVE

For the past two weeks, Steve Brickman had been living dangerously as an illegal immigrant in a foreign country whose people spoke an incomprehensible language and acted with extreme hostility towards strangers. It had quickly become obvious that he could not have chosen a worse disguise. The Iron Masters treated Mute journeymen as slaves who, when not working under the whips of overseers, were herded into prison compounds; the groups he had seen moving along roads had been chained together and closely guarded. He had not come across any renegade Trackers but, on the evidence so far, they were probably getting a rough ride too.

Unable to make contact with anybody who could help him, Steve had become a scavenger, stealing scraps of food whenever he could. But there were soldiers and officials everywhere checking the movement of goods and people. It was like trying to move around one of the Federation's underground bases without an ID card. Steve's basic dilemma was this: he could not move openly without becoming part of the system, but if he *did* find a way to become part of it as a Mute he risked ending up in a chain gang unable to move at all.

In one of his more successful sorties he had managed to steal a padded cotton blanket to help ward off the bone-chilling hours before the dawn, but on his last two scavenging expeditions he had almost been caught and had only escaped by the skin of his teeth. To evade his pursuers, he had taken refuge deep in the forests and there he had remained, living on whatever wild game he could catch, and moving mostly at night. Steve had discovered that the hours between dusk and dawn were the only time the Iron Masters ceased their relentless round of activity. Even so, it was too dangerous to light a fire; anything edible he managed to catch or steal had to be eaten raw.

The day, now drawing to a close, had been warm and sunny but, for Steve, it had been as tense and frustrating as the day before. And the day before that. The mission that had brought him to the land of the Iron Masters – and which he had entered with hopelessly inadequate preparation – seemed doomed to failure. Steve had come to Ne-Issan to find Clearwater and Cadillac. His only lead was a reported conversation which had mentioned a place called the Heron Pool. With no idea where that might be, he had been working his way across country in a more or less easterly direction in the vague hope that something might turn up. Up to now, his luck had failed him and there was no point in trying to kid himself any longer. He had no idea where he was or in which direction he was supposed to be heading, and the only thing he had to look forward to was another night of fretful sleep on an almost empty stomach.

When darkness fell, Steve curled up under the stolen blanket with his bladed quarterstaff clasped in his arms. His excuse for not being on his feet and on the move was the clouds which, for the second night running, covered the sky; the truth was that his body yearned achingly for a brief respite. One half of his brain agreed; the other half refused to co-operate, keeping one ear open and the alarm bells jangling. For a time it worked, causing Steve to twist and fidget, but finally, when it became clear that he was no longer responding, the obstinate grey cells turned in for the night and whiled away the hours with dreams of food: hot, spicy Mute stews, dried meat twists, new-baked flatbread and juicy yellow-fists. The menu even included a mountainous, mouth-watering pile of soya bean-burgers fresh from a giant microwave.

Steve woke as the new day dawned, springing to his feet with the alertness of a wild animal, all six senses attuned to danger. He slowly relaxed his grip on the quarterstaff. The only sounds that filled the air were the natural sounds of the forest: the cries of birds, some shrill, some harsh, some melodic; an improvised pastorale underscored by the staccato chatter and snuffling grunts of their four-legged neighbours and played to a whispering audience of leaves stirred by the wind. The keen listener could also hear the creaks and groans of trees flexing their sap-filled timbers as they continued their yearly cycle of growth; trunks thickening inch by imperceptible inch to support the upward climb and outward spread of youthful branches; roots forever seeking a firmer foothold, wriggling snakelike through the earth, splitting buried rocks with a primeval power that defied comprehension.

The next move, now part of his daily ritual, was to check the tiny radio transceiver hidden in the handle of his combat knife. Under the wooden side-pieces was a marvel of microcircuitry with an alphanumeric keyboard on which you could enter text or data for high-speed transmission at a pre-set time. Incoming messages were preceded by a signal that switched on the electronic memory. Steve unclipped the tiny stylus and activated the recall button which caused any stored messages to scroll across the fifteen-character liquid crystal display. Eleven familiar letters marched across the screen from right to left and halted. MEMORY CLEAR.

Side-Winder, the undercover agent who had helped him stow away on the wheelboat, had hinted that Karlstrom had been concerned by Steve's failure to keep in contact. There had been reasons for that, but now he had been given the means to do so he had no excuses – and no wish to increase the nagging doubts about his loyalty to the Federation. Unaware that the device had been rigged to transmit his call-sign at regular intervals, Steve had programmed it to broadcast HGFR in Morse code for ten minutes twice a day so that a fix could be obtained on his position.

When giving him the knife, Side-Winder had said, 'The Family always keep one ear close to the ground.' Steve, ever curious, had been trying to figure out how.

The maximum range of the radio knife was fifty miles. But he was now, at the very least, more than a *thousand* miles from the nearest way-station or wagon-train. If the First Family *were* able to track him, they must have installed some kind of secret network on Iron Master territory which allowed them to pick up and relay the signals he was pushing out. So far, he had drawn no response. Okay. Maybe that was because he had not filed any progress reports or asked for help. Even so, they could have let him know that somebody was on the other end of the line.

Despite his years of training at the Flight Academy, Steve's knowledge of radios – like that of most Trackers – was limited to their performance specifications, how to operate them and how to replace faulty circuit boards. Elementary stuff. All you needed was to be able to read. The communications equipment issued to Trackers contained diagnostic displays which told you which bits needed replacing. You got a requisition order, drew them from the stores, and plugged 'em in. It was with the circuit boards that the mystery began. The knowledge, skills and processes that had led to their design and manufacture, and the fundamental scientific principles on which it was all based remained the exclusive preserve of the First Family.

Steve closed up the handle of his knife and replaced the strip of rag that had been wrapped around it. He knew his transceiver was operational but was the network? The only sure way to find out was to send a mayday call – the one thing he dared not do. He was in urgent need of a map of Ne-Issan with a large 'X' marking the location of the Heron Pool, and a videotape containing an instant course in Japanese. But AMEXICO could supply him with neither. Even if Karlstrom condescended to bail him out, a skyhook – MX slang for an airborne rescue – would serve no useful purpose, and the arrival of a back-up squad would only make things more complicated than they were already. No. He was responsible for the present situation and the only way to come out looking good was

95

to solve it on his own.

Steve made a long roll of the blanket, tied the ends together so that he could carry it looped over his shoulder, and set off in search of a stream. In these hills they weren't hard to find. He filled his small drinking-skin, then slapped water on his face and arms and attempted to rub off some of the accumulated grime. The black and brown markings on his body remained intact. Once applied, the paste-like dye, first concocted by a long-lost generation of Mutes, was impervious to sweat, did not stain or fade, and resisted normal wear and tear. Mr Snow had told him it could only be removed with the aid of special five-fingered pink leaves. When scrubbed vigorously against the skin, the crushed fibres released a chemical substance that changed the nature of the dye so that it was no longer waterproof. Steve had not had time to check out the removal process himself, but he knew it worked and had brought a bundle of the leaves with him in case he needed to make a quick identity switch.

He thought back to the memorable day he had secretly watched Clearwater and Cadillac 'come clean' and re-ran the subsequent events across the screen inside his head. Connecting with her eyes on the night he had bitten the arrow had been a fantastic sensation, but the discovery of her unflawed beauty was the moment when his life had changed; had taken on new meaning. Events had conspired to force them apart but on his return to the Plainfolk, Mr Snow had revealed they were destined to come together. Knowing what he had been sent to do, Steve had tried to push her from the forefront of his mind, but whenever he saw sparks of sunlight trapped in the ripples of a crystal-clear stream her name sprang to his lips. When he knelt to drink in its coolness, the reflection that rose to touch his lips was hers, not his own. She was everywhere. The unbroken blue of a cloudless sky recalled her calm, unwavering gaze; the slim-legged deer carried themselves with the same, lithe, sure-footed grace, the scent of wild flowers recalled the garlands in her hair. Nothing had changed. His feelings now were just as strong, just as overwhelming as on their last night together when she had slid her naked body between his sleeping-furs . . .

Hard-edged reality staged a comeback, bringing the curtain down on his soft-focus reverie. The unfulfilled longings aroused by such thoughts were better buried. Rising from the stream, Steve fastened his combat knife to the inside of his left forearm, then wound a second grimy strip of rag around it, making it look like a rudimentary splint. By the time an assailant got close enough to see what it really was, the blade would be at their throat.

The rising sun had not yet cleared the crest of the hill in front of him. There was still enough time to find a safe vantage-point from where he could observe the lie of the land and spend the rest of the day plotting out his next moves. As he set off through the trees, Steve made a conscious effort to clear his mind. Dwelling on the past did nothing to resolve his present predicament. The rescue of Clearwater and Cadillac was only one part of the problem. When that had been accomplished a stark choice awaited him. If he made good his promise to Mr Snow then Roz, his kin-sister, might end up dead. The alternative was to do what the Federation had demanded and risk losing Clearwater for ever. The situation was made worse by the fact that he was equally bound, for differing reasons, to both women. The prospect of losing either was something he steadfastly refused to contemplate. He would find a way to save both.

Or a way would be found for him . . .

Since graduating a year last April from the Air Force Academy under the sands of New Mexico, Steve had seen and heard enough to convince him that his life was being shaped by forces that neither he nor the Federation had the power to control. According to Mr Snow, he had been born in the shadow of Talisman, the Thrice-Gifted One; the all-conquering hero who, according to Mute prophecy, would enter the world as the Saviour of the Plainfolk. The Federation did not believe in prophecy; the Mutes did. For them, the Path was already drawn. The Wheel turned. The Federation also had a dream of the future, but Trackers used computer modelling and critical-path analysis to make it happen. Mutes had faith in invisible spirit beings; Trackers had faith in themselves, in the system. For them, the physical world had finite dimensions and properties which could be quantified, potential resources that could be exploited. For the Mutes, the world of nature was like a walled garden with a door, beyond which lay a vast cloud-rimmed land offering everchanging vistas of unparalleled splendour: snowcapped mountains with swift-running streams, tree-lined valleys heavy with fruit, carpeted with sweet-smelling earth and tall bread-grass, rolling plains rich with game. Their cosmos stretched beyond the ceiling of the stars, beyond time and space, to encompass spiritual realms of immeasurable dimensions. Trackers might agree that earthly life was as a spark rising from a fire, flaring briefly as it spirals heavenwards to be snuffed out an instant later, but the Mutes believed the sparks were constantly reborn in the leaping flames. Birth, death, rebirth – the cycle was endless: the ocean of being at the end of the river of time revolved around an eternal sun, whose fiery radiance was at the heart of all creation.

In the past few months, and especially during the last few weeks, Steve had had few opportunities to ponder these mysteries. Everything he had been taught as a Tracker ran counter to such ideas. The Federation dealt in facts, not abstractions. But his conversations with Mr Snow still echoed through his mind. Despite past and present dangers, they had triggered something within him, sympathetic vibrations which had brought his body into tune with the overground. The alien world which he felt instinctively was his real home.

As he continued his upward journey through the woods, Steve saw a small furry animal with a bushy tail clinging to the trunk of a tree a few yards ahead of him. He froze in his tracks and slowly drew his hidden knife.

Raising his arm with the stealth of a praying mantis, he took aim and – *thwokk*! The knife hit the exact spot vacated by his breakfast in the previous millisecond with the speed of greased lightning. A few minutes later Mo-Town, the great Sky-Mother, offered him a new target of opportunity. His roving eye glimpsed the tail end of a snake sliding away under a layer of rotting leaves. Steve took a firm grip of his quarterstaff, swept it round at shoulder height and – *whap*! Although the snake had vanished between the leaves, the blade struck the head off cleanly. Once again the quarterstaff moved with a speed that surprised him – he'd first noticed it in the fight with the doomed back-up squad. It had vibrated in his hands and seemed to be pulling the wooden shaft after it – almost as if it had a mind of its own.

Trembling with excitement, Steve quickly skinned and gutted the snake and sank his teeth into the flesh along its spine, oblivious to anything but the sensation of filling his mouth and gullet with something he could chew and swallow. He gasped with pleasure, and nearly choked. Oh, bliss! Slinging his quarterstaff across his back, he moved on, gnawing his way out from the middle of the snake towards both ends.

Reaching the crest, Steve climbed into the upper branches of the tallest tree he could find and took stock of his surroundings. The sun now hung above a tree-covered ocean. Wave after wave of forested hills stretched away towards the eastern horizon, their undulating crests running north and south as far as the eye could see. Along the floor and lower slopes of the adjacent valley were scattered clearings, some with dwelling places; others enclosing square ponds and terraced cropfields.

Smoke climbed from the chimneys of the dwellings, reminding Steve that others, more fortunate than himself, were preparing to face the day fortified by something more appetising than raw snake meat. If he decided to traverse the valley he would have to take great care to keep out of sight. Safer to wait till dark and hope for a clear sky. The moon was a thinning crescent and would soon disappear altogether, but that didn't matter. If the stars were out, he could use the roads. Provided he kept clear of dwelling-places and the guard-posts that controlled access to bridges and ferry crossings, it was not as dangerous as it sounded. And it was a lot faster than blundering through a pitch-black forest. The Iron Masters rarely moved along the roads at night. When they did, the travellers were always accompanied by several dozen foot-soldiers and everyone carried lanterns on the end of long poles. They also made a surprising amount of noise, banging sticks and small drums, blowing on horns and talking at the top of their voices. The din they created could not have endeared them to the people living along the route who were trying to grab some hard-earned shut-eye, but it meant that Steve always had plenty of warning of their approach.

From his perch at the top of the tree, Steve saw a stretch of the winding highway that cut through the mountains. Its western end met the Allegheny River, running on, via the ferry, towards navref Pittsburgh – the Fire Pits of Beth-Lem. Since it was wider than the other roads he had encountered and surfaced with tightly packed stones, Steve had concluded, not unreasonably, that it must lead to other places of similar importance. Persuaded – for want of a better idea – that the Heron Pool might be located at or near one of them, Steve had steered a course roughly parallel to the highway, dividing his attention between the landscape and the sky. Cadillac and Clearwater had been here for a good six months. If the Mute *had* picked his brains he ought to have something airborne by now. Something that he, Steve, could get a bearing on. So far, there had been nothing up there but the birds – and today's dawn patrol wore feathers too. He drank in the fresh breeze sweeping through the treetops, and headed for the ground.

Since beginning his eastward journey, Steve had made a point of spending part of each day noting the type and level of traffic along the highway and the behaviour patterns of the people at work in the fields and around their dwelling places. What he saw confirmed the impression he had formed of the Iron Masters back at the trading post. They ran a tight ship – afloat and ashore – and they were highly organised. Perhaps over-organised. And it had occurred to Steve that he might have discovered their weak spot. Field-work and domestic activities were dovetailed into a strictly daily routine, but their schedule also included rest periods when people gathered in groups to chew the fat and – to judge from the faint sounds of laughter that reached him – generally have a good time. Whether their Mute slaves found anything to laugh at was another matter.

Having now walked and run nearly 200 miles – much of it over difficult terrain – Steve had begun toying with the idea of waylaying one of the lone horsemen who sometimes passed by. If he found himself unable to ride the beast, he could always eat it. It was an agreeable fantasy but nothing more. The handsomely dressed warriors who rode back and forth – sometimes singly but more frequently in groups – were a superior kind of Iron Master whose appearance caused local pedestrians to hit the dirt. To take one of them out would cause the shit to hit the fan in triplicate.

Steve had seen video pictures of horses, but the discovery of their continued existence had been the biggest surprise to date. The Federation archives listed them as one of the many species that had become extinct during the Holocaust. But it was not true. In the past three weeks he'd seen close to fifty – always with samurai in the saddle. Horses were clearly a status symbol, reserved for the privileged classes. Everyone else walked, or rode on pushcarts or on larger four-wheeled vehicles drawn by smooth-skinned buffalo. Really important people – to judge by the accompanying procession – were carried shoulder-high in lavishly decorated palanquins. Iron Master society obviously had a pecking order just like the Amtrak Federation, running down through the ranks from their version of the First

101

Family and the high-wire Execs in the Black Tower to the greaseballs in the A-levels. Despite the vast cultural and technological gap, Trackers and the Sons of Ne-Issan were cast from the same mould. The arms and accoutrements of the samurai showed they were gripped by the same unbridled passion for hardware: they also subscribed to the idea of a master race – and thought they were it. But despite this potential source of conflict it was not beyond the bounds of possibility that, at some point in the future, the Iron Masters might decide to cut out the middleman and deal directly with the Federation. If they did, Talisman and the Plainfolk would have to get their act together. Fast.

Keeping to the western flank of the mountain – still shaded from the sun – Steve headed in the direction of the highway. It lay at the bottom of a man-made gorge whose smooth sloping sides were now covered by a tangled carpet of vegetation. At some time in the past, a wide band on either side of the highway had been cleared of trees, but the forest above was slowly reclaiming the lost ground. Several generations of saplings had sprung up amid the bushes and the long grass, and the strongest were beginning to elbow the weaklings out of the way in the race to grab the biggest chunk of sky.

Before Steve could select a proper hiding place, a motley group of horsemen burst out of the trees on the far side of the highway and zigzagged down through the belt of saplings. Caught on the wrong foot, Steve froze awkwardly, unsure whether to duck or run. His surprise turned rapidly to panic as the riders clattered across the road and came thundering up the slope towards him, their slung weapons bouncing off their backs. The fact they kept looking over their shoulders suggested that they, and not he, were the quarry but Steve was not about to hang around for confirmation. It was time to get the hell out. *MOVE it, Brickman!*

Powered by a surge of adrenalin, Steve turned and sprinted back up through the trees, pausing to check the scene behind him as he reached the crest. The rising steepness of the slope had obliged the riders to cut back and forth across its face, slowing their mad gallop to a laboured canter. The wild bunch had become a strung-out line and now the home team – approximately double in number, and decked out with banners and matching armour – were streaming out of the woods, firing volleys of arrows across the gorge as they galloped down towards the highway.

And scoring hits. Ouch! A horse reared up and fell backwards on top of its rider. Steve accelerated rapidly. There was no point in getting caught in the crossfire. His frantic dash through the trees reminded him of the afternoon he had been chased through another forest by a posse of Mutes. He had given them the slip by diving into a rock pool and hiding close to the bank among the reeds. Given the chance he'd have done the same thing now but he was too high up. Every stream he came across was no more than ankle-deep. The only thing he could do was keep going. He settled down into the loping stride he'd picked up from running with the M'Call Bears. The accumulated aches and pains of the past weeks merged, becoming an exquisite burning sensation that enveloped him from head to foot as he pushed his body to the limits. It went past the point of being unbearable and induced a strange kind of euphoria that damped down all physical sensation. He could barely feel his feet thudding against the ground, or his pain-wracked lungs that, only moments before, had felt as if they were about to explode inside his chest. He was conscious of being outside himself. It was as if his brain had parted company with his body and was floating just above and behind him, saying, 'You go right ahead and do what you have to do, fella. Don't worry about me. I can't feel a thing.'

Steve had been there before and knew from experience that he could maintain the same relentless pace for several hours. But he could not outrun a galloping horse – and that was fast becoming his most pressing problem. He had changed direction several times but whichever way he turned, the fugitive riders –

who were obviously as confused as he was – always seemed to end up heading in the same direction!

The only solution was to take to the trees and stay there till the excitement died down. But what would he do if the home team spotted him and took him for one of the opposition? He would be trapped, out on a limb – like a treed mountain-cat. But then, if they caught him it wouldn't matter *who* they thought he was. The jig would be up. It was a chance he'd have to take. He shinned up the leafiest tree he could find, pulling his legs up out of sight as the ground shook under the hooves of the front runners.

The gaps in the leaves provided Steve with a few brief snapshots of the riders as they sped by, crouched low over their horses. Their faces and arms were smeared with dirt, and their dress was as varied as the ragtag uniforms worn by Malone's renegades. Some wore armour, but nobody seemed to own a full set. Two or three had small square shields fixed to their shoulders. Most had helmets of one sort or another, some with wide sweeping brims and what looked like metal horns or crescent moons attached to the front. A few had a tangled mess of shoulder-length hair streaming out from under headbands of cloth. All the riders Steve caught a glimpse of wore curving swords – the mark of samurai – plus a variety of other weapons: spears, halberds, two-bladed axes and bows and arrows. Were these outlaws? Did the Iron Masters have their own brand of breakers?

Moving to a higher branch, Steve saw another sizeable bunch gallop through the small clearing, followed a short while later by a handful of stragglers. The last one had turned round in his saddle and was shouting hoarsely in the Iron Masters' nonsense language. From his gestures it was clear he was urging on someone who had fallen behind. He paused briefly, his sweating horse pawing the ground nervously, then rode on. A few seconds later Steve caught sight of another rider. But this guy was in trouble. His horse had slowed to a trot and he was hunched up in the saddle with two arrowshafts sticking out of his back. Now that, thought Steve, must hurt. He lost sight of the rider as he crossed the clearing, then heard a sharp crack and a dull thud rolled into one.

Peering down the line of the trunk, Steve saw that the guy had fallen off and now lay at the foot of the tree. His wide-brimmed helmet and the shanks of long hair that went with it had rolled to one side, revealing a head that was completely bald. The riderless horse moved restlessly back and forth near by, snatching hurried mouthfuls of grass. Steve was filled with a strange feeling. This has to be fate, he thought. It was totally mad. Insane. But a voice that was not his own urged him on. Quickly! Before it's too late! His mind resisted. But I don't know how to ride these things! *Never mind,* said the voice. *Just do it!*

He dropped out of the tree and took a quick look at the fallen Iron Master. He had landed on his back, flattening the lacquered wooden arrowshafts beneath him. The impact had driven the bladed points out through his chest. He wasn't dead, but he soon would be. Steve relieved him of his sword, then scooped up the long-haired helmet and put it on his head. Pulling the plaited strap firmly under his chin, he gathered up the reins of the horse, took a deep breath and hauled himself aboard.

Okay, sweet Sky-Mother, let's go!

The horse took off with Steve bobbling around in the saddle like a ping-pong ball in a shooting gallery. But Mo-Town – or some other benign deity – kept him in his seat until his feet found the stirrups and some innate sense of rhythm brought his undulating backside into partial phase with the rise and fall of the horse beneath him. What Steve wanted to do most of all was stop and get off, but he didn't know which buttons to press. The alternative was to throw himself off, but he was too scared to try. The horse was going too fast and he was too high off the ground. If he failed to get clear and fell under its hooves . . .

Steve drove the thought from his mind. It was clear he had made a serious tactical error. He had shinned up the tree to get out of the way of the wild bunch – and here he was hard on their heels! In fairness, it had to be said it was not of his own volition. His entire energies were concentrated on staying upright in the saddle and avoiding getting his brains knocked loose by low-hanging branches. There was no way he could steer at the same time – even if he had known how. Steve had, in fact, lost the reins and was hanging on, white-knuckled, to the front edge of the saddle. His feet kept springing out of the stirrups and every time they banged against the horse's ribs, it tensed up and made another wild surge forward. Christo! What on earth had persuaded the Iron Masters to use such a capricious means of transportation? No wonder they had no hair. They must have torn it all out trying to figure out how to stay on top of the goddamned things.

Steve could see that a horse offered certain advantages: if you had a lot of ground to cover it was the animal that did most of the work in getting you there. But *jeeezzz* – the pain! The sinews in his thighs were zinging like overstretched rigging wires, and every time his ass collided with the horse it felt as if a red-hot knife had been driven into the base of his spine. The discomfort was something he could cope with. What worried him most was the fact he was now the meat in the sandwich: if he tried to slow the horse down the home team might catch up with him; if it went too fast, he could land himself in the arms of the wild bunch.

Unaware of the problems it was causing its rider, the horse galloped on, weaving its way through the trees without the slightest hesitation. Since there was no trail beneath its feet, it must have been following an internal route map. Which indicated the animal was not as stupid as it looked – even if the route did not always contain sufficient headroom for the person on its back. Within a short time, Steve's face and limbs were striped, bruised and bleeding from the searing whiplashes delivered by bush and branch along the way. The headlong dash for freedom was also taking its toll of the horse. Its

106

breathing was harsh and laboured, and its quivering flanks were covered with a soapy lather, but somehow the animal found the stamina to keep going mile after mile, driven on by the same herd instinct Steve had seen demonstrated by fast-foot and buffalo. Rider and mount were possessed by the same urgent need to reach some place of safety. But where might that be? It was the kind of situation he always did his utmost to avoid.

So what's happening here, Brickman? I mean, aren't you the guy that likes to plan ahead? Y'know – figure out all the angles . . .?

Yeah, right, but –

Never mind the 'buts'! Come on! 'S about time you got a handle on this situation. Let's see some positive action here!

Easier said than done. Steve was still the guy who liked to figure out all the angles, but he had noticed that ever since Clearwater had crossed his path he had become prey to sudden, dangerous impulses. The off-the-cuff decision to stow away on board one of Yama-Shita's wheelboats without asking even the most elementary questions about what he might find when he got to wherever they were going was a prime example. Leaping astride this animal was another. It was just not like him. Or was it?

From the very beginning, entering the blue sky-world was like coming home. What he had experienced ran counter to everything he had been taught. It was like being torn in two. He had become impatient and increasingly rebellious, had discovered feelings he could not put into words and was now driven by the need to find his rightful place in the whole great scheme of things. This inner conflict had given birth to the sure and certain feeling that it was the overground that held the key to the questions which plagued him. It was here that he would discover not only the truth about himself but also the dark secrets so jealously guarded by the First Family. Perhaps, in allowing the horse to carry him wherever it had a mind to, he was being given a sign. A gentle warning to stop trying to manipulate people, to always be in control. Perhaps he was being asked to put his life in someone else's hands – to allow them to manipulate *him*. It was an interesting proposition, and one he would definitely give some serious thought to. But not right now.

The shouts and trumpet calls of his pursuers slowly died away, and there was no sign of the wild bunch up front. The fear that had turned Steve's balls into frozen walnuts slowly melted away. After a while, the forest began to thin. Soon there were more bushes than there were trees, more sky than leaves, and the only thing smacking him in the face was fresh air. Ahead of him was a rise in the ground. Steve gathered up the reins and managed to get the horse to stop short of the crest so that, by standing up in the stirrups, he could take a peek at what lay on the other side.

The ground fell away unevenly into a rock-strewn river valley. On the far side there was more broken ground rising up to meet a heavily forested slope which ringed a mountainous, flat-topped chunk of bare rock. Its deeply fissured sides were only a few degrees off the vertical and, from a distance, it looked like the stump of a giant stone tree rooted in a mound of red moss; a fossilized relic of some bygone age.

Anxious to reach its chosen destination, the horse moved forward, straining at the bit. At the same instant, the wild bunch – or at least some of them – made their second appearance of the day. This time, however, they were not heading towards him – at least not yet. They came out between the trees on the far side of the river, angling down from left to right across his front. Once again they were closely pursued by flag-carrying comrades, although now the numbers looked roughly equal.

Steve hauled back savagely on the reins, pulling the horse's head round to the left. The animal circled, stamping its hooves nervously and tossing its head in an effort to tear the reins from his grasp. Steve fought back, cursing the wretched beast for making him divide his attention at such a crucial moment.

Twisting from side to side in his saddle, he caught brief glimpses of the wild bunch as they raced along the river bank to where the broad, placid current rippled over a pebble bed. He felt a sudden pang of anxiety as they crossed over towards him in a cloud of spray, but they promptly veered off to his right, fanning out in three different directions – presumably in an effort to throw off or divide their pursuers.

The ruse didn't work because the home team also had a few tricks up their sleeve. With a dramatic suddenness which took Steve totally by surprise, a second group of beflagged samurai burst out of the forest from which he himself had just emerged. Fortunately, they were way over to his right and, by some miracle, had failed to spot him. Even so, the unexpected chorus of blood-curdling yells was a real heart-stopper. Co-lumbus! To think he had just been sitting there – right out in the open!

Having now discovered how the reins worked, Steve urged the horse towards the river, going down to his left, away from the action. Looking over his shoulder, he saw that the samurai's pincer movement had cut off the wild bunch's escape route, causing them to wheel about in confusion, swords waving in the air. A fold in the ground blocked Steve's view of the ensuing clash of arms, and by the time he had managed to get safely across the river the sight and sounds of battle had faded.

Yeah, well, you win some, you lose some . . .

Whichever side carried the day was immaterial to Steve. He had no reason to believe that renegade Iron Masters treated Mutes any better than their law-abiding kin. Only one thing mattered: he, Steven Roosevelt Brickman, was still up and running.

And so was the horse. Once they were clear of the fire-fight, Steve had allowed it free rein and it now moved forward purposefully along the steepening forest trail towards the forbidding ramparts of the rock tower which Steve had mentally christened 'Big D' in affectionate memory of Buck McDonnell, the crewcut, granite-jawed

Trail Boss on the wagon-train known as The Lady.

The great stretch of landscape that now lay below and beyond the trees reminded him of the view from the cockpit of his Skyhawk. His thoughts drifted back to the moments of danger he had shared with McDonnell and the rest of the crew during the Battle of the Now and Then River. Jodi Kazan, his Flight Leader, swept overboard, wrapped in a white-hot ball of fire while attempting to land her Skyhawk during the height of the storm. Gus White, fellow-graduate wingman, who had flown away leaving him to die in a blazing cropfield. And the rest of the flight section who had all perished on the same fateful day. Booker and Yates, consumed like moths in a flame when their aircraft were hit by lightning. Webber, killed in the take-off ramp. Caulfield, his head transfixed by a crossbow bolt, hauled from the cockpit with his eyeballs hanging out of their sockets. Ryan plunging to earth, incinerated on impact by his own planeload of napalm. Lou Fazetti and Naylor who, seized by a sudden, inexplicable madness, shot each other down.

By a combination of luck and circumstance, Jodi, her face and neck now disfigured by scar tissue, had survived with the help of a band of Tracker renegades. But her luck had run out at the same time as theirs. She was now in the hands of the Iron Masters and on her way to Heron Pool. Prior to her capture and trade-in by the clan M'Call, she had saved Steve's life, and he had made up his mind to rescue her along with Cadillac and Clearwater – just as he had vowed to get even with Gus White. And the others. The people who had conspired to deny him the graduation honours that were rightfully his. The memory of past injustices, and the cynical way he had been pressured by the threats against his kin-sister Roz, put the iron back in his soul.

So many scores to settle. So much still to do . . .

As the horse emerged above the tree line, Steve looked down towards the valley. Most of it was obscured by the forested slope he had just climbed, but he could see, almost directly below him, the stretch of broken water where the wild bunch had crossed over the river. From his previous flight experience he judged himself to be some 800 feet above it. The horse moved on, picking its way along an increasingly precipitous trail through the scrub that clung like a red foam to frozen cascades of fallen rock.

Trees and rockfaces held no terrors for Steve. He had a good head for heights and flying like a bird was the greatest thrill of all. But this was something different. He was not standing on his own two feet and his hands were not firmly on the controls. He was balanced precariously on top of a strange beast that might stumble and lose its balance at any minute. That unsettling thought, plus the constant swaying back and forth, was making him feel distinctly queasy. More than once he felt compelled to get off and bring up his snake-meat breakfast but, by the power of positive thinking, he succeeded in holding down the bile that kept rising in his throat and stayed on board.

The horse worked its way slowly towards the eastern flank of the rock tower. Steve looked up and scanned its weathered face. Big D looked unassailable – like the man it was named after. The animal must know what it was doing but, as far as Steve could see, there was nothing up there and no way to go but down. He had the impression the horse had come to the same conclusion. It was certainly not in any shape to go much higher. Its pace had slowed to a plodding walk and its neck sagged under the weight of its head. With increasing frequency it missed its footing, causing Steve to rock alarmingly in the saddle, but it just wouldn't give up. An admirable stubborn streak drove the exhausted animal onwards and upwards until they reached a deep fissure. They had already passed several, but it evidently knew which one it was looking for.

Steve glanced back down towards the river as they turned off the trail, but a curve in the rock slope now blocked off the valley, leaving only a distant view of the surrounding landscape. They were now about 1,000 feet up and, at a rough guess, had climbed two-thirds of the way towards the summit. Once they were a few yards inside the fissure all he could see of the outside world was sky and, pretty soon, not much of that. The fissure was not just a narrow vertical fault-line; it was a deep cleft that went not only into the rock tower but all the way up to the top. At another time and place it was the kind of feature Steve might have been tempted to explore – except for one unsettling detail. During, or after the formation of the cleft, several hundred tons of rock had come loose from the sides and were now wedged some fifty feet above the narrow floor. The ceiling of rock appeared to be anchored in place by several enormous boulders, but all it needed was a sizeable jolt of what the Mutes called 'earth thunder' and the whole lot could come crashing down.

Heedless of the possible danger, the horse plodded along a series of rising S-bends. A leaden gloom replaced the last vestiges of daylight, and as they climbed deeper into the belly of the mountain the jagged ceiling of boulders got lower and lower, until its menacing bulk was only a few feet above Steve's head. After a few more twists and turns, he found himself sitting hunchbacked in the saddle facing a wall of rock. It was a dead end.

Brilliant . . . There was not even room to turn the horse round. Which bit did you have to kick or pull to engage reverse gear? What a pain!

While Steve fumed silently, his borrowed helmet jammed against the roof, the horse stood patiently with his nose against the rock wall. Then, when his ungrateful rider failed to take the appropriate action, he pawed at the wall, first with his right hoof, then with his left. Steve got the message. The horse wasn't as big a dummy as he thought. It was trying to tell him this wasn't a dead end. What looked like a solid wall of rock was a door – but how the eff-eff did you open it? He slithered out of the saddle and discovered he was unable to stand upright. Arching his back, he staggered about bent-legged, clutching his kidneys as he tried to get his knees together. His thighs had locked and his butt-bones were . . .

Kerr-istopher Columbus!

112

Gritting his teeth, Steve ran his hands over the rock, testing its surface. It was the real thing all right, but when he ran his fingers down the corners where it met the side-walls he thought he detected a slight draft. Cunning bastards . . . it *was* a door! Steve pulled out his knife and tried to insert it between the end wall and the uneven rock surround. Whoever had put it together had done a good job. It was a real tight fit. But there *had* to be a handle or a secret catch somewhere. Steve pushed the horse back out of the way and scrabbled around amongst the loose rocks and rubble lying against the foot of the wall. He then checked the side-walls again and peered up at the ceiling. No rope pulls, no hidden levers or handles. Nothing.

Shit . . .

Steve sagged against the wall bent-legged, still unable to straighten up. The pain that began at his knees had now spread all the way up his spine and out through his shoulder-blades.

Fucking horses . . .

He eyed the foam-flecked animal as it returned to scrape a hoof against the end wall, tossing its head impatiently. Just you wait, fella. If we get through this and clear of whatever's behind it, I'm gonna turn your ass into beefburgers . . .

The horse snorted dismissively.

Steve mastered his frustration and tried reasoning with himself. Come on, Brickman! A smart guy like you should be able to figure this out. These dinks may know how to join two pieces of wood together but their technology is still in the stone age. There are only so many ways this stone can move and you can bet your last meal credit they've gone for the simplest solution. If this *is* a secret entrance then you've got to be able to open it in a hurry.

The first glimmerings of a possible solution came into Steve's mind. Elbowing the horse out of the way, Steve re-examined the rock face inch by inch. The fact that the passage was in semi-darkness didn't help, but he eventually discovered something he'd missed first time around. The rock face was made up of irregular terraced layers whose edges ran mainly in a vertical direction. About eighteen inches from the right-hand wall his fingertips encountered an edge that was a little deeper than the others and appeared to be undercut at chest height.

Tingling with excitement, Steve probed the undercut section with his knife. With the handle laid flat against the rock face, the blade slipped in easily. By working it around he quickly discovered a V-shaped slot which narrowed as it went in. The sides of the V were angled at roughly ninety degrees. As he pushed the blade all the way in, Steve heard the sound of metal on metal. He moved the tip of the knife around the obstruction in an effort to divine its shape and function. It was rectangular and hollow. Some sort of tube or . . . socket – that pointed downwards at the same angle as the bottom edge of the V-shaped slot.

Sockets had only one function – they were made to have things stuck in them. This was it.

Scarcely daring to breathe, Steve found the opening and tried to insert the blade of his knife. The point went in and then stuck fast. Held flat, the main part of the blade was too wide to go in. Steve pulled it and tried inserting it on the diagonal. It fitted perfectly, leaving only the handle protruding from the V. There was only one way it could go – and that was up. Steve wriggled his fingers between the handle and the rock face, got as firm a grip as he could, took a deep breath and pushed. It took some effort and removed the skin from his knuckles but, as the knife handle came into line with the top edge of the V, Steve felt the right-hand side of the rock face move.

The horse dug his nose between Steve's shoulder-blades. He leant back and tried to brush it aside. The horse persisted, this time sticking its muzzle under the rim of his helmet, pushing it forward over his eyes. Steve turned and threw a punch but the horse jerked its head out of the way.

Bloody animals . . .

He threw his weight against the door. The massive slab swung away from him on groaning timbers and came to rest against the left-hand wall, revealing the passageway on the other side. It was still roofed in but the jagged ceiling of boulders didn't get any lower. And it wasn't dark any more.

Ye-ess . . . it's all so simple when you know how . . .

As he stood there, hands on hips, admiring his handiwork, the horse brushed past him and trotted on up the narrow cleft and out into the daylight beyond.

Good riddance . . .

Having sat astride the beast for close on six hours, Steve was in no condition to catch it – and he certainly didn't intend to get on again. He turned back and took a closer look at the door. The slab of rock matched its surroundings perfectly but it was only a few inches thick. It had been fixed to a massive timber frame which was lined with several densely packed layers of cotton waste – presumably to stop the slab sounding hollow. It pivoted on thickly greased black iron bearings, its weight being partly supported by a line of wheels running on radiused timbers buried in the floor.

The door was locked in position by two vertically mounted timbers that engaged square sockets in the roof and floor. A lever on the inside face of the door performed the same function as Steve's knife. When lowered, the lever caused the iron-shod bolts to engage, and to retract when raised. Steve made a mental note of the locking mechanism, tested it once more, then withdrew his knife and put it away.

Swinging the door back across the pathway, Steve wedged a small rock in front of it, leaving himself enough space to slip through in case he had to get out in a hurry. Up to now, he had let the horse carry him in whatever direction it chose and, by a combination of luck and circumstance, he had managed to stay on it and out of serious trouble. But from here on in he had to move carefully. Steve's knowledge of horses did not extend much farther than knowing they had a leg at each corner, ate grass, drank water and were absolute murder to ride, but he was bright enough to realise that the animal's urge to get through the rock door was fuelled by a homing instinct. The upward path the horse had followed could only lead to one place – the hide-out of the wild bunch. You don't need to have graduated from the Flight Academy to figure that out. But that obvious conclusion merely led to another question. Was anyone at home?

The answer – if affirmative – was likely to appear at any moment. The horse, which he had been glad to see the back of, would soon – if it had not done so already – come to the attention of whoever was up there. And since it could not open the door by itself, someone – whether driven by idle curiosity or neighbourly concern – was bound to come looking for the rider. Yet another bad tactical error. Hence the partly open door.

Steve weighed up the options. From the way things were going when he left the valley, it was highly unlikely that any of the wild bunch would make it back home. That left their reserve team, or supporters, if they had any, or . . . maybe servants. Slaves. Plainfolk Mutes, who might give him a hand. The horse's eagerness to get through the door was proof there was something up there. And it was crazy to have come all this way without taking a look. Especially after enduring so much discomfort. An unattended base might yield rich pickings. Like food, for instance. Steve's mouth watered at the prospect. It was no good staying where he was. The distance between the walls was less than the length of his quarterstaff and, with no place to hide, he would be an easy target for a bowman. He could either beat a hasty retreat or go forward to give himself room to manoeuvre.

Acting on the dictum that attack was the best form of defence, Steve advanced swiftly, quarterstaff held at the ready. Fifty long-legged strides brought him out into the daylight beyond the rockfall that had turned the cleft into a tunnel; another thirty brought an amazing sight into view. The flat-topped mountain had a hollow core with a roughly circular base fringed with fallen rocks. Steve clambered quickly up into the untidy pile of huge boulders that lay to the left of the entrance ramp and made a rapid appraisal of the scene that now confronted him.

The interior walls of the mountain rose steeply upwards like the sides of Tennessee Valley Deep – the accommodation shaft at Roosevelt/Santa Fe where Steve's kinfolk were quartered. The resemblance was heightened by the three tiers of caves which ringed the uneven rock floor. Whether they were man-made or natural was hard to tell, but the network of inclines and terraces that allowed access to the upper level was, without doubt, the work of Iron Masters – and there were dozens of them, swarming all over the place!

The horse which had carried him into the heart of Big D was walking slowly towards the far side of the arena. Steve shrank back into a small pit formed by three massive chunks of rock as several Japs ran out to meet the exhausted animal.

Well done, Brickman. This time you really have excelled yourself . . . He checked the skyline in case any guards were posted round the rim. Nope. No danger from that direction. If there had been anyone on top of Big D he would have been met by a reception committee at the door. Had they caught him in possession of the horse, helmet and sword of one of their compatriots they would, in all probability, have put two and two together to make five, and gone on to mark his card in no uncertain fashion.

To prevent any future misunderstandings, Steve stuffed the helmet and its straggling hairpiece into a nearby crevice and slid the sword into another. Having got over the initial shock of the latest twist to an event-filled day, his brain began to register the finer details.

As far as he could tell, there were only four fully active members of the wild bunch on duty; a fifth was hobbling towards the animated group around the horse with the aid of a stick, helped by a sixth who had what looked like a bandage around his head. All the rest – maybe fifty or sixty people in all – were women and children of various ages, some babes-in-arms. There was no need to make an accurate head-count. All that mattered was that there were just too goddamn many!

Steve mentally kissed goodbye to the prospect of several square meals and a night in a comfortable bed, and started to climb out of his hiding place. Two of the able-bodied men were now striding purposefully across the arena towards the entrance where he lay hidden, followed by two women and a small group of kids.

It was time to get going. When they found that the missing rider was not lying in the passageway and that the door had been propped open, alarm bells would start ringing.

Steve started to ease himself out of his hidey-hole. The two Japs at the head of the search party were still about fifty yards away. Just enough time to get clear. When he was halfway towards the rear edge of the rockpile he heard what sounded like several horses clattering up the passageway. Christo! He dived back under cover and watched with a mixture of horror and surprise as eleven be-flagged samurai galloped up the entrance ramp and skidded to a halt in the arena. From the way they jerked around in their saddles they were clearly as surprised as he had been. Pulling out their swords, they wheeled about, jabbering excitedly. Steve couldn't understand a word but it was clear that these guys realised they'd hit the jackpot.

Their sudden appearance on the scene caused everybody else to panic. With shrill cries of alarm, the women with the two front men picked up the two smallest children and herded the rest towards the caves around the edge of the arena. Everybody else ran for it too, including the remaining men – presumably to get something to fight with.

The pair that had been walking towards the entrance

froze and went for their swords. There wasn't much else they could do. They were only yards away from the leading horses. It was a brave but futile gesture. Before their swords were clear of their scabbards both were cut down with blows that severed one side of their neck from shoulder to clavicle.

The first wave of horsemen split into two and swept round both sides of the arena, riding down the stragglers; panic-stricken kids and women who had stopped to gather them up. Unable to reach safety, others ran back towards the centre and were mown down when several samurai in the second wave started firing arrows with deadly accuracy. Two dismounted and rapidly got to work with their swords on the people who had been bowled over by the charging riders. Some women reappeared with halberds and attempted to fight back, but it only made things worse. Barely thirty seconds had elapsed and there were now bodies everywhere.

Steve felt torn in two. It wasn't his fight and there were no medals to be won by sticking his nose in, but he couldn't stomach the way these gooks were enjoying themselves. A year ago he had dropped napalm canisters on a cropfield which Mute children were trying to defend by throwing stones at his Skyhawk. He had done so with some hesitation, but he had still pulled the release handle. A lot had happened since then. But what could he do? He couldn't take on all eleven of them!

The leader of the samurai wheeled his horse and shouted to one of the riders. Once again, Steve could not understand the words but he was able to grasp the meaning as the rider sheathed his blood-stained sword and headed back towards the entrance. He was being sent back to announce their find to the rest of the home team.

It was now or never.

CHAPTER SIX

Steve leaped out of his hiding place and dropped down behind the rockpile on to the entrance ramp. He would hide behind the door and nail the messenger as he dismounted to pass through. He had to take sides. At the back of his mind was the nagging thought that he was responsible for the massacre now taking place. The samurai had probably been on his tail all the time. Not only had he unwittingly led them to the camp, he had obligingly left the door open!

Taking a firm grip on his quarterstaff, he sprinted down the shallow incline, passing under the rock ceiling into the darkened section of the narrow passageway. As he rounded the final curve and came in sight of the door, he skidded to a halt. The door had been jammed wide open, and there was a twelfth samurai, armed with a bow and arrow, standing guard on the other side!

Shee-itt!

For a split second, the samurai was just as surprised as he was, then he shouted to Steve in Japanese and prepared to fire.

At that range and in such a confined space there was no way he could miss. For Steve, faced with certain death, everything went into slow motion. He knew he couldn't turn and run – the horseman behind him would be coming round the last bend at any second!

Everything came into extra-sharp focus. He saw, with dreadful clarity, the samurai raise and draw the bow; saw the faint glint of light on the wide-bladed, razor-sharp steel point, felt his heart miss a beat as his chest tensed in anticipation of the fearful, piercing blow. And all he could hear was the thunderous crescendo of hoof-beats as the rider came racing down the tunnel behind him.

120

In that same split second, the quarterstaff came to life, vibrating in his hands, filling his limbs with a tingling energy that swept the ice-water out of his veins. Brain, hand and eye reacted with undreamt-of speed and precision as his body became a supercharged fighting machine. Steve was less than ten yards from the archer, but as the bow-string was released and the arrow sped towards his chest, he advanced the curving blade of the quarterstaff and swung his body to the left.

The steel-tipped point struck the angled blade and was deflected upwards. Steve saw it as a moving streak of light as it flashed past his right shoulder, then heard a strangled cry. Looking back, he saw that the arrow had embodied itself in the throat of the rider behind him. The sword which he had been intending to plunge into Steve's back fell from his hand as he toppled backwards out of the saddle.

Steve flattened himself against the wall as the horse's forward momentum carried it past him towards the open doorway where it collided with the samurai. The Jap, who was in the process of fitting another arrow to his bow, was thrown against the opposite wall as it clattered past, and the impact knocked the arrow loose from the bowstring.

Realising he was suddenly at a disadvantage, the samurai cast the bow aside, drew his sword and rushed towards Steve with a fearsome yell. A bad move. Just as in the fight with the back-up squad, Steve's blade moved faster than the eye could register. The first forward thrust severed the samurai's sword hand at the wrist, the second drove the curved end of the blade sideways through his throat, cutting his neck clean through to the spine.

Two down, ten to go . . .

Ordinarily, such odds would have given him pause for thought, but Steve's killer instinct was now well and truly roused. He dragged the blood-drenched body of the samurai out of the way, shut the door firmly and headed back up towards the arena past the second casualty. The

Jap lay on his back, choking on his own blood as he clawed feebly at the arrow in his throat. Steve eyed him without compassion.

Boy . . . what a fluke shot that had been.

An image of Clearwater came into his mind and a voice told him it was she who had used her gifts as a summoner to give the bladed quarterstaff its power. But was it a finite charge? If so, how long would it last? Was that the gist of the message her clan sister, Night-Fever, had been unable to remember when she had presented the staff to him on his return to the clan? Jeeezz! Steve ran on, hoping like hell that the Mute magic was not about to fade out on him like the power in a battery pack. With the kind of odds he was facing he needed all the help he could get.

Racing back into the centre of the arena, Steve saw that the odds had dropped to seven to one. A considerable number of arrows, fired by unseen defenders, were now flying in all directions without finding a target. An intermittent series of loud bangs followed by puffs of smoke told him that somebody was using one of the primitive drum-magazine rifles that the Iron Masters had supplied to the M'Calls. The smoke issued from the mouth of a cave on the third tier but the rifleman's aim was bad and his ineffectual shots only served to increase the samurai's anger and blood-lust. Only the leader now remained on horseback, directing operations. Two archers covered him, firing at anything that moved on the terraces. Armed with burning brands, the other four were now systematically attacking the ground-floor caves on the right of the arena. Smoke billowed from the interiors of those that were already alight. As the panic-stricken women and children ran out in a vain effort to escape the flames, they were struck down.

This, thought Steve, has gone on long enough.

Running towards the centre of the arena, he planted his feet firmly on the rocky ground and yelled defiantly at the mounted samurai. There was no more than fifty yards between them. To judge from the shrill reaction, the sight of an armed Mute seemed to give the rider apoplexy. Wheeling his horse round to face Steve, the samurai ordered the two archers to cut the insolent lumphead down.

Once again, Steve made two incredible deflections, catching the converging arrows on either side of the blade and sending them winging past him with an adroit flick of the wrist. And again. And again! *Zzzikk – zzzokk! Pow-Pow!* Away they went. His reaction time and his perception seemed to have speeded up by several thousand per cent. The arrows appeared to float slowly towards him, giving him plenty of time to bat them out of the way.

Hhhhawwww! The head samurai practically fell out of the saddle. His startled archers had another cause for worry. With all the previous mayhem they were now out of arrows. And Steve was closing in the gap between them, moving in for the kill. Out came the swords, but neither man was keen to make the first move against what was clearly a serious contender. The rider, however, figured he had a clear advantage, and spurred his horse forward, psyching himself up with a tongue-twisting battlecry.

Steve waited until he got up some speed, heaved a rock at him, then sprinted rapidly off to the left towards the terrace of boulders that formed the edge of the arena. His path was angled past the oncoming samurai, forcing him into a choice between making a wide galloping turn, or hauling back on the reins in order to hang a sharp right. Unsettled by the rock that bounced off his breastplate, he made a manoeuvre which fell somewhere in between, by which time Steve was standing on top of a boulder, brandishing his quarterstaff above his head as if he was playing king of the heap.

The boulder on which Steve was standing was about the same height off the ground as the rider's stirrups. The size of the boulders and the manner in which they were clustered together made it impossible for the samurai to pursue Steve over them, should he decide to retreat further. He had to take him to where he stood. To make sure Steve stayed there, he ordered the two archers to get round behind him. The Japs split up and began their pincer movement as the samurai positioned his horse for another charge. Meanwhile the mindless slaughter over on the other side of the arena continued.

Pow! The rifleman in the upper cave finally got a round on target. One of the advancing archers was knocked flying by the heavy metal slug. He stayed down, sprawled across a rock, one leg jerking feebly.

Six down, six to go . . .

Riding in from right to left across Steve's front, the samurai curved in towards the rocks, sword poised, the shield on his left arm raised to parry Steve's counter-blow. He and the horse were clearly used to working together. Steve, who now stood head and shoulders above the samurai, guessed correctly that his attacker would try to cut the legs from under him. The slashing blow when it came was lightning fast, but Steve was even faster. Leaping clear of the sweeping blade, he twisted his body round to the left, spinning like a top as the samurai sped by. The quarterstaff, extended at a downward angle, and rotating with the speed and force of a helicopter blade, passed under the rear of the samurai's helmet and came out under his plaited chin-strap. With the head still seated inside, the wide-brimmed helmet lifted into the air and described several backward somersaults before hitting the ground. The rest of his body swayed drunkenly in the saddle as the horse galloped on. Steve did not have the time to watch what happened to it. His attention was now focused on the surviving archer.

Realising he was next in line, the Jap turned in his tracks and beat a hasty retreat. Steve raced after him, leaping effortlessly over the jumbled heap of rocks like a mountain goat. The archer fell awkwardly off the last rock into the arena, picked himself up and scuttled towards the four remaining samurai, yelling at the top of his voice.

With a few, swift, bounding strides, Steve caught up

with him. Realising he had to make a stand, the Jap gave one last despairing shout to his companions, then turned and assumed a fighting stance, with both hands on the hilt of his sword. But by this time, Steve was moving forward like a steam train. As the Jap began to bring his sword down, Steve – who was holding his quarterstaff level across his chest – punched both arms upwards to parry the blow.

Yahhh!! The thick wooden shaft hit the underside of the Jap's arms with the impact of an iron bar, shattering both elbows. The force of the blow, added to Steve's initial momentum, lifted the Jap off his feet and sent him flying backwards.

By the time he hit the ground, Steve was already bearing down on his next target: a samurai who had just cut down a young woman fleeing from a burning cave and was about to kill another who had tripped and fallen with a small child in her arms. She was now on her knees, pleading for mercy. Some chance.

Out of the corner of his eye, Steve saw more trouble on the way. The three other samurai, now fully alerted to his troublesome presence, were running towards him. But first things first.

The nearest samurai had also seen the danger from Steve but his mind was already committed to making a killing stroke that would dispatch both woman and child. For a fleeting instant, his raised sword wavered. It was the chance Steve needed. Coming in from the side, he thrust his quarterstaff forward, driving the full length of the blade in through the Jap's exposed armpit into the chest cavity beyond.

Nine down, three to go.

He turned to face the final trio. They were a gruesome sight. With the samurai who had just had his card cancelled, they had done most of the close-quarter killing, and their body armour and swords were smeared with blood.

And the next blood to be spilled will be yours, thought Steve. Come on staff! Don't fail me now!

Emboldened by his spirited attack and the dwindling number of samurai, the camp-women began to reappear. Some of them picked up the halberds lying by the bodies of the earlier defenders; others gathered up arrows and fitted them to bows. Over on his left, two women finished off the stunned samurai whose arms he had broken. The rest formed a ragged but resolute semi-circle behind the trio of swordsmen facing Steve. The scent of victory was in the air and they wanted to be in at the kill. Steve waved to them to stay back. After the way those arrows had been flying around earlier, he did not want to risk getting in the way of a near miss at this stage of the game.

While the two outside samurai edged outwards, figuring how best to take Steve, the guy in the middle spun on his heel and advanced on the women, hopping from one foot to the other like a bandy-legged bogey man, shouting angrily and brandishing his sword. For a minute it worked. Two or three turned and fled. The rest wavered and took a few paces backwards but then rallied and held their ground.

Steve knew he had to strike while the middle man had his back turned. The two on his right and left were clearly planning to take him from both sides. A frontal attack on one would leave him exposed to the other. Steve leapt through the space between them, twisting round in the air so that he landed squarely on his feet behind both men, facing his previous position. It was a tremendous jump. From a standing start he had cleared over twelve feet. If his body had not been energised by the power in the quarterstaff he would have been lucky to cover half that distance.

As the startled Jap on his right turned to bring his sword to bear, Steve swung the iron-shod butt of his quarterstaff up and round, delivering a lethal uppercut to the base of the jaw. It landed at the point where the hangman places his knot and produced the same effect – a broken neck. Then, in one continuous movement, he caught the sword blow from the second Jap on the cross-piece set below his own blade, and swung the butt forward and upwards in between the samurai's splayed legs. The impact lifted him clean off the ground. As he came back down and crumpled forwards under the pain, Steve snapped his head back with another iron-butt-blow under the chin, then, sensing danger, he spun round to face the attack of the advancing middle man.

The last samurai's sword was still poised above his head as Steve's blade punched deep into his stomach. It was only when he toppled forwards that Steve saw why the Jap's reactions had been so slow. A shower of arrows had turned his back into a pin-cushion.

Well done, ladies . . .

Steve turned back to make sure the other two were out for the count and was just in time to see the woman whose life he had saved plunge the first Jap's sword into the throat of the second.

*

Noburo Naka-Jima, leading the forty-six survivors from his band of *ronin* through the secret door to his camp, was alarmed to find the bodies of two of Lord Se-Iko's samurai lying in the passageway beyond. Urging his horse into a gallop, he raced up the entrance ramp into the arena just in time to see a tall Mute plunge what looked like a spear into the belly of yet another of Se-Iko's samurai. Smoke poured from five of the ground-floor caves and –

By the blessed kami, there were bodies everywhere!

His men, following in single file with their three prisoners, spread out on either side of him and cried out in horror as they caught sight of the dead women and children. *Iiyyyehhh!* And alongside them, their comrades who had been left to guard the camp! Old Ishido, who had slipped from the upper terrace after drinking too much sake and had broken his leg; Narita, who had been thrown from his horse and had split his head open. But they had given a good account of themselves. Twelve of Se-Iko's samurai had also fallen.

127

The *ronin* cantered forward and hurriedly dismounted as their womenfolk and the surviving children rushed towards them uttering heartrending cries. The tearful lamentations and the mournful howls of women bearing the limp bodies of their young offspring alternated with shouts of joyous relief as the unharmed found their kinfolk. Fathers gathered up their precious sons and hugged them fiercely as they listened to shrill accounts of the dreadful slaughter that had taken place – and the courage of the mysterious intruder who singlehandedly had killed five of the blood-crazed attackers.

And the two in the secret passageway?

Ah, in that case, *seven!*

And who was this base individual who dared to court the wrath of the Iron Masters by bearing arms?

No one knew. He had appeared, as if by magic, when Ishido and Narita and the other men had been killed and the terrible wrath of Se-Iko's samurai had been turned against young and old. And despite his base origins, the outlander had conducted himself like a true warrior, with the martial skills and courage that only samurai were thought to possess.

And there was more! He had saved Kiri, Noburo's wife, and their son, Itada as they lay helpless under a samurai's blade! Was that not so? Kiri Naka-Jima agreed it was so. The crowd parted to make way for her as she carried Itada towards his father. One hand supported her child, the other gripped the hilt of the samurai's sword, red with the blood of the Se-Iko. Noburo took charge of the boy and embraced him. Their tears mingled as he showered kisses on his tiny face. Placing the point of the sword on the ground, Kiri folded her hands together over the hilt and inclined her head respectfully. Noburo reached out and gripped her shoulder. Normally samurai did not embrace women or display any signs of affection in public. It was deemed unseemly but, on this occasion, he found himself overcome by emotion.

*

As Steve stood there, in the midst of the carnage, he realised that he had won a hollow victory. There was little cause for celebration and he was unlikely to be given a hero's welcome. If anything, his intervention had placed him in an even worse predicament than before. Not only was he an armed alien intruder, he was now an uninvited guest at a wake, who would soon be called to account for his presence.

The unkempt warriors – who must have belonged to a different group from the one he had seen trapped in the valley – were clearly aghast at what had taken place in their absence, and those whose kin had been killed soon gave vent to their grief. And there were many women who were visibly distressed when they failed to find their menfolk among the horsemen. Questions were asked and answers were given. Mainly about him. In between bouts of grief-stricken gobbledegook, the women kept pointing in Steve's direction, and when the men had got over the initial shock of the devastating attack on their camp he was quickly surrounded.

With so much sharp iron pointed in his direction, the only thing Steve could do was to keep absolutely still and hope that he'd done enough to earn himself a fair shake. From the fierce glares he was getting he had the feeling he was supposed to be on his knees. *Screw 'em . . .* He had done nothing he needed to apologise for. He stayed right where he was, feet apart, body nice and loose, and with the quarterstaff cradled against his chest.

Since he was almost a foot taller than the group around him, Steve was able to look over their heads and thus avoid direct eye contact. Three of the group hadn't dismounted. Two were small dark-haired, olive-skinned dinks, the other was a taller, cowled figure whose face was covered by an oval chalk-white mask. All three were blindfolded. Their wrists were bound to a rounded post at the front of their saddles and their ankles had been fastened together by a rope passed under the horse's belly. Something drew his eyes back to the figure in the white mask. The quarterstaff vibrated in his hands,

129

causing a shiver to run down his spine. Not of fear, but of excitement.

No – surely – it couldn't be. It just wasn't possible!

The ring of sweat-stained warriors around Steve parted to let through the man who had led them into the arena. He was bigger than the rest and was followed by the woman and the small boy. The child was now back in her arms, his face buried shyly against her neck. Now and then his small, slanted black-button eyes would dart towards Steve. His guard-mother's gaze was more steady, but it was hard to tell what she was thinking. Her dark eyes reflected neither gratitude not hostility. Now she had recovered her composure, her face was completely devoid of expression.

They were all the same. Side-Winder had told him Iron Masters had amazing self-control. They prided themselves on their ability to suppress all outward signs of emotion. And, apparently, they were pretty cool characters on the inside as well. As a result, it was virtually impossible to tell from their faces what they were thinking – or what their next move might be.

Steve realised he must present a weird sight. Apart from his patterned skin, he had dark, tangled hair, and a golden four-week growth of beard. Plus hair on his forearms and the exposed parts of his legs. Whereas these dinks had, as far as he could see, absolutely no hair of their own at all. The straggling pieces the wild bunch wore must have come from Mutes. And Steve remembered that several sackfuls of hair had been among the items that the M'Calls had carried on their trucking poles to the trading post by the 'great river'.

The big man circled Steve slowly, then came back and stood in front of him. He was about six inches shorter than Steve, but his stock frame was all muscle and bone and his dark eyes didn't waver. 'You understand my words, grass-monkey?'

'Yes, I do '

'You kill these samurai?'

'Some of them.'

Noburo Naka-Jima held out his hand for the quarterstaff. Steve gave it to him. He passed it on to one of the men standing near by, then took hold of Steve's left arm and ran his eyes over the dirt-stained bandage. Steve let his arm hang loose. This was no time for last-ditch heroics. Noburo slid the combat knife out of the hidden scabbard, pulled the strip of rag from around the hilt and inspected the finish and sharpness of the blade.

Without waiting to be asked, Steve unwrapped the scabbard and removed it from his arm.

Noburo handed both items to another of his sidekicks. 'How did you find way in here?'

Steve was ready for that one. The whole story had started to come together in his mind. 'I was on the mountain. I saw a horse with no rider go into a split in the rocks. The twelve samurai were following it.' He shrugged. 'So I followed them.'

'Why?'

Steve shot a quick glance at the white-masked figure sitting astride the horse about ten yards from where he stood. The strange sixth sense that had helped him from time to time in the past put the words on his tongue. 'You were someone I had to meet.'

Noburo nodded, but his face gave no indication as to whether or not he accepted Steve's explanation. Reverting to his own language, he delivered a staccato string of nonsense-words to his gang.

Four of the men surrounding Steve grabbed him and hustled him across the arena towards one of the ground-floor caves. Steve looked over his shoulder towards the three bound riders. They were being pulled down from their horses.

The cave mouth towards which they were heading was wider than it was high. The interior was screened off from floor to ceiling by a wall made of slatted timbers, with two split doors constructed in the same manner. Judging from their height, they were designed for diminutive dinks. One of the guys unbolted the lower

131

half of the right-hand door and gestured to Steve to enter. Steve toyed with the idea of asking them to open the top half as well, then swallowed his pride and crawled in on his hands and knees.

The accommodation was spartan, but not as bad as he expected. At least the walls and floor were dry and the place wasn't crawling with bug-uglies. The only items of furniture were a woven straw mat and a box with a hinged lid. Inside it was a plank seat with a cut-out beneath which was a two-handled pot. It looked like a primitive type of john, but Steve decided not to use it in case it turned out to be something the dinks served soup in. The fact that he had ended up in the slammer was proof they weren't about to hand out medals but Steve – who, despite the snake, had a huge backlog of hunger to assuage – was persuaded that, at the very least, his efforts on behalf of the camp-women deserved to be rewarded by a square meal. Christo! Back home, even guys in the condemned cells got a bite to eat before they got the bullet.

Steve sat cross-legged on the mat with his back against the slatted partition that separated the two cells, and recalled some of the delicious odours he smelt wafting on the night air when he'd been prowling around the dinks' dwelling places in search of some scraps to eat.

His reverie was broken by the sound of bolts being withdrawn. Peeping through the finger-wide gap between two planks, Steve saw both sections of the door to the next cell being opened. The two small dark-haired women walked in carrying bedding rolls followed by the taller cloaked figure in the white mask. She held a bedding roll too.

All three were still blindfolded but, as the door slammed shut, one of their gaolers shouted something in Japanese. The two women dropped their bedding rolls and quickly removed the cloth covering their eyes, then removed Whitey's blindfold. The cells were in semi-darkness, but now that she was closer Steve could see the details on the mask – the tiny, pouting mouth, the two thin strokes representing the eyebrows, raised in perpetual surprise, the red blush on the cheekbones, and the angled eye slits. And behind them, a tell-tale flash of blue.

Clearwater laid her bedding roll against the partition and sat down with her back to Steve. She pulled back the cowl. Her flowing dark hair – which, when he last saw it, reached down to the middle of her back – was now drawn up and pinned with combs in the style of the Iron Masters.

Steve caught his breath. The smooth, olive-tinted skin on the back of her neck was unmarked. What had caused her to remove her body-paint? A whiff of her natural body odour reached his nostrils. The memories it brought back sent a zing through his loins and made his mind reel.

Clearwater pulled off her glove, placed the fingers of her right hand on her shoulder and rested the chin of her mask on them.

Steve's movements mirrored hers. Leaning back against the partition, he slid his left forefinger through the gap in the planking and breathed – 'Hello, stranger . . .'

The only answer was a slight pressure on his fingertip. But it was enough to send a megavolt charge up his arm. Oh, Mo-Town! You sweet mother! The Amtrak Federation's vocabulary did not include the word 'love', and the education syllabus did not include any reference to sexual chemistry, but this was the real thing right enough.

Yess-sirrree . . .

'What happened to your –'

Clearwater dug a fingernail sharply into his skin.

Steve interpreted it as a warning not to talk to her while the two women were there. For the next hour or more, he had to be content with maintaining fingertip contact. It was no hardship. When the chemistry is right, it is amazing how suggestive ten digits can be, and when he rang the changes by tracing tiny circles on her shoulder her body sent the same ardent message through the layers of cloth.

The sun had disappeared from the circle of sky above the campsite a long time ago, and now the light began to fade as Mo-Town drew her dark cloak across the world. Within a short time, the gaps between the planks were almost as dark as the planks themselves. No one came to check up on them, but every so often yellow lanterns wandered by, proving they had not been totally abandoned.

Steve tried to master his frustration. Less than twenty-four hours ago he had gone to sleep tired, hungry and dispirited, his mission doomed to failure. Now here he was, only inches away from one of the two people had had come to rescue!

He knew why *he* had been thrown in the slammer, but why had Clearwater been taken prisoner? And why was she now clear-skinned and dressed up like a Jap? The questions crowded in. Who were the two women with her? Both wore identical outfits made of plain dark brown material: baggy trousers gathered into cuffs just above the ankle, and high-collared smocks with full sleeves fastened in similar fashion around the wrist. The full-length cape hid what Clearwater was wearing, but the cape itself was made of the same glistening material used to clothe Yama-Shita – the top Iron Master that Steve had seen at the trading post.

From his observations so far, he knew that Iron Masters were dressed according to rank – unlike the almost-universal Federation jumpsuit. The drab uniformity of the women's clothes indicated that their status was inferior to Clearwater's – so why was she unwilling to talk in front of them?

Steve sensed something was going down. She had been captured by a raggedy-assed bunch of Iron Masters who had been vigorously pursued by the forces of law and order. Taken in transit, perhaps, from one of those groups of drawn vehicles and people he had seen moving along the east–west highway. He deduced this from the

134

mask and the outer clothing that concealed the fact that – to an uninformed observer – she had the body of a Tracker; an outlander whose social rating was only marginally higher than the Mutes.

Why had someone been at pains to conceal her identity? Whoever it was had to be someone important; her clothes were proof that she was in contact with at least one high-flyer. And the two women – were they there to see she didn't give the game away? The fact that it was they, and not she, who had removed her blindfold, plus her reluctance to speak in their presence, suggested this was the case. There was something else. All three had been brought into the camp blindfolded. That could only be for one reason: to prevent them from identifying their captors and describing where they had been held prisoner. Which meant they were due to be released at some future date.

The plot thickened – and became even more intriguing when Steve began to consider the reasons why Clearwater's mask had not been removed. Her blindfold had been tied over it and around the *outside* of the cowl that concealed her dark, lustrous hair and her neck, whose skin-colour would have revealed it all. To his devious mind, it suggested that only *some* of the wild bunch were supposed to know the true nature of the person they had carried off. Or, alternatively, perhaps *none* of them knew. Either way, it implied that they had not captured Clearwater for themselves but for someone *else*.

From what Side-Winder had told him, Steve knew that the life of a Tracker – or a Mute – was not worth a soyabean. Yet here she was – a Mute who, in terms of appearance, was indistinguishable from a Tracker – dolled up like an Iron Master out of the top drawer, with two personal minders to do the fetching and carrying.

Oh, yes . . . something was going down all right. There was a lot more Steve needed to know, but the big question was – could he get in on the action and turn the situation to his advantage?

A pair of approaching lanterns cast their warm glow through the slatted timbers. Steve glimpsed a quartet of orange faces fringed with shanks of Mute hair. Four hard cases from the wild bunch. Clearwater quickly pulled the cowl back into place and replaced her glove. The Japs stopped outside the door to the adjacent cell and shouted something in Japanese. Peering through the slats, Steve saw the diminutive female minders adjust each other's blindfolds. When the knots were securely tied, the door was unbolted and they were led away.

As darkness enveloped them once again, Steve knelt facing the partition and thrust both sets of fingers through the gaps in the timbers. The middle fingers got no further than the second knuckle. There was a rustle of garments on the far side of the wooden wall; a cool swish of limbs moving inside rich silk brocade – something he had never heard before.

This time she had taken off the mask as well as the gloves. She kissed the tips of his fingers then slid her face against them. Her own slim fingers wriggled through the gaps and touched his nose, then caressed his mouth. He held each one in turn, lightly between his teeth.

'Oh, cloud warrior,' she whispered. 'If you only knew how much I have longed for this moment.'

'Me too,' said Steve. 'All I've thought about is being alone with you in the dark, but . . . this isn't quite what I had in mind.'

'Be patient, beloved. Our journey together has just begun.'

Yeah . . . Question is – where are we headed . . . ?

Steve saw a single lantern approaching – held aloft by a man.

'Watch out, someone's coming!'

They both moved away from the partition. Steve looked through the slats of the door. The Jap wore a mask like the samurai at the trading post, but Steve recognised his build. It was the stocky guy who had ordered him to be thrown into the slammer. He unbolted the door to the other cell and entered, closing it behind

him. Steve kept well back but was able to see Clearwater –
mask, cowl and gloves now back in place – shuffle round
on her knees to greet her visitor with a respectful bow.

The Jap transferred the lantern to his left hand so that,
from where Steve sat, Clearwater was thrown into sil-
houette. 'Stand up.'

She did so.

'Remove outer garment . . .'

Clearwater unfastened the collar that kept the cowl
closed tightly round the edges of her white mask, lifted it
over her hair and let it fall back. She then undid the front
of the cape and cast it aside to reveal another long robe
underneath with wide three-quarter-length sleeves and a
low-cut collar that showed off her pretty neck. A deep
sash wrapped round her waist and midriff was tied in a big
bow at the back. The white gloves that hid her unblemished hands and forearms reached up inside the sleeves
of her robe.

'Now gloves and mask.'

Clearwater removed them and stood with her chin
lowered. What's this guy going for? wondered Steve. A
complete strip-down? He was seized by a sudden, irrational wave of anger at the pending violation of what he felt
was his own private preserve. Irrational to Steve, that is,
because jealousy and possessiveness were two more of the
many word-concepts that did not feature in the Federation's vocabulary. Once again, as when he fell in love
and could not describe the feeling, he did not know what
was eating him.

The Jap raised the lantern, lifted Clearwater's chin and
inspected her face and throat closely. He then walked
around her, peered at the back of her neck, ran his fingers
over the roots of her swept-up hair, then came around the
front and examined her hands and arms.

'Now you will dress as before.'

He watched silently as Clearwater became the white-
masked woman again, then, as she knelt submissively
before him, he uttered a grunt of approval and left,
bolting the door behind him.

Ahah, thought Steve. So that's how it plays. It's only the boss man who's got the inside track on this. The rest of the bunch are just spear-carriers. When the light faded away, he moved back to the partition and re-established contact with Clearwater.

'Did you ride across the waters on one of the wheelboats?' she whispered.

'Yes. How did you know? And why are you whispering?'

She raised her voice slightly. 'I felt your presence near by soon after I came ashore.'

'You – you were on one of the boats?' stammered Steve. 'You actually *came* to the trading post?!'

'Did Mr Snow not tell you? Did he not show you the box?'

'What box?'

'The box with the hidden pictures that were to guide you to the place where Cadillac and I are held. I gave it to him the night before we sailed back to Ne-Issan.'

Steve began to understand. 'When he came out to Yama-Shita's vessel . . .'

'Yes – with Rolling-Stone and Mack-Truck.'

Steve responded with a dry, sighing laugh. 'So that's what he was up to. Trust me to do things the hard way. When I saw him go by I was already on board one of the other wheelboats. I found a place to hide and stayed out of sight until we docked at Pi-saba.' Steve didn't volunteer any further details. 'Did the Old One know he was coming to see you?'

'No. He seemed taken aback. Perhaps because I was unskinned.' 'Unskinned' was the term Mr Snow had used to describe the true appearance of Clearwater and Cadillac in the brief period between washing off their camouflage and applying a fresh coat of paint.

'Yeah, I wanted to ask you about –'

Clearwater cut in quickly. 'Yama-Shita was present. We were not free to say what we wished, but his hidden words told me you had returned and would try to rescue us. He did not say how or when.'

138

'I was going to travel with the M'Call journeymen but Mr Snow wouldn't let me take any weapons on board. So I made my own travel arrangements. There was no way I was going to leave my quarterstaff behind – not after what you'd done to it.'

'Did it help?'

'Are you kidding? If it wasn't for your magic act, I wouldn't be here. You've saved my life several times over.'

'Not I, golden one. The power was given to me by Talisman.'

'Maybe. You I know, him I don't.' Steve's voice lightened. 'If he's so keen on helping me he could at least have arranged for us to be on the same boat. We could have spent some time together. Would have made the trip a lot more enjoyable.'

'It would have been utter madness. What you did was dangerous enough.' She sounded concerned – and a touch severe.

Steve kept it casual. 'No worse than the jam I'm in now. But – on the other hand – here you are. Fate, I guess.'

'Did you get back to your own people?'

'Eventually.' There was no point in lying. He had already told Mr Snow the whole story. Or most of it. 'They weren't too pleased to hear that the Plainfolk weren't as stupid as they thought.'

'Did you tell them about me?'

The lie tripped easily off his tongue. 'No, I didn't. You're my secret weapon. When I'm with you I feel as if I could conquer the world.' That part, at least, was true.

'Perhaps you are meant to,' she whispered.

'Is that what Cadillac has seen in the stones?'

'He has seen many things.'

Steve felt his skin prickle. 'Such as . . .?'

'That you would return in the guise of a friend, with Death hiding in your shadow, and carry me away on a river of blood. Is that why you have come back? To take me down into the dark world of the sand-burrowers beneath the deserts of the south?'

'Are you crazy? I came back to be with *you*!' He squeezed her fingertips. 'Are you sure the stones said I would take you back to the Federation?'

'No. Cadillac didn't say where to. Just that you would carry me away.'

'That's right,' said Steve hurriedly. 'That's why I'm here now – because I promised Mr Snow I would get both of you out of here! The rest makes sense. I *am* in the guise of a friend because I'm hoping to do a pretend-deal with these people. As for the "death hiding in my shadow", I'd say that fits the hidden power you poured into the quarterstaff. Take it from me, it's lethal. I'm sure these Japs won't let us get away without a fight, so maybe I *will* carry you away on a river of blood. But that blood will be running out of the veins of the Iron Masters. And the only place you're going is back where you belong.'

'I belong to you, cloud warrior. As long as we are together I do not care where you take me. But Cadillac must go back to the Plainfolk.'

'You're *both* going back. Trust me.'

She drew her finger down over his lips and found the tip of his tongue. 'Do you think Talisman would put his power into your hands if you meant to harm us?'

It's not Talisman I'm thinking about. It's the other people in this game. And they're not using the same rule book . . .

Steve answered with another dry laugh and changed the subject. 'Amazing, isn't it – the way things work out? I came to the trading post because I wanted to be the first to welcome you back. I must have spent hours pacing up and down that beach, staring at those boats, willing you to appear. Why didn't you show yourself?'

'I was not allowed to do so. In the last two months I have seen almost nothing of the outside world.'

'Who's been keeping you locked up – this guy Yama-Shita?'

'When I was on the boat, yes. But since I came to Ne-Issan with Cadillac I have been held by another.'

'Held how? Who by?'

Her voice faltered. 'A lord who lives by the Eastern Sea.'

'Is he the guy who gave you those fancy clothes?'

She answered by kissing the tips of his fingers.

'And is that why you washed off your body-paint?'

His question met with a pregnant silence. He tried again. 'You want to tell me about it?'

Her reply, when it came, was in a barely audible whisper. 'What has . . . happened is . . . is the will of Talisman.'

'Yeah, sure, I understand all that,' said Steve. 'Just take me through it from the top of page one.'

*

They did not have long before Su-Shan and Nan-Khe returned with three trays of hot food, but it was time enough to make Steve wish he hadn't pressed her for an explanation. Knowledge might indeed be power, but whoever coined the maxim omitted to mention that there were some things it was better not to know. Steve was learning that young men who seek truthful answers to every question often find the process extremely painful. On top of which, the delicious aroma from the assortment of goodies the trio next door were preparing to tuck into was absolute torture.

He did not have to endure it for long. As the door to the next cell was slammed shut, the bottom half of his door was opened and he was ordered out. Mentally bracing himself for some sort of physical assault, he exited on his hands and knees – and was not disappointed. A leg hooked his hands away and a kick in the butt sent him sprawling face down in the dirt. It didn't look promising, but the subsequent flurry of blows proved to be something less than a serious attempt to injure him. If the four armed dinks had wanted to break a few bones they could have done so easily. No. They were just out to ruin his composure. Show him who was boss.

Grinning broadly, they hauled him to his feet and continued to roust him all the way across the arena. Steve could not see much of anything beyond the circles of light cast by the swaying lanterns, but it looked as if all trace of the earlier mindless slaughter had been removed. His escort pushed him up a flight of rough-hewn steps on to the terrace linking the second tier of caves and brought him face to face with the main man. He was sitting cross-legged on a mat laid against the side-wall. There were another ten or twelve guys with him. The cave was lit by more yellow lanterns and the air was thick with smoke which caused Steve to cough on entering.

Several of the dinks had pipes like the one used by Mr Snow. They weren't smoking rainbow grass, but Steve's nose told him that a touch of the old happy valley weed had been added to the mixture. The wild bunch were also swallowing capfuls of the pale yellow liquid Side-Winder had introduced him to. *Sake*. His escort pushed Steve down on to his knees in front of the honcho and helped themselves to some juice.

In view of what had taken place earlier everyone seemed cheerful enough, but Steve could sense an undercurrent of tension. The jovial atmosphere had a brittle, knife-edge quality which gave him the feeling that they could – at any minute and with equal cheerfulness – tear him limb from limb. One misjudged word or gesture was all the pretext they needed. Mindful of Mr Snow's warning to avoid prolonged eye-contact, Steve tried to ignore the ring of strange, hairless faces with their dark, almost jet-black eyes. He focused through on to the wall behind them and willed himself to stay calm.

Come on, Brickman! You've been in tight corners before. You can face these guys down. They're like the death-birds. Show yourself weak and defenceless and they move in for the kill. You've already shown them you're a top gun. Be strong!

Nothing to it . . .

His hairless host drained his cup and held it out sideways for someone to fill it. 'Do you have a name, grass-monkey?'

Steve looked him straight in the eye. 'Yes. Brickman.'

'A-barick a-man-uh . . .'

'No, it's all one word. BRRickmaNN.'

'Ahh-so . . . Barickmann-uh.'

'Right.' *What the hell . . .*

The stocky Jap snapped his fingers and pointed to Steve. A hand came out of left field and stuck a cup of *sake* under his nose.

'I'd rather have something to eat.'

'Later, perhaps. First we drink to your courage, then we talk. After that – who knows?'

One of the dinks said something. Everybody fell about.

'What's so funny?' asked Steve.

'He say you may find you have no stomach for food.'

Ohh, yeah. Boy . . . what a terrific sense of humour . . .

Steve took the offered cup and raised it level with the Jap's.

'Kanpai!'

Steve took his cue from his host and downed the contents of the cup in one gulp.

In introducing him to *sake*, Side-Winder had omitted to warn Steve about the alarming impact alcohol can have on the central nervous system when poured into an empty stomach. The sake exploded inside him like a small bomb. Steve felt the heat rise back up his gullet and set fire to his ears. His eyes went out of focus. He swivelled his head round sharply in an effort to unclog his brain and regained a measure of control by sheer willpower. He had to squint in order to see straight but, when the smoke cleared, he was left feeling extra-sharp, supremely confident and utterly fearless.

Steve favoured his host with a gracious bow from the waist. 'May I be permitted to know who I have the honour of addressing?'

The Jap hesitated. It was probably the first time a Mute had asked him a question. 'I am samurai-captain Noburo Naka-Jima.'

'Then permit me to salute you, Captain.' Steve bowed again, then met Noburo's eyes as he straightened up. 'And which domain-lord do you serve?'

Noburo chewed over his response. This grass-monkey would pay dearly for his insolence but first, it was necessary to ask him certain questions on a man-to-man basis, however distasteful that might be. Torture could have produced the answers and might yet have to be used by others, but Noburo was constrained by the samurai code of behaviour. The reason this outlander now sat facing him instead of being skinned alive then slowly dismembered a joint at a time was because he had single handedly vanquished seven of Lord Se-Iko's samurai. However honourable his motives, he would eventually have to be put to death, but his redoubtable courage and skill as a fighting man and his proud bearing demanded a certain measure of consideration from his peers.

'We have no domain-lord,' he said finally. 'Lord Naka-Jima is dead, his family dispossessed. We are *ronin*. Wanderers who owe allegiance to no one.'

'You surprise me, Captain,' replied Steve. 'You say you are a samurai – but do the noble warriors of Ne-Issan venture forth to capture women? And can one believe that you would sacrifice thirty to forty of your valiant men to secure such a worthless prize?' He saw the puzzlement in Noburo's eyes and added: 'I saw them fall to their pursuers in the river valley. Samurai from the same house as the men who found death here.'

The Jap's face hardened. 'The fate of my kinsmen is none of your business, grass-monkey. Let us discuss yours.'

Steve set down the empty cup and bowed. 'I am at your service, Captain.'

'Grass-monkey,' began Noburo, 'I find myself in, uhh –' He broke off to search his limited Basic vocabulary for the right word – 'delicate, uhh – situation. You saved many here from certain death. In particular, my wife and son Itada. Because you did so at risk of your own life, I am bound to you by a debt of honour – from which I can only be released by performing similar action. You understand me?'

'Yes. What's the problem?'

'Grass-monkeys are forbidden, under pain of death, to carry arms in Ne-Issan. And it is even greater crime for slave-person to kill Iron Master – especially samurai. So there is conflict here. As long as the debt of honour remains, uhh . . . undischarged, I am obliged to defend your life – even at the cost of my own. But, equally, you cannot be permitted to go unpunished.'

'I see what you mean,' said Steve. 'It's a tough one.'

'Tough?'

'Hard. Difficult.'

'Ahh, so . . .' Noburo held out his cup for a refill. 'Tough for both of us, grass-monkey. It would have been better if you had let my wife and son die under sword of samurai.'

'I don't understand.'

'Obligation to inferior slave-person cause loss of face. Only honourable solution for samurai family in such situation is to die by own hand.'

'That's crazy,' said Steve. 'There must be some other way.'

'There is,' replied Noburo. 'You can kill yourself.'

'Kill myself . . .?'

'Yes, now.' Noburo drew his short-sword, then leant forward and placed it reverently in front of Steve. 'Your death by your own hand will release me from debt of honour and lift shame from my family. Samurai of Lord Se-Iko will also be avenged. Satisfactory, uhh – solution for everyone.'

Except me, thought Steve. No wonder Noburo's wife didn't look overjoyed. 'Loss of face' . . . what the eff-eff was all that about? Someone reached out to give him a refill. Steve laid his right hand over the cup, pinning it to the floor as he waved Noburo down with his left. 'Hold on a minute. You've got this all wrong.'

'Ahh, how so?'

'First, I am not a slave – second, as a warrior I could

145

not stand by and let the sons of samurai be slaughtered – and third, I venture to suggest, Captain, that killing samurai can only be considered a crime by those *who live within the law.*'

Noburo nodded soberly then translated Steve's spirited reply for the benefit of his companions. It caused a great deal of laughter and slapping of thighs. When the merriment subsided, he addressed Steve with the hint of a smile. 'Well said, grass-monkey. But you now pose another problem. If you are not slave – what are you doing here?'

This was the crunch point. Steve took a deep breath and went for it. 'I came to prevent a war between our two nations.'

Noburo mastered his surprise and laughed. 'Between the Sons of Ne-Issan and the grass-monkeys?'

'No, Captain. Between the Sons of Ne-Issan and the Federation. The warriors from the underground world beneath the deserts of the south.'

The faint smile faded from Noburo's face. 'The long-dogs make war on grass-monkeys. Why do they send you as peace messenger?'

Steve straightened his back and looked the head ronin right in the eye. 'I am not a Mute, Captain. I am a cloud warrior from the Amtrak Federation. One of thousands whose sky-chariots will darken the skies of Ne-Issan and rain fire upon the earth if the enemies who now shelter in your midst are not handed over to us.'

Noburo's bewilderment appeared genuine. 'What enemies?'

'I seek the masked woman you took from the road convoy and her male companion who is to be found at a place called the Heron Pool in the lands by the Eastern Sea.'

Noburo eyed him impassively for a while, then retrieved his short-sword and issued a lengthy order in Japanese. His men got up and filed out, leaving only two guys sitting on either side of him and a third standing guard by the door-screen fitted across the mouth of the cave.

Steve smiled inwardly. His programme was up and running.

The chief *ronin* squared his shoulders and adopted a forbidding expression. 'You have the means to prove truth of your words?'

'Yes. But I will need the knife you took from me.'

Noburo asked the man sitting on his right to fetch it.

Leaving the knife in the scabbard, Steve pressed the concealed catches securing the wooden side-pieces to the hilt and removed them to reveal the microcircuitry inside. He held it out for the chief *ronin* to see, then took out the tiny stylus, pressed the recall button and placed the knife in Noburo's hands.

Holding the knife gingerly between his fingertips, Noburo reacted with wide-eyed astonishment as the eleven familiar letters marched across the liquid crystal display. The two *ronin* on either side of him looked equally impressed. '*Hhhaawww . . .*'

'What you see there is an example of the power of my people,' said Steve. 'Those signs which appeared represent the sounds of words I speak. With that device I can send messages to my masters in the space of a single heartbeat.'

Noburo dropped the knife on the mat in front of Steve with a curious, almost involuntary gesture – as if he had suddenly received an electric shock. He muttered something to his companions. All three looked vaguely uneasy.

Steve couldn't figure it out. He clipped the wooden side-pieces back into place and laid the sheathed knife before Noburo. 'Let us forget the debt of honour, Captain. We both have more important matters to attend to.'

His forthright manner took Noburo's breath away and rocked the other two back on their heels. It seemed to indicate that they also had some knowledge of Basic. Noburo pointed to the knife. 'What do you wish me to do with this?'

'Show it to your masters.'

'We have no masters, Barickaman.' Noburo seemed unable to get his tongue around words with an 'r' in them. 'We are outlaws.'

Steve bowed. 'With respect, Captain, in your nation and mine, there are men who assume many guises in the service of their lord. I am one of them and I believe that you too are such a man. Show your master this knife, explain what has passed between us, and tell him that there are things he and I need to discuss.'

Noburo roared with laughter and slapped his thigh. He quickly translated the gist of the conversation, then turned back to Steve as his companions shared his amusement. 'I never thought I should say this to outlander, but you honour us by your presence, cloud warrior! And we applaud your courage in face of death! Your message will be passed to those who have interest in this matter. I cannot promise you, uhh . . . deliverance, but – if all your comrades are as valiant as you – it would be most foolish man who did not give serious consideration to the words you speak here today.'

*

Clearwater sat up as she saw the light of the lanterns. The cloud warrior was returning. He was carrying a tray of food, and when they reached the cave his escort opened both sections of the door to his cell, allowing him to walk in upright. She glanced at Su-Shan and Nan-Khe as narrow bands of yellow light swung to and fro across their faces. Both were still fast asleep.

The cloud warrior sank down slowly with his back against the partition as the door was barred, and laid the tray across his lap. Darkness filled the cave as the lanterns receded. She heard him let out a long, heartfelt sigh. Clearwater slipped her fingers between the plans and touched Steve's shoulder. 'Oh, cloud warrior . . . when I saw them beating you I feared I might never see you again. Are you hurt?'

'Can't feel a thing.' His voice sounded slurred.

'Ssshhh!'

He lowered his voice. 'Don't worry. It's all going well. We're on our way, lover.'

'On our way where?'

'Out of here.'

'How? I don't understand.'

'Explain-a-you la'er,' gurgled Steve, as he scooped up hot rice with one hand and vegetables with the other. 'Can' spea' now. Goh my mou' full . . .'

CHAPTER SEVEN

At some point during the middle of the night, Steve was roused by his gaolers. They gave him a moment to shake off the torpor induced by fatigue, *sake* and a bellyful of hot food, then instructed him in sign language to gather up his meagre possessions: the stolen cotton quilt, his water-skin and the waist-bag containing the bundle of pink leaves that could turn him back into a long-dog.

Emerging from the cave into a pool of lantern light, Steve saw that Clearwater and her two minders were back in the saddle, bound and blindfolded. A fourth horse awaited him. Steve hauled himself aboard, gritting his teeth as his butt hit the unyielding leather. Deprived of the electrifying energy that flowed from the quarterstaff, all his accumulated aches and pains had returned to plague him. Steve drew some comfort from the fact that he was now able to cross hunger cramps off his list of ailments and that – for the moment at least – no one was threatening to cancel his card.

That had been a bad moment but, with some fancy footwork, he had been able to sidestep disaster yet again. He shuddered to think what would have happened if he had taken a second shot of *sake*. He would have to watch that stuff. Noburo and the other *ronin* were able to knock it back like there was no tomorrow, but that first cup had practically pulled the floor out from under him. It was true it had given his tongue a reckless edge, but there had been a terrifying moment when it had almost lost its way around his mouth.

Close!

A dink carrying a length of cord came around the head of the horse. Steve offered his wrists to him and was tied to the pommel of the saddle. They left his feet in the stirrups and made sure they stayed there by looping a second length of cord round both ankles. Steve experienced a moment of anxiety as he thought about the steep descent they had to make on leaving the camp. If the horse went down, that was it. He would go down with it.

Noburo Naka-Jima and eleven mounted *ronin* appeared out of the darkness. Four riders gathered up the reins of the waiting horses and prepared to lead them out. Noburo and the three men who had attended the private interview positioned themselves at the head of the column and moved off in single file across the arena. The other four came into line behind Steve.

The door was opened and shut by one of a small group who had been sent ahead to make sure that it was safe to exit through the cleft on to the slope beyond. There was a muttered exchange with each of the mounted *ronin* as he passed by, then the foot patrol withdrew, closing the door behind them.

Clearwater, Su-Shan, Nan-Khe and Steve were led down the bare precipitous trail under a thinning moon which hung in a cloudless sky. Steve felt they were helplessly exposed, and what made it worse was the realisation that he was sitting there with his hands tied. But there was no deadly shower of arrows, and no sudden trumpet blast to signal a ferocious charge like the one he had witnessed in the river valley. The nerve-wracking descent seemed to go on for ever and he remained on edge, his stomach freezing every time his horse missed its footing, until they entered the tree-line.

For the next three hours they headed north-eastwards, along narrow winding forest trails, over hill and valley, across streams and small rivers until finally, in the grey twilight that preceded the dawn, they descended a tree-covered slope and came in sight of the highway. The old Pennsylvania Turnpike that Steve had been keeping an eye on since leaving the wheelboat at Pi-saba.

Noburo raised his hand, signalling the column to halt. Clearwater, Su-Shan and Nan-Khe were untied and lifted off their horses. Still blindfolded, they were led to within about a hundred yards of the road, then pushed into a kneeling position and harangued at some length in Japanese by six *ronin*. The female minders bowed repeatedly, bobbing up and down as if their bodies were on springs, then prostrated themselves at the *ronins'* feet, pulling Clearwater to the ground between them.

Steve, who loved to know everything, found himself wishing he could understand what was being said.

The six *ronin* closed in and loosed off a final tirade, underlining their words with several toe-jabs to the ribs and thighs. Nan-Khe and Su-Shan lay there, silent and unresisting. Satisfied that the women had got the message, the *ronin* swaggered back to the rest of the party and mounted their horses. Noburo led them back up the forested slope. Steve glanced back as the trees closed round them and saw that all three were still lying flat on their faces, their heads towards the road.

*

Nan-Khe and Su-Shan counted to one hundred twice as instructed, then sat up and removed their blindfolds. The *ronin* had disappeared. Untying the cloth covering Clearwater's masked eyes, they ushered her on to the highway, and set off towards the east.

The *ronin* had told them they were less than five miles from the nearest post-house. Once there, they would be able to discover the fate of the convoy from which they had been kidnapped. If it was still in one piece and had not travelled too far along the road, they might be able to catch up with it and continue their journey. After attacks like these, there were always delays while the local authorities took statements from eye-witnesses and recorded details of the stolen goods.

Had they been able to reveal that they were trusted servants of the Consul-General of Masa-chusa and Ro-diren, brother-in-law to the Shogun himself, every assistance would have been offered to them without delay. But they could not do so. Their employer had threatened to have their tongues torn out if they dared to utter his name. Their papers identified them as house-women of a dried-fish merchant residing at Nyo-poro. If anyone asked, they had been told to say they had escorted 'Yoko Mi-Shima' to visit her relatives at Kari-faran and were now returning with her to join said merchant at Firi, where he was due to attend the next slave market.

But no one had told them what to do if they and their charge were carried off by *ronin*. No one had foreseen a situation in which 'Yoko Mi-Shima' might be taken from the sealed carriage-box and released on to the highway where she would be exposed to the prying eyes of the general public – and to official scrutiny.

It was all very worrying, and things were made even more precarious by the fact that Su-Shan and Nan-Khe were duty-bound to report their kidnap and release to the local magistrates' office – and answer any questions put to them. The greatest danger lay in the fact that they had been left stranded in one of the western domains which easterners such as themselves regarded as the boon-docks. If one of these unsophisticated provincial clerks insisted on seeing who was under the mask, instead of treating the 'lady of pleasure' with the customary discretion, it could prove extremely awkward. And it was bound to happen, because their charge could not speak Japanese and thus could not answer any questions put to her. Once the long-dog was discovered, it would be immediately obvious that her papers were forgeries.

Su-Shan and Nan-Khe both knew that the use of false documents was a serious criminal offence. Trusted servants they might be, but as Vietnamese, they were permanently relegated to the lower half of Iron Master society. In essence, that meant they had neither the social leverage nor the money needed to halt any legal proceedings. If the deception was discovered and they were arraigned before the magistrates for questioning, they could find themselves facing the removal of their ears, noses and other extremities if they refused to answer – and losing their tongues if they did.

Aie-yie-yieee . . .

*

The risks were real enough but, on this occasion, their fears proved groundless. Unbeknown to them, a member of the Se-Iko family who was linked through various business enterprises with both the Ko-Nikka and Lord Yama-Shita had ordered his samurai-captains to keep a discreet watch on the road convoy as it passed through the areas under their command. It was for this reason that, when the raid took place, the response had been unexpectedly rapid. It was only Noburo's tactical skill and experience in covert operations that had prevented it from turning into a disaster.

Hideyoshi Se-Iko, the good neighbour whose task it was to ensure peace and tranquillity in the domain's southern sector, had not been informed of the reason why this particular convoy was of interest to Yama-Shita. He had merely been asked by the Ko-Nikka to use his good offices to ensure its unhindered passage through his family's domain. When the news of the raid reached him, he dispatched two trusted officials at the gallop to advise magistrates and other officials stationed along the route that any enquiries into the affair were to be made with the utmost circumspection.

Translated into Basic that meant: 'Don't ruin your career prospects by trying to solve this one, boys. If the case lands on your desk, just close up the office and take a long time over lunch.'

*

For the nervous Su-Shan and Nan-Khe, it meant that when they reached the post-house at Kara-li and explained what had happened, they found the innkeeper both sympathetic and concerned. Although not officially part of the law and order system, innkeepers were required to keep a beady eye on all comings and goings. It was in their interests to do so. As a result, they usually got the word on any sensitive issues or investigations ahead of everybody else. Such was the case now.

Ordering a room to be placed at the disposal of their mistress – who was so distressed by the experience that she was unable to speak – the innkeeper arranged for them to be conveyed to the nearby magistrates' office and insisted on coming with them.

Filled with trepidation, Su-Shan and Nan-Khe presented their papers to the clerk, together with those of their mistress, and recounted their ordeal at the hands of the *ronin*. The innkeeper confirmed that the lady Yoko Mi-Shima was in no fit state to answer questions. To their utter surprise – which they hastened to conceal – the clerk appeared to accept this without demur. He made a note of what little they were able to tell him about the raid on the convoy and the *ronin* who had carried them off, made a cursory examination of their papers, then handed them back without comment.

Su-Shan and Nan-Khe could hardly believe their luck. The good *kami* had certainly favoured them today. Bowing gratefully, they enquired about the fate of the convoy from which they had been taken.

The clerk told them that the remaining travellers and wagons had reassembled and, after giving evidence and filing a list of the valuables that had been plundered, had been allowed to proceed. Did they intend to rejoin the convoy? They did. The clerk promptly provided them with a *laissez-passer* to get them across the ferry.

It was all quite bewildering. From past experience, both women knew that any procedures involving the issuing or examination of documents usually took hours, sometimes the better part of a day – no matter how piffling the transaction might be. Their audience with this particular clerk had taken less than an hour and they had not even been required to 'polish the table' – the phrase used to describe the payment of bribes. Billed as voluntary donations to assist the widows and orphans of low-paid clerks, such payments were on a scale which varied with the importance of the document required, and ensured that paperwork did not go astray. It was an entrenched tradition and everybody, from the top man down, had a hand in the pot.

Bobbing up and down from the waist, Su-Shan and Nan-Khe withdrew from the clerk's presence and turned to beg the assistance of the kindly innkeeper. They had some money that the *ronin* had not found. Was it possible to hire a pushcart for themselves and a *jinrikisha* for their mistress? It was. The goddess of good fortune had smiled on them yet again. Both vowed to offer gifts and burn many joss-sticks in her honour at the next shrine they came to.

Having released the captives, Noburo now led the column on a circuitous route which took them across the highway west of the three women and into the trees on the other side. Dawn came, and soon the forest was pierced by slanting rays of light. Pausing only to feed themselves and the horses, the *ronin* pressed on throughout the day and the following night, riding first north, then east across the Susquehanna River where it swept into a narrow right-hand bend on its way south to Harrisburg – now a ferry-crossing known to the Iron Masters as Ari-saba. The Susquehanna was the border between the domain of the Se-Iko and their eastern neighbours, the Mitsu-Bishi – staunch allies of the Shogun. Provided they kept a low profile, Noburo and his men were relatively safe here.

They camped on the top of a forested ridge – one of the many hundred that Steve had glimpsed from his tree-top perch and had likened to the wave-crests of an endless tree-covered ocean. Noburo allowed his men three hours' sleep then, after a pre-dawn breakfast, the column swung south in a wide curve around Ari-saba.

Steve, who had been noting the various changes of direction, sensed that their present course would eventually lead them back to the highway. As on the previous day, they stayed on the back trails and rarely broke cover. Each time they had to cross open ground, they sent a scout on ahead to spy out the terrain, and when they stopped to water the horses and let them crop patches of grass, everyone stayed in the saddle.

In the middle of the afternoon, Noburo gave the signal to halt and dismount. Apart from a few mild canters, the horses had covered the ground alternately walking and trotting, and were thus in fairly good condition when they were unsaddled. The same could not be said for Steve. As soon as he was released he slid to the ground, sank gratefully against the nearest tree and stayed there. Over the last three days, at his reckoning, he had been in the saddle for almost a day and a half. At this point, death would have been a blessed release and the direst threats his captors could utter would not have persuaded him to get up on a horse again.

As it happened, his mood of grim determination coincided with their arrival at the place Noburo had chosen to lie up for the rest of the day. So for the next eight hours, the only movement demanded of him was to sit up on the one occasion he awoke to find that a bowl of food had been thrust under his nose.

While Steve slept, Noburo stripped off his dusty clothes and washed himself from head to foot in the stream that ran past their camp site. After a vigorous towelling, he opened a saddlebag and took out the travelling dress and wig of a samurai. Two of his men helped arrange the folds in his tunic and made sure the wig was seated properly. Several more swapped the harness on his horse for a more elaborate set decorated with blue tassels, and laid a black cloth trimmed with blue over the horse before replacing the saddle. Noburo slid his two swords through the folds of the sash around his waist and, when he was assured that his appearance was correct in every respect, he mounted his horse and rode away accompanied on foot by two *ronin* dressed up as red-stripes.

Their destination was the post-house at Midiri-tana where he had met with the Herald Hase-Gawa some ten days earlier. Hase-Gawa had stepped out of the darkness swathed in black from head to foot like a *ninja*, and would no doubt appear in similar guise tonight.

Noburo smiled at the role the Herald had adopted. Despite his obvious, flair for intrigue, the young man was a romantic at heart, with a taste for drama. In Noburo's view, an ill-fitting combination. Nevertheless he was a Herald – and only the brightest and most capable young men were selected for that prestigious post. Noburo concluded that Hase-Gawa must have other, less obvious, qualities to recommend him.

Flanked by the two red-stripes – the customary escort for a single samurai – Noburo arrived at the post-house around six in the evening, intending to make his usual careful check of the location and the travellers who were planning to stop there overnight. He knew Hase-Gawa was anxious to hear his report on the outcome of the raid and his examination of the masked courtesan. The Herald would not be disappointed – but what would he make of the valiant grass-monkey who claimed to be a long-dog?

Entering the courtyard of the post-house, Noburo was surprised to see a large number of loaded ox-wagons, some of which looked vaguely familiar. Parked alongside them was a carriage-box. Passing the reins of his horse to one of his red-stripes, he dismounted and strode boldly around the veranda and terraces of the post-house, eyeing the faces of all those he encountered. One of them belonged to the master of the convoy his *ronin* had raided! By the sacred *kami!* It had reassembled and was stopping here for the night!

Noburo knew there was no danger of being recognised and accused of banditry. He had been masked during the attack and dressed as a disreputable, down-at-heel character. But what an odd coincidence! Making his way back to the courtyard, he met with an even bigger surprise. Only yards from where his own horse stood between the two disguised ronin, the two Vietnamese house-women were helping the masked courtesan down from a *jinrikisha*!

This was no longer mere coincidence, decided Noburo. Fate had conspired to bring the players in the drama together on the same stage. He would make his promised report to the Herald, but he would also arrange for the young man to discover the truth for himself!

Noburo watched discreetly from a distance as the two house-women were brought to the convoy-master, who welcomed them back into the fold and helped them secure the best possible accommodation for their 'mistress'. When she had been whisked out of sight, Noburo sought out the innkeeper and his wife and announced that he wished to discuss a matter of some importance with them in private.

The innkeeper, who – like all men who plied his trade – was the social inferior of the samurai, led Noburo into his private quarters with the usual bowing and scraping, to which his wife added her abject apologies for the miserable state of their abode, et cetera, et cetera.

Once the niceties had been observed, Noburo adopted a cross-legged position facing the kneeling innkeeper. His wife knelt in her traditional place, facing her husband's left shoulder. Noburo began by explaining that his previous visit to the post-house had been to verify its reputation as a clean, well-run establishment. He had been gratified to discover that everything he had heard was true. The high standards of service and heart-warming hospitality offered to weary travellers reflected nothing but credit upon its proprietors. Their honesty and zeal was, said Noburo, an example that the rest of their profession would be hard put to emulate.

Praise indeed.

While the surprised couple searched for the correct form of words to express their unworthiness to be the recipients of such a fulsome accolade, Noburo produced a wad of high-denomination notes and placed them on the mat in front of the innkeeper. The man and his wife exchanged a startled glance, then both stared open-mouthed at what was clearly a small fortune. Unable to believe his eyes, the innkeeper reached out towards the notes with trembling hands, then jerked them away. By the rules of etiquette he could not pick up the money until Noburo gave him permission to do so.

After receiving solemn assurances that they would treat what he was about to say with the utmost discretion, Noburo revealed that he was acting on behalf of a young nobleman of high birth who greatly desired to meet the masked lady – who they had only just received into their house.

Warming to his tale, Noburo painted a tragic picture of a young man's awakening love – in this case reciprocated by the lady in question. But because of his family's exalted rank the liaison could not be allowed to continue. Arrangements had been made for the young man to marry a daughter from one of the many branches of the Toh-Yota family – the rulers of Ne-Issan.

Hhhhaaaawwww . . .! The innkeeper and his wife looked impressed. To think they were caught up in such great events!

For this reason, continued Noburo, the lady had been banished from court circles and was now on her way to become the chattel of some common east-coast merchant. This meeting – assuming that the innkeeper and his wife would graciously allow it to take place under their own roof – was their last chance to be together.

The innkeeper's wife, a warm-hearted woman whose life had been entirely devoid of such grand passions, listened avidly to the *ronin's* story. Her husband only had one aim: to make a profit out of every transaction. His fingers, which could flutter with incredible grace and speed over his abacus, no longer knew how to caress her body. As a consequence, her romantic appetite fed vicariously off the details of other people's love affairs. The gift of money satisfied the husband, and the heart-rending tale brought tears to the eyes of his wife.

On retiring to bed she would be able to close her eyes and project herself into the role of the courtesan locked in a last desperate embrace with her noble young lover. Always providing, of course, that her dull lump of a husband did not shatter the illusion by snoring his head off.

But, in the meantime, how could they help? The question was put timidly to Noburo through her husband. Noburo explained that the two women acting as her chaperones were in the employ of the merchant. The fact that he had provided two Vietnamese women was an insult in itself and showed what an uncouth fellow he was.

The innkeeper and his wife, who were both of Chinese descent and thus superior to everybody except the Sons of Ne-Issan, were quick to agree.

Having ascertained that he could rent the small pavilion he had used on his previous visit, Noburo produced a small vial of powder – a potent sleeping draught that was to be mixed in two cups of *sake* that the innkeeper would generously offer the courtesan's servants with their supper. When they were soundly asleep, and the other travellers had retired for the night, he would, with their consent, introduce the lady into the pavilion where her noble lover would be waiting in the hope that she would receive him with a generous heart and a giving nature. By morning he would be gone, never to see her again, the lady would be back in her chamber and her chaperones would be none the wiser.

The innkeeper gazed misty-eyed at the money and agreed it was a most excellent plan; his wife swore to guard the secret with her life and managed to convey by a lingering sidelong glance that while the master lay in the arms of his loved one she would not be averse to pleasuring his trusted servant. For Noburo, nothing was less likely but, aware she was his principal ally, he responded with an equivocal glance and withdrew, leaving her in a lather of pleasurable anticipation while her husband's eager fingers riffled through the sweet-smelling pile of new dollar bills.

*

By the time the wafer-thin crescent moon had risen, Steve's body felt rested and his mood had mellowed considerably. Which was just as well, because the *ronin* had begun to saddle their horses.

With a huge yawn, Steve got to his feet and stretched his limbs, then leapt up to grasp an overhanging branch and hung there to loosen his spine. Ohh, yeah, that's better . . . Just what the doctor ordered. Dropping down, he did a few more limbering-up exercises, then scooped some water out of the nearby stream and splashed it over his face and down the back of his neck.

Okay, world, I'm good and ready. Do your worst . . .

The worst the world had to offer was another slow night-ride. But now there were only nine *ronin*. Noburo was one of those who had gone missing, leaving his two sidekicks to head the column. Steve, whose saddle-sore butt was soon sending out a new wave of distress signals, switched his thoughts away from the means of locomotion and tried to work out what might lie ahead.

Even without understanding the language, it was obvious to him that Clearwater and her two minders had been set free and left to find their own way home. But what had been the point of the exercise? From the little she had been able to tell him, Steve knew she was now the 'body-slave' of one of the top Iron Masters; a certain Nakane Toh-Shiba who had just moved into the No. 1 spot on Steve's hit list. He also knew she had been transported across Ne-Issan in conditions of great secrecy, had sailed with Yama-Shita to the trading post and had then been put back in the box for return to Toh-Shiba. At which point, Noburo's *ronin* had spoiled everything with their raid on the convoy: a convoy which also contained two long-dogs. Clearwater had only caught a fleeting glimpse of them, but she had seen enough. The itinerant duo were Jodi Kazan and Dave Kelso, en route for the Heron Pool where Cadillac was now busily at work trying to build imitation Skyhawks.

162

But not for much longer, amigo. Your old friend Stevie, who you so kindly shafted by first picking his brains, then assuming his identity, is aiming to throw a nice big spanner right in the works.

Thanks to Clearwater, Steve now had three names to work with: Yama-Shita, old Golden Nose, who had set up the deal with Mr Snow; Min-Orota, another high-wire in whose domain the Heron Pool was located and who, apparently, was funding the operation; and Nakane Toh-Shiba, the Jap who now 'owned' Clearwater. He was some kind of top-level government official based in Min-Orota's territory.

Three interesting pieces that all linked together, but how did they fit into the rest of the puzzle? Steve had coaxed Noburo into admitting he was an agent of 'those who have an interest in this matter': his exact words. Was that the purpose of this present journey – to meet the person, or persons, running what amounted to a covert operation against the trio led by Yama-Shita?

As the column continued its slow progress across the forested terrain, threading its way from one dimly lit clearing to the next, Steve mulled over the known elements of the present situation. If a meeting *did* materialise he had to look and sound confident, and be poised to exploit any opportunity that presented itself. If he failed to make the right connections, he was unlikely to get another chance. The biggest problem was his crippling lack of knowledge of the present set-up inside Ne-Issan. Without these facts it was virtually impossible to figure out who was doing what to whom. He had to rely on the winning combination that had served him so well in the past: intuition – his elusive sixth sense, the voice that sometimes made itself heard in the recesses of his mind, and his incredible luck – what Mr Snow and Clearwater kept calling the will of Talisman.

The more Steve thought about it, the more evident it became that it was Clearwater, not Cadillac, who was the key element in the equation. For reasons he did not yet fully understand, her transformation from patterned grass-monkey to clear-skinned long-dog had made her a valuable asset; a prize that Yama-Shita and his friends had gone to considerable lengths to conceal. But why? What made her so different from all the other Tracker renegades held prisoner in Ne-Issan? Was it because she was the only female, apart from Jodi, that had fallen into their hands? Or was it because this Nakane Toh-Shiba found her as stunning to look at as he did? Was it the Jap's present physical relationship with Clearwater that was the cause of all this clandestine activity? Was Toh-Shiba breaking the rules – and were his friends Yama-Shita and Min-Orota involved in the cover-up?

The raid on the convoy was proof that somebody was on their case: somebody with sufficient clout and resources to employ close on a hundred '*ronin*' operating from a secure, well-established base-camp. That 'somebody' – Mr X – was opposed to or, at the very least, concerned about what was going on: concerned enough to gamble men's lives in order to find out who was behind the mask. And powerful enough to command the loyalty of men prepared to die, as more than forty of them had, in order to satisfy his curiosity. Noburo had asked Clearwater no questions; the house-women had been ignored. He had merely inspected his hard-won prize and, to judge from his outward reaction, had not been overly surprised to find what looked like a long-dog, clothed in Iron Master finery.

Steve thought back over what Side-Winder, his fellow-Mexican, had told him about Ne-Issan, searching for clues as to who 'Mr X' might be. Toh-Shiba, the Jap now waiting to repossess Clearwater's body, was a government high-wire. Yama-Shita and Min-Orota were domain-lords. Were they plotting something? Were the aircraft that Cadillac was attempting to build to be used in a bid to seize power? Side-Winder had talked of an 'undercurrent of conspiracy'. Were they plotting against other domain-lords or . . . against the government? Could the 'someone' whose identity Steve was trying to establish . . . could 'Mr X' be . . . the Shogun?

164

Steve felt his brain quiver as he came to this realisation. It was as if an ice-cool electric current had suddenly connected all of his several billion brain cells.

Yep . . . that's how it plays, Brickman. You just hit the jackpot.

The column halted. Two *ronin* appeared out of the darkness and untied Steve's wrists and feet. Through the trees, Steve could just make out several faint points of orange light arranged in a regular cluster. From his scavenging expeditions he knew they came from the lighted windows of dwelling places. This, then, was the rendezvous point.

The two *ronin* brought Steve to the head of the column where Noburo Naka-Jima now stood illuminated by a thin ray of light from a masked lantern. He had dispensed with the ragtag look and was now dressed like a man of some distinction. He wore a black outfit trimmed with blue. Several white word-signs and symbols were arranged across the chest and back of his jacket. His bald head was partly covered by a wig swept up at the back into the top-knot that was the exclusive hallmark of the samurai.

'You will now take off clothes and wash body,' he said, pointing to a wooden bucket full of water.

Steve stripped off his walking skins and stood shivering in his blue wingman's underpants. Noburo motioned to him to take those off too. The sight of the hair that ran down from his navel then spread out across his pelvis brought some muttered comments from the dinks standing around him. Someone handed him a square block of fat and made rubbing motions as another guy emptied some of the water over his head. Steve worked up a rich lather. The block was a solid version of the liquid soap the Federation provided in push-button dispensers. More water was thrown over him. Christopher, it was cold! He worked the soap over his body until he reached his toes, got another drenching, then was handed a towel. A good hard rub got rid of most of the goose pimples.

Noburo sniffed the air coming from Steve's direction

and gave a nod of approval. 'Now you dress in different manner.'

One of the *ronin* handed Steve a cotton loincloth and showed him how to wrap it around his private parts, then another guy brought over a sack to put his dirty clothes and his other belongings in. With that task completed, Steve was provided with a pair of white cotton socks, a brown, loose-fitting cuffed jacket and trousers like those worn by Clearwater's minders and a pair of flat-soled shoes. A square straw mask with two eye-slits was placed over his face and fastened at the back of his head and round his throat, then a hooded waist-length cape made of woven straw was draped over his shoulders and closed by means of a loop and toggle just below the collarbone. Finally, another pair of white socks was slipped over his hands and tucked up his sleeves to hide the tell-tale patches of coloured pigment.

Steve's wrists were tied together again, but his horse-riding days were over. Two *ronin* who had changed into red-stripe outfits rode up as Noburo remounted. All three horses had been dolled up by the addition of tassels attached to the harness, their tails had been partly braided and the body of Noburo's mount was now draped with a black cloth decorated to match the outfit of its rider.

One of the red-stripes took the free end of the rope that ran around Steve's wrists and hitched it to his saddle; the other took charge of the sack containing his old outfit. Noburo's party waved goodbye to the nine *ronin* they were leaving behind and set off towards the distant points of light. Steve didn't have time to wave. He was too busy trying to keep up.

*

Near midnight, as the inhabitants of the now-silent post-house slumbered, a figure swathed in black, with only his eyes visible through a gap in the strip of cloth wound around his head, entered the darkened pavilion through the half-open screen that gave on to the garden, and sat down cross-legged opposite the waiting *ronin*.

It was Toshiro Hase-Gawa. A small lantern placed on the floor to Noburo's left provided the only illumination. Revealing his face to the *ronin*, the Herald exchanged the customary greetings and then listened intently to Noburo's account of the raid and his subsequent discoveries. The loss of some forty men was regrettable, but it was reassuring to know his informants had not lied. The love-object was indeed a long-dog.

As requested, the *ronin* had sent separate confirmation of this fact directly to the Shogun by courier pigeon. Noburo then announced that the *kami* who had snatched them from the jaws of death following the raid on the convoy had intervened in their favour yet again. The Herald could now examine the merchandise himself: 'Yoko Mi-Shima' and her two chaperones had rejoined the road convoy and were spending the night at the same post-house!

Mastering his surprise, the Herald asked how the examination could be conducted without giving the game away. Noburo explained the arrangement he had made with the innkeeper and his wife who, if she was as good as her last whispered word, was now abed with one ear cocked for the three owl-hoots which would summon her to the silent steam-laden bath-house and into Noburo's arms. She was destined to be cruelly deceived, but Noburo intended to make a handsome apology in the morning. He would blame his non-appearance on the need to guard the ill-starred couple during their midnight tryst, then leave with a backward glance that hinted at unfinished business.

Toshiro listened with an amused smile and laughed in all the right places, but his light hearted manner concealed mixed feelings at learning of the long-dog's presence in the post-house. The fact that she was now here and, thanks to Noburo, could be viewed whenever he desired called into question the wisdom of his original plan. Had it been a rash and futile action? Had men's lives been uselessly squandered?

He decided they had not. Gazing surreptitiously at the body of the long-dog through a bath-house screen, or from behind the door to her bedchamber with Noburo beside him as an independent witness, would have proved his accusations were well founded but it would not have thrown the conspirators into disarray.

That was the real purpose of the kidnapping. It raised doubts, it hinted at the possibility that at least one of their secrets was now known to others and fuelled the ever-present anxiety that their conspiracy had been uncovered. Perhaps Lord Yama-Shita would decide that the long-dog was now too great a risk and arrange to have her assassinated. That would certainly eliminate one problem – but it would also end his hold over Nakane Toh-Shiba. It might even cause the Consul-General to turn against him.

Yes . . . either way there were interesting times ahead.

Toshiro maintained his show of good humour and congratulated the *ronin* on his artful handling of the situation. 'So when may I be permitted to see the lady who has led me to risk all for a last passionate encounter?'

'Soon, sire,' replied Noburo. 'But first, there is another person I must bring to your attention.' Without further explanation he unwrapped a piece of cloth to reveal the combat knife, and proceeded to tell the Herald about Steve's intervention to halt the slaughter of the camp women and his subsequent revelations.

Toshiro listened impassively, then reached out and touched the knife. 'Why do you show this to me?'

'Because it is more than a knife. It is a weapon filled with the power of the long-dogs. The . . .' Noburo hesitated '. . . power whose name we dare not speak.'

The Dark Light . . .

Toshiro examined the knife cautiously. It was well crafted but the quality and sharpness of the steel blade was markedly inferior to the swords and daggers produced in Ne-Issan. He offered it back to the *ronin*. 'Show me . . .'

Noburo released the hidden pressure catches and removed one of the wooden side-pieces revealing the

168

device hidden inside. He had observed Steve's actions and had practised opening the hilt several times in order to avoid looking clumsy in front of the Herald. He had even taken out the stylus and used it to press various buttons just as the cloud warrior had done, but he had not found out how to make the moving word-signs appear.

What Noburo had done – although he did not know it – was to cancel the automatic broadcast of Steve's call-sign programmed by Side-Winder, plus the brief twelve-hourly transmissions Steve had keyed in himself. The result was to take Steve completely off the air. For the last two days, the high-flying ears of the First Family had searched for his signal and drawn a blank. The last fix AMEXICO had on him was in the area of Big D – the *ronin*'s secret hide-out – but now, no one knew where he was, or what had happened to him.

Toshiro inspected the microcircuitry inside the handle but was none the wiser. 'Did the cloud warrior explain the purpose of this device?'

'Yes. It is like a courier pigeon without wings. He uses it to send messages through the skies – and also to receive the commands of his masters.' Noburo shook his head in wonderment.

Toshiro also found the idea fascinating, but he was acutely conscious that they were playing with fire. The hidden contents of the knife made it a forbidden object whose power might destroy those who tampered with its mechanisms. He was obliged to take it with him in case the Shogun expressed a wish to see it, but its presence in the room made him feel uneasy. Toshiro got the *ronin* to show him how to release and replace the wooden side-pieces, then told him to wrap the knife up and place it in another room until they had concluded their business.

When Noburo returned he had the mysterious cloud warrior in tow. The tall dark-haired figure whose wrists were tied together went down on his knees before the Herald and bowed respectfully.

'Remove the mask,' said Toshiro, in Japanese.

Noburo untied the straw mask and adopted a cross-legged position facing them, on the Herald's right.

Steve sat back on his heels and kept his eyes lowered until the black-clad figure addressed him. Noburo had given him a crash course on how to behave, stressing that this high-flyer did not owe him any favours and was apparently a stickler for protocol. Social inferiors – and especially outlanders – did not sit in the company of samurai. They knelt. Above all, they did not come on like Jack the Bear.

Toshiro studied Steve's patterned face and forearms with a mixture of suspicion and distaste. He had never been this close to a grass-monkey before. He paused, uncertain what tone to adopt in this situation. He thought over what the *ronin* had said about his extraordinary martial skills and his fearless responses when questioned and decided to address him in a firm, but not overbearing, manner. 'I understand you call yourself a cloud warrior. What is that exactly?'

Steve was surprised to hear the fluency with which his interlocutor spoke Basic. 'That's the name the Mutes give to the wingmen of the Federation. They are a special kind of soldier. Cream of the crop. But instead of being mounted on horses like samurai, they ride into battle on flying machines called Skyhawks.'

'Got it. So tell me – why would someone as special as that dress up as a grass-monkey?'

Steve hesitated.

'You find that a difficult question to answer?'

'No, sire, I was just wondering what words to use. You speak Basic amazingly well, but the system you operate here is so different to ours we may not share the same kind of vocabulary.'

'Try me,' said Toshiro.

'The supreme ruler of your country is known as the Shogun. Is that correct?'

The Herald's throat tightened. He had not foreseen that the outlander might have the effrontery to ask him a question. He mastered his anger without changing his expression. 'Go on . . .'

'The supreme ruler of my country – the Amtrak Federation – is known as the President-General. I have the honour to be one of a small number of soldiers selected personally by him to carry out highly sensitive undercover assignments. The unit, over which he exercises direct control, is known as AMEXICO. The AMtrak EXecutive Intelligence COmmando. Its operatives are known as mexicans. We are the eyes and ears of the President-General, and it is he who sent me here.'

'In pursuit of two long-dogs, I believe –'

Steve hit him with the big one. 'You are mistaken, sire. The couple I seek are not long-dogs. They're Mutes.' As he inclined his head, he saw the eyes of his masked questioner flicker with alarm.

Toshiro exchanged glances with the *ronin*. If what this outlander said about himself was true, then the position he held in his own country was more or less equivalent to Toshiro's own as a Herald to the Inner Court. If that was the case, it was little wonder that he had fought so well and spoken with such assurance. But what he had just said about Clearwater and her companion could totally demolish the scenario he had constructed for the Shogun. And that could be very embarrassing. A firm response was necessary.

He slapped his thigh and laughed mockingly. 'You spin a good story, cloud warrior, but I advise you to tread carefully. You come here uninvited, threaten to make war on us with fire from the sky if we do not hand over the two criminals you seek, and now you ask us to believe that, despite your appearance, you are really a long-dog, and those who look like long-dogs are grass-monkeys!'

Steve bowed. It was obvious this guy hadn't heard about super-straights. 'Yes, sire, I know it sounds far-fetched, but that's the way it is. They are a special kind of Mute that you may not have come across before.'

Toshiro's mouth tightened and went down at the corners. Was this possible? *Hhhawwwwh!* This conversation was taking a dangerous turn. He would have to find some excuse to get rid of the *ronin* so that he could talk privately with the cloud warrior. It was vital that this disturbing piece of news did not reach the Shogun's ears until he had had an opportunity to prepare the ground.

'Can you prove you are not a grass-monkey?'

'Yes.' Steve indicated Noburo. 'I gave the samurai-captain my radio-knife.'

Toshiro nodded. 'Yeah, I've seen it,' he said flatly.

'The Plainfolk do not possess such devices. Neither do the Sons of Ne-Issan. Only the Federation has the knowledge and the power to create these things. I can show you how it works.'

And who knows, maybe this time I might get Karlstrom on the other end of the line. That would rock them back on their heels.

'The device is of no interest to us.'

Steve found his reply bewildering, but then the *ronin* had also shown a certain reluctance when presented with the knife. Steve recalled Side-Winder telling him the dinks didn't have electricity. Okay. Neither did the Mutes. But these guys were different: they were into making things in a big way. They should have been falling over themselves to find out about it but instead they gave the impression they couldn't care less. Maybe they were just scared of new ideas – like the M'Calls not wanting the Iron Masters' rifles. Never mind, if he couldn't blind this guy with science he still had a couple of cards to play. 'This skin colour comes off. But I need some water and some leaves that are in my bag.'

Toshiro looked across at the *ronin*. Noburo got up and left the room.

As the screen door slid shut behind him, Toshiro said, 'What else do you know, cloud warrior?'

Steve raised his eyes, hesitated for a moment, then decided to play his hunch. 'I know that you and the samurai-captain serve the Shogun and that there are those who seek his downfall. Lord Yama-Shita is one, his friend Min-Orota is another.'

172

Toshiro's eyes gave nothing away. 'Go on . . .'

'If I'm right, maybe you and I can do business.'

'What kind of business?'

'I was sent here to take out the Mute who is building flying machines for Lord Min-Orota.'

' "Take out" . . . you mean kill?'

'My orders were to bring him and his female companion back alive if possible. If not . . .' Steve completed the sentence with a shrug. 'If I fail, the Federation will be obliged to resort to other . . . more destructive means. We do not seek a wider conflict, but we cannot allow this enterprise to succeed. It's also possible that what is going on at the Heron Pool does not have the wholehearted support of those you represent. If this is the case, you may feel that perhaps it would be in the best interests of all concerned if it was closed down. Permanently.'

'Mmmmm . . . interesting thought. Are you making me an offer?'

'It would save everybody a lot of grief.'

'Who gave you all this information – my colleague?'

Steve shook his head. 'Apart from disclosing that his name was Noburo Naka-Jima, he didn't tell me a thing. He didn't need to. The Federation has ears and eyes all over the sky.' That last part was pure invention, but Steve was closer to the truth than he realised.

Noburo returned with a small bucket of water and the deerskin waist-bag. When his wrists had been untied, Steve spread out the fingers of his left hand towards the man in black and pointed at them in turn. 'Pick one.'

Toshiro said nothing until Steve switched hands and reached his right middle finger. 'Stop right there.'

Pulling one of the five-pointed pink leaves from the bundle, Steve wet it thoroughly, then scrunched it up in his left hand. He then dunked the chosen finger in the bucket and screwed it around vigorously inside his closed fist. A couple of minutes and several rinses later, no trace of the dye remained. Stretching out his arm, he closed his fist and extended his middle finger upwards in front of Toshiro's face for him to examine.

The Herald, who was unaware of the symbolic meaning behind the gesture, stared silently at the pink-skinned digit.

'Satisfied?'

Toshiro managed to control his anger, but it took a great deal of effort to do so. He would dearly have loved to cut off the cloud warrior's arm to punish him for his insolence, but this was not possible. Not yet, anyway. But he had to let this outlander know he was not dealing with an ignoramus. 'Don't push it, sport.'

'Sire, it was your facility with my language that led me to use a more colloquial form of address. By doing so, I meant to pay you a compliment, not to give offence.'

'Spare me the bullshit,' said Toshiro. 'I may not be up on the Federation but I know when someone's trying to put me down.'

There was only one thing to do: bow gracefully.

'Okay,' said Toshiro. 'You have the skin and the face of a long-dog. But so has the woman you seek. She was painted like you.'

'That's true.' Steve indicated the pattern on his arm. 'This stuff is specially made by the Mutes to disguise those born with clear skins.'

'Unfortunately we only have your word for that.'

Steve shrugged. This guy's attitude was beginning to get his back up. 'It's a pity the samurai-captain let the woman go. If she was here now she could prove I'm speaking the truth.'

The Herald digested Steve's reply then looked at the *ronin*. Noburo responded with a slight nod. 'Very well. We'll see what she has to say.'

It was Steve's turn to be surprised. 'She's here?'

'Yeah. It's your lucky day.'

A real wise guy . . .

Toshiro turned to the *ronin* and spoke again in Japanese. 'My friend. If it is still possible, bring the woman here without delay and hold her in the next room until I am ready to question her.'

Noburo replied in their native tongue. 'Shall I secure

the wrists of the outlander?'

Toshiro suppressed a smile. 'No. He is a venomous serpent, but I think I know how to handle him. If we could find a way to place him in the bosom of our enemies he could be of great use to us.'

'And afterwards . . .?'

'I shall have great pleasure in drawing his fangs.'

Not understanding your opponents' language was like playing Shoot-A-Mute with your eyes shut. Steve watched Noburo bow, then pad softly towards the door. For some reason these guys took their shoes off every time they came inside. He had been made to leave his out on the veranda too. Strange people. He turned back to the man in black and wondered what the rest of his face looked like.

'Look, uhh . . . may I speak frankly?' No response. Steve tried again. 'The samurai-captain warned me that outlanders such as myself are not supposed to ask questions but there are a few things we need to clear up.'

'Like what?'

'Well, it would help if I knew your name.'

'That's not necessary.'

'Okay, then – just tell me where you fit into the picture.'

'You don't need to know that either,' replied Toshiro. 'What you have to fix clearly in your mind is this. Your life is in my hands. If I decide to make use of you then your execution will be delayed. If you follow my orders and help bring this situation to a successful conclusion it *may* be postponed indefinitely.'

'Does that mean I get to go home?'

'That's up to you.' At this stage it was best to keep things fluid.

'Okay. But let me give you some advice. I'm happy to work in with you, but I've been on this case for some time. I know these two. I know how their minds work. So I may be able to come up with a few ideas you haven't thought of.'

The cloud warrior's brash confidence was really quite

insufferable. From the way he spoke anyone would think they were equals! Toshiro gritted his teeth and took a deep breath. 'I think you're getting a little ahead of yourself, sport. As yet, there is no deal. If you don't manage to convince me that the masked lady is a Mute, you'll be dead before morning.'

*

Clearwater experienced a moment of alarm when she woke to find a masked samurai in her bedchamber. She shrank away as he went down on one knee beside her, but he indicated by gestures that he wished her no harm. Putting a finger to his lips, he told her in fractured Basic that a gentleman who was concerned for her future was waiting near by and wished to speak with her. If she came of her own accord, he would ensure her safe return. Seeing her hesitation, the samurai assured her that both her guardians had been drugged and would not wake until dawn at the earliest, by which time she would be safely back in bed. Clearwater put her travelling cape over the thin cotton shift she was wearing, pulled the cowl over her head so that her face was shadowed and picked up a pair of wooden-soled sandals.

The samurai, whose voice and build she thought she recognised, slid open the door to the antechamber and ushered her past Su-Shan and Nan-Khe. Both women lay sprawled on their futons, breathing heavily through their mouths. Stepping barefoot on to the veranda, Clearwater followed the samurai to the far end past several other guest rooms and then slipped on her sandals as they stepped down on to a winding path. The moon had disappeared, leaving the post-house shrouded in almost total darkness, but as she was being taken to her room earlier in the day, Clearwater had noticed that the path led to a small pavilion set apart from the other buildings. No light came from the windows but as they drew closer she saw two red-stripes standing guard outside. One of them slid open the door-screen and bowed as she and the samurai mounted the steps, parked their footwear and went inside.

Standing in the light of a masked lantern was a man swathed in black. Only his eyes were visible. As the door slid shut the man stepped into the shadows. 'Take off your cape and stand in the light.'

Clearwater let the cape fall to the floor. The ankle-length cotton shift she wore hung from the points of her breasts, moulding itself softly over her belly and thighs. Her hair, now unpinned, framed her face and throat. She swept it up with her hands and pushed it back over her shoulders.

The shrouded eyes of the Man in Black glistened briefly in the lantern light. He motioned her to lift the hem of her shift. Clearwater reached down and gathered it up around her thighs.

'Higher.'

She lifted the hem clear of her pelvis. The Plainfolk had no complexes about nakedness. They dressed and observed a certain decorum, but to be without clothes was viewed as neither shameful nor embarrassing. Plainfolk were vigorous and lusty but they were not filled with prurient curiosity.

'Higher.'

Clearwater calmly hoisted the shift up over her breasts. She felt nothing because exposing her body to these cold-eyed strangers meant nothing. It was the same with the Consul-General. Even though she had lost count of the times he had penetrated her she remained inviolate. For Mutes, it was the inner self that was sacred. Her soul was pledged to the cloud warrior and would remain so.

'Turn round.'

Clearwater turned to face the masked samurai. She was sure he was the same man who had inspected her when she had been held in the cave. She sensed that neither of the Iron Masters lusted after her. If anything, they viewed her with a certain repugnance. So why were they so curious about her body? The fact that she had hair on her head and belly where they had none could not be the real reason why she had been carried off, released without any explanation, and was now once again in the hands of the same man and yet another of his accomplices.

Yama-Shita and his friends had kept her hidden in a carriage-box and windowless rooms. If these men hid their faces behind masks and wrappings of black cloth then they must be adversaries of Yama-Shita. Her clear-skinned body had, in some way, become important to both sides.

'Cover yourself.'

Clearwater pulled the shift down over her hips and let it fall. The masked samurai handed her the cape. She wrapped it round her shoulders and turned to face the Man in Black.

Toshiro switched to Japanese and addressed the *ronin*. 'Send one of your men to keep an eye on the house-women. If they should wake and raise the alarm . . .'

'I'll make sure it doesn't happen.'

'Good. I want you to stay out here and keep watch while I talk to these two. If I need any assistance I'll call. Otherwise, there are to be no interruptions. Is that understood?'

Noburo bowed. 'Absolutely.'

The Herald slid open the door-screen to the adjoining room and motioned Clearwater to enter. She bowed respectfully to both men, then went through. Her hand flew to her mouth as she saw the cloud warrior kneeling on the mat by the masked lantern.

Steve was equally surprised to see her.

Toshiro pointed to a spot on Steve's right. 'Move over there.'

As Steve shuffled round, the Herald motioned Clearwater to take his place. When they were both kneeling with bowed heads, he sat down facing her, cocked his elbows outwards and placed his hands on his splayed thighs. 'Okay, straighten up! Let's get this over with.'

They sat back on their heels.

Toshiro flicked a hand towards Steve. 'This individual has made certain allegations which I wish to verify. You will answer me fully and with the utmost truthfulness. Is that understood?'

'Yes, sire.'

'Good. This may not concern you in the slightest but I may as well tell you that –' he pointed towards Steve again – 'if this person has lied to me in any material particular you will be a witness to his immediate execution.'

Clearwater bowed and stole a sideways glance at Steve. *Oh, my beloved cloud warrior! What have you said . . .?*

'Let us begin,' said Toshiro. 'Do you come from the underground world they call the Federation?'

'No. I was born under the sky.'

'So you are a Mute . . .'

'I have never claimed to be anything else, sire.'

'What is your true name?'

'Clearwater.'

'And the names of your parents?'

'I am the blood-daughter of Sun-Dance. My father was Thunder-Bird – a great warrior.'

'To which clan do you belong?'

'The M'Calls, from the blood-line of the She-Kargo, first-born of the Plainfolk.'

So far so good. Round Two.

'The individual who came with you from the sky and now works at the Heron Pool – is his name Steven Roosevelt Brickman?'

'No. His name is Cadillac. Like me, he is of the Plainfolk and the clan M'Call. His mother was Black-Wing. His father was Heavy-Metal.'

'What were you hunting when Cadillac first "chewed bone"?'

'Fast-foot.'

'What was the name of the warrior who challenged him?'

'Shakatak D'Vine, from the blood-line of the D'Troit.'

'Did Cadillac kill him?'

Clearwater hesitated. 'He fought bravely and well.'

'I shall only ask you once more. Did he kill him?'

'No, sire. I did.'

'What is your relationship to Mr Snow?'

'He is my teacher and guardian.'

'Is he an agent of the Amtrak Federation?'

'No, sire. He abhors the Federation and all its works. He has sworn to pit his strength against it until the last breath leaves his body.'

Toshiro's outward stance did not change one iota but inwardly he was crumbling as fast as the scenario he had laid before the Shogun. Every answer this grass-monkey gave confirmed the claims made by the accursed mexican. Instead of giving him *sake* when he started shooting his mouth off, Noburo should have cut his tongue out . . .

He rallied his flagging confidence and tried again. 'Have you or Cadillac, acting without the knowledge of Mr Snow, entered into league with your enemies?'

'No, sire. Such treachery would be unthinkable. We were sent to help you in exchange for new, long sharp iron.'

'Rifles.'

'I have not seen these objects but I have heard that word used by the clan elders.'

'Why do you and Cadillac paint your skins?'

'Because we wish to be like our clan brothers and sisters. To us, who are of the Plainfolk, it is not a disguise. That is how we truly wish to be.'

'I see. Then why – if these are your "true colours" – did you remove them?'

Clearwater hung her head. 'Out of weakness, sire. When I saw the reduced condition of the Plainfolk that are held here I hoped to improve my lot by pretending to be a long-dog.'

'Is that why Cadillac came here dressed as a cloud warrior from the Federation.'

'Yes, sire. Besides not knowing that some of us are clear-skinned, Lord Yama-Shita thinks of the Plainfolk as ignorant and slow-witted. If he were to discover all the things we know and are capable of he might not be so eager to trade with us.'

Her reply, delivered so mildly, sent a chill running up the Herald's spine. By the sacred *kami*! He thought of the thousands of Mutes spread throughout Ne-Issan. Several subservient generations who had been breeding quietly in increasing numbers. Over the last few decades, the *bakufu* had been doing its sums and had come to the realisation that the economy was now dependent on them. The news that they might not be dull-eyed, ox-brained slaves but a silent, vengeful army waiting patiently for the signal to rise up against their masters put a different complexion on things.

If it were found to be true, the blame could be laid squarely at the door of the Yama-Shita family, for it was they who had introduced these outlanders into Ne-Issan, growing rich and powerful on the proceeds. Perhaps it might form the basis of a new charge that could be levelled against them – economic sabotage.

'Have you heard of the Dark Light?'

'No, sire. The words mean nothing to me.'

Round three. You're moving well, champ . . .

Toshiro pointed to Steve. 'Who is this man?'

Clearwater saw the veiled warning in the cloud warrior's eyes and understood. 'His skin is marked like that of my clan brothers but he is not of the Plainfolk. He is a sand-burrower.'

'Sand-burrower . . .?'

'It is the name we give to the warriors from the dark cities beneath the deserts of the south. You call them long-dogs.'

'Do you know his name?'

'Yes.' Clearwater gazed at Steve. 'His name is Brickman. Steven Roosevelt Brickman.'

'The name your clan brother chose as part of his disguise –'

'That was an act of revenge. My people call this man the Death-Bringer.'

181

Toshiro's interest reawakened. 'He has been among you?'

Clearwater nodded. 'Last year. He and the other cloud warriors burnt our land with fire from the sky. And the iron snake devoured the flesh of our people. Many died.'

Toshiro turned to Steve. 'You certainly get around.'

Steve accepted this with a nod. 'That's my job, sire. And after watching the way you operate I've got a feeling we're in the same line of business.'

Toshiro's fingers itched to seize the hilt of his long-sword. Once again he controlled the murderous impulse that welled up within him. He had to find ways to build a new case against Yama-Shita and his co-conspirators. But to achieve this he might have to make use of the outlander. It was not a prospect he relished, especially since it appeared that the only way to keep the ill-mannered dog in his place would be to nail his knees to the floor.

'Did anyone ever tell you you've got a big mouth?'

'Frequently,' said Steve.

*

Noburo rose to meet the Herald as he brought out the clear-skinned woman. Glancing through the doorway, he saw that the cloud warrior had been left kneeling on the mat.

Toshiro addressed him in Japanese. 'I am deeply indebted to you for bringing these outlanders before me. It has been most instructive. Please make sure she is returned safely and without incident.'

Noburo bowed.

Toshiro turned to address Clearwater. 'It would be in your best interests to say nothing to anyone of what you have seen or heard tonight. And in case you and your clan brother cherish any hopes of returning home, let me alert you to the fact that Lord Min-Orota personally assured me that when Cadillac's usefulness comes to an

182

end he is to be stripped of the gifts and pleasures with which he has been provided and plunged into utter degradation. And when he has had sufficient time to fully appreciate his fall from grace, he will suffer a lingering death. Your position is equally perilous. Your master's friends regard his desire for your company as a dangerous weakness that threatens them all. Do I make myself clear?'

Clearwater bowed from the waist. 'Yes, sire.'

Noburo ushered her out on to the veranda and handed her over to the waiting red-stripe. 'Put her to bed, make sure everything is as it should be, then bring Tenno back here.'

The red-stripe and Clearwater disappeared into the darkness.

'I shall take the outlander with me,' said Toshiro as the *ronin* re-entered the pavilion. 'Mask him and tie his hands behind his back. And hang that bag of leaves on him somewhere.'

Noburo brought Steve to him with the waist-bag hanging round his neck. The length of rope that had been used to secure his feet while riding was now tied round his waist. Noburo offered the loose end to the Herald. 'Shall I escort you to your horse?'

'No, you've done enough,' said Toshiro. 'Thank you again, my friend. It has been an honour to know you. Be assured that I shall commend you and your men most highly to the Shogun.'

Noburo bowed. 'To serve him is reward enough. May the *kami* grant you safe passage through these troubled waters.' He followed Toshiro out and watched as the Herald led his prisoner down the planked steps on to the path, then turned right, going round towards the trees that lay behind the pavilion. Noburo walked along to the end of the veranda but, in those few seconds, they had vanished into the night.

*

When they had covered a distance of some hundred yards, the Man in Black who was leading Steve by the rope tied round his waist turned back to face him. Steve had a sudden premonition of danger, but even his reflexes weren't fast enough to cope with the speed of Toshiro's fist. The blow, aimed with pinpoint accuracy, landed on a nerve centre in Steve's neck just below the ear, knocking him senseless to the ground. Toshiro quickly bound Steve's feet together, then ran back towards the pavilion.

*

Tenno, the other red-stripe who had been given the task of keeping guard outside the rooms occupied by the courtesan and her house-women, sprang into an attacking stance on hearing the scrunch of feet on gravel, then relaxed as he was greeted by three froggy croaks. He replied in similar vein. Shida, his colleague, stepped up into the terrace with the woman. The cowl of her cloak was pulled forward, making it impossible in the darkness to see her face. While Shida kept watch, Tenno motioned her to keep silent, then slid open the door to her quarters and guided her past the sleeping house-women to the shuttered inner room.

Although it was even darker inside than out, Clearwater was just able to make out the sleeping forms of Su-Shan and Nan-Khe; neither had moved in her absence. The red-stripe waited while she hung up her cape and slipped back under the quilt, then made his exit.

Tenno and Shida returned to the pavilion. Now that their mysterious visitor had gone, neither was unduly surprised to see light coming from the central doorway. Mounting the steps, they saw that the two masked lanterns had been hung from the ceiling with the single vertical slit raying its light towards the open door. It was then that they saw Noboro's body. He lay with his feet towards them, his head pointing towards the sliding screen that gave access to the veranda at the back of the pavilion. It was now wide open – a threatening black square full of unseen dangers.

Tenno and Shida dropped down on one knee on either side of Noburo. His throat had been cut from ear to ear. A square of writing paper had been pinned to his chest by a needle-like stiletto. The legend read: 'Thus perish all *ronin* who dare to challenge the Se-Iko.'

Hhhawwwww!

Both men leapt to their feet, hands flying to their long-swords. As they began to move across the room towards the opening at the rear the deathly silence was broken by two sharp, overlapping sighs – like the hiss of two rival snakes. It was the last sound Tenno and Shida heard and it was made by two razor-sharp throwing stars that flew out of the darkness and embedded themselves in the centre of their foreheads, killing them stone dead in mid-stride.

A few seconds after they hit the floor, Toshiro's black-clad figure vaulted over the railing on to the veranda. Entering the room, he closed the front door-screen, then dragged the bodies of the red-stripes into line on either side of the dead Noburo and pinned them to the floor with their own swords. With that task completed, Toshiro doused the lanterns and went out the way he came, drawing the two screens together behind him.

Noburo's assessment of the Herald had been characteristically shrewd and uncannily correct. There was a great deal more to Toshiro Hase-Gawa than met the eye. As well as the less obvious qualities with which he was endowed, he also possessed unsuspected skills, and tonight they had served him well.

Reaching the spot where he had left the outlander, Toshiro found his prisoner was still unconscious. He untied Steve's feet first, then massaged the pressure points on his neck and shoulders to bring him round. The process took two or three minutes and Steve was still a little shaky when Toshiro hauled him to his feet.

'Come on, time to get going.'

'Yeah, okay. I'm on my way.' Steve shook his head to clear away the lingering dizziness and worked his jaw around. 'I don't know what I did to deserve it, but that was a neat trick. You must show me how you do that sometime.'

The black-clad figure took a step towards him. Steve tried to step back out of range and found himself up against a tree. He was a good head taller than the Jap but there wasn't much he could do with both hands tied behind his back. And even if they'd been free he wasn't looking to take him on. This guy was his ticket to ride.

'Listen, Brickman. To have got this far, you can't be as dumb as you look. I keep giving you the message but from the way your mouth is acting your brains must be out to lunch. So let me lay it out for you one last time. You've already said enough to get yourself killed several times over. The only reason you're still here is because I'm hoping that maybe you and I can work out a deal that could earn you a reprieve and give both of us what we want. But don't think that makes you fireproof. Nobody's indispensable. Not even you. If you don't start showing me some respect, I'll cut you loose and go it alone. And if that happens, you're going to end up as a pig's breakfast. Got it?'

Steve bowed to show a little respect. 'Yes, sire.' *You pint-sized, slant-eyed yellow asshole.* The straw mask concealed his mocking smile and his voice carried no hint of triumph. But inwardly he was cheering. 2102-8902 Brickman, S.R. had cleared another hurdle. Despite all the blood-curdling threats, he would live to see another dawn.

CHAPTER EIGHT

In the Federation, there had been no sunrise for close on a thousand years: or sunset either. Year in, year out, the lights stayed on wherever people were working. Life for Trackers was geared to a twenty-four-hour cycle. The machinery that made life possible underground was constantly serviced by succeeding shifts of generation upon generation of technicians. For those not engaged on 'night' work, the passing day was marked by a lowering of the illumination level in accommodation areas and public plazas to what was called 'twilight'.

The thing that Trackers feared most was darkness. And some old hands, who were the subversive guardians of an alternative history that was not to be found in the video archives, spoke in hushed whispers about a time known as the 'Black-Out' when an apparently well-planned but ill-fated attempt to mount a revolt against the First Family plunged the underground into total darkness that lasted – according to some accounts – for several decades.

Thousands suffocated as the ventilation shafts ceased to function, thousands more went mad and tore each other to pieces like starving rats trapped in a concrete cellar; the innocent dying with the guilty. The few who survived owed their salvation to the First Family – Creators of the Light, the Work and the Way; Keepers of all Knowledge, Wisdom and Truth.

From that moment on, their authority became absolute. The elimination of dissident elements, the ungrateful, the greedy and the disloyal, removed the worm from the bud that would one day flower in the Blue-Sky World. And the progress that had been made towards that dream confirmed their fitness to lead the

Federation, provided visible proof of the genius that lay behind their vision of the future, and underlined the sureness of their guiding hand and the truth in the immortal words of the Founding Father, George Washington Jefferson I: 'Only people fail, not the system.'

Amen . . .

*

In the Paul Revere Medical College, which formed part of Inter-State U – itself an annexe of Houston/Grand Central, Roz Brickman came out of the neurological lab along with the rest of her classmates to find John Chisum leaning against the wall opposite the door. Because of the heavy workload imposed by the curriculum, Roz had begun to skip some of the regular Saturday night java-and-jive sessions hosted by Chisum, but she made a point of visiting the apartment at Santanna Deep at least once a month.

Chisum had a line into some good grass, and although Roz had cut down on the amount she smoked, the occasional reef still helped to take the pressure off. Chisum also provided the best in blackjack – illicit music tapes that could earn you a spell in the slammer or, for repeated offenders, drug therapy and worse. And there was always the chance that he might have some news of Steve.

Chisum eased himself off the wall as Roz sidestepped through the milling crowd of white-coats and gave his outstretched palm a friendly slap. 'Hi. What brings you here?'

'Didn't see you last Saturday.'

'No.' She grimaced. 'May not be able to make it this week either.'

'Same here.' Chisum checked the activity in the corridor, then laid a hand on her elbow. 'You got a minute?'

'You can walk me to my next lecture. Will that do?'

'Guess it'll have to.' They headed after her classmates. 'What's the problem?'

'Did I say I had a problem?'

'No, but I'm picking up some bad vibrations.'

'You're right,' sighed Chisum. He looked back over his shoulder, then gnawed at his lower lip. 'I'm being leaned on.'

'Who by?'

'This guy.'

'You'd better get to the bottom line soon, John. We're running out of corridor.'

'He didn't give me his name!' hissed Chisum. 'All I know is he's some high-wire from the Black Tower.'

The headquarters of AMEX – the Amtrak Executive.

Roz eyed him cautiously. 'I've got a feeling I'm going to regret this but . . . why is he coming down on you?'

Chisum replied with an awkward shrug. 'Somebody must have blown the whistle on me.'

'For shipping grass? Christopher Columbus!'

Chisum motioned her to keep calm. 'It's not as bad as it sounds. These guys aren't Provos. They promised not to press charges if I was prepared to give them certain information.'

Roz felt her stomach turn over. 'About what?'

'About you and Steve.' Chisum saw the look on her face and spread his hands defensively. 'I had to do it. Roz! They got me over a barrel! It wasn't much, honest.'

'What did you tell them, John? About that night Steve and I were together before he was sent down?'

'They already know everything there is to know about Santanna Deep.'

'Columbus! Does that include the guys from here who've been tunnelling out every Saturday night?'

'Na, don't worry. These people aren't interested in piddle-shit stuff like that. There's only one thing they want to know about – what goes on between you two. C'mon . . . you know what I mean.'

'Maybe. What was your story?'

'I just gave 'em the few things Steve told me about the way you and him, uhh . . .'

Roz turned to face him as the group in front reached

the appointed lecture room and began to file in. 'About connecting?'

'Yeah,' said Chisum hurriedly. 'Stuff like that. Thing is, they want to see you. Ask questions.'

'So why didn't they just pick me up? Why send you, John?'

'Maybe they thought you might not co-operate. When it comes to thought transfer, I don't know from shit but it seems to me that it would be pretty difficult to prove one way or the other. You could tell 'em anything you liked.'

Roz treated him to a cold-eyed glance. 'What makes them think I'll talk just to save your skin?'

Chisum shrugged. 'You don't have to do anything, but – ' A new, sharper note of desperation entered his voice. 'Be fair, Roz. The only reason why I'm mixed up in all this is because I stuck my neck out to bring you and Steve together.'

'Yeah.' Roz glanced over her shoulder and saw that they were alone in the corridor. 'Gotta go.' She backed off. 'You sure know how to make a girl feel good, John. Have a nice day.'

'Listen –'

The door to the lecture room swung shut in his face.

Chisum turned away with a quiet smile and made his way down to Level One-1. It shouldn't be as easy as this – especially with someone who was supposed to be telepathic.

Despite her mental bond with her kin-brother, they had both proved soft targets. After the meeting Chisum had set up between them, Steve had lost his coveted wingman status and had been transferred to the A-levels. Steve had been told it was as punishment for expressing sympathetic concern for Mutes – his former captors and the perpetual enemies of the Federation – but, in reality, it was part of a softening-up process to get Steve in the right frame of mind for his next 'assignment'.

Near the end of the third month of his three-year sentence, Chisum had dressed up as an A-level medic

190

and contrived a 'chance meeting'. When Steve had asked the reason for his demotion, Chisum had put the blame on Roz. He had swallowed the story hook, line and sinker. And later, when Karlstrom, the head of AMEXICO, had told Steve that Roz had come forward voluntarily and confessed everything he had told her about his time with the Mutes, he had believed that too.

But none of it was true. Roz had said nothing to anyone. She didn't need to: her meeting with Steve at Santanna Deep had been videotaped. All the lies were part of a plan evolved by the faceless puppet-masters in the Black Tower. Roz and Steve were just two of an unknown number of Trackers whose lives had been manipulated from birth and who would probably die without ever knowing they were on the Special Treatment List.

Steve Brickman was a strange young man. When Chisum had been softening him up prior to the meeting with Roz, he had been bursting with tales of Mute magic, yet he seemed wilfully intent on neglecting the mental powers that he and his kin-sister possessed. Perhaps that was why it had been possible to play them off against each other. Roz's mind was open and eager to communicate, whereas Steve had pulled the shutters down.

And who was to say he was wrong? thought Chisum. With the First Family telling you what to think every moment of the waking day it was hard enough just trying to get your own mind sorted out, without having someone else roaming around inside your head.

Chisum was an undercover agent of AMEXICO, the top-secret organisation that Steve had joined at the beginning of March. With only four months' service under his belt, Steve was still what the organisation called a 'wet-back', and would be for some time yet. Chisum had been a fully fledged mexican for years but, unlike Steve, he had never been overground. He was employed by the section handling internal assignments – and two of his current files bore the names of Steve and Roz Brickman.

Following Roz's arrival at Inter-State U to complete the second, more advanced stage of her medical studies,

Chisum had been put on her case, then when her kin-brother had returned to the Amtrak Federation in the fourth quarter of 2989, Chisum had gone to work on him too.

The fact that Chisum had a 'file' on them did not mean he knew all about them. The First Family, which controlled access to the data stored on COLUMBUS, only dispensed information on a 'need-to-know' basis. No one had thought it necessary to explain to him why he was required to deceive these two young people. Apart from being provided with their basic bio-data and training profiles, the only piece of inside information he had managed to acquire was the fact that they had both been programmed at an early age and were classified as 'sensitives'.

That rare attribute was enough to gain them an ST-Listing, but there might be other factors of which he had not been advised. They might not, for instance, be kin-brother and -sister. The presence of mind-blocks suggested that maybe it was not the President-General's seed which had fertilised the eggs placed to hatch in Annie Brickman's womb. Or it could be that neither had been implanted in Annie and carried to term. They could have been changed without her knowledge for her own babies at birth – or she might have agreed to act as their surrogate guard-mother.

The possibilities were endless. Chisum knew from previous assignments that some strange things went on at the Life Institute, and most of the work was carried out behind closed doors.

Only Fran – their controller and his present boss – had access to the full story. And like all controllers, Fran was Family. Not only that, she was closely related to the President-General – an indication that Roz and Steve might be far more important than he realised.

*

During the evening of the same day, Roz Brickman was

summoned to the Principal's study. Entering the outer office where, during working hours, several administrative assistants formed a defensive line against visitors seeking to enter the inner sanctum, Roz found the Principal, Russell Waxmann, bent over one of the VDUs, pecking away at the keyboard. Roz waited until he tore his attention away from the screen, then introduced herself and presented her ID card. He gave it a cursory glance and told her to go on through, promising to join her directly.

Waiting for her in the wood-lined, carpeted room were a man and a woman dressed in black and silver-blue jumpsuits – the standard outfit worn by AMEXecs.

Roz recognised them as the special investigators from AMEX's Legal Division who had visited her in the medical school's private hospital ward, following the appearance of the mysterious wounds in her right arm and head. And she realised why Waxmann had elected to stay outside. If she was in trouble, he wanted to stand well back to avoid the fall-out.

The man asked her to hand over her ID card. Roz produced it without demur. The female exec then told her that her assistance was required in connection with an ongoing investigation. Roz indicated her willingness to help in any way she could, then, without more ado, she was ushered into the Principal's private elevator and taken down to the medical school's own subway station.

After a journey which involved two shuttle interchanges, Roz and her silent escort reached an unnamed subway station whose walls were clad with black marble. An elevator ride took them up to Level Three-1 and into an office which, to judge from the colour scheme of the subway station marbled corridors, carpeted elevator and the sleek room furnishings, was almost certainly in the Black Tower. This was the lair of the organisation men and women, the high-wires with the top-rated ID cards and spacious quarters in the new flashy accommodation deeps.

'Go on through,' said the male exec, breaking his silence. 'We'll pick you up later.'

Roz was inwardly relieved to know that there was going to *be* a 'later'. It was the first encouraging word that anyone had offered her since Chisum had dropped his bombshell earlier in the day. From that moment on, her mind had been in a turmoil. She stepped into the turnstile door and was rotated through into the adjoining office.

Standing behind the desk was another man wearing a black and silver-blue jumpsuit. But this one had sleeves laced with gold wire, a sign she was dealing with someone from the top deck.

Roz snapped to attention. The man, who had a high forehead and lean, angular features, motioned her to sit down in the chair facing the desk. The high-wire stayed on his feet. Placing his hands behind his back, he stalked slowly round her like a predator circling its exhausted prey.

'You don't need to know who I am,' said Karlstrom. 'But I can assure you that I know everything there is to know about you and your kin-brother and you should bear that in mind before replying to the questions I shall put to you. Any attempt to conceal information will have unpleasant consequences. Is that clear?'

Roz nodded.

'Steven is no longer in the A-levels.' Karlstrom fixed her with his deep-set penetrating gaze. 'But then I expect you already know that.'

Roz paled but did not reply.

'As I thought.' Karlstrom passed between her and the desk, then snaked round behind it. 'I have studied the taped reports of the psychosomatic wounding you experienced when your kin-brother was shot down last June. And I am aware that you have been subjected to further distress since.' He paused expectantly. 'I see. You prefer to make no comment. Very well. Take a look at this.'

Karlstrom swivelled a pedestal-mounted video screen

towards her and hit a button on the desk console. A coloured line appeared and expanded to fill the entire screen. It was a picture of Roz, taken by a concealed video camera. She lay on her side asleep in her bunk, the covers pulled up to her chin. The image was sharp, every detail clear; people studying for medical doctorates slept with the lights on like everyone else.

Roz saw her sleeping self open her mouth, saw her face muscles tighten to issue a soundless scream, then saw an invisible arrowhead punch a hole through her cheek. The screen Roz rolled her head from side to side, revealing an exit wound on the other cheek, then she sat up and clutched her face. The blood seeped through her fingers and trickled down on to the back of her wrists. Kicking aside the duvet, she ran barefoot out of camera range in the direction of the washroom.

The picture changed. This next camera had been positioned to cover the line of hand basins and the communal showers. Roz found herself wondering what other activity the watchers had recorded since the cameras were installed. Or were these hidden eyes everywhere – not just for her, but to keep tabs on the whole class? The whole school . . . ? Where did it end?

Her screen self entered and hurried across to examine her face in the wall-to-wall mirror mounted above the hand basins. The palms of her hands and cheeks were coated with blood. She opened up both taps, spat out a mouthful of blood, then pulled some cotton tissues from the nearest dispenser and swabbed her face and hands. Roz saw herself pause and stare at her mirror image, and she silently recalled the moment and the surprise she had felt then and which her screen self now displayed.

The hidden camera zoomed in as she examined her face closely. The wounds were closing before her eyes. A minute later, the skin was whole; only a bruise remained to mark the point where the arrow had pierced her cheeks. She took a closer look, clearly doubting the evidence of her own eyes, then accepted the event with a shrug and rinsed her mouth to get rid of the last traces of blood.

The tape then switched back to a wide-angled view from the camera aimed at her bunk-space. The digital time display in the top right-hand corner of the screen showed that it was 0630. Other students moved past in various stages of undress and alertness. Roz saw and heard herself explaining to Gina Blackwell – the student in the next bunk – that the blood on her pillow was the result of a sudden nosebleed.

Karlstrom hit the 'Off' button. 'Remarkable.' He sat down behind the desk and gazed at Roz over his steepled fingers. 'May I now take it you are prepared to concede that this is a true record of what happened?'

'Yes,' whispered Roz.

'Yes, *sir*,' said Karlstrom.

'Of course. I'm sorry, sir. I didn't mean to –'

Karlstrom silenced her with an abrupt wave. 'Would I be correct in assuming that when these woundings have taken place you also made mental contact with your kin-brother? Would you say, for example, that you were able to visualise his location as well as the, ahh . . . stressful conditions he finds himself in?'

'To some extent, yes, sir. Sometimes it's just a vague out-of-focus impression, at other times it's like actually being there.'

Karlstrom accepted this with a thin smile. 'As when Clearwater entered the hut where your kin-brother was spending the night. That was one picture that came over very well.'

Roz felt the colour rise to her cheeks. Her questioner had not been lying when he said he knew everything. Which meant they probably had pictures of her trying to get inside Steve's jumpsuit. The thought that cold-eyed strangers had been secretly watching her every move, listening to every word, made her feel sick.

'Can you speak to each other?'

'Sometimes I hear a voice, but it's not like a conversation. I feel his thoughts enter my head, share his emotions, see what he sees. But I think it's my own mind that puts it all into words.'

'Can he do the same?'

'Sometimes. It depends.'

Karlstrom looked amused. 'On what?'

'On whether he's in a receptive mood. He doesn't understand why we are bound together or how it works, and that scares him. Most of the time he tries to shut me out.'

'But he heard you clearly enough when he was being brought back to Grand Central on the shuttle. "They are watching me", I think you said. Who were you talking about, Roz?'

Oh, Christopher! They had taped every last word! 'I – I don't know,' she stammered. 'It was just a feeling that . . . that built up after the first time it happened. When Steve was shot down, those two people who brought me here came to see me over at the medical school and –'

'And asked you a lot of questions.'

'Yes, sir.'

'To which you gave evasive replies.'

'I was scared. I – I didn't want to say anything in case they took me off the course. I didn't know what to do. Nothing like this had ever happened to me before.'

'Not the wounding, perhaps. But don't play games, Roz. You've known about this special gift you and Steven share for a long time. So let's have nothing but the truth from now on. A lot of people are depending on you. Do you understand what I mean?'

'Yes, sir.' Play ball or Steve, Annie and Poppa-Jack will get shafted. Along with John Chisum and her fellow students who had been 'tunnelling out' with the aid of his Saturday Night Specials.

Karlstrom got up, came round the desk and hoisted his butt on to the front edge. He was now only a few inches away from where she sat with her hands nervously clasped together. 'Can you read *my* mind, Roz?'

She looked up at him. This time her eyes and voice didn't waver. 'No, sir.'

'Pity . . . ' Karlstrom laid a fatherly hand on her shoulder. 'I would have liked you to discover for yourself the very positive feelings we have for you and Steven.'

'We'? Who was 'we'? The First Family?

'You two have always been regarded as . . . very special people. People with extraordinary gifts who – one day – might be able to place the powers they possess at the service of the Federation. It would not be an exaggeration to say that you and Steven, along with . . . certain others . . . could one day tip the scales in our favour in the battle for the Blue-Sky World.' Karlstrom paused, then placed both hands on her shoulders. 'Steven is already engaged in that battle, Roz. He's out there now and he may be in trouble – although if it was serious, I imagine you would already know about it.'

Roz felt her heart skip a beat. 'What do you want me to do?'

'We've lost contact with him. It could be simply because his radio has stopped working. Or it may be something else entirely.'

Like the fact that the devious sonofabitch may have sold out on us . . .

Karlstrom's fingers tightened their grip. 'I want you to get in touch with him, Roz. I need to know how he is, and where he is. It's very important.'

'I'll do my best, sir,' she whispered.

'Good girl. I have something here which may help.' Karlstrom went over to a wall-storage unit, pulled a map out of a tube and unrolled it across the desk top. 'Bring your chair in closer.'

Roz slid the chair forward so that her knees touched the inset front panel of the desk and took a look at the map. It was printed in greens and browns to show the physical features of the terrain. The right-hand edge met a slab of pale blue. 'Where is this?'

'It's part of the north-east coast of America. That blue area is water. The Atlantic Ocean. This map shows the way it was before the Holocaust. Before the Mutes came and burned everything to the ground.' Karlstrom

198

pointed to a navref point named Pittsburgh. 'This is where Steve landed . . . ' His finger moved from west to east along the Pennsylvania Turnpike. 'We think he went along this road and – ' His finger stopped at the feature that Steve had christened 'Big D'. 'And we lost touch with him somewhere around here.'

Roz ran her fingers along the route traced by Karlstrom and described several circles around Big D, then she closed her eyes and reached out towards Steve with her mind.

Karlstrom's voice continued to filter through. 'He went out to capture Clearwater, Roz. That's why we need you to help us. We want to do everything to make sure he gets back safely. If you can help us do that I promise we will never allow Clearwater to come between you and Steven again . . .'

Roz's body suddenly went limp. Her head dropped backwards, eyes closed, lips parted. Karlstrom caught her as she swayed and laid her gently against the back of the chair, then stood by ready to catch her in case she was seized by convulsions. He had never been involved this closely with a sensitive before, and watching her made him feel uneasy. The Federation needed people with these powers in case the Talisman Prophecy turned out to be an accurate picture of future events. That was why the secret breeding programme had been initiated. The question was – once their powers were officially recognised and unleashed – would the First Family be able to control them?

Karlstrom came out of his reverie as Roz stirred. Her eyes snapped open, widening into an unblinking stare. Whatever it was she was looking at was far beyond the confines of the room. Without looking down at the map, she reached out and found Big D, then traced her way unerringly along the circular route Noburo had taken to reach the post-house at Midiri-tana.

From there, her fingertips moved north along a route that passed through a series of navref points – pre-Holocaust urban areas known as Mahandy City,

Hazelton and Wilkes-Barre – to Scranton, then over the border into Lord Yama-Shita's domain to Binghampton, then to Albany on the western bank of the Hudson River – now a busy ferry crossing known to the Iron Masters as Ari-bani.

'He is here,' murmured Roz.

Karlstrom looked over her shoulder. The map he had given her to work with did not show the various domains or the limits of Iron Master territory, but he knew from the data fed back from mexicans such as Side-Winder that everything west of the Hudson river at this point belonged to the Yama-Shita. On the eastern side lay the lands of the Shogun's family – the Toh-Yota – and beyond that, Lord Min-Orota's domain.

'What's he doing?'

'He sleeps. He has been running.'

'Running? Running away? Is someone after him?'

'No, he runs because he chooses to. He . . . ' Roz frowned as she concentrated on deciphering the images she was picking up. 'He has been given messages to carry.'

'Who for?'

Roz tried again, then shook her head. 'I cannot say. The man who has given him this task has no name.' She made another attempt. 'His face and body are hidden in darkness. Only his eyes . . . ' She pressed her hands against her forehead. 'He makes false promises. My brother knows this man is dangerous but he is also powerful. By agreeing to work with him he is able to go where he wishes.'

'What kind of shape is Steve in?'

Roz smiled to herself. 'He is tired, but he is fit and well. He has found Clearwater –'

'Is she with him?' asked Karlstrom abruptly.

'Not any longer. They have met but have not . . . been together.'

'Does she still feel the same way about him?'

Karlstrom saw Roz's eyes screw up tight. The blunt question upset her. It was meant to. Her hatred for

Clearwater was the McGuffin that would keep this little pixel in a co-operative frame of mind.

'Yes, she does.'

'How about Cadillac? Has Steven pinpointed his location?'

'Not exactly. But he knows the . . . general area.'

'Show me.'

Roz's fingers trembled over the map, but the information failed to come through. 'Near the Eastern Sea. He must take the road to the east to the place where the birds are . . .'

Birds . . . the feathered or the man-made variety? wondered Karlstrom. He looked at the map. The road that caught his eye was the old Massachusetts Turnpike that met the Hudson south of Albany and ran east through Springfield and Worcester to Boston and the Atlantic Ocean. Hmmmm . . . 'Does he have his radio – or any weapons?'

'No. They were taken from him.'

'Does he think of you? Does he . . . want to come back home – to the Federation?'

After a long pause, Roz said, 'His thoughts are only for what he must do. I see images of death and destruction. They – ' She broke off and tried to shake them from her mind. 'They frighten me.'

As she spoke, Karlstrom saw her eyes come back into focus. She stared at him with surprise, then looked nervously round the room as if trying to work out what she was doing there. A moment later, Karlstrom saw her relax as the part of her mind that had reached out to her kin-brother returned and settled into place.

'Uhh, have I . . . did I?'

'Don't you remember?'

'I know I made contact with Steve, but – did I say anything that made sense?'

Karlstrom laid his hand on her shoulder. 'A great deal. I'm very impressed.' He motioned her to rise and ushered her over to the turnstile. 'You will, of course, speak to no one about this meeting.'

201

'No, sir. But, uhh . . . the thing is, I don't want for anybody to get into trouble over this. John Chisum said –'

Karlstrom cut her short. 'Your friend Chisum has been very foolish and should know better. Still, I'm sure we all do things we shouldn't from time to time. That doesn't mean to say I approve of what has been going on at Santanna Deep. I don't. But –'

Roz opened her mouth, searching for the words to lift the blame from Chisum and excuse her actions.

Karlstrom motioned her to remain silent. 'The important thing is to do whatever has to be done for the Federation and the First Family when the call comes. Like the way you have helped me this evening. That won't be forgotten. Indeed, I may ask for your help again. Steven is a very resourceful young man, but he may not be able to make it back here in one piece without our assistance. So remember, I'm counting on you.'

'Yes, sir. Thank you, sir. I'll do whatever I can.'

'I'm sure you will. The people outside will give you a special number to call if you should "hear anything" from Steven.' He patted her on the back and guided her into the turnstile. 'Now off you go back to college. Oh, and, uhh . . . congratulations on those good grades you've been getting. Keep up the good work!'

Karlstrom pressed the button which caused the cylindrical compartment to rotate, carrying Roz back into the adjoining office suite. The two execs rose from their chairs to meet her.

CHAPTER NINE

'Roz?'

Steve woke with his kin-sister's name on his lips and his nostrils filled with the soap-scented smell of her hair. For a split second or so he was convinced she was in the darkened room with him. Or had been, and had just left. Slowly that certainty faded. It had been a dream, nothing more. He shivered, quickly retrieved the padded quilt that had slipped off his naked body and snuggled down beneath it.

It was amazing how the brain could create a mental landscape as real as anything you could see with your eyes open, right down to the smallest detail. It could bring you face to face with images of people you could speak with, reach out and touch, draw to you and embrace. Not only that, the dream state allowed you to savour the same emotions, the same sensations as when you were wide awake: the taste and the moist softness of their lips, the electric tingle of their skin under your fingertips, the delicious all-enveloping warmth generated as your body joined with theirs.

Did *their* sleeping minds, he wondered, share the same dream? Did they merge with yours on one of the invisible planes of existence Mr Snow had often referred to? In his dream, Steve had been with Clearwater. They were back in the hut where she had visited him only hours before he had made his escape from the M'Calls – the Mute clan that had held him captive during the summer of 2989. Clearwater's naked body had been locked round his, but as she drew his mouth down on to hers he found himself embracing Roz. And they were no longer in Cadillac's hut. He and his kin-sister were lying naked under a quilt in his bunk-space in the quarters allotted to the Brickman family at Roosevelt Field. The room seemed much bigger than he remembered it, and so did the bunk. It was then he realised that his kin-sister's breasts had shrunk back into her body. Her skin was patterned like a Mute's and she was now no more than ten years old.

As he drew back from her with mixed feelings of guilt and surprise he became aware that Karlstrom, the head of AMEXICO, was sitting on the end of the bed watching them with an amused smile. A man and woman dressed in black and silver-blue jumpsuits suddenly appeared. The man pulled the quilt from the bed. Steve tried to hold on to it but his fingers wouldn't grip properly. His hands had become weak and boneless. The woman exec picked up Roz, only now his kin-sister had become a five-year-old. They wrapped her in the quilt and took her away. By the time they reached the door Roz was a little snub-nosed baby, eyes screwed up tight, her toothless mouth wide open – screaming . . .

Had Roz been trying to get in touch with him? Was she trying to tell him something, or was this another message from the furtive stranger who haunted the dark recesses of his own brain?

Jumbled fragments of his dream drifted through his mind as he began to doze off again. The world outside the shuttered log cabin lay quiet and still. Inside, the only sound to break the silence was the sonorous breathing of his sleeping companions – fourteen Mutes who lay head to head on two neat rows of mattresses.

The cabin in which Steve was passing the night lay near the post-house at Ari-bani, and he was here as a result of the deal he had struck with the man in black – or someone who sounded very like him. Within four days of leaving the post-house where he had met Clearwater, Steve had acquired the papers and ID plaque of a roadrunner. These were foot-messengers, the first tier in the centrally-controlled postal system which had been set up by the Toh-Yota Shogunate to keep the endless stream of paperwork flowing smoothly round the country.

The job of roadrunner was now the exclusive preserve of Mutes – selected for their ability to run tirelessly mile after mile, hour after hour. It was the best job a Mute journeyman could aspire to, and a much coveted position. Provided you didn't get lost or lose the precious satchel of mail and arrived within the time allowed, you were clothed and fed, and while you were out on the road you tasted the nearest thing in Ne-Issan to the freedom that was the birthright of the Plainfolk. But if you fell sick, or committed some minor infraction, they took away your badge and sent you back down the road to work on the nearest dung-heap.

Since they were government employees, roadrunners were based at the Consul-General's residence – where they were housed in a special compound – and at small depots attached to certain post-houses on the major highways, which acted as distribution points. The post-house had become synonymous with the wayside inn, because the more enterprising owners had set up their establishments next door in the hope of attracting the passing trade. The arrangement proved mutually beneficial and, as a result, post-houses and inns moved progressively closer together. Now, three-quarters of a century later, the majority had ended up sharing the same roof.

Roadrunners acted as two-footed packhorses. They delivered the bulk mail, which was then collected by local residents. Official documents for district functionaries were relayed to the addressee by couriers – a job usually awarded to a 'mainlander' of Korean or Vietnamese descent. Top-level communications were carried by a kind of 'pony express' staffed by samurai. Alongside this, the ruling families in each domain had their own messenger service to ensure that 'sensitive' private communications to relatives and friends did not pass through the hands of government agents.

Taken together, the system comprised a veritable army of mailmen, from the lowly roadrunner to the mounted samurai, and above them flew the courier pigeons bearing cryptically worded ribbons of rice-paper from government spies to the Shogun.

Steve was unaware of this last tier of communication, but the sheer size of the system and the volume of traffic caused him to wonder why they had not opted to go for a hi-tech solution. Iron Master society seemed to be suffering from arrested development. They had raised their craft and mechanical skills to an impressive level but seemed unwilling – or incapable – of making the next leap forward. He was sorely tempted to show them how, but that would only make it harder for the Federation to win the battle for the Blue-Sky World. Better to leave them with their Stone Age way of doing things. And to make sure they stayed there by putting an end to this 'flying-horse' project which – according to the man in black – Cadillac had succeeded in getting off the ground . . .

*

In coming to an arrangement with the cloud warrior, Toshiro Hase-Gawa was acutely aware that (a) he had put his whole future on the line and (b) he had done what he had wrongly accused Lord Yama-Shita of doing – making a deal with the long-dogs. Nevertheless he felt justified in doing so, for the basic charge against Yama-Shita still stood. He and Min-Orota had conspired together to subvert the Shogun's brother-in-law, and Toshiro still hoped that he would soon be able to produce some hard evidence to back up the rumours that Yama-Shita was making preparations to recapture the Dark Light.

In his own mind, Toshiro did not see himself as acting on behalf of the Shogun, and he did not view Brickman as representing the Federation. The deal with the cloud warrior was a private contract between two individuals: a purely tactical manoeuvre to get himself out of an awkward corner. He had let it be understood that if Brickman did all that was asked of him, he and his two

Mute prisoners would be granted safe passage out of the country. Brickman had accepted this with suitable expressions of gratitude, then had the effrontery to demand safe passage for another long-dog!

Once again, Toshiro had swallowed his anger, agreeing without demur. Four, fourteen, forty – the number was academic. Toshiro had not hesitated to kill Noburo and his two red-stripes in order to conceal his previous error of judgement; these three troublesome outlanders would meet the same fate. Once they were disposed of, there would be nothing to weaken his case. The conspirators would be either dead or fatally compromised, his own position in relation to the Shogun would be strengthened and he would be one step nearer to achieving that which he most desired.

From the post-house at Midiri-tana, Toshiro had ridden north through what was left of the night towards Ari-saba, with the cloud warrior slung face-down over the back of his horse like the carcass of a stag brought home by a huntsman. With dawn approaching, the Herald had taken the precaution of blindfolding his prisoner. For his scheme to succeed and to protect his own position, it was vital that Brickman did not discover the identity of his benefactor.

The twelve-mile journey did not take long. Waiting for him on the outskirts of Ari-saba were his own pair of red-stripes – part of the disguise obligingly provided by Ieyasu, the Court Chamberlain, second most powerful man in the Toh-Yota Shogunate. While his men held Steve, Toshiro swapped his black assassin's garb for the travelling costume of a samurai, then remounted and led the two foot-soldiers and their prisoner through the dawn mists to the post-house where he had rented rooms the previous day. They arrived before the first servants had begun to stir, and were able to slip back into their quarters unobserved.

Steve was kept securely bound and blindfolded for most of the following day. He knew from the unintelligible conversations that he was guarded by two

Japs, and he could hear the muffled voices of people in movement outside, but none of it made any sense. The only thing that marked the passage of time for Steve was the arrival of two bowls of rice topped with vegetables. These were delivered several hours apart by his unseen captors, who freed his right hand and guided it to the bowl placed on the floor between his knees.

Toshiro, meanwhile, remained in his own quarters and worked out his next moves. When he was satisfied he had every angle covered and knew what he would say in advance to the cloud warrior, he made his way to the room occupied by the red-stripes and told them to stand guard outside while he interrogated the prisoner.

Before he switched into Basic, the Herald rolled up two small strips of cotton and stuck them inside his cheeks to alter the sound of his voice. Adopting the identity of an unidentified colleague of Noburo and the man in black, Toshiro laid out his plan of action. The blindfolded cloud warrior listened attentively and did not raise a single query or objection. The Herald found this new-found reticence so unsettling he felt obliged to enlarge upon the possible dangers, stressing the points at which he felt extreme caution would be needed. Brickman greeted these strictures in the same offhand manner, dismissing potential problems with the phrase 'Let's cross that bridge when we come to it.'

The young man's assurance was breathtaking. Toshiro realised that he would have to be careful not to be misled by his own innate feelings of superiority into underestimating this ill-mannered individual. Brickman might come from a different world with totally different values, but he was endowed with an intelligence that was every bit as penetrating and devious as his own.

The Herald proceeded to outline his scheme to integrate Steve into the labour system as a roadrunner. As soon as he was registered, arrangements would be made for his immediate transfer to the government's chief postal depot in Lord Min-Orota's domain. This would enable him to move openly and legally across Ne-Issan.

The Heron Pool lay some four hundred miles from their present position. The journey would take several weeks to accomplish for, in his new role, Steve would be required to carry mail along the route that would be mapped out for him. However, upon reaching his destination he would be at the heart of the action, attached to the residence of the Consul-General Nakane Toh-Shiba – towards whose aching arms Clearwater was presently being conveyed. He would also find himself delivering and collecting paperwork from the Heron Pool where his prime target, Cadillac, was busily building a small fleet of flying-horses.

The next meeting, promised Toshiro, would take place in the domain of the Min-Orota, after Steve had joined the postal staff of the Consul-General. When he had had the opportunity to assess the situation on the ground for himself, they would then consider how Steve could shed his grass-monkey disguise, and join the staff of the Heron Pool as a long-dog.

'Supposing I need to get in touch with you before then?'

It was the question Toshiro had been expecting. 'You can't. From here on in, it's a case of "Don't call me, I'll call you".'

'I see . . . I thought we were working together on this.'

'We are, but that's the way it has to be, sport. Don't worry. I'll make sure someone keeps an eye on you.' Toshiro was lying. He could not put the spies and informers who worked for him in Lord Min-Orota's domain on to Brickman's case. It was too risky. But there was no harm in letting the cloud warrior think he would be under surveillance from here on in. It might minimise the chances of him trying to pull a fast one.

'Okay,' said Toshiro. 'That about wraps it up for today. We have to go on to Ari-dina to get you registered as a roadrunner. That's where the Consul-General for this domain is located. After that you're on your own. Provided you watch that lip of yours, there should be no problem.'

'I'll try and remember that. This, uhh . . . place we're going to – is it a long way from here?'

'Fifty miles.' An alarming thought struck Toshiro. 'Can long-dogs run that far? Since you're disguised as a Mute I assumed . . .'

Steve nodded. 'That's why they picked me for this job.'

There was one last piece of business Toshiro had to attend to. 'My colleague who met with you and Samurai-Captain Naka-Jima told me what happened when the Se-Iko hit the *ronin's* base camp. How about telling me your side of the story?'

'Do we have time?'

'Sure. We don't leave here until tomorrow morning.'

Steve began with the surprise appearance of the *ronin* crossing the highway with the Se-Iko in hot pursuit, and fed him everything up to the moment when he had sung for his *sake* in front of Noburo. The one thing he omitted to mention was the fact that he had been held in a cell next to Clearwater for several hours. Since he was not questioned about her, Steve could only presume that his unseen interrogator was unaware that the only thing separating them had been a slatted wooden screen – or did not view it as important.

Toshiro did not know this but, in any case, his interest had waned by the time Steve reached the point where he had handed over his weapons. The Herald had discovered all he needed to know: the location of the *ronin* camp and how it could be entered. These details would be sent in a letter addressed to Hideyoshi Se-Iko, the military commander of the southern district, and signed 'A Well-Wisher'. Since his samurai had failed to catch all the raiders of the road convoy, Hideyoshi could be counted upon to take the appropriate measures.

With the last survivors eliminated, Brickman would be the only person who knew of his mistake over the true identity of the 'love object' and the fake 'cloud warrior'. The secret was safe with him. He was unlikely to reveal details of his mission to anyone else. If it was successful he would vanish; if it was not, he would be dead.

*

The Mute roadrunners attached to the depot at Ari-bani and their transient colleagues were accommodated in a sturdy log cabin in the courtyard behind the post-house. Food, lodgings and laundry services, all paid for by the *bakufu*, were provided by the inn-keeper, who usually kept a Mute family, or a group of Mute women, for this task. The idea of higher social orders cooking for the lowest was out of the question. That was why Clearwater's two housewomen had been taken away to prepare their own food. The reason Steve had been subsequently fed by the *ronin* was that they considered him to be a special case.

Steve was roused at 0500 along with his fourteen overnight companions. Reveille was sounded by one of the cabin staff, a stocky, strong-armed female Mute equipped with a stout pole that came up to her shoulder. The woman walked up and down the length of the hut between the two lines of mattresses, pounding the three-inch-thick pole on the planked floor. Since everyone was required to sleep with their head towards the middle of the room, the shock waves generated by the quivering timbers battered the ear drums and were almost strong enough to shake your teeth loose. To a brain dulled by sleep it also sounded like earth thunder – a noise guaranteed to get a Mute up and running in nought seconds flat.

Steve jumped to his feet and headed across the cobbled yard to the bathing shed set aside for Mutes. This was one of the perks of being a roadrunner: as an employee of the *bakufu*, in daily contact with Iron Masters, you were required to maintain the same standards of cleanliness.

Finishing off with a bracing bucket of cold water emptied over his head by a cheerful boy-child, Steve dried himself vigorously and donned a clean cotton loincloth as the boy refilled his bucket and got ready to douse the next Mute out of the steaming tub.

211

The boy was an 'iron-foot', the term used to describe Mutes born in Ne-Issan. It came from the metal leg-restraints that Mute journeymen and Tracker renegades were often made to wear. Steve – who had not yet had an opportunity to converse at length with any adult 'iron-foot' – wondered if these second- and third-generation journeymen still identified with the Plainfolk. Since becoming a roadrunner he had discovered that, in Ne-Issan, the unbridgable gulf between the various clans had been forcibly broken down. The D'Troit, mortal enemies of the She-Kargo, the San'Paul, San'Louis, C'Natti and M'Waukee had been thrown together without any regard for the enmity they felt towards one another.

In talking with other roadrunners he had met up with en route for Ari-bani, he had learned that the Iron Masters dealt harshly with inter-clan disputes – especially where makeshift weapons were involved. Steve had encountered some latent hostility from D'Troit and M'Waukee roadrunners during his over-night stops, but it was all low-key. There had been none of the provocative posturing and bragging insults that had triggered the outbreaks of violence he had witnessed during the week when the clans had gathered at the trading post.

Mute journeymen still preferred the company of their clan brothers and sisters, but the decades of slavery had weakened the age-old traditions. Living under the heel of the Iron Masters had taught the Plainfolk something they had failed to learn throughout the centuries of fratricidal violence – the positive benefits of peaceful coexistence. It would be ironic, thought Steve, if the sense of nationhood spoken of in the Talisman Prophecy was to be born here, among those to whom Mr Snow had referred as 'The Lost Ones'.

Did one have first to lose freedom in order to gain it? What did the word – which did not appear in the Federation dictionary – *really* mean? Steve knew it had something to do with an absence of control by a central authority – such as the First Family. But it was precisely this lack of control which, according to the Family, had brought the state of anarchic violence and degeneracy that had led to the Holocaust.

Was freedom without a collective sense of purpose forever destined to self-destruct? Did absolute freedom mean that the monolithic tyranny of the Jeffersons was replaced by the equally tyrannical behaviour of individuals, or small groups, each fighting to protect and propagate their own narrow self-interests at the expense of everyone else? Did this kind of freedom lead, in the end, to chaos and a point where the greatest number of disadvantaged people in such a society came to regard any form of protest as anathema, and demand a return to autocratic rule by a central authority?

Perhaps this was the true wisdom of the First Family. In the closed underground world of the Federation, the unquestioning obedience which was demanded, and almost universally accorded, gave everyone a role, a sense of purpose and satisfaction derived from the knowledge that, through planned, collective action, the efforts of each individual brought their society one step nearer to the realisation of the great dream – the return to the Blue-Sky World. An ordered, peaceful world under the continuing stewardship of the Jeffersons, not the factional chaos that had led to the Holocaust. Ordered not through coercion, but because everyone shared the same goals, the same ideals: peaceful because the enemies of mankind (of which Trackers held themselves to be the sole survivors), who had brought the world to the brink of total destruction, had been wiped from the face of the earth.

The Mutes believed the Talisman Prophecy was a forecast of things to come but perhaps, as Steve had first thought, it was an empty pipe-dream; a yearning for a long-lost sense of purpose.

While the Trackers had carved out their subterranean empire, the Plainfolk and the southern Mutes had run free across the overground for close on 1,000 years. They had enjoyed the freedom that the hardier renegades found so seductive – but what had they done with it? Nothing. And yet, and yet . . .

Despite the fact that the Plainfolk had not managed to build anything to compare with the magnificence of the John Wayne Plaza, owned few material possessions, and were still fighting hand to hand with 'sharp iron', they were in tune with the external world and in touch with the primal forces that had led to its creation. They could not write or read, but their eyesight was flawless and their minds were open to visions of other worlds. They made music on primitive wind, string and percussion instruments, and they sang songs which they made up for themselves.

In the Federation, this area of creativity was the exclusive preserve of the First Family – except, of course, for the illegal trade in blackjack. But the Family might even be producing this, controlling the market for its own devious purposes.

In Ne-Issan, they also made music on hand-operated instruments and since electronic communications remained to be discovered, a huge army of scribes penned the data transmitted through the postal system, recorded transactions and chronicled events for posterity. But there was also another class of scribe who freely composed strings of 'ideograms' – the name for the incomprehensible signs used by the Iron Masters to make a permanent record of the spoken word – and, apparently, these people did not record data, they invented it, drawing details from life to create imaginary situations in which imaginary people interacted. They were like recorded dreams, and when they were written down they were called 'poems' and 'stories', and they were given to other people to read.

Steve had seen these various scribes at work, seated in some of the small open-fronted buildings that lined the main streets of the villages and townships he had passed through on his way from Ari-dina to Ari-bana. Other 'shops' had housed a staggering variety of traders and

214

craftspeople: candle-makers and lantern-makers, basket and mat weavers, dyers, carpenters, furniture-makers, saddle-makers, wheelwrights, potters, fine metalworkers, blacksmiths, merchants selling cotton cloth and silk brocades and purveyors of *sake* and all kinds of food. The list was endless.

And he had also glimpsed Iron Masters creating coloured images with brushes on folding screens made of paper and silk, and on wooden panels. The images depicted scenes from the natural world, animals prowling through forest grasses, birds perched in trees, horsemen in pursuit of mountain cats, serene landscapes with waterfalls and views of distant, snow-capped mountains; images filled with life that surpassed anything created by COLUMBUS. And there were others carving strange beasts and squat figures with fierce expressions out of blocks of wood and stone.

Steve could not understand why anyone would choose to produce objects which appeared to serve no useful purpose, but something within him responded to the skill and dedication they brought to their work. The forms they produced were pleasing to the eye, but what impressed him most was the fact that the ruling powers in Ne-Issan allowed their subjects to create words, images and objects and pass them on to others.

In the Federation, such a thing would not be allowed – indeed, it was not possible. Trackers were involved in construction and production processes, but everything was created and designed by the First Family – including life itself.

'Art' and 'literature' were two more word-concepts that could not be found in the Federation dictionary. The only pictures Trackers had to look at were those that could be accessed through the Public Archive Channel – plus the obligatory wall-mounted holograms of the Founding Father and the current President-General. No one played instruments; the music, produced electronically, came through the loudspeakers. Trackers did not 'write', they typed on keyboards. Besides, even if the

215

idea had occurred to them, there was nothing to write *on* – or with. Paper did not exist. The nearest thing to it was the plasfilm used to produce the maps issued to the commanders of wagon-trains.

Apart from the spoken word, the only method of communication was through the network of video screens controlled by COLUMBUS. The Jeffersons did not produce fiction. They only dealt in facts, and every object created by them and produced under their supervision was designed to perform a specific function.

In the past year, Steve's overground experiences had caused him to doubt the truthfulness of much of the information fed to ordinary Trackers by the First Family. But he did not question their right to secrecy. The need to conceal information seemed to be an ingrained part of human nature. His personal crusade to discover the truth was not inspired by a desire to blow the lid off for the good of people in general: he just wanted to be one of the select band of people who knew what was *really* going on.

At least, the darker side of him did. But there was another side of his nature that responded to the overground and filled him with rebellious thoughts. This other Brickman had begun to view the benevolent guiding hand of the First Family as an iron fist clamped around the collective throat of Trackerdom, stifling all independent thoughts and feelings. And it was this half of his psyche that wanted to break their grip, to blow their underground world apart and start all over again from the beginning.

*

Returning to the cabin, Steve folded up the straw mattress and quilt and placed them in a neat pile against the wall. When the other occupants had done the same, four low tables were pulled into the centre of the room, and the cabin staff proceeded to serve breakfast. It was the established custom for the roadrunners to eat all

216

meals wearing only loose cotton vests and their loincloths in order to keep their uniforms as clean as possible. As part of the deal between the innkeeper and the post-master, the Mute cabin staff held a small stock of uniforms as well as providing a laundry service, so that incoming roadrunners could exchange travel-stained garments for clean ones before setting out again. The one thing the runners did not part with was their gorget, a plaque of copper shaped like a fat banana that hung round their neck on a chain. Stamped into the metal were Iron Master word-signs and numbers. This was their ID card, meal-ticket, and passport to the good life – as good, that is, as a Mute could hope for in Ne-Issan.

The roadrunners sat cross-legged, four to a table; Steve shared the table furthest from the door with a brooding member of the San'Louis – friends of the D'Troit – and another She-Kargo Mute, the first he had come across leaving the trading post. Deer-Hunter, from the clan M'Kewan, had been a roadrunner for the last two of his four years as a journeyman. He told Steve he had three more years on the road before his term came to an end.

'What happens after that?' asked Steve.

Deer Hunter frowned. 'Didn't anyone tell you?'

'Nobody told me anything. I just got off the boat.'

Deer-Hunter raised his eyebrows. 'You move fast . . .'

Steve tried to sound modest. 'Just lucky, I guess.'

'Ain't nothin' to do with luck,' grunted the San'Louis. 'The friggin' She-Kargo get the biggest share of the best jobs 'cause they got their noses stuck right up the jappo's ass!'

Steve and Deer-Hunter eyed the Mute but didn't rise to the bait.

'You were saying . . .'

'You get the chop,' said Deer-Hunter.

'You mean you end up back on the chain-gang?'

'No. You end up dead.' The prospect did not seem to spoil Deer-Hunter's appetite.

Steve stared at him. 'Sweet Sky Mother! Why?'

Deer-Hunter shrugged. 'Search me. Maybe it's

because they didn't want too many Plainfolk who know their way around Ne-Issan. A man who keeps his eyes open gets to see a lot of what goes on. These dead-faces are holding down a big piece of turf, but they're awful thin on the ground.'

'Even so, they seem to have things well under control. In fact it's so tight you almost need permission to breathe round here.'

'True, but if things keep going the way they are, pretty soon there are going to be more of us than there are of them.'

'Interesting thought,' said Steve. 'And thanks for putting me straight. If I'd known my neck was on the line I probably wouldn't have taken the job.'

'You'd have been crazy not to. It's the best there is.'

'Yeah, but . . . doesn't it get to you? I mean, knowing you've only got three years left?'

Another shrug. 'Nobody lives for ever.'

'Mo-Town thirsts, Mo-Town drinks . . .'

'Exactly.' Deer-Hunter scooped the last fingerful of rice out of his bowl and licked the rim. 'And in case it still hasn't sunk in, let me spell it out for you, one last time. You don't have to do anything wrong to get into trouble around here. If one of these dead-faces feels like killing you, he doesn't need to ask for permission. He'll just do it. And you look like a prime candidate.'

'Why?'

'The eyes.' Deer-Hunter snapped his fingers at the young iron-foot who had doused Steve in the bathing shed.

The boy hurried over with a bowl of water and held it out obligingly.

'It's the way you look at people.' Deer-Hunter rinsed his hands and mouth, then wiped them dry using the cloth draped over the boy's forearm. 'The dead-faces don't like sassy Mutes.'

'I know.' Steve dipped and dried his hands. 'Several people have already warned me about that.'

The San'Louis Mute, a lumphead called Purple-Rain

from the V'Chenzo clan, took his turn with the bowl, then got to his feet. The boy moved on to the next table.

Deer-Hunter weighed up Purple-Rain as the Mute moved away, then turned his attention back to Steve. 'Maybe you like to live dangerously. If not, do something about it.'

'I will. Thanks.' Steve rose from the table and began putting on his uniform – a loose saffron yellow jacket and trousers, and a matching bandanna which, when folded to the required width, was wrapped round the forehead and knotted at the base of the skull.

Deer-Hunter got dressed alongside him. 'Do the M'Calls have many smoothies like you?'

'A few.' Steve tied the black sash round his waist and pulled on his shoes. They had extra-thick rope soles sewn to heavy-grade cotton uppers, and laces that fastened round the ankle.

'I'm surprised they let someone like you come here. They'd have got a much better deal from the sand-burrowers. If they'd traded you in as a yearling –'

Steve cut him off. 'The M'Calls don't do deals with the sand-burrowers.'

'Maybe it's time they started. Were you in that battle last year? Against the iron-snake?'

'Yes.' Steve picked up the waist-bag containing the precious bundle of pink leaves. 'How come you know about that?'

Deer-Hunter smiled. 'Word travels fast. They say the M'Calls had a Storm-Bringer whose magic cut the snake in half. Many sand-burrowers died, but their beast escaped by breathing white fire. It is also said that Mo-Town drank deep that day.'

Steve nodded. 'We'll do better next time.' He left the cabin and headed across to the post-house. He did not want to get into a rerun of the battle between the clan M'Call and wagon-train known as the 'Lady from Louisiana' – especially when he had been fighting on the other side.

Within a few minutes, Deer-Hunter and the other

roadrunners joined Steve outside the post-house and stood in a respectful line with downcast eyes: displaying what Mr Snow, in his parting lecture, had called 'a little humility'. As a fellow Mute from the blood-line of the She-Kargo, Deer-Hunter had felt obliged to urge Steve to tone down the challenging and often contemptuous way he looked at people. After three years at the Flight Academy, where student wingmen were constantly urged to think of themselves as the brightest and the best, and where Steve was convinced he had been top of the heap, it was not something that came easily.

Responding to a single hammer-stroke on an iron bell, the diminutive Iron Master in charge of the depot and his two principal clerks appeared and went through the usual jut-jawed, mean-eyed routine, swaggering slowly down the line and back up the rear, making sure that everyone was properly and cleanly attired, and comporting themselves with the required degree of deference.

Once the inspection and roll-call was completed, the roadrunners were allowed to sit on a long bench made out of a single sawn log placed on the veranda next to the post-house door. From there, the roadrunners were called in four at a time to receive the sealed black satchels of mail they were to deliver.

Deer-Hunter was in the first quartet. After a short while he emerged carrying the bulging leather bag on his back. He drew the hooks on the shoulder straps together, fastening them across his chest, and walked back to bid farewell to Steve.

'Where are you headed?'

'Uti-ka,' said Deer-Hunter. 'Regular run of mine. Know it like the back of my hand.' They slapped palms, warrior-fashion. 'See you around, blood-brother.'

'Maybe. Mind how you go.'

Deer-Hunter grinned, then vaulted over the rail of the veranda and ran off down the road.

Steve was among the third group to be called inside. Aside from the fact that his job as a roadrunner was bringing him ever closer to the Heron Pool, being part of the postal service gave him access to detailed maps of Ne-Issan. Hanging on an inside wall of every post-house was a large panel bearing a hand-painted map of the territory served by that particular depot. On the facing wall was another equally large map of the Iron Masters' world, showing the domains, the major highways and the network of post-houses. Not only that, the family names of the domain-lords and the names of places, mountain ranges and rivers had been carefully recorded in Japanese *and* Basic.

Since Mutes had no written language, Steve had been obliged, at the start of his journey, to pretend he could not read, allowing himself to be taught how to pronounce and recognise the name of his given destination and any places en route. He had then repeated them for the benefit of the clerk, hesitantly at first, then with increasing confidence until the dink was satisfied and sent him on his way. He had gone through the same routine at each post-house, gradually improving his 'reading skill', but taking care to make a mistake now and then so as not to give the game away.

With the help of his photographic memory, Steve now possessed a clear picture of the country and knew precisely to which part and in which direction he was heading. He had also grasped the relative size and disposition of each domain.

Instead of the arbitrary straight-line divisions between the states of pre-Holocaust America, the domains of the Iron Masters tended to follow the more natural boundary lines of rivers from their source to their confluence with other, larger waterways or to where they met the sea. Yama-Shita's domain was the only one which ran from the Great Lakes in the west to the Eastern Sea at the mouth of the Uda-sona River. It was here that the lands of the Toh-Yota was split in two, and the northern half – a narrow strip which ran up the west bank of the Uda-sona to the Sanoransa River – was sandwiched between the Yama-Shita and the Min-Orota.

The maps gave no hint as to who would back whom if it came to a fire-fight, but from the strategic point of view the Yama-Shita were well placed. They could not be encircled, and the rivers and lakes which formed the greater part of their borders severely limited the number of points where a frontal attack could be launched against them. It was not surprising that the mystery 'colleague' of the man in black had opted for a covert operation which, if it went wrong, could be blamed on renegade Trackers and Mutes.

One of the clerks beckoned Steve over to the district map and pointed to a location west of the Uda-sona. 'Today a-you go this-a place. Sapirina-fida. Unna-stan'?'

Steve bowed. 'Sapirina-fida.'

The clerk then pointed to a third map showing the street layout of Ari-bani. 'Go a-river this a-way. Take ferry to uh-thah side. We give a-you spe-shawl pa-pah to make car-rossinah. Now a-you show me way a-you mus' goh.'

After pretending to think hard, Steve swiftly traced the route from the post-house to the ferry, then switched to the larger map and ran his finger over the road from Albany to the pre-Holocaust urban centre of Springfield, Massachusetts.

With a grunt of satisfaction the clerk went back behind the counter and wrote the word-signs stamped on Steve's gorget on to a ferry pass which he handed over with the satchel of mail.

Steve accepted both with a grateful bow and, keeping his eyes on the floor, took five backwards steps towards the door, bowed again, turned left and made his exit.

Slimy little worms . . .

Steve adjusted the sit of the mailbag so that it lay snugly across his shoulder-blades, giving the remaining roadrunners a farewell wave and set off towards the ferry.

Although traditionally regarded as the lowest form of life, Mutes serving as roadrunners were, nevertheless, servants of the Shogunate. Acting on the dictum 'the

222

mails must go through', the *bakufu* had decreed that roadrunners were not required to kowtow to anyone en route except mounted samurai and palanquins carrying nobles or high court officials. Since these were always escorted by samurai they were easy to spot. It was a sensible arrangement: if roadrunners had been obliged to prostrate themselves every time they encountered a social superior, the whole postal system would have ground to a halt.

As it reached the river, the road came out on to a long wooden wharf. Several vessels of varying shapes and sizes were moored alongside. Upstream to his left was a two-funnelled wheelboat. Steve glanced at it casually as he turned towards the boarding point for the ferry which lay at the far right-hand end.

After he had gone a few yards it suddenly dawned on him that the wheelboat was decorated in the same colour scheme as the one which had carried him to Ne-Issan. He turned back and ran towards it. It *was* the same one! The same pennants and banners fluttered from the masts and gallery posts. Side-Winder had said, in parting, that the boats went to all parts of Ne-Issan. And here it was! It was an incredible stroke of luck. All he needed now was to find Side-Winder and his day would be made.

And lo and behold, there he was – standing with his back to Steve, talking to a group of Mute stevedores, his red bandanna knotted round his shaven head. Approaching to within a few yards of the group, Steve turned his attention to the wheelboat. As he ran his eyes along its bulk from stem to stern he slid his left forefinger up behind his left ear, located the tiny dime-sized transceiver that had been implanted under the skin just below the line of his skull, and pressed down on it, activating the transmitter. The second touch switched it off. He pressed it on and off again, sending his call-sign in Morse code: H–G–F–R. Hang-Fire . . .

To anyone watching, Steve appeared to be scratching his neck. Side-Winder glanced casually over his shoulder as he heard the faint but unmistakable mosquito-like hum in his ear, and caught sight of Steve. He rubbed his neck, sending out the letters M–X to acknowledge the message had been received and understood.

Steve sauntered slowly back down the wharf. Now that he was 'legal' he was in no danger of falling foul of the authorities, but he couldn't afford to hang around for ever. He felt a tap on the shoulder as Side-Winder caught up with him.

'You're the last person I expected to run into.'

'Same here,' said Steve. They slapped palms.

Side-Winder looked him over. 'You wanna know something? When you left the boat at Pi-saba, I wouldn't have given a rat's ass for your chances. In fact, I told Mother I figured you'd last a week at the most. But I gotta hand it to you, amigo. For a guy who came on like he didn't know from shit you've wired yourself in real good.'

'Just happened to be in the right place at the right time . . .'

'Maybe.' Side-Winder gave him a shrewd glance. 'I have a feeling there's more to you than meets the eye.'

'Listen,' said Steve. 'I don't have time to tell you how and why but I lost my radio-knife. You still in touch with Mike-X-Ray One?'

MX-1 was the code-name for Commander Karlstrom, Operational Director of AMEXICO. 'Mother' was a sobriquet used by mexicans.

'Yeah, what d'you want me to tell him?'

'Tell him I'm still on the case. I've located my targets near Bosona and I'm on my way there now.'

'To the Heron Pool?'

'That's right. You did me a big favour by picking up on that.'

'All part of the service. Need any help now?'

Steve grimaced. 'I might, but – the trouble is, I won't know until I get there.'

'Yeah.' Side-Winder sucked on his teeth. 'It's a tough one.'

'There is one problem you can help me with.'

'Okay, let's hear it.'

Steve wondered how much he could tell the mexican without compromising himself. He decided he had to take a chance. 'Here's how it plays. I've got to pull two people out of here. The Heron Pool is at a place called Mara-bara – west of Ba-satana. Without going into details, I think I can handle that end of it. The problem is how to get out of this place. I've been taking a long hard look at the post-house maps and the distances are gi-normous!' He threw up his hands. 'I just don't know how I'm gonna do it!'

'Where d'you wanna get to?'

'Back to the Federation but – here's the killer – I have to go via Wyoming.'

Side-Winder responded with a low whistle.

'Wyoming . . .?'

'I have no choice. That's where my third target is.'

'You're right, you *do* have a problem. They sure gave you one hell of an assignment for your first time out.'

Steve let it pass. 'By my reckoning it must be what – about five hundred miles from Ba-satana to the shores of Lake Iri?'

'Something like that. And from there, you got another fifteen hundred miles to Wyoming. At least.'

'I figured twelve hundred but – what the heck . . . another three hundred more or less . . . ' Steve raised his eyes skywards. After a moment's silence he eyed the boat and turned back to Side-Winder. 'How did this thing get here?'

'Through the canal.'

'The same one that took us to Pi-saba?'

'No. This one runs across Yama-Shita's domain. Used to be the border between the Yama-Ha and the Matsu-Shita before the families linked up. It starts at Bu-faro on Lake Iri runs through Uti-ka and comes out at Taro-ya a few miles upriver from here.'

Steve's eyes followed his pointing arm, then swung back on to Side-Winder. 'Supposing I managed to get my two targets from the Heron Pool to here, what are the chances of getting a boat ride?'

'To Lake Iri?' The mexican pursed his lips. 'Are these guys going to be kicking and screaming?'

'No. If everything goes as planned, they're going to be in a hurry to leave. That goes for me too. Is it possible?'

'In theory, yes, but – I may not be here. But even if I was, I couldn't handle *three* stowaways. I was able to help you get a free ride, but you'd already managed to get on board by yourself.'

'I realise that. The thing is, there might be four of us. Do the Iron Masters ship Mutes and Trackers along that waterway?'

'Yes, now and then. But you'd need papers. A travel pass and a document certifying you've been purchased by someone in Bu-faro. A slave-dealer would be best.'

'*Shee-iit*. This is more complicated than I thought.'

'It always is.'

Steve chewed it over and had the germ of an idea. 'Okay, let's assume I can get the papers we need. What do they have to say?'

Side-Winder gave him the standard wording and the name of a slave-dealer in Bu-faro. 'I don't see what use this is. You can't even speak Japanese, let alone write it.'

'Let me worry about that.'

'Okay, suppose you *do* get to Bu-faro. What are you gonna do then?'

Steve grinned. 'Ahh, that's where you come in. I'm hoping you're going to be able to set up a skyhook.'

'Jack me! You don't stop, do you?'

'I know it's asking a lot but – you're my only contact with the Federation.'

'Yeah, okay . . . when's this likely to be?'

Steve threw up his hands again. 'Can't say. How long are you going to be working this route?'

'Barring earthquake, flood, shipwreck, acts of war and civil disorder, we should be on this run for the next four months. The turnround point is 150 miles south of here. A place called Nyo-yoko. That's where this river meets the Eastern Sea.'

'Yeah, I saw it on the map. There's a bunch of islands

down there.'

Side-Winder nodded. 'The Shogun has a palace on one of them. Did you know that, before the Holocaust, over twenty-five *million* people lived there? Twenty-five million jammed into a few square miles. Can you imagine that?'

Steve shook his head. 'That's probably why they ended up killing each other.'

'Maybe . . . Anyway, for what it's worth, we sail at midday for Nyo-yoko, two days later we call back here, then go all the way to Bu-faro. There and back takes about three weeks. Bear that in mind. If you can time it right, you can hitch a ride with us and I'll do whatever I can to help. These dinks can be unpredictable. The trip might be easier if you have a friend on board.'

'You're right.' Steve fisted Side-Winder's shoulder. 'Gotta go, but – I really appreciate this. If it hadn't been for your help on the way in –'

Side-Winder waved away his thanks. 'If we ever meet up back home when I've got these lumps out of my face we'll split a Korn-Gold and swap case notes. Buena suerte!'

'You too, amigo. Hasta la vista!' Steve set off towards the ferry.

'Hey! I forgot something!'

Steve halted as Side-Winder ran to catch up with him.

'You'll have to pay for the boat ride.'

'What with?'

'Money. Didn't anyone tell you about that?'

Steve stared at him, uncomprehending.

Side-Winder grinned. 'Obviously not. It's like the credit ratings on our ID cards, only different. Never mind. Looks like you got a steep learning curve ahead of you. Find out about all that and get your hands on some. The trip'll cost you five dollars a head.' He began to back away. 'Plus the extras! Bring another twenty dollars, just to be on the safe side!'

'Sure! No sweat!' Steve signed off with a confident wave and ran down the wharf past the line of moored boats. Money . . . dollars . . . Columbus! As if he didn't have enough to worry about!

Side-Winder stood watching until Steve reached the ramp that led down to the ferry. The small twin-paddleboat had just left the far side of the river and was chugging its way back to the west bank. In a few minutes Brickman would begin the next stage in his journey – though in view of the distances involved, 'odyssey' might be a better word. Meeting him had been a lucky break, but it was not entirely unexpected. AMEXICO had alerted him to the fact that Steve had secured a job as a roadrunner and might be heading in his direction.

How Mother had managed to figure that out remained a mystery, and how Brickman had managed to get on board the system so fast was an even bigger one. Side-Winder had been forced to endure two years of hard labour and brutal treatment, before being selected to work on the wheelboats, and it had taken him a further twelve months to claw his way up to head overseer. And he had only achieved that distinction by being the meanest mother on board. No . . . Brickman's rapid advancement had to be an inside job. Clearly a man to watch.

As he walked back towards the stevedores, Side-Winder realised he had forgotten to tell Brickman that Mutes and Trackers were not allowed to possess money. Slaves didn't own anything and couldn't earn anything: food, clothing and housing came with the job but the rice in your belly, the shirt on your back and the roof over your head belonged to your master – and so did you.

Whilst it was less serious than carrying a weapon, to possess money was still a punishable offence – as Brickman would soon discover if he did his homework. The boat tickets would have to be paid for, but they could only be purchased by an Iron Master.

Side-Winder was not unduly worried. Anyone smart enough to get himself promoted from illegal immigrant to roadrunner in less than six weeks should be able to figure his way round a little problem like that.

CHAPTER TEN

While Steve was heading north for his unexpected meeting with Side-Winder, the much-delayed road convoy to which Jodi Kazan and Dave Kelso had been assigned finally reached Firi on the banks of the Delaware. The bricks used to build Firi came from the ashes of Philadelphia, city of brotherly love, incinerated in AD 2015 – the year that marked the end of what the Mutes called The Old Time.

For many of the travellers who had joined the convoy in the latter stages of its journey this little riverside town – now awash with merchants and traders drawn in by the forthcoming slave-market – was the end of the line, and as soon as their presence had been registered by the officials at the western toll-gate, they hurried away in search of lodgings in one of the already overcrowded inns.

For Jodi and Kelso the long march, which had begun with their capture by the M'Calls in Western Nebraska, was not yet over. The two Tracker renegades were collected from the toll-gate by a pair of sturdy Korean clerks working for a shipping agent who enjoyed the trust and commercial patronage of the Min-Orota family. The clerks, their eyes compressed into slits by prominent slanting cheekbones, conducted them through the crowded streets to the agent's office for yet another round of paperwork.

Through an opened screen which served as a door and window, Jodi could see a bustling food market crowded with buyers and vendors. The stalls had a staggering variety of food stacked on counters and hanging from their roof frames. Some were selling raw items, others were cooking portions to be consumed on the spot. A delicious stew of odours drifting on the summer breeze reached Jodi's nostrils and made her feel faint with hunger.

A glance at Kelso showed he was similarly affected. They had been adequately fed en route, but they had covered more than 300 miles since leaving Pi-saba – all of it on foot. The trek had left them leaner and tougher than before – and permanently hungry. They were destined to remain so for some time. The agent fed his family and staff and wined and dined his clients, but he was not in the catering business. As far as he was concerned the two long-dogs were just another consignment to be forwarded.

Armed with the necessary passes for themselves and their charges, and a monosyllabic command of Basic, the two clerks herded Jodi and Kelso back out on to the streets and down to a ferry plying back and forth across the broad stretch of river which snaked past the eastern edge of town on its southward journey towards the open sea.

As they waited on the jetty for the ferry to complete its return journey the two Trackers witnessed the arrival of a now-familiar sight; the sealed carriage-box with its mysterious white-masked occupant and her two diminutive female attendants, who, like them, had joined the convoy on its formation at Pi-saba. Halfway through the journey, a strong force of mounted bandits had staged a dawn raid on the convoy, carrying off the White Lady and her two women as part of their plunder. Their kidnappers had evidently had a rapid change of heart, because all three had been put back into circulation and had caught up with the convoy at Midiri-tana towards the end of the following day.

With no understanding of the Iron Masters' language, Jodi and Kelso could not make head nor tail of what had taken place, beyond what they had seen with their own eyes. And since no one had seen fit to offer an explanation in Basic they had been left guessing as to what it all meant – and whether it had any connection with what had followed. For the violent assault by close on a hundred *ronin* in which a handful of drivers and travellers had been killed had not been the end of the alarms and excursions. The morning after the kidnapped trio had rejoined the convoy, its progress had been further delayed by the discovery of three dead bodies – one of them a samurai – in the grounds of the post-house where the drivers of the plundered goods-wagons and the shaken travellers had paused to take stock and regroup.

For the Iron Masters, the unlawful killing of a samurai was a serious matter. Within minutes of the alarm being raised, a mini-hierarchy of officials descended on the post-house and unleashed a frenzied investigation, haranguing each other and everyone in sight with a stream of gobbledegook. To the untrained ear, it sounded like the shrill clamour raised by a flock of nesting crows alarmed by a marauding buzzard.

Staff and overnight guests were rounded up, questions were asked and statements taken; rooms and baggage were searched; the murder site was combed for clues. Jodi and Kelso caught a brief glimpse of the corpses as they were removed from a garden pavilion and carried back to the main building, but were not called upon to give an account of themselves. Since they had each spent the night in the customary fashion, bedded down under a wagon with their feet shackled to one of the wheels, they were not regarded as potential suspects. Eventually, after everyone's papers had been scrutinised for the umpteenth time, the road convoy was allowed to proceed.

Whips and prods were applied to the oxen drawing the wagons in an effort to get back on schedule, but the efforts of the perspiring drivers came to naught. Bellowing under the rain of blows, the big-boned beasts reluctantly changed up from a leisurely plod to a lumbering trot, but proved unable to cover more than fifty yards before dropping back down through the gears. At which point, the process began all over again.

After several punishing miles which found the animals

in better shape than their masters, it became clear to Jodi – to whom all this was a new experience – that the oxen had already made a major concession in allowing themselves to be put into harness and were temperamentally opposed to being run off their feet. The convoy-master evidently reached the same conclusion and, after a brief confab with the despairing drivers, they permitted the yoked pairs to proceed at their own measured pace without further molestation.

Looking back towards the town and the land beyond it that stretched away westwards to the horizon, and to an infinity of horizons beyond that, Jodi wondered what fate had befallen the other captured renegades from Malone's group. In particular, she wondered about Medicine-Hat, who had nursed her broken body back to health after three breakers from Malone's group had found her half buried in mud deposited by the flash-flood in the Now and Then River.

Kelso had been one of the guys who had helped to dig her out. A lot had happened since then. She had become a renegade through circumstance, not choice, but her experience of overground life had awakened new feelings which had left her troubled and confused. Meeting up with Steve Brickman again hadn't helped. She had done everything she could to save her former crew-mate's life and then – jack me – he had painted his body, plaited his hair and decked himself out in a Mute pebble-suit! The argument they'd had over that, and over some of the things she had learned about how the First Family kept control over the Amtrak Federation, still bothered her.

Jodi had heard a lot that seemed to make sense – but how much of it was true? Brickman had dismissed her accusations and had pleaded with her to trust him. But how could you trust a Tracker who chose to bed down with the enemy rather than stick with his own kind?

But then – who *could* you trust?

According to the First Family, it was the Mutes who were poisoning the air with their presence. That was why they all had to be killed – to make the air safe to breathe again. But what about the Iron Masters? Theirs might not be a hi-tech world, but they were a highly organised, industrious and inventive bunch and quite clearly in a different league from the Mutes. And a lot more dangerous. Where had they come from? Did the fact that they were surface-dwellers mean they were poisoning the atmosphere with their presence too? If they were, it meant they were next in line for extermination in the battle for the Blue-Sky World. So how come there was no mention of them in the public archives? The First Family must know about them. The Family knew all there was to know about everything.

Before being swept overboard from the Lady in a ball of flame and then half drowned in the flash-flood, everything had been so simple. The world had been neatly divided into us and them; Tracker and Mute. A guy knew who the enemy was, and why he had to do what the Family asked of him. But the presence of the Iron Masters confused the issue; spoiled the brutal symmetry. Okay, they might be flat-faced, squatty-assed runts but they could hardly be categorised as sub-human. They were kind of halfway-in-between. And that made it a whole new ball game. Because if there was a third race, then there could be a fourth and a fifth out there somewhere who had staked a claim to a piece of the overground.

How would the Federation react if some of these other human-type beings turned out to be even further up the evolutionary and technological tree than the Iron Masters? The Mutes were easy to classify – they were made-to-measure fall-guys – but what did the word 'sub-human' really mean? Who laid down the criteria – and how did they know where to draw the line?

Once you began picking away at it, the whole concept started to look distinctly flaky. And that was dangerous, because it called into question the historical basis for the First Family's claim that Trackers were destined to inherit the earth and be the sole masters of all therein.

Yeah . . . somebody, somewhere, had a lot of explaining to do.

*

The Delaware marked the eastern boundary of the Mitsu-Bishi domain. Once across the river you were in Nyo-jasei. The territory, together with Aron-giren, had once belonged to the Da-Tsuni, but following their defeat at the hands of the Toh-Yota they had been dispossessed. As a result of that victory, the Shogun's family now held a slice of land stretching from the St Lawrence at Quebec to Cape Charles at the mouth of Chesapeake Bay. The remnants of the Da-Tsuni, their desire for revenge neutered by marriage ties with the new ruling family, now occupied a domain carved out of the virgin hill forests on the south-west frontier.

When the ferry docked on the far shore, the sealed carriage-box was loaded on to a two-wheeled chassis which could be hired for that purpose, along with a pair of porters to man the poles front and back. The serving-women and the two Korean clerks rode in open hand-carts – a downmarket version of the *jinrikisha*, lacking weather cover, padded seats and the luxury of sprung axles. Jodi and Kelso, as usual, were obliged to hoof it.

They found themselves at the western end of a fifty-four-mile stretch of highway that ran in an almost straight line through forests of sweet-smelling pine and white cedar and across marshlands carpeted with cranberries. The small party rested at a post-house some thirty miles along the road at which the two breakers got their first meal of the day. It came courtesy of the White Lady, whose carriage box was lifted off its wheels and carried inside her room so that she could alight safe from prying eyes.

At the other end of the road, which they reached in the late afternoon of the following day, lay a bare sandy coastal plain. The wide beaches running away to the north and south were sheltered from the breaking waves by a chain of narrow sandbars and scattered islets. The few trees that had managed to get a foothold were not so lucky. Their twisted trunks and stunted branches had a bent and beaten look which bore witness to the brutal force of the winter gales that swept in from the Eastern Sea.

A wooden bridge, with a split middle section that was cranked up by capstans and plaited ropes as thick as a man's arms, spanned a narrow waterway between the mainland and a large island, called Atiran-tikkasita. A fishing village with a sheltered harbour had been built amongst the ruins of pre-Holocaust buildings whose shrouded sand-filled shapes gave no clue to their former function. Succeeding generations of scavengers, whose occupation of the island pre-dated the arrival of the Iron Masters, had long since pillaged the collapsed structures of any useful items.

Beyond the village, the fossilised stumps of squared timbers stuck out of the sand in rows like the broken ribs of half-buried dinosaurs. The weathered boardwalks they had once supported had also vanished long ago – torn up to fuel cooking fires and warm the freezing limbs of the few grey phantoms who had found the mental and physical strength to survive the un-numbered years known to the Mutes as the Great Ice Dark.

The harbour was home to a motley fleet of small fishing boats and a port of call for several slab-sided ocean-going junks. It was towards one of these that the Korean shipping clerks directed their human cargo. The jetty was lined with wooden shacks that came in a variety of shapes and sizes. As they drew level with the moored vessel, the local leg-man for the agent in Firi emerged from his shoebox of an office to help speed the paperwork through the various layers of officialdom. Identity documents and travel passes were checked and stamped, names were taken, details noted. And since they were travelling to another domain, their modest baggage was searched for any undeclared items on which an export tax might be levied.

Trade and tariffs were the twin preoccupations of the Iron Masters in time of peace. The Toh-Yota family was now immensely rich, but it hadn't always been that way. As supreme rulers of Ne-Issan, they were merely profiting from a time-honoured tradition that had enriched their predecessors, the Da-Tsuni – whose liquid assets had been expropriated along with their domains. 'To the victor the spoils' was a maxim that still held good.

Government was an expensive business, and any opportunity to raise additional revenue was eagerly seized on – no matter how piffling the sum. When you took into account the number of transactions, it all added up, thereby justifying the existence of the huge army of tax-gatherers and customs men – and also providing the means to pay their wages.

The documents of 'Yoko Mi-Shima' were presented by Su-Shan. After he had knocked respectfully, the door of the carriage-box was opened far enough to enable the harbour-master to satisfy himself that its sole occupant appeared to be a courtesan dressed in the traditional manner. After bowing politely, he signalled the door to be closed. No attempt was made to search the carriage-box or come face to face with the person behind the mask. As long as the papers were in order, such people were always passed through on the nod.

And with good reason. The masking of courtesans who had won the favour of domain-lords and the Shogun dated back two centuries and was a status-symbol granted by their noble masters, along with certain other privileges – such as being able to travel incognito. As a result of the discretion they were accorded it had become the custom among high-born ladies to adopt the same protective colouring when indulging in illicit liaisons. It must also be said that, on occasions, the white mask and heavy silk kimono had concealed high-born gentlemen. In order to avoid embarrassing discoveries, it was now standard practice to treat such travellers with the utmost circumspection. All professions have their cautionary tales, and it was common knowledge that, in the past, a number of over-zealous customs officials and toll-gate keepers had ended up knowing far too much for their own good.

Jodi and Kelso, who possessed nothing beyond what they stood up in, had been provided with small flapped document-cases made of woven straw that hung around their necks, where they could be read at a glance. Together with their numbered armlets, it provided all the relevant details: departure point and issuing authority to travel, route to be followed, final destination and name of their new owner. Any Tracker or Mute found wandering about the countryside without a 'yellow card' faced arrest and speedy execution as a runaway. They had already been stamped with indelible ink on entering Atiran-tikkasita and, now they were about to exit, the harbour-master's cachet was added to the growing collection on the inside of their forearms.

After the customary round of haggling between the junk-captain and the local leg-man, an all-in package price for the trip to Porofi-danisa was agreed upon and sealed with cups of *sake* and smiles all round. The Korean clerks coughed up the cash, the leg-man took his cut – which included a rake-off for the harbour-master and his opposite number in the customs house – and, when all the niceties had been observed, the travellers were invited to mount the gangplank.

Su-Shan and Nan-Khe preceded the porters bearing the sealed carriage-box on its carrying poles; Jodi and Kelso, as befitted their station, brought up the rear. The box was set down opposite the door leading to the stern deck cabins – one of which had been reserved for the White Lady. The two house-women stood either side of the doorway to mask Clearwater's exit, then followed her below. Jodi and Kelso – who had been booked on board as deck cargo – were allotted the fresh-air suite between the raised bow-section and the forward hold.

The next two days on the water were spent wearing leg-irons, but they drew some comfort from the fact that the sea was relatively calm, and they were able to keep warm at night by burrowing in between the bales of cotton stacked on the foredeck. The spartan diet of boiled rice and chopped vegetables was also easy to digest, and this time, in contrast to their trip across the Great Lakes, they managed to keep most of it down.

The junk-captain made a brief stop at a small harbour further up the coast, then headed out to sea on a curving course that kept them well to the south of Aron-giren, before swinging northwards past Baro-kiren into what was once known as Rhode Island Sound.

Block Island – to use its old name – was the eastern limit of the protective zone set up around Aron-giren when the Shogun was in residence. Swinging wide around it meant they would not be intercepted by the inquisitive crews of the Shogun's patrol vessels. On this occasion, the junk-captain had nothing to hide, but he and his crew had been born and raised in their home port of Ba-satana, which meant their primary allegiance was to the Min-Orota family. They therefore regarded it as a matter of honour to keep the Toh-Yota's lackeys off the decks of their vessel whenever possible – a sentiment shared by all seafarers from Ro-diren and Masa-chusa.

It was at Providence that Jodi and Kelso parted company with the White Lady. Taking advantage of a moment when everyone on board seemed to have forgotten about them, they leaned on the deck rail and watched as an Iron Master, whose imperious gestures and style of dress suggested he was a man of some substance, took charge of the sealed carriage-box and had it carted away by a quartet of energetic porters. Jodi never ceased to be amazed at the staggering size of the loads some of them carried, the weight borne partly on their backs and partly by a cloth band looped round their forehead. It was not surprising they were all bandy-legged.

The man was, in fact, the same dried-fish merchant who had arranged for Clearwater to be convoyed to Kari-faran; his task now was to ensure her discreet return to the Consul-General's island love-nest.

Three white-stripes armed with whipping canes collected the two Trackers from the junk and marched them out of the harbour and northwards through the town on to the open road beyond. Jodi and Kelso, now without leg restraints but bound loosely together by a rope around their necks, marched side by side. One dink led the way, the other two followed on behind, gingering their charges with a stinging stroke of the cane whenever they broke step or started to flag, and sometimes – to judge from the guffaws of laughter – just for the hell of it.

The two Trackers bore it stoically. *Just wait fellas*. One of these days . . .

After a brisk thirty-five-mile hike, Jodi and Kelso reached their appointed destination: the Heron Pool, situated close to the small farming community of Mara-bara. Had they had access to a post-house map, they would have discovered that they were about twenty-five miles west of Boston on what had once been Highway 20. The area was dotted with ponds and reservoirs. The largest, which lay just to the south and contained two islands, formed part of the estate of Nakane Toh-Shiba, Consul-General for Ro-diren and Masa-chusa. And it was to his back door, by a devious, roundabout route, that Clearwater was now being delivered.

As they covered the last mile down the dusty road, under the curious gaze of people working in the nearby fields, Jodi Kazan and Dave Kelso were totally unaware of the deal between Mr Snow and Yama-Shita over the delivery of a flying-horse, and the plots and counter-plots which were now afoot. And apart from the realisation that they had been singled out from the other breakers because they knew how to fly, no one had told them where they were going, or why.

It was only when they both looked up almost simultaneously and caught sight of a glider whose shape was clearly inspired by the Federation Skyhawk that they got the first glimmering of what they were getting into. The glider, covered in white silk tinted rose-pink by the rays of the setting sun and bearing a solid red disc under each wing, circled almost directly overhead, then dropped its right wing, making a deep, sideways descent before straightening out to land beyond the cluster of buildings that were now in sight to the left of the road.

Kelso looked across at Jodi with raised eyebrows. 'Are you thinking what I'm thinking?'

'I doubt it – but they sure as heck didn't bring us all this way just to sweep the yard.'

'Right. All that thing needs is an engine and you and I could be on our way out of here.'

Jodi smiled. 'Don't get too excited, Dave. If they're aiming to let us near those things then you can bet your sweet ass they've already got that angle covered. These guys aren't idiots, y'know.'

'Neither are we,' said Kelso. 'Neither are we . . .'

By one of those coincidences with which both life and fiction abound, Steve had also been watching the glider's descent. Approaching from the west with a sack of mail on his back, he had picked up the old Highway 20 at Awo-seisa and was, at that very moment, about three-quarters of a mile behind Jodi and Kelso. Steve's heart quickened as he saw the swept-wing craft drift lazily across the cloudless sky, then dip towards the ground. This was it. The Heron Pool. He was within reach of his first objective.

Steve saw a small party ahead of him on the road. By the time he passed the compound, the marchers had turned in through the open gates. Shortening his stride to a slow jog, he took a look at the courtyard beyond. There were a number of buildings, some people moving round, but nothing of any interest and no clue, apart from the fact that the glider had landed close by, to indicate what was going on there. *Never mind, he'd be back . . .*

In the meantime, he had mail to deliver to Consul-General Nakane Toh-Shiba, whose official residence lay a few miles down the road. This was to be his new base until the Man in Black came out from behind the woodwork and fixed him up with the promised job at the Heron Pool. At that point he would cease to be a roadrunner. With the aid of the precious bundle of pink leaves he would lose his stripes and become the newest recruit to the small team of Tracker renegades led by Cadillac.

And then things would start to happen . . .

Passing beneath a tile-roofed timber lintel that kept the rain off the ten-foot-high gates, Jodi and Kelso found themselves in a walled compound containing two brand-spanking-new single-storey accommodation units. Like most Iron Master dwellings, they were built clear of the ground and used a modular system of rectangular frames, lattice screens and paper panels. The roof was made of overlapping wooden shingles, suggesting that they might not be intended as permanent structures. There were also the usual support facilities they'd observed at the various post-house inns along the way: bathhouse, cookhouse, laundry, et cetera, plus several older structures.

The two new arrivals were relieved of their 'yellow cards' and booked in with the usual flurry of paperwork. The ink and paper had a pleasing odour, and from the wide-eyed way the dinks went to work it was clear they got a big buzz out of handling the material. Once they were officially 'on strength', the armlets which the Trackers had been fitted with at the trading post were prised loose and replaced by a metal identity disc, fastened round their neck with a loop of thin wire. The pint-sized chief clerk, faced with the choice of looking up their noses or remaining on his perch behind the high desk, stayed put and wagged a warning finger. 'You wear a-disc all-uh time. Remove this an' we-uh remove head. Hoh-kay?'

Jodi and Kelso swallowed hard and hung their heads meekly.

A female Mute was summoned to take them to the bathhouse, where the sight of hot water triggered a yell of delight. Casting aside the straw cape, bedding roll

241

and bag of eating utensils issued to them at Pi-saba, they peeled off the threadbare remnants of their Tracker uniforms and leaped into the steaming tub. After the cold water sluices they had had to make do with since Columbus knew when, it was an undreamt-of luxury.

Wallowing up to their ears, they ducked each other playfully, then got down to the serious business of scrubbing the accumulated grime off their bodies and off each other's backs. The sand-glass which measured the time they were allowed emptied all too quickly. Just as well: had they been left to soak much longer, the all-embracing warmth would have lulled them off to sleep. To make sure they stayed alert, the Mute – who remained silent and detached throughout – gave them the standard cold-water treatment, then handed over big, sweet-smelling towels. Oh, boy! The pain and discomfort they had suffered during the past weeks was temporarily obliterated by the sheer joy of being squeaky clean again.

At the adjacent clothing store – also staffed by female Mutes – they were issued with two sets of clean clothes of the type worn by the lower orders: draw-string bikini-type briefs, loose V-neck work shirt and baggy trousers, a padded jacket fastened with toggles and loops, and rope-soled canvas sandals to cover their bare feet.

The sandals were dark brown, everything else was a smoky blue. An eight-petalled flower symbol enclosed in a circle was printed in the same dark brown on the back of the padded jacket and the shirt. The white-stripes who had collected them from the boat had carried the same design on their headbands, likewise the brush-boys in the admin block. Jodi guessed it was the equivalent of a divisional sign, and she was not far wrong. The brown flower was the emblem of the Min-Orota family, their new masters.

The next stop was the bedding store. Armed with a mattress and a new padded quilt, Jodi and Kelso followed their guide across the compound and into one of the accommodation units, where she gestured towards a couple of empty places to the right of the entrance.

'Thanks,' said Jodi. 'What happens next?'

The Mute eyed her with a mixture of resentment and resignation and left without saying a word.

Jodi and Kelso exchanged a raised-eyebrow look, then folded and positioned their mattress and quilt to match the others ranged at regular intervals down the length of the room, and placed the spare set of clothes and their eating utensils on the shelves above their bed space.

In essence, it was the same procedure they had followed during their years of training in the Federation. No matter how tired you were you didn't just breeze into a new base, toss your gear in a corner, then take it easy on the mess desk until the guy in charge of your section came and winkled you out. If he wasn't on your back already, you stowed everything shipshape and went looking for *him*.

A Tracker wearing the same blue work clothes appeared in the doorway. He had a lean, haggard look and the eyes of a man who had seen hard times. 'Hi. Are you all there is?'

'As far as we know,' said Jodi.

The Tracker stretched out a hand. 'Welcome to the Heron Pool. I'm Ray Simons. Reagan/Lubbock.'

'Jodi Kazan. Nixon/Fort Worth. This here is Dave Kelso.'

'Houston/G.C.' The two men shook hands. 'You the honcho?'

Simons gave a dry laugh. 'Some chance. One of the hired hands. You just get off the boat?'

'Yeah, how about you?'

Simons grimaced. 'Into my third year.'

'At this place?'

The Tracker responded with a bitter laugh. 'No . . . I was drafted here in March. Before that it was the Pits.'

'Pits?' queried Jodi.

'The Fire-Pits of Beth-Lem.' Simons shook his head. 'Acre upon acre of brick blast furnaces. It's where they

243

melt down ore to make iron and steel. For the first year I was a stoker, then they put me in charge of a gang of Mutes tapping the molten metal. We'd run it out into shallow ditches cut in beds of wet sand – arranged like a tree with a thin trunk and short fat branches.

'When it solidifies you have to cut off the branches – which are still red hot – and tong 'em over to the rolling mill. Making sure you don't bump into the guys doing the same thing on each side of you – and for as far as you can see. Twenty-four hours a day, three hundred and sixty-five days a year.

'The heat blisters your skin and the smoke rips out the inside of your lungs. Run the melt out too fast and she'll jump the mould and torch your feet off. Dump her in sand that's too wet and the steam'll blow half of it up in the air like golden rain. Looks real pretty but it can burn a hole right through you –'

Kelso cut across the well-rehearsed tale. 'No shit. You must tell us about it sometime.'

'Is that where most breakers end up?' asked Jodi, trying to compensate for her companion's withering disinterest.

'Either there or in the mines.'

'Sounds like you were lucky to get here,' said Kelso.

'Not as lucky as you.' Simons sounded a mite aggrieved.

Jodi let it pass. 'So what's going on, Ray?'

'We're building airplanes. Well – just starting to.'

'Who's "we"?'

'Couple of dozen guys like you and me. They pulled us in from all over.'

'You from Big Blue?' asked Kelso.

Simons shook his head. 'Lineman. Tech-4. None of us have been near a flight-deck, but we've all got Tech grades of one kind or another. It's the only reason I can think of for drafting us here. What are you – ground-crew?'

It was Jodi's turn to shake her head. 'Wingmen. I went over the side last year after five up the line.' She pointed

244

to Kelso. 'He's been off the hook for longer but . . . I never did get the whole story.'

'Who cares?' said Simons. 'It's past history. Waste of breath. When you step off the boat the tapes are wiped clean. The dinks don't give a shit who you are or where you're from – and neither do we. It's what you do from here on in that counts. And Rule One is to keep faith with your fellow-breakers.'

'That's good enough for me,' said Kelso.

'What's Rule Two?' asked Jodi.

'Do as you're told, keep your head down, don't try to buck the system.' Simons's grin had a bitter twist to it. 'That's optional – depending on how long you can stand the heat. If you want out, the dinks will be only too happy to oblige. Just remember Rule One. Whichever way you choose to go, don't screw it for everyone else.'

'Gotcha.'

Simons gave them a second appraising glance. 'So . . . wing men, huh? They must have drafted you in to help the other guy with the flight-testing.'

'Could be,' admitted Kelso. 'We saw some kind of a glider fly over as we came down the road. Was that him?'

'Yeah . . .'

'Brought her in real neat,' said Jodi. 'Is he another drop-out from Big Blue?'

Simons nodded. 'Yeah. He runs the project.'

Kelso exchanged a puzzled glance with Jodi, then said, 'Did I hear you right? I thought the Iron Masters gave the orders round here.'

'They do. It's . . . a . . . kind of interesting arrangement.'

Jodi's throat tightened. 'What's this guy's name?'

'Brickman.'

Kelso opened his mouth to speak, but his lips couldn't decide which way to go.

Jodi asked the question for him. '*Steve* Brickman? From Roosevelt-Santa Fe?'

'Yeah,' said Simons. 'D'you know him?'

'Do we ever,' growled Kelso. 'Jack me! That

245

lump-sucker's the reason we're standin' here! Last time we saw him he was struttin' around with a bunch of Mutes, dressed up like a monkey's uncle – and now he's got his nose right up the ass of *these* meatballs!'

'Cool it, Dave.'

'Yeah, I'd listen to your friend,' said Simons, grabbing the opportunity to score a few points off Kelso. 'I don't know what happened out there and I care even less, but it sounds like good ol' Stevie's a lot smarter than you –'

Kelso made a lunge towards Simons, but Jodi blocked him with her shoulder. 'I said *cool* it, Dave! This won't get us anywhere!'

'That's right,' said Simons. 'Brickman's carved himself out a sweet little number. I don't know how long it's going to last, but every day spent working here is one day less in the Pits, or doing some other lousy, backbreaking job. Me and the rest of the guys *earned* this free ride and we're not about to let some wet-behind-the-ears shithead mess it up for us.'

Kelso saw red again. 'That does it! I ain't takin' any more of this!'

Simons stood his ground as Jodi wrestled Kelso to a standstill. He was bigger and heavier, but she was fast and wiry.

'Kaz! Get the hell offa me, will you!'

She turned to Simons. 'Don't worry. I'll straighten him out.'

'You'd better,' said Simons, turning towards the door. 'Otherwise he's going to be late down for breakfast.'

'Oh yeah!' roared Kelso. 'We'll see about that. Don't worry, I got your number!'

Simons paused on his way out. 'And as of now, me and twenty-three other guys have got yours.' He underscored the threat with a jabbing finger. 'Think about that before you go to sleep tonight.'

Kelso shoved Jodi aside and went over to the window. They both saw Simons walk across the compound.

'That wasn't very smart, Dave.'

'Yeah? A good smack in the mouth would have done

246

him the world of good. Would've made me feel better too. Fuckin' Brickman . . . ' He eyed her sullenly. 'Whose side are you on, anyway?'

'Yours. But this is not the time or place to try to get even. These dinks'll come down on us like a ton of bricks. Promise me you won't rock the boat.'

'Maybe.' Kelso stared moodily out of the window, then shrugged as his anger subsided. 'We'll see how it goes.' He watched her cross over to the door. 'Where're you off to?'

'To mend a few bridges.'

'Nehh, screw 'em. I don't need you brown-nosing for me. If you're not prepared to back me up, just stay out of it. Okay?'

Jodi clamped her jaw shut and counted to five before replying. 'You're fucking impossible – you know that?'

Kelso treated it as a compliment. 'Part of my fatal charm. Nobody ever got to the top by being Mr Nice Guy.'

'No shit,' said Jodi, mimicking his delivery. 'You must tell me what it's like up there sometime.'

*

In terms of its physical components – acreage, installations and personnel – the Heron Pool did not give the impression of being a major enterprise. Despite Cadillac's industry, it was still very much in the embryonic stage; an experimental project, no more.

This was due, in part, to the caution exercised by Lord Kiyo Min-Orota. His estimation of Cadillac's potential had not changed in the slightest, but he knew that developments at the Heron Pool were being closely monitored by the Herald, Hase-Gawa. From the reported use made of such craft by the long-dogs it was clear that just a few regiments of flying-horses could dramatically alter the present balance of power – a possibility that could not have escaped the attention of the Shogun.

The Sons of Ne-Issan did not yet possess the rapid-fire guns and explosive devices that made the flying-horse such a deadly weapon, but that day would come. Meanwhile, their speed meant that a strong force of samurai could rapidly reach any part of the country regardless of the intervening terrain. They would, literally, drop out of the sky like swooping falcons. The ability to execute such manoeuvres would demand a complete revision of military tactics.

Lord Kiyo Min-Orota was aware of the delicate line he had to tread. The task of building these craft had been given to his family because they were regarded as *fudai* – trusted allies of the Shogunate. But success had its dangers. If the Heron Pool expanded too rapidly and its importance was inflated by loose talk and wild speculation, it might cause the young Shogun to think twice, and perhaps withdraw the licence in favour of his own family – a situation to be avoided at all costs. If the Toh-Yota became the sole possessors of such a weapon they would use it to hold their opponents in check, thus ending all hopes for a new age of progress.

As a key participant in the 'modernist' conspiracy, Min-Orota had therefore been at pains to create the impression that, whilst he was prepared to back the flying-horse project, it did not have his unqualified support. To this end he had slowed down the pace of development by trimming back Cadillac's constant requests for more manpower and resources, and he had let it be known in court circles that even if a craft capable of sustained powered flight *was* eventually constructed, he feared that, in the long term, its impact on Iron Master society would be more adverse than beneficial.

All lies, of course, but it bore the appearance of a face-saving exercise whilst expressing his support for traditional values. And it also provided him with an escape hatch if Yama-Shita's plan to recapture the Dark Light backfired – an enterprise which certainly did *not* have his wholehearted support.

Translated into Basic, the message he was beaming

towards the Shogun read thus: 'I'm only going along with this because you guys twisted my arm.'

It was a neat ploy. The whole deal had, of course, been put together on the back-stairs by Yama-Shita, but the records would show Kiyo Min-Orota hadn't pitched for the business. It was Ieyasu, the wily old Court Chamberlain, who had advised the Shogun to grant the manufacturing licence to the Min-Orota family without going through the usual process of soliciting the highest bid from other interested parties. All that remained now was to find some way, short of death, to prevent Nakane Toh-Shiba, the Consul-General, from screwing things up – both literally and figuratively – and everything would fall into their hands.

Jodi caught up with Simons as he passed through an archway in the back wall of the compound, opposite the main gate. There were more buildings beyond. Simons paused expectantly.

'Listen,' said Jodi. 'Before this goes any further I just want to say that Dave is okay – y'know what I mean? I know things got a little out of hand back there, but the truth is, uhh . . . neither of us expected to run into Brickman again so soon.' Jodi shook her head in wonderment. 'I don't know how the guy does it, but he certainly gets around.' She fell into step beside Simons. 'Are you *sure* his name's Steve Brickman?'

'That's what he calls himself. I can't see why he would want to lie about something like that, but what difference does it make? He's giving the orders and he seems to know what he's doing. It's only you guys who seem to have a problem.'

Simons led her down an alleyway between two long single-storey structures. The facing walls had matching sets of sliding doors at regular intervals and they were all wide open, giving Jodi a clear view of their interiors. They were both large, airy workshops. The one on the left contained stacks of sawn timber and rows of benches for making sub-components; the one to her right contained several trestle jigs on which ribs and spars were assembled into wings, while on the others, formers and stringers were turned into fuselages.

Running down the centre was a primitive production line on which the various pieces were mated together. In all, Jodi counted a dozen airplanes at various stages of completion. Several Trackers in blue outfits were putting tools back into racks and tidying up workbenches; others were sweeping the floor. The job looked as though it demanded skill and intelligence, the whole environment looked clean and healthy and, above all, the atmosphere appeared relaxed – with not a white-stripe or a whipping-cane in sight. Jodi could understand why Simons and his co-workers didn't want anyone spoiling things.

But there was something that didn't add up. Simons had been drafted to the Heron Pool in March and had implied that Brickman had already set up the operation. But she and Kelso had first run into Brickman when still part of Malone's renegade band back in the early part of April, and they had last seen him at the end of May, hob-nobbing with their Mute captors at the trading post. Jodi was not sure of the exact dates; her standard-issue calendar watch had been ripped from her wrist when she was washed downstream in the tangled wreckage of her Skyhawk. But a day or two either way didn't matter, the questions remained: if Brickman was in Plainfolk territory during April and May, what in Columbus's name was he doing there when he was supposed to be running the Heron Pool – and how the eff-eff had he gotten back here so fast?

Before she could ask Simons, her attention was drawn to a swept-wing glider taking off from the big field beyond the workshops. Another, of the same type, was being pushed towards them aboard a wheeled trolley. The craft now airborne rose steeply on a line attached under the nose. The other end ran down to a lump of machinery on the far right-hand corner of the field.

A faint *tuff-tuff-tuff* reached Jodi's ears.

'Steam-driven winch,' said Simons.

Jodi watched the ascent with interest. She was conversant with the principles of thermals and soaring flight of which Skyhawks were designed to take advantage, but purpose-built gliders didn't exist in the Federation. You learned to fly with the aid of a propeller and battery-power from Day One.

When the glider was about a thousand feet up, the pilot released the cable. The falling end was marked by a fluttering blue pennant. The glider banked gently to the right, nosed down to gather speed, then went up into a stall turn. It stood on its tail for a brief moment, then cartwheeled over its port wingtip into another dive and swept back over their heads towards the perimeter of the field.

'Neat,' said Jodi. 'But why gliders?'

'The dinks don't have electricity,' replied Simons.

'They didn't have airplanes before you guys started building them. How come nobody's told them what they're missing?'

'No need to. The dinks have known about it from way back. They call it the Dark Light and, as far as they're concerned, it's bad news. According to Brickman, Iron Masters are forbidden by law to mess around with any kind of electrical equipment. On top of which, the subject is absolutely taboo.' He shrugged. 'I know. It sounds crazy, but there it is.'

Jodi looked up at the glider. 'May be a good thing in the long run. These things aren't going to be much of a threat to anybody.'

'Don't be too sure. Brickman's working on the power problem. He's developing a lightweight steam engine.'

'*Steam* engine . . . ?' The idea made Jodi laugh.

'Don't knock it. We're running bench tests right now. Just having problems developing enough power.'

'What are you using for fuel?'

'Oil. But we're trying to find something that burns faster and generates more heat.'

Jodi sniffed dismissively. 'It'll never get off the ground.'

'It hasn't so far,' admitted Simons. 'But we're working on it.'

The six Trackers wheeling the grounded glider back to the right-hand workshop passed by close to where they were standing. While Simons asked them how the test flight had gone, Jodi cast a professional eye over their handiwork.

The silk-covered wings were not swept back as far as the Skyhawk's and were of rigid construction instead of being inflated to the correct shape by helium gas. The slim fuselage pod, lacking the rear-mounted engine and pusher-prop of the original, was attached directly to the underside of the wing, with the cockpit just ahead of the leading edge.

The Skyhawk was a pure-delta wing design, with no tailplane or rudder; Brickman's craft had a boom running back from the centre section with a cruciform tail assembly mounted on the end. That was not the only departure from the original; on the Skyhawk, banking to left and right was affected by means of control wires that warped the outer trailing edge of the wings. On Brickman's glider, there were inset panels that pivoted up and down: ailerons – as used on the two-seat Skyrider and the Mark-2 Skyhawk.

But Jodi didn't know about those yet. The Skyrider was used exclusively by AMEXICO, whose existence was a closely guarded secret, and she'd been lost overboard, presumed killed before the Mark-2 had been issued to Big Red One – the Red River wagon-train, flagship of the Amtrak Federation overground forces.

There was one other obvious difference – the tricycle undercart had been replaced by a central wooden skid. Two small runners had been fitted at an angle on either side to prevent the glider from angling over and snagging its wingtips on landing. But it didn't eliminate the problem. A rookie pilot could still rip those beautifully crafted wings apart every time he made an iffy landing.

'No undercarriage,' said Jodi, as Simons returned.

'No. The dinks don't have any rubber to make the

tyres with. And without electricity there's no chance of making aluminium, or any other of the lightweight alloys. We have to make do with iron, steel, copper and brass. For take-offs we use a launching trolley. It's kinda primitive – like lots of things around here – but it works.'

'Provided you land back at the same field.'

'You got a point there,' conceded Simons. 'If you've got any bright ideas, don't be shy about speaking up. Brickman runs a tight ship, but he's always open to suggestions. And as wingmen, you guys know a lot more about this stuff than we do.'

'Yeah . . .'

'What's the connection?'

'With Brickman? Oh . . . we shipped out together on the same wagon-train. The Lady from Louisiana. I was his section leader. We ran into all kinds of trouble – that's when I went over the side. From what he told me when we met up, he was shot down the next day. But he's a survivor. Smart too. Doesn't miss a trick.'

'You can say that again.'

Jodi watched the glider now under test drift gracefully across the evening sky. 'I'm surprised he hasn't taught any of you to fly.'

Simons laughed. 'Are you kidding? You wouldn't catch me going up in one of those things. Took me long enough to get used to standing out here on the ground all by myself without getting the shakes.'

The glider, now way over on the right, swept southwards across the road running past the compound, then circled back towards the field. As he drew near the road, Brickman dropped the starboard wing and applied top rudder, making the same steep approach they had watched first time round. It seemed like he was going to slide right into the workshops, but when he was down to about fifty feet, he levelled out and kicked the nose straight, swishing over their heads to land a short distance away.

Kelso walked down the alleyway in time to see the touchdown. Positioning himself between them with folded arms, he rocked gently back and forth on his heels and pointedly ignored their presence. Simons glanced up at him, then aimed a questioning look behind his back at Jodi. She raised her eyebrows and shoulders in reply.

The glider slid to a halt about a hundred and fifty yards away, then tilted gently over on to its starboard runner as the Tracker ground crew ran a trolley out on to the field. A figure dressed in an all-white outfit climbed out of the cockpit and stood, hands on hips, as the sleek craft was lifted gently on to its carrying frame, then walked behind the six-man crew as they wheeled it back towards the workshops.

'Is that it for today?' enquired Kelso. 'Or is this where we start hanging out lanterns?' His voice carried no hint of rancour.

'No. We don't start night flying till next week.'

The joke was lost on Kelso. 'Good. How about introducing us?'

'I thought you already knew each other.'

'We do. But since he isn't expecting us it might be better if you break the ice. Don't want him to get the wrong idea.'

Simons looked at Jodi. 'Is he always this difficult?'

'Only when his feet hurt.'

The ground party pushing the glider drew closer. Brickman was now walking level with the tailplane, his face partially obscured by the starboard wing. He wore a white headband bearing the brown petal motif of the Min-Orota and looked thinner than the last time Jodi had seen him. His crewcut hair looked darker too.

Simons set off towards the plane. Jodi and Kelso let him get ten yards ahead, then followed.

'Steve! Got the new boys here. They'd like to meet you.'

The white-clad figure gave an answering wave then motioned to the ground crew to take the glider back inside the workshop. The intervening wing moved out of the way, enabling Jodi and Kelso to get a clear view of their fellow alumnus. He *was* slimmer. His hair was not just

254

darker, it was jet black.

And the guy it belonged to wasn't Brickman.

Kelso faltered in mid-stride. 'Wait a minute –'

'Keep going,' whispered Jodi. 'Just play it by ear.'

They approached to within arm's length in time to hear Simons identify them by name, adding. 'They tell me they're old friends of yours.'

Cadillac found himself in something of a quandary. In 'borrowing' Steve's acquired memory, and later assuming his identity, he had not considered the possibility that he might encounter Trackers who actually knew the *real* Steve Brickman. There was no danger of them guessing he was a Mute, but they would know he was an impostor – and that might prove awkward.

If they had not been wingmen, he would have arranged for their removal on some trumped-up charge of sloppy workmanship or insolent behaviour. But that was not possible. He was in urgent need of people with flight experience to help move the project along, and these two new arrivals were the only ones available in the whole of Ne-Issan.

Cadillac squared up to the new recruits and cast his eyes over each of them in turn. He was sure that Steve would have known exactly how to turn a situation like this to his advantage. He had to try and do likewise. But knowing everything that Steve knew was not the same thing as knowing how Steve would act in any given set of circumstances. Not the same thing at all . . .

And there was another problem he hadn't foreseen. The transfer of information had ceased the moment that Steve had finished teaching him to fly. Cadillac had then gone on a long journey with Mr Snow, arriving back at the settlement in time to witness Steve's flight to freedom. He only knew at second hand the events leading up to Steve's escape, and was unaware of what had happened since. He was thus able to recall everything Steve knew about Jodi up to the moment of her dramatic disappearance: Kelso, on the other hand, was a total stranger.

'Jodi Kazan . . . Yeah, the name's familiar. She was the flight section leader aboard The Lady from Louisiana. But she was killed trying to land during a thunderstorm.'

'Uh-uh,' said Jodi. 'Almost.' She motioned to the disfiguring sheet of livid scar tissue that covered the left side of her face and neck. 'I got the marks to prove it.'

'So I see . . . ' 'Brickman' eyed her keenly. 'You still look a lot different to the Kazan I remember.'

'I *am* a lot different. You've changed quite a bit too.'

'You must have me mixed up with someone else,' said 'Brickman'. 'I heard about what happened to Kazan and The Lady, but I wasn't on board at the time. I'm not saying you aren't who you claim to be, but I joined Hartmann's crew after the refit. The Plainfolk gave The Lady a real pounding.'

'True. Yeah, well . . . that explains everything,' said Jodi.

'Brickman' suppressed a smile and turned his attention to Dave Kelso. 'Are you *sure* we've met? I've been trying to place you but your name doesn't ring a bell.'

'That doesn't surprise me,' said Kelso. 'When Simons here mentioned your name, I thought I knew you but, uhh . . . like Jodi . . . I've obviously got you confused with some other guy.' He shrugged. 'It happens.'

'All the time,' said 'Brickman'. Never mind. We'll have plenty of time to get acquainted in the next few weeks. Welcome aboard.' He shook hands with both of them. 'Ray Simons will put you in the picture. We've got a good little team here, but now that you two have arrived we can really start moving.' He signed off with a snappy parade-ground salute and strode away. It had all gone much better than he expected. He hadn't fooled either of them, but they both had enough savvy not to make waves.

Simons eyed Kelso. 'Well, I'm glad that's over. What d'you say – start with a clean slate?'

Kelso grasped the offered hand. 'Sure. No hard feelings?'

'None whatsoever.' Simons began walking backwards. 'See you back at the hut – okay?' He turned and hurried

256

after 'Brickman'.

Jodi and Kelso watched them disappear round the corner of the far workshop building, then exchanged blank stares. Jodi was the first to find her tongue.

'Well, well, well . . .'

'Exactly,' said Kelso. 'Just what the fuck is going on?'

*

Precisely the same question – phrased somewhat more elegantly in Japanese – was being posed with equal urgency by Consul-General Nakane Toh-Shiba, Lord Min-Orota and, with the aid of fleet-winged courier pigeons, by Lord Hiro Yama-Shita. But they too found themselves obliged to draw speculative conclusions from the few facts available.

The Consul-General, concerned by reports that the road convoy had been twice delayed before arriving at Firi, asked the two house-women to explain exactly what had happened. Su-Shan and Nan-Khe, who had been living in terror of this moment, recounted their part of the story in a shrill falsetto, fluttering their hands and twittering like panic-stricken canaries.

Listening to them was like having his head pierced with long needles, but Toh-Shiba bore it stoically, then sought out Clearwater, whose luminous presence once again graced the bedroom of the lake-house. Now bathed and freshly clothed in a gossamer-light kimono bearing a design of wild flowers and dew-soaked summer grasses, she was invited to soothe her master's troubled spirit by renewing her acquaintance with his pleasure-machine. Only then, when the weeks of pent-up passion had been spent and he was left lying on his back with the deliciously painful feeling that his balls were about to catch fire, did the Consul-General ask for her version of the same event.

Called to account for each moment of captivity, Clearwater admitted to being unmasked and subjected to a physical examination but swore on her life that the

257

ronin had asked no questions and she had volunteered no information of any kind. She said nothing about her midnight encounter at the post-house with Noburo, Steve and the Herald, Toshiro Hase-Gawa. To have spoken of this would have placed the cloud warrior in mortal danger. But the subject never came up. Nakane Toh-Shiba's questions were based on what the house-women had told him – and they had slept throughout the entire episode.

During one of his regular official visits to Lord Min-Orota's fortress at Ba-satana, the Consul-General recounted the details of the kidnapping and volunteered the opinion that it was an ill-fated enterprise based on faulty intelligence. Anxious to put the best gloss on things, Toh-Shiba plumped for the simplest and most obvious explanation: a group of *ronin*, alerted to the presence in the convoy of a sealed carriage-box, had made off with its occupant in the hope of extracting a hefty ransom then, finding the mask hid a worthless long-dog, had promptly abandoned her and the two house-women by the roadside.

Kiyo Min-Orota listened carefully, nodding in agreement as the Consul-General concluded that, while all such acts of criminality were regrettable, this particular incident was, essentially, a minor upset that need not worry any of them.

'It is, without doubt, a convenient theory which I would be happy to embrace were it not for one, small, irksome detail.' Kiyo paused to let his opening shot sink in, drawing a certain satisfaction from watching Nakane Toh-Shiba's bullish confidence become tinged with fear, uncertainty and doubt. The Consul-General might be a well-connected fellow-nobleman, but he engendered scant respect and Kiyo always enjoyed taking the over-fleshed cocksman down a peg or two.

'I'm not sure I understand . . .'

'Oh, come now, isn't it obvious? The *ronin* lost forty-six horsemen in the course of capturing their prize –'

The Consul-General reacted with astonishment. 'You know of this already?'

The lie came easily. 'I heard in a roundabout way that *a* convoy had been waylaid and that the *ronin* had been hotly pursued. But until this moment I had no idea they had made off with, ahh . . . goods belonging to you. The point is, the *ronin* lost a great many men only to find themselves in possession of a long-dog and two Vietnamese house-women. Three worthless individuals, that they fed, then escorted back to within sight of the main road – risking more of their men in the process.'

'Yes – but they did move under cover of darkness.'

'Even so, doesn't it strike you as odd?'

Toh-Shiba looked perplexed.

'Why let them go? Why weren't they killed out of hand or, at the very least, kept as slaves?'

Toh-Shiba's brow became increasingly furrowed as he grappled with the implications of the domain-lord's questions. With his brain almost totally geared to the needs of his nether regions, logic was not his strong point. 'Mmm, yes, now that you mention it, I suppose it *is* rather strange . . . ' He scratched his navel absent-mindedly. 'I suppose they must have had a reason, but for the life of me I can't think what it could be.'

'You should try harder, my friend,' said Kiyo severely. 'Because your life and mine could depend upon the answer! By the great *kami* – it's staring you in the face! These three individuals should have vanished, never to be heard of again!'

'Ye-ess, I see that now.'

'To my mind,' continued Kiyo, 'there is only one explanation. They were set free because they are by no means as worthless as they appear. *Someone* places as much value upon the long-dog as you do yourself.' He paused to give his words time to sink in, then added. 'As this is your affair, I leave you to consider who that someone might be. But I think you've been rumbled, my friend, and I suggest it's time for some rapid house-cleaning.'

Domain-lord Yama-Shita who, if anything, was faster on the draw than Kiyo Min-Orota, arrived at exactly the same conclusion when presented with the bare facts by courier pigeon. Through his close links with the Se-Iko, he had learned of the raid and its bloody aftermath two days after it had occurred, and he had promptly dispatched one of his own winged couriers to alert Lord Min-Orota.

Yama-Shita was furious. Despite his best efforts, the long-dog had fallen, albeit briefly, into unknown hands. Fortunately, the Consul-General was not privy to the plot to recapture the Dark Light, but Yama-Shita now found himself wishing he had kept to his rule of never becoming involved with people he disliked, mistrusted and, above all, did not respect. He had allowed Kiyo Min-Orota to persuade him that, as the Shogun's brother-in-law, Toh-Shiba might be a useful pawn, but despite their vigilance the degenerate clown had finally managed to compromise them as well as himself!

No one knew the true nature of the *ronin* who had held the long-dog overnight, but those few hours might prove perilous. It was not unknown for criminal bands to act on orders from above. When laws and common usage did not provide the means, the rulers of Ne-Issan did not hesitate to use unorthodox methods to achieve their ends – and neither did ambitious domain-lords. According to the dispatch sent by Min-Orota, the gutter-bitch had not been interrogated by her captors. But the account she had given Toh-Shiba had not been elicited under threat of torture. Who could say, without putting her to the test, that she was telling the truth? Allowing her to live once she had become Toh-Shiba's painted whore had always been a risky decision; but now she was the subject of outside interest she was an even greater danger than before.

Yes . . . steps would have to be taken . . .

Yama-Shita had also been told of what the

house-women had said regarding the samurai and two red-stripes, found dead at the Midiri-tana post-house. There was a suggestion that the men might have been killed by *ninja*, but the two women knew next to nothing about the incident and Yama-Shita did not have any independent source of information that would have enabled him to link the killings with the raid on the road convoy. The paper placed on Noburo's chest identifying him and his two companions as *ronin* and enemies of the Se-Iko had been spirited away before it could become public knowledge. Midiri-tana was in the domain of the Mitsu-Bishi, allies of the Shogun, and they had responded to an appeal from the summer palace at Yedo to lay a veil of secrecy over the whole affair.

*

The contents of the anonymous letter, penned by the Herald Toshiro Hase-Gawa and addressed to a member of the Se-Iko family, might have helped Yama-Shita make the connections which would have confirmed the suspected identity of the puppet-master. But the letter revealing the location and method of entry to the *ronin*'s hidden base camp never arrived at its destination. Someone who had been ordered to keep a discreet watch on the Herald's movements observed him entrust a shopkeeper at Ari-dina with the task of dispatching a sealed document via the postal service, and it was intercepted soon after being handed over the counter.

CHAPTER ELEVEN

Having used his position as a Herald of the Inner Court to secure Steve a job as a roadrunner, Toshiro Hase-Gawa left Ari-dina and returned to the Summer Palace on Aron-giren. By changing mounts at post-house inns along the way, he was able to ride at full gallop for hour after hour. Even for a seasoned rider like Toshiro it was an exhausting exercise, but he pressed on into the evening of each day, snatching a hot bath and a few hours' rest before rising at 0300 to resume his journey through the same grey twilight world he had left the night before.

Arriving at Yedo, the Herald exchanged the customary round of greetings with Kamakura, the ever-hopeful guard-captain, then, as protocol demanded, he presented his credentials to the Court Chamberlain's office. Ieyasu was unable to receive him personally, being indisposed with an intestinal complaint which had begun to plague him with increasing frequency.

To the principal private secretary who was holding the fort in his absence, Toshiro expressed his profound regrets at hearing of his illustrious master's ill health, and he asked him to convey personally to Ieyasu his respectful, yet heartfelt, good wishes and fervent hopes for a speedy recovery. The secretary responded in the same fulsome manner, assuring the Herald that the Chamberlain would be deeply gratified by his expressions of concern and goodwill. Et cetera, et cetera.

The ritual exchange ended with a series of bows and with Toshiro wondering if the Shogun had finally managed to find a poisoner with sufficient knowledge and subtlety to slip something past the troublesome old fox.

Yoritomo, the twenty-eight-year-old Shogun, received the Herald in his study on the first floor of the palace, overlooking the landscaped pool dotted with lilies and alive with red and white carp. The last message from samurai-captain Noburo, sent by carrier pigeon on the same day that Clearwater had been released, had put an end to the speculation about her identity. Once again, the Herald's sources of information had proved utterly reliable.

Toshiro knelt before the raised section on which the Shogun sat with five of his bodyguards. As soon as the usual formalities had been dispensed with, the Herald assumed a cross-legged position and proceeded to relate his own face-to-face meeting with Clearwater at Midiri-tana. It was, of course, a highly edited account: he said nothing about her admission that both she and her companion were unmarked Mutes. But he did reveal that Noburo Naka-Jima had brought another long-dog with him, and gave a brief outline of how he had fallen into the *ronin*'s hands.

This individual, explained Toshiro, was a 'mexican', a secret agent of similar rank to his own, working on the direct orders of the Federation's 'shogun'. 'From his responses to my questions, it became clear that I had drawn the wrong conclusion from the reports previously available to me. Lord Yama-Shita has not entered into league with the Federation or their agents. To date, he has dealt solely with the grass-monkeys and the renegade long-dogs.'

Yoritomo's face darkened as he lost a good 10 per cent of his cool. 'So, apart from proving that the gutter-bitch currently being humped by my dear brother-in-law is a long-dog, it now appears that your remaining charges are totally without foundation.'

The young Shogun abhorred uncertainties. The conspiracy had been clearly defined, containment strategies had been planned, understandings with trusted allies had been reaffirmed, wavering loyalties had been bolstered by promises of hard cash and quid pro quos, everything had been neatly tied together – and now it was all starting to unravel.

It was the thought of Ieyasu's reaction that annoyed Yoritomo more than the fact it had all been a pointless exercise. The ageing Court Chamberlain had never accepted losing control of the Office of Heralds, and seized every opportunity to discredit the present arrangement of direct access. When the old fox learned, as he most assuredly would, that the latest round of fence-mending and buy-offs – in which he had been actively involved – had been based on a faulty premise of which he had not been advised or asked to comment upon, he would be laughing all the way to the nearest whorehouse.

'I'm not happy about this, my friend. Not happy at all. I was reluctant to believe these stories from the very beginning, but I relied on your judgement – and it now appears you totally misread the situation.'

'Not entirely, sire. Given time, I believe I can still provide you with first-hand evidence that –'

'Given time? Hah! What for? To weave more fairy tales? Kiyo Min-Orota, whom you named as Lord Yama-Shita's principal partner, is involved in building these flying-horses because Ieyasu advised me to award the licence to someone we could trust! Are you proposing to come back in a month's time and tell me that the Court Chamberlain – the only person it seems I can rely on – is involved in this conspiracy too?'

The Shogun appeared to have conveniently overlooked the fact that Ieyasu – suddenly promoted from tiresome meddler to peerless sage – had also advised him to grant Nakane Toh-Shiba the hand of his fourth sister and the post of Consul-General.

Toshiro bowed deeply. This was the make-or-break moment. His life now depended on how the Shogun reacted to what he would say next. 'Sire, permit me to state once again that to serve you in death, as in life, is an equal honour, but I beg you to consider this. When the Seventh Wave reached these shores, the blood of the

264

Hase-Gawa coloured the Eastern Sea – mingling with that of their brothers-in-arms, the lofty Toh-Yota.

'No samurai born to such an ancient line would knowingly sully the name of another noble house with baseless accusations. To do so brings dishonour upon his family and upon himself – a stain that can only be removed by the act of *seppuku* as tradition demands.

'Whether I live or die does not alter the fact that the power and ambitions of the house of Yama-Shita pose a growing threat to the present era of peace and stability. My conclusion, based on the evidence presented to me, was incorrect, but my error was an honest one, a product of natural caution and an all-consuming desire to protect the Shogunate.

'But my intentions, however well founded, are of little consequence. A samurai, worthy of the name, does not plead mitigating circumstances. If he has conducted himself correctly, his actions speak for themselves. Whatever the verdict, be it harsh or merciful, a servant must always accept the judgement of his sovereign lord gratefully and without question, for he is the sole arbiter of justice and his authority must always be upheld.'

'Well said. I wish everyone felt the same way.'

Toshiro accepted this comment with another deep bow from the waist. So far so good, but he wasn't out of the woods yet. 'Sire, if I had found myself obliged to return empty-handed, I would have chosen to kill myself rather than lose face by confessing this grievous error of judgement. But I stayed my hand because the news I now bring is more important than anything we have hitherto spoken of.'

'Go on . . .'

The Herald hesitated, his mouth suddenly dry. He ran his tongue around his teeth to moisten it, then said, 'The threat of a possible alliance between the Yama-Shita and the Federation has been replaced by a direct threat from the Federation itself.'

The Shogun's lips and eyes narrowed into three thin lines.

'The ruler of the Federation knows of the arrangement between the grass-monkeys and Lord Yama-Shita – right down to the terms of the trade-off. A shipment of repeating rifles in exchange for one flying-horse complete with rider. The "mexican" also knew when and where the weapons were delivered. He claims his masters possess secret devices which allow them to spy on us from afar. The phrase he used was – "They have eyes and ears all over the sky".'

'Did he explain what he meant by that?'

'No, sire. I assumed he was referring to devices fashioned by those versed in the secrets of the High Craft. So even if he had explained I doubt if I would have understood.'

'Do you believe him?'

Toshiro reached inside his robe and pulled out Steve's radio-knife – now wrapped in a strip of black silk. 'The mexican offered this as proof of his identity. It was taken from him by samurai-captain Naka-Jima.' Holding the ends of the slim package between his fingertips, he reached forward and laid it gently on the mat near the foot of the dais.

The five guards seated cross-legged in a semicircle behind the Shogun lifted their butts off the floor and craned their necks to take a peek.

Yoritomo gave it the once-over. 'What is it?'

'Something which I fear to touch or even speak of, but which duty requires me to lay before you.'

'Are we talking about a device powered by the Dark Light?'

Toshiro bowed his head.

'Very well. You are hereby pardoned unconditionally for taking possession of such an object and bringing it into my presence,' said Yoritomo. 'And you are also absolved from any future charge of high treason arising from its subsequent retention or disposal as ordered by me. Does that make you feel happier?'

'A little less uneasy, perhaps.' Toshiro would have preferred to have been offered this crucial dispensation in writing.

'You worry too much. Open it up.'

Toshiro unwrapped the package, taking care not to touch the contents.

The Shogun gazed down at the combat knife. 'I hope, for your sake, there's more to this than meets the eye.'

The Herald operated the pressure-catches that released the wooden sections of the handle, revealing the microelectronics mounted on the metal frame beneath.

Yoritomo, who had never seen any kind of electrical device, eyed the tiny radio transmitter with the caution of someone who half expected it suddenly to come to life and fill the room with death-dealing rays. 'What is it supposed to do?'

Toshiro repeated Noburo's explanation, adding that he had not questioned Steve further on the matter, preferring to keep him off balance by displaying a total lack of interest in what the disguised long-dog clearly thought was an attention-grabbing item.

'So, if I understand you correctly, by means of this device, the masters of this "mexican" can reach him anywhere at any time, day or night – and know exactly where he is?'

'That was the situation up to the moment he fell into the hands of samurai-captain Naka-Jima. The device has been in my possession since then.'

The Shogun accepted this with a nod. 'Did you manage to find out what the "mexican" had been sent here to do?'

'He was only too eager to tell me, sire. His orders were twofold: kidnap or kill the renegade long-dog directing the work at the Heron Pool and, if possible, destroy the entire set-up.'

'Singlehanded? Extraordinary . . .'

'Sire, I hate to admit it, but he is an extraordinary individual. His martial skills earned him the grudging admiration of samurai-captain Naka-Jima, he is quick-witted, imprudently courageous, insufferably confident about the superiority of the system he represents and utterly unconcerned as to whether he lives or dies.'

'And there might be others like him?'

'It's a possibility we have to consider,' admitted Toshiro.

'Did he say *why* he'd been sent to do this?'

'Yes, sire. The Federation view the decision by us to build flying-horses as a threat to the status quo. By kidnapping or killing the renegade who is passing their secrets to us they hoped to wreck the project. Were the mexican to fail, the Federation would be obliged to bring greater forces to bear, making a massive pre-emptive strike which, in turn, could trigger a wider conflict.'

The prospect of war with an enemy armed with weapons whose power came from the Dark Light destroyed the inner calm which the Shogun had achieved during his precious hour of contemplation in the stone garden. The veins under his temples became visible as his pulse rate soared.

'So . . . what action did you take?'

'I offered to assist him.'

The Shogun's eyes hardened. 'I trust you had a good reason for doing so.'

Toshiro bowed his head. He had thought long and hard before deciding to reveal Brickman's presence, and had carefully worked out each move. 'I believed it to be in your best interests, sire.'

The Herald went on to describe how he had arranged for the mexican to work as a roadrunner in order to have him assigned to the Consul-General's residence, from where, at the appropriate moment, he could – if the Shogun so desired it – be transferred to the Heron Pool.

'By placing this individual within the system, we now have him under our control. And he cannot change his present identity unless we allow him to do so.' Toshiro opened up the bag of pink leaves he had taken from Steve and explained their purpose to the Shogun.

'By agreeing to assist him, I have been able to learn his

intentions, and can aid or hinder them depending on what suits us best. Knowing who he is and where he is means he can be kept under surveillance and his contacts investigated. And he can be eliminated the instant you so command.

'On the other hand, should you for any reason decide to take out one or more of your . . . "opponents", or halt work at the Heron Pool, you may find that this particular long-dog could be used to achieve the desired result – and then be set up as the fall-guy.'

Yoritomo placed an elbow on the lacquered arm-rest standing next to his left thigh and pulled throughtfully at his lower lip. 'Mmmmm. Interesting idea.'

'It would be seen as intervention by a foreign power. And if Yama-Shita wasn't the target, he couldn't miss being hurt by the fall-out. Let's face it, it *is* his family who've been importing all these outlanders. And if, for instance, there was some "incident" which resulted in the death of, let's say . . . the Consul-General of Ro-diren and Masa-chusa . . .'

'It could be interpreted as an attack upon the Shogunate –'

'Which, at the very least, would require from those involved – however unwittingly – a *major* act of restitution.'

'Right . . .'

There was a lengthy silence while the Shogun mentally reviewed various scenarios. Toshiro kept his eyes averted in the customary fashion until the Shogun spoke.

'I feel bound to tell you that when this conversation began I had serious doubts about your career prospects. And when you started to tell me about the deal you'd struck with this "mexican" I really thought you'd gone over the edge. But I can now see this has a lot of possibilities. Well done.'

Toshiro bowed gratefully and sat back feeling extremely pleased with himself. His reading of the situation had been faultless. Even though the long-dogs were armed with the Dark Light, the samurai-warriors of

Ne-Issan might find ways to repulse an attack by the Federation. But victory could still result in a defeat for the Shogunate. The debilitating effects of an all-out war would upset the present delicate balance of forces, creating a turbulent situation where the Toh-Yota family could find itself displaced by the Yama-Shita – the apostles of progress.

Faced with that stark prospect, Toshiro knew the Shogun would choose to sacrifice the Heron Pool project – settling a few scores in the process. And that suited the Herald very well indeed.

*

After four days of running mail back and forth between the numerous houses of the Min-Orota family and the Consul-General's residence, Steve learned he had been assigned to the route which included the Heron Pool. No explanation was given, but he suspected that his masked benefactor had been pulling a few strings.

On his journeys to and from Ba-satana and down to Nyo-poro, Steve had kept his eyes peeled but had seen no aerial activity – an indication that the range of the glider Cadillac had constructed was fairly limited.

From his own knowledge of aeronautics – and he had been the best in his class – it seemed to Steve that without the aid of helium gas you needed an entirely different wing form to provide the lift for sustained soaring flight. If the young wordsmith had, as Mr Snow claimed, filched all the theoretical and practical knowledge Steve had worked so hard to acquire, then he must be aware of that too. The fact that Cadillac hadn't acted upon it suggested he was intending to add a power-plant at some stage. In which case, the swept-back wing design Steve had seen on his way past the Heron Pool made sense. Cadillac was obviously testing the stability of the basic airframe while he figured out how to build an efficient engine using whatever materials and tools were available.

Terrific. Couldn't be better. Had things progressed faster Steve might have found himself surplus to requirements. As it was, he still had a chance to make a useful input. There might be some initial hesitation but, providing Cadillac could be assured that he would get the sole credit for any bright ideas the two of them came up with, Steve was confident he would be able to persuade the Mute to take him on board. Cadillac might have picked his brains but he didn't think the same way. The flaws in his psyche prevented him from using the stolen information to gain an insight into Steve's thought processes. The knowledge he had gained was a valuable asset; knowing how to use it was a different matter entirely.

As Cadillac had already discovered.

This comforting realisation put an extra bounce into Steve's stride as he headed west along the highway towards Mara-bara and the Heron Pool. Drawing closer to the small hamlet, he caught sight of something that gave him an even bigger kick. Three white-winged gliders flying in tight arrowhead formation broke out into the blue from behind a fluffy mound of low-lying cumulus.

Steve judged their altitude to be around 2,000 feet. It was a hot day, so there were plenty of thermals rising from the surrounding cropfields, and once at cloud level a Federation wingman knew how to use the updrafts within to get a further lift.

Flying in perfect unison, the three gliders pulled round to the right in a vertical bank, then slid nose-down as their leader took them into a steep dive. Realising they were going for a loop, Steve stopped to watch, holding his breath as he waited to see if they had enough speed to make it all the way over the top. With an engine behind you there was never any worry about being able to power your way round, but these guys could stall before they went over the top and – being so close together – could find themselves in all kinds of trouble. Steve doubted whether the craft had airspeed indicators and

271

wondered if Cadillac had made sure the airframes were stressed for aerobatics.

Steve's fears proved groundless. The gliders stayed in one piece and nobody fell out of the sky. They went over the top in the same tight formation as if they were glued together, then banked out of the ensuing dive, crossing overhead towards his left.

Steve moved off again, settling down into the long, easy stride he'd picked up from running with the M'Call Bears. The three gliders had lost about 1,000 feet in that last manoeuvre. If they kept to their present curving course it would bring them back towards the road on the far side of Mara-bara, where the Heron Pool was situated. Provided he didn't have to stop and kowtow to a passing samurai, he might just manage to arrive in time to watch the landing – and maybe see more of the general set-up.

The roofs of the buildings clustered along the left side of the road momentarily blocked his view of the formation, but as he cleared the hamlet he saw it was heading in the direction he'd expected. As he rounded a bend in the road, the Heron Pool came into sight way down over on the right.

Looking across at the approaching formation, he saw the glider on the left of the leader rock wildly and then break away, diving under the tails of the other two aircraft. There was something trailing from its port wing. Steve leapt over the irrigation ditch and ran across the cropfield as the glider wobbled drunkenly towards him, losing height rapidly.

The something trailing from the port wing was the shredded outer third of the fabric covering. There was still enough in place to generate some lift, but the glider was slipping and sliding all over the place. The pilot, who had to keep dropping the undamaged starboard wing to correct the imbalance, was obviously in a hurry to put the plane down before more of the fabric came adrift. If that happened the glider might flip over and go in nose-first.

In his instinctive haste to help a fellow-pilot, Steve had rushed forward blindly, only to find himself in danger of being mown down as the glider, now some fifty feet up, suddenly swerved towards him and came down steeply, one wing low. Unable to decide which way to run, Steve stood there, open-mouthed. For one gut-wrenching moment, it looked as if the whole caboodle was going to land on his toes, but it turned out to be further away than he thought. At the last instant, the pilot managed to bring the wings level. The glider hit the ground with a sickening crunch less than ten yards away from where he stood, then bounced back into the air, skimming over his head as he threw himself out of the way.

She-eh! Jack me! Breaking his fall with outstretched hands, Steve got a worm's eye view of the glider as it dropped back to earth. It cut a wide swath through the standing grain and came to rest sideways on, with its right wingtip only inches from the banked edge of the field. Apart from the broken skid, which had ripped an untidy furrow in the topsoil, the pilot had got the plane down in one piece. With only one and a half wings that was no mean feat.

Steve ran forward, ducking between the ragged strips of white fabric hanging from the trailing edge of the port wing as the pilot eased himself gingerly out of the cockpit. He, or rather *she*, wore a white headband and a loose blue tunic and trousers. And she had a livid slab of scar tissue down the left-hand side of her face.

'You wanna watch where you're going,' said Steve amiably. 'Almost ran me over.'

Jodi Kazan froze with one leg over the side and did a rapid double-take. 'Sweet Christopher! What the eff-eff are you doing here?'

'I was about to ask you the same question.'

'I got in first. Let's hear it.'

'It's a long story but, among other things, I came to see you. I promised I'd look out for you – remember?'

Jodi threw him an old-fashioned look and swung her other leg out of the cockpit. As both feet hit the ground

273

she buckled slightly at the knees.

Steve grabbed her arm. 'You okay?'

Jodi straightened up stiffly. 'Feels like my asshole's been rammed halfway up my spine.' Throwing off his hand, she cast her eyes over the stripped wing, walked round behind the tail boom to check the undamaged starboard wing, then knelt down to inspect the underside of the fuselage and the wrecked skid.

Steve peered into the cockpit. It was fitted with a woven cane seat, joystick and rudder bar, but, as he had correctly surmised, contained no instruments of any kind. He knelt down and took a look at the damage from his side. The laminated wooden skid was badly split and the supporting struts had been driven up through the underside of the fuselage pod. He straightened up and leaned over the nose of the glider.

'Could be worse. When that wing started to unravel I thought you might not make it. But I see you haven't lost your touch.'

Jodi raised her head but stayed on her knees. 'Just what are you after, Brickman?'

'Nothing.'

'Come on, I wasn't born yesterday.'

'I was just on my way to deliver some mail to the Heron Pool. I work around here now.' He smiled. 'Just like you.'

'You got some nerve, you know that?'

'Not really. I meant what I said back in the Big Open.' Steve looked over his shoulder and saw a small crowd of blue-and-white-clad figures running towards them from the direction of the Heron Pool. They were still a long way off. He turned back to Jodi, his voice taking on a new urgency. 'Listen, we don't have much time. Who else was up there with you?'

'Kelso –'

'How about that? Good ol' Dave . . .'

'Don't count on it. If you run into him stand well back. He still blames you for being here.'

'Who was the third man?'

'You mean Number One.' Jodi was unable to resist a smile. 'He's the guy who runs the project.' She paused, then let him have it. 'Goes by the name of Steve Brickman.'

Steve took the news in his stride. 'Good. Any more wingmen on the project?'

Jodi, who had been hoping to see Steve knocked sideways, was completely thrown by his matter-of-fact reply. 'No . . . ' She got to her feet while her brain was putting the rest of the sentence together: ' . . . just the three of us and a couple of dozen linemen.' She paused, still bewildered. 'I don't get it. You *know* about this guy?'

'Yeah. He's the reason why I'm here. His name's Cadillac. He's a Mute. You've heard of straights – this one's a super-straight.'

Jodi hid her surprise behind a sarcastic laugh. 'Really?' She cast her eyes over Steve's black and yellow outfit and the swirling skin patterns on his face and arms. 'And just what are you supposed to be?'

'Hey, c'mon – don't let's go through all that shit again. What you see is what it takes to stay alive. Underneath it's still me.'

Jodi eyed him suspiciously. 'Yeah? I've only got your word for that.'

Steve glanced over his shoulder to check on the progress of the rescue party. 'Wave to them. It may slow 'em down a little if they know you're in one piece.'

Jodi stepped clear of the glider and waved both hands across her head, looking at Steve as she did so. 'I really don't know what to make of you, Brickman. But I'll say one thing. You're certainly full of surprises.'

'Yeah? Well brace yourself. There's another one coming up right now.' Steve took a deep breath. 'I didn't give you the full story when we met up in Nebraska –'

'You bastard. Malone was right. You *are* an undercover Fed!'

'I'm not! I swear it!' cried Steve. He dropped his voice to a harsh whisper. 'But I *am* on an assignment.'

Jodi took a step back.

'I had no choice! They threatened to kill my kin-sister and strip Poppa-Jack! I *did* escape from the Mutes just like I said, but I made it back home.' He threw up his hands. 'Biggest mistake of my life. Thought I'd be a hero. Instead of which the shit hit the fan and I ended up in the A-levels! Christo! Can you imagine what it's like for one of us to have to live down there?' He paused. 'How far away are they?'

'About a hundred and fifty yards.' Jodi's voice had lost its hard edge. 'But they're not running.'

She's bought it. I'm in with a chance . . .

'I made a big mistake when I was preparing to escape from the M'Calls. In order to get them to trust me, I persuaded this guy Cadillac to help me put this plane together from some bits and pieces they'd salvaged from Fazetti's rig and that other guy's . . .'

'Naylor.'

'Yeah. Naylor. Anyway, this Mute agrees to help – on condition I teach him to fly.'

'Wowww . . . ' breathed Jodi. 'I bet the Assessors were thrilled to hear that.'

'I didn't tell 'em. But they found out anyway. The thing is, besides being a straight, unmarked Mute, this guy is also a wordsmith –'

'They're supposed to be the bright ones.'

Steve nodded. 'This one is more than just bright. He's got some of that Mute magic you've heard about but aren't supposed to believe in. Don't ask me to explain how it's done, but if you teach him anything, he's able to tap into your brain and siphon off everything you know just like sucking Korngold through a straw.'

'*Shee-ii-ittt . . .*'

'My sentiments exactly. Fortunately, no one back home knows about that yet. If they did, I'd still be in the A-levels. But after I'd done three months on the sewage detail, some high-wire gave me the chance to put things right –'

'Or else they'd shaft little sister . . .'

Steve spread his hands. 'I had to do it, Jodi.'

She nodded soberly. 'Okay, assuming I buy that – how does it play from here on in?'

'I have to find some way to lift that Mute out of here and get him back home in one piece. With his friend. There's two of 'em.'

'Sounds interesting. You planning to do this all by yourself?'

'No. I'm hoping you'll help me. For old time's sake.'

Jodi's eyes narrowed. 'Jeez . . . you've got a fucking nerve.'

'I know. You already told me. But let's stop pretending. You don't deserve to be here any more than I do. You're not a breaker, Jodi, you're a True Blue. If Malone's gang hadn't found you, you'd have made it back home – broken arm an' all.' Steve glanced over his shoulder at the advancing rescuers. 'Look, just think about it. And in the meantime, why don't you go weak at the knees so I can pretend to revive you and look as if I'm doing something useful.'

'I've got a feeling I'm going to live to regret this.'

Steve treated her to one of his winning smiles. 'What can you lose? If you don't like the idea you can always turn me in. I'm in your hands.'

'You're right . . . ' Jodi let her legs fold under her.

Steve ran round the nose of the glider and cradled her limp body in his arms. 'Trust me,' he whispered, patting her face. 'If we pull this one off we'll both be heroes.'

*

'I can't stay long,' said Steve.

'Don't worry, you'll be okay for a while.' Cadillac led the way into what he called his 'study'. 'I've fixed things with the head man. He's sent one of our Mutes down to the post-house at Wah-seisa with a message telling them you've been delayed.' He smiled. 'You offered invaluable assistance at the scene of an accident and are now answering questions that may help us discover what went wrong. So relax. Make yourself at home.' He swept a hand around the room. 'What d'you think?'

Steve made a quick appraisal of the interior. Sliding wall screens afforded a view of the neatly trimmed areas of grass and various other types of vegetation that surrounded Cadillac's dwelling place. The floor, on which they stood in stockinged feet, was covered with the ubiquitous *tatami* – rectangular straw mats that the Iron Masters produced in prodigious quantities and traded with the Mutes. A narrow raised section down one side of the room was fitted with storage space underneath.

The main floor area contained a low, box-type table and two sitting mats, a large drafting table set at an angle on trestles, a stool, a stand holding jars of what Steve presumed to be drafting implements, and a rack which held rolls of what the dinks called 'paper'. Apart from the drafting table set-up which indicated an untidy human presence, the room bore the usual stamp of stripped-down anonymity that Steve had come to associate with Iron Master interiors.

'Not bad.'

Cadillac responded with a dry, mocking laugh. 'Not bad! It's fantastic! Can you imagine what it's like, after all those years living on your hands and knees in a skin hut, to actually be able to stand up and *still* not be able to touch the roof?' He shook his head dismissively. 'I tell you – these people know what living is all about.'

The dwelling place Cadillac had taken him to lay outside the Heron Pool compound, some two hundred yards down the road towards Mara-bara. Set amidst shrubs and trees on a well-tended patch of ground, it reminded Steve of the stand-alone unit at the post-house where he had met with Clearwater and the Man in Black.

For some time now, Steve had been wondering if there was a 'hidden' Basic vocabulary that held the word-concepts to describe the things he had seen since entering Ne-Issan. Coming, as he did, from the underground world of the Federation where military

278

organisation and terminology shaped the lives and thoughts of everyone from the President-General down, Steve had been unable to give full expression to what he had seen and felt during his travels across the overground.

Even something as simple as the small collapsible huts used by the Plainfolk Mutes had been a new idea to assimilate. The wheelboats had been less of a problem. Although they were totally alien structures, they could be viewed as primitive, sea-borne wagon-trains and thus understood in terms of past experience. But the bewildering variety of Iron Master architecture which was the outward expression of a totally different lifestyle opened up a whole new world. Palaces, houses, pavilions, cottages, shops, markets, towns, villages and hamlets were word-concepts Steve had never encountered before, just as he had once been unaware of the existence of words, states such as 'love' and 'freedom'.

Meeting Clearwater had changed all that, and he was conscious that the memory of her stood between Cadillac and himself at this very moment: invisible yet as tangible and as disturbing as if she had been physically present in the room.

Cadillac slid open a wall panel, revealing a row of shelves. He took out a porcelain bottle of *sake* and two small bowls bearing the same glazed design. Placing the bowls on the drafting table, he filled them with a professional flourish and motioned Steve to pick one up.

They raised their bowls to each other and touched rims.

'To old times,' said Cadillac. His voice and face gave no hint as to whether he viewed them as being good or bad, but he swallowed the contents of the bowl at one gulp – an indication perhaps that he needed something to kill the pain or to give himself an extra boost in order to deal with his unexpected visitor.

Mindful of the tongue-loosening effects of the *sake* he'd drunk with Noburo, Steve took it nice and slow and

279

concentrated on reading his rival. He hadn't anticipated meeting Cadillac this early, and in this fashion, and wasn't quite sure how to play it.

Cadillac refilled his bowl, stoppered the bottle and bolstered himself with another big swallow. 'So . . . what brings you here?'

Steve adopted the same low-key approach. 'Ohh, various things. I brought you a message from Mr Snow.' He saw Cadillac's eyes flicker at the mention of his teacher's name. A guilty conscience, fond memory, a lingering sense of loyalty, it didn't matter. It was a gap in his defences that could be exploited.

'He sent you here?'

'Not exactly. He was worried about you. When he discovered you hadn't come back on the wheelboat –'

'You were at the trading post?'

Steve had a simple rule in situations like this. Stick to the truth wherever possible, deflect the awkward questions by appearing dense, save the lies for real emergencies. And if you had to lie, go for the big one – and frame it in a way that would exploit the weakest aspects of the recipient's character.

'Yes. That rig you and I built gave up on me. I never made it back to the Federation.'

'I didn't think you would – not without a motor.'

'No. Mr Snow told me you did a first-class job on that.'

'Yes. Even you would have been impressed.'

'I am. Anyway – there I was stuck in the middle of nowhere. Got picked up by some redskins. We holed up during the snows, then, sometime during what you call the New Earth, a whole bunch of us were captured by the M'Calls.'

Cadillac reacted with surprise. 'Mr Snow sold you down the river?'

'No,' laughed Steve. 'I offered to come and find you. He was worried about something you'd seen in the stones and –'

'I have seen many things in the stones,' said Cadillac darkly.

280

Steve ignored the interruption. 'He asked me to find out if you were okay, and to tell you that time was running out. When he learned you had decided to stay here – apparently of your own free will – it really knocked him sideways.'

Cadillac responded with a non-committal shrug. He poured the rest of the *sake* down his throat and refilled the bowl.

Steve, who was still only halfway through his first helping, couldn't understand how the Mute was still on his feet. 'Hey – don't you think you ought to go a little easy on that stuff?'

'Don't worry, I can handle it. Practice makes perfect, isn't that what they say? Besides, it's good for you.' Cadillac's voice had thickened noticeably, but his drinking arm and his legs were still steady. He raised his bowl. 'Drink up. There's plenty more where this came from. Just one of the many fringe benefits.'

'What are the others?'

Cadillac swept his free arm round the room as his lips reached out for the rim of the bowl. 'How many Mutes get to live in a place like this?'

'Not many, that's for sure.'

'I've got another room to sleep in, one for eating and entertaining, a kitchen, bathroom, you name it. Plus a couple of guys who cut kindling wood and look after the garden, a cook and what they call a scullery-maid, and four body-slaves who keep house, clean my clothes, serve my meals, make my bed, and lie in it.'

'Sounds too good to last . . .'

'On top of which I'm finally doing something I really enjoy. Something useful, demanding – that really stretches me. Y'know what I mean? And for the first time in my life I'm *somebody*. Anywhere else in this country, Mutes and Trackers are treated like dirt. But the Heron Pool's different. The people here respect me.'

'Glad to hear it,' said Steve.

Cadillac sank some more *sake*. 'Anyway, my work here's nowhere near finished yet. But even if it was, why in the name of Columbus should I give all this up in order to play wet-nurse to a bunch of snot-brained louts who smell like they just took a bath in buffalo shit?'

'Yeah, well, it takes all kinds. When we first met I'd have said pretty much the same about you.'

'Except I turned out to be smarter than the average Bear.'

'A whole lot smarter,' admitted Steve. This guy's ego was insatiable. Never mind. If praise was what he wanted, that's what he'd get. By the bucketful. 'Is that how you think of Mr Snow?'

'No. Of course not.'

'So what's going to become of the clan when he dies? You saw his death in the stones, remember? Right where it's due to happen.'

Cadillac shrugged off the question. 'Maybe I did, maybe I didn't.'

'Well he seems certain enough. He told me he only had a few more months to live.'

'All the more reason for not going back.' Cadillac's drunken defiance crumbled a little. 'Look, reading the stones is not an exact science. I'm just a new boy. I'm not infallible – any more than he is. Okay, yeah – I *did* see a lot of blood, sweat and tears in the stone. Death and destruction too. Mr Snow was in there somewhere, but so was the rest of the clan. And you put in an appearance too. But I may have mixed up two separate events – and the timing could be way out. It could be this year, or next – or ten years from now. Not that it makes any difference.'

'What makes you say that?'

Cadillac drained the bowl. 'Because that part of my life's over. And soon there'll be nothing left to go back to. They're finished.' He picked up the bottle and sat down at the low table, plonking the *sake* down in front of him.

Steve cast his eyes over the sketches and drawings on the drafting table, then lowered himself on to the mat facing the young wordsmith. 'Who are finished – the M'Calls? The Plainfolk?'

'I don't want to talk about it.'

Steve pushed his bowl forward for a refill. He didn't really want any more, but it meant there would be less for Cadillac to pour down his throat. So far, apart from the slurring voice, he was holding up well. But Steve had the feeling that the Mute might go out like a light at any minute. And he didn't want that to happen just yet. They still had a lot more ground to cover.

Steve raised his second helping to Cadillac's fourth, took a sip, and let it slide down gently. However well Cadillac thought he was doing, Steve knew he must be feeling threatened by his sudden arrival on the scene. And he knew the next bit would be like walking on thin ice. 'I'm sorry. I really messed things up for you.'

'On the contrary. Things couldn't have turned out better. If it wasn't for you, I wouldn't be here.'

'I wasn't talking about picking my brains. You're welcome to whatever's in there. I meant Clearwater.' Steve paused, hoping for some reaction. Cadillac's face gave nothing away. He tried again. 'I feel bad about what happened. You saved my life, offered me your friendship and . . . I betrayed you. It wasn't a deliberate act, but – ' He gave a helpless shrug. 'That's why I had to cut and run. There was no way I could hide my feelings for her, and . . . I was too ashamed by what I'd done to face you and Mr Snow.'

'It was meant to be. It was the Will of Talisman. He who seeks to be a true warrior must find the inner strength to accept these things.'

'All the same, it must have hurt.'

'For a while,' said Cadillac. 'But now I don't feel a thing.'

Yes, it shows . . ., Steve watched Cadillac knock back some more *sake*. 'Is that why she's no longer with you?'

'No. The Iron Masters separated us soon after we arrived.'

'Doesn't that bother you?'

'Why should it? I'm not in any danger, and as long as she can call on the power of Talisman neither is she.'

'Do you know where she is now?'

'Yes. She was handed over to your present employer.' Cadillac saw Steve's reaction and smiled. 'Amazing, isn't it? All three of us together again. So close – and yet so far.' He topped up his bowl of sake, but this time he spilt some on the table. 'One might almost think it was meant to be.'

'Yeah,' said Steve. 'Amazing . . . ' He got up and wandered over to the drafting board and took a closer look at what Cadillac was working on. Everything had been painstakingly drawn out by hand with the aid of straight-sided wooden shapes.

In the Federation, drawings like this were stored in COLUMBUS. The central computer that served the Federation had a vast library of drawings for every part of every machine that had ever been built. People with access to the right level could call up stored images and incorporate them in new designs right there on the screen, then transfer the information into fully automated machine tools that would make all the bits and pieces.

The sheets of paper Steve was looking at contained several rough sketches showing proposed modifications to a design for a small, lightweight steam engine. This had been drawn life-size on a larger sheet beneath, in three elevations, plus a cutaway showing internal detail. It was an ingenious design, but required a great deal of precision engineering, and it would take forever to get into even limited production.

That was the real problem. Time was the critical factor. They couldn't afford to wait around while the Iron Masters upped the level of their machine-tool technology. There were too many hands stirring the conspiratorial pot. The longer they were here, the more chance there was of something going wrong. With Jodi's help, and maybe Kelso's, he had to get Cadillac and Clearwater on that boat to Bu-faro. And to reach the Hudson in one swift bound, the propulsion problem had to be solved quickly and simply using existing techniques. Steve, basking in the glow of the *sake*, felt he knew the answer.

'This is a nice idea, but it's going to take too long to put together.'

'I know. I've got to come up with something soon, otherwise the Japs may start to lose interest.'

'Mind if I make a suggestion?'

'I doubt if I'm going to be able to stop you.'

'Y'know what you need?'

'Yes, another bottle of *sake*.' Cadillac hurled the empty one through the open screens into the garden.

Steve took another bottle from the wall cupboard and brought it over to the table. He refilled Cadillac's bowl, then sat down and topped up his own. 'What you need is an assistant. Someone to toss ideas around with. Someone reliable who can also take care of the nitty-gritty while you work on the big concepts.'

'Just who do you have in mind?'

Steve responded with a modest shrug. 'Why look any further? I know as much as you do. We managed to build Bluebird using little more than hope and fresh air. With a set-up like this, if we put our heads together we could really go places.' He raised his bowl. 'You'd get all the credit, of course. What d'you say?'

'I'll think about it,' said Cadillac. He managed to pour half of his fifth helping of *sake* into his gullet, then spilled the rest down his shirt front as his coordination went. An instant later, his forehead hit the edge of the table with a dull thud.

It was evidently a sound that his female staff knew well – and had been waiting for. A wall screen slid open and four small dinks, dressed in colourful ankle-length wraps, padded in on white-stockinged feet. They bowed respectfully to Steve, then took hold of Cadillac's arms and legs and hauled his senseless body out of the room.

Some warrior . . .

Steve poured the contents of his bowl back into the bottle, shouldered his sack of mail, and hit the road. It had been a strange encounter, like talking to a slightly warped mirror-image of himself. But provided Cadillac hadn't forgotten everything when he woke up,

Brickman, S.R. might be in with a chance. With plenty of soft-soap and hard work he would soon make himself a key member of the team.

As he passed the gates of the compound he wondered what was going through Jodi Kazan's mind. She had promised to say nothing to Kelso about the real reason why he was here, and Steve was 99 per cent sure he could rely on her. He felt he'd touched a responsive chord when he'd told her that deep down she was still a True Blue. Kelso remained to be won over, but that was not impossible. He just had to be fed the right story. All Steve needed now was the blessing of the Man in Black and the precious bundle of pink leaves.

And Clearwater. He needed to see her too. His first run from his new base had taken him along the shore of the lake with the island on which she was held. At the *ronin*'s camp he had made a rash promise to pay her a visit and, despite her pleas to him not to risk his life on such a foolhardy venture, it was a promise he intended to keep. On becoming a roadrunner he'd discovered that it was possible to 'go over the wall' during off-duty hours, but so far he'd been denied the opportunity. Since he had arrived on the scene, the pattern of deliveries had obliged him to spend his nights in other, more distant post-houses – putting her beyond reach.

The act of running swept away the stupefying effects of the *sake*. Steve felt a sense of elation as he kicked into top gear. *Yeah . . . All in all, not a bad day's work.*

*

A few days later, Steve found himself heading south again, along the western shore of Two Island Lake. In pre-Holocaust times, it had been known as Sudbury Reservoir. The lake, some three and a half miles long and a mile and half across at its widest point, lay on a north-south axis. Its meandering coastline was shaped like a floppy, high-heeled boot, like the toe of Italy, but nipped in tight at the ankle. Clearwater was housed on the larger island which lay in the crumpled leg of the boot, close to the eastern side where a small jetty had been built. The second island lay just above the slim ankle, where the opposing shores swung inwards to within some three hundred yards of each other.

Steve cursed his luck at being so close and yet so far. He had no qualms about swimming across from the west bank, but it was crazy to attempt it in broad daylight. There was also his present job to consider. If he lost that through being late with his deliveries and wound up shovelling shit he might ruin his chances of getting into the Heron Pool. He let off a string of breathy obscenities and ran on down the trail that led to Wunasaka, the first of several mail-drops he would make on the way to Nyo-poro.

Near the ankle of the lake, the trail swung away from the shore and climbed through a stand of tall pines. The morning sun cast slanting shafts of light and shadow across his path, turning the red grass into pools of fire. Motes of dust and pollen, caught in the golden beams, drifted aimlessly through the air like newborn fireflies mesmerised by the beauty of the world around them.

This was one of the riches of the overground; the play of light and shadow, varying in colour and intensity through the day, the month, the year. In the Federation, there was an artificial twilight but there were no shadows, no cool dark corners, nowhere to hide. The illumination, which shone down from all sides, was cunningly balanced to match the essential components of sunlight but it could never replace the real thing, just as – despite the genius of the First Family – the man-made rock-roofed underground world with its gleaming marbled piazzas and cool landscaped deeps could never compete with the vastness and splendour of the overground, its beckoning blue-hazed horizons and ever-changing cloud-filled skies.

Steve's thoughts were jolted back to the present by the sight of an approaching rider decked out in red and black armour and with two tall narrow banners fixed to his back. A samurai – and from the look of him, no ordinary one at that.

Stepping off the trail, Steve went down on his knees, then bent forward, forearms on the ground, palms together, nose pressed between his thumbs. As someone ranked below the bottom strata of Iron Master society, he was required to stay there, eyes averted, until the samurai went past, then count *very* slowly to ten before getting up. To his surprise, the hoofbeats stopped before the rider reached him.

Oh-oh . . . what's all this about?

Glancing sideways, he caught a brief glimpse of the samurai as he dismounted and looped the reins of his horse round the trunk of a sapling about fifteen yards away. The animal, which was between Steve and the rider, blocked off a view of the Jap's face. Not that it mattered all that much. They all looked alike to Steve, and the rules about when and when not to make eye-contact made it even harder to tell one dink from another.

Steve turned his attention back to the ground and waited, all six senses finely tuned for the samurai's next move. His eye caught the moving pattern of light and shade as the Jap strode slowly towards him and, cutting across the sound of a moving suit of armour, he heard the faint, chilling swish of a long-sword being drawn from its scabbard.

Ohh, shit . . .

The shadow cast by the samurai stopped directly in front of him, darkening the grass on either side of his fingers to a deep blood-red.

Steve mentally invoked the name of Talisman but didn't move a muscle as the ice-cold blade brushed against his right cheek, then slid under his ear. He didn't need to see it to know that it was sharp side up. After pausing there for a brief, agonising moment, the tip of the blade traced a chilling line across the back of his neck and came to rest under his left ear. He didn't feel the cut as the blade was withdrawn, just the trickle of blood warming his skin as it flowed down the line of his jaw.

'So . . . how's it going, sport?'

It was the Man in Black. Only this time, he was wearing fancy dress.

Steve was seized by a reckless desire to look up, and an equally pressing need to discover what remained of his left ear, but managed to resist both. His bloodthirsty benefactor was operating on a hair-trigger, and the overall situation was so ill-defined, he could not gamble on being indispensable. The razor-sharp blade now hovering inches from his head served to remind Steve he'd already pushed his luck close to the limit. Easing his nose clear of his thumbs, he began to recount his chance meeting with Cadillac.

'Louder!'

Steve raised his head a notch, cleared his throat and delivered the rest of his story without further interruption, ending with his offer to help Cadillac produce a suitable power-plant for the flying-horses.

'And what did he say to that?'

'He said he'd think about it.'

'No hard feelings about your, uhh . . . previous encounter?'

'None whatsoever. He was quite pleased to see me. Especially now he has the upper hand.'

'I know the feeling,' said Toshiro.

Steve watched the armoured feet of his interlocutor describe a semicircle from left shoulder to right then back again, each slow step preceded by the angled tip of his long-sword.

'The "interests" I represent have given me the go-ahead to insert you into the operation. You are now free to carry out your sabotage mission. But first, before you wreck the Heron Pool project, you have to help make it a success.'

'Sire, the pleasure will be all mine.'

'Yes – I thought that might appeal to you. Are you sure you can make these craft work properly?'

'Once I get my feet under the workbench, I can have one flying under its own steam inside a month.'

'Good. That's very important. In fact, your life may depend upon it.'

You're telling me, thought Steve. 'May I beg to ask if our original . . . "understanding" still holds good?'

'And what was that?'

'Safe passage out of the country with Cadillac and the Mute woman who came with him – Clearwater.'

'Ahh, yes, well . . . that may be difficult to arrange.'

'I'll make the arrangements,' replied Steve. 'All I need from you is your personal assurance that the "interests" you claim to represent won't stand in the way.'

The long-dog's insolent manner continued to amaze and anger Toshiro, but he had now fully mastered the murderous impulse to kill him out of hand. It was deeply wounding to have to treat Brickman as if he were an equal, but those were his orders. For the moment, he was obliged to swallow his pride. If this self-styled 'mexican' managed to do what was being demanded of him it would humiliate and confound the Shogun's enemies and clear the way for Toshiro to gain what he most desired.

'Very well, you have my word on that. However, there is one other matter you will need to attend to. We require you to arrange the demise of a certain Nakane Toh-Shiba, the Consul-General for this region. He is also, coincidentally, the, ahh . . . custodian of the second individual you wish to recover.'

That too will be a pleasure, thought Steve. But if you ask me, it's no coincidence. He was going to have to watch this guy.

'If you undertake to get rid of him, I will make sure that the woman is delivered to you unharmed. Is it a deal?'

Steve gazed at the samurai's lacquered toes and weighed up the proposition. For someone normally accorded slave-status to be asked to kill a high-ranking Iron Master was pretty damned extraordinary. Apart from hinting at further intrigues he didn't know about, it seemed to indicate that the Man in Black and the 'interests' he represented had swallowed his story and were prepared to take him seriously. He was back in the game and, now that they'd asked him to do some of their own dirty work, had even acquired a little leverage. When added to the make-and-break assignment at the Heron Pool, it meant he had room to manoeuvre and the time he needed to put his own plans in motion.

Yeah . . . it was all coming together. But there was no point in going overboard.

'I feel honoured at being given such a task, but someone in my position is going to find it difficult to even get near a man who, by the sound of it, is a high-ranking official.'

'Don't worry, sport. When the time comes, you'll get all the help you need.'

They were the right words, but they did not have a comforting ring. Steve ached to straighten up, but decided it would be unwise. Better to keep talking to the grass. 'How soon do you want this to happen?'

A pregnant pause, then: 'The instructions I have received are quite specific. The Consul-General is to be taken up in a flying-horse. When it has attained the greatest possible height, he is to fall from the sky. His body is to be split and broken like that of a stray mongrel crushed under the wheel of a passing cart. This is the death which has been chosen for him. No other. Is that clear?'

'Yeah, sure.' It sounded like a real suicide mission, but this was no time to go weak at the knees. 'Dumping him overboard is the easy bit. It's getting him up there that's going to be the problem. First of all I have to get transferred to the Heron Pool. Once I'm in there I'm pretty sure I can put together a propulsion system. In fact I *know* I can. And once we're over that hurdle, it shouldn't be too hard to persuade Cadillac to let me get involved in the flight testing. So I'll have access to an aircraft. *That's* where it gets difficult. According to Cadillac, the Heron Pool belongs to the local domain-lord –'

'Lord Kiyo Min-Orota.'

'Right. Cadillac is in nominal charge of the project, but he's just a hired hand like the rest of us. It's Lord Min-Orota's people who really run the show. I don't have to tell you what the set-up is, you're part of it. If I can't look you in the eyes, they're not going to let me even breathe the same *air* as the Consul-General. But okay – let's assume for the moment they did – how do I persuade him to go for a joyride?'

'Don't worry about it, sport. When you're ready to go, he'll be there.'

The samurai's reply confirmed Steve's hunch about the identity of the man with his finger on the button. There was only one person with sufficient clout to order a Consul-General into the air with an outlander at the controls. The Shogun.

Yeah . . . better watch out, Stevie, he told himself. You're back in the game all right, but this is not like trading shots in a Shoot-a-Mute video gallery for a glass of Korngold. You're at the high-stake table with the big boys. The kind that eat people like you for breakfast . . .

The fact that the Man in Black had been less than forthcoming about the relationship between Clearwater and the Consul-General was proof that he could not be trusted. 'Promises to Mutes don't count.' Wasn't that what Karlstrom had said? You could bet your last meal-credit that this overdressed dink felt the same way about Trackers. Yeah . . . if he was going to get home in one piece he would need more help than Jodi or Kelso could provide. He had to enlist the help of a big gun. And there was one close at hand, eager and willing to be pressed into service.

Clearwater.

She might not be able to move mountains, but she had shown she had the power to rearrange large chunks of the landscape. He had to find a way to get her off that island when the crunch came. With her by his side there would be nothing to fear from Yama-Shita's boys or from the friends of the Man in Black. At the first sign of danger she would blow them right out of their socks.

The samurai's voice cut across his machinations. 'Okay. That about wraps it up.' His feet disappeared from view, then returned. 'You'd better have this. I'm sure you'd like to let your friends know what's happening.'

A slim bundle wrapped in black silk dropped into the grass a few inches from Steve's forehead. It could only contain one thing – the combat knife with the radio hidden in the handle.

'Are you serious?'

'Sure. You can tell them how well you're doing. We don't want anyone making a rash move at this stage, do we?'

'No, I guess not . . .'

'That stuff inside the handle. Is it possible to take that out and throw the rest of the knife away?'

'No. I can't explain how it works, but the set's powered by a layer of special crystals sealed into the blade.'

'Okay. Stow it at the bottom of your mailbag until you can find a better place to hide it.'

'Thanks,' said Steve. 'Any chance of getting my bladed staff back?' He already knew what the answer would be, but what the hell? It was worth a try.

The question triggered a snort of laughter. 'Are you crazy? That knife is enough to get you killed in under ten seconds flat. What d'you want to do – hang a sign round your neck?'

'You're right. Okay, forget the staff. Just give me back the bundle of pink leaves. I can't start work at the Heron Pool until I've washed this gunk off.'

'Don't have 'em on me, sport.'

Steve cursed silently. 'So when am I going to get them?'

'When the time's right.'

'I'm not going to be able to get into an airplane decked out as a Mute.'

'I know that.'

'Okay. How soon can I get a transfer?'

'I'm working on it.'

This guy's stringing me along, thought Steve. 'Are you trying to tell me there's a problem?'

'Nothing serious. It's just that, because of the "interests" I represent, I can't be seen to intervene directly on your behalf. To do so would compromise your position as a "free agent" – and might even endanger the whole operation. I have to work, ahh . . . obliquely, through my contacts on the Consul-General's staff and key officials in the main post-house. It's they who have to okay the move.'

Terrific . . . 'Let's hope they don't lose the paperwork. When will we meet again?'

'When it's necessary.'

'Yeah, but time's –'

'Don't worry. I know where to find you. Just stay cool, hang loose and keep trucking.'

Steve heard the curved long-sword whisper its way back into the scabbard, followed by the soft clack of the layered plates of armour as the feet walked away.

Keep trucking . . . What a nitwit.

Steve watched out of the corner of his eye as the samurai remounted, turned his horse towards him and urged it into a canter. The top half of the Jap's face was shadowed by the wide-brimmed helmet; the lower half was obscured by a narrow white scarf held in place by the plaited red silk chinstrap. Steve kept his nose close to the ground until the hoofbeats faded, then got up and rubbed the cramp out of his knees.

It had been another instructive encounter, but Steve was in no mood to hang around while the Man in Black inflated his already overblown ego by scoring debating points. Time was running out. Side-Winder's wheelboat would not be on the Hudson River run for ever and that trip to Bu-faro was a crucial part of the escape plan. If the Man in Black was unwilling or unable to move things along at a high rate of knots then he, Steven Roosevelt Brickman, would have to go it alone.

CHAPTER TWELVE

When Clearwater woke to find Steve kneeling by her pillow, she was neither surprised nor alarmed. Her subconscious mind, which had already registered his presence, inserted his image into the last few seconds of her dream, causing illusion to merge seamlessly with reality. Despite the fears she had expressed at the *ronin* camp, her mind and body had yearned to be reunited with his – and now, at long last, he was here.

Steve had towelled himself dry before entering the lake-house to avoid leaving any tell-tale tracks, but his skin was still damp and cool to the touch. Clearwater ran her fingers slowly along his arms and shoulders, then cupped his face in her hands and drew his mouth down on hers.

The chemistry was still as potent as ever. The touch of her lips and the warmth of her embrace brought the memories of their one night together flooding back. The desire to possess her, body and soul, and the inexpressible feelings aroused by her nearness over-whelmed his senses, sweeping aside all thoughts of his own safety.

Clearwater too seemed oblivious of the mortal danger he had placed her in. Removing one hand from his neck, she lifted the edge of the silken coverlet and silently invited him to join her beneath it.

Steve was sorely tempted, but managed to cling on to a vestige of self-control. He hadn't swum across the lake just to fall into her arms. Taking hold of her hand, he gently pulled the coverlet back into place to form a safety barrier, separating his naked body from hers. He knew as surely as the First Family were born to rule that once they touched thighs, skin to skin, he'd forget everything, including his name, rank and number. 'We have to talk.'

'Later . . .'

'No, *now!*' Steve grabbed both her hands to stop them from spoiling his concentration. 'Don't *do* that!' he hissed.

Clearwater lay back and contented herself with tracing the contours of his face and occasionally stroking his hair.

The last hands to slide below his waist had belonged to Roz, back in Santanna Deep, the previous year. They'd both crashed out through smoking some bad grass, so he wasn't sure how far things had gone, but he still felt bad about it. Roz had known about Clearwater before he'd got around to telling her, and he had an uneasy feeling that part of her mind was inside his own head right now.

Forgive me, little sister. This is how it has to be . . .

Steve gave Clearwater a quick rundown on everything that had happened since their midnight meeting at the post-house in front of the mysterious Man in Black, ending on the *sake*-swilling session with Cadillac.

Except it was not *quite* everything. He made no mention of his chance meetings with Side-Winder on the dockside at Ari-bani and Jodi Kazan in the cropfield opposite the Heron Pool, and he also kept back his latest head-down encounter with the Shogun's contact-man. That would come later.

'Listen, what are we going to do about Cadillac? I tried to reason with him, but he seems determined to stay here. He says he's got everything he ever wanted. Well . . . everything except you.'

'Did he tell you that?'

'He didn't need to. Why else would he be hitting the knockout drops? He's sinking the stuff like there's no tomorrow.'

'Did he ask what had happened to me?'

Steve hesitated. 'He knows where you're being held and who by but, uhh . . .'

'Did he say anything else?'

Steve chose his words carefully, 'Not very much. He, uhh . . . seems to think you can take care of yourself. But maybe that was just to get back at me.' He shrugged. 'Let's face it. Like I said to him, if I hadn't come along –'

'But you did. And it was meant to be. Cadillac knows that too. He read it in the seeing-stones.'

'Maybe he did. But he still needs something to help kill the pain.'

'The pain was there from the moment you left us. And it is a pain that I share, for I have no wish to make him suffer. But even if we had been allowed to stay together I would have been of little comfort. Our life-threads are no longer as closely entwined as they once were. One day he will understand why all this has happened. And so will you.'

'Yeah, well . . . I'm sure you're right. But I have to deal with Cadillac as he is here and now. He may not be hostile, but as long as he's within reach of a bottle he's going to be unpredictable.'

'So what are you going to do?'

'At the moment, that's up to Cadillac. He told me he'd run into a few problems building an engine, so . . . I offered to help him out. Listen, it's a start. If I can get close to him, maybe I can talk him round. Between you and me, I don't want to stay here a day longer than I have to, but it's gonna make life a lot simpler if he goes quietly.'

'What was his answer?'

'Well, he didn't say "yes", but on the other hand he didn't say "no". Despite everything that's happened he still seems eager to pick my brains.' Steve gave a low, husky laugh. 'By that I mean the few bits he hasn't picked already.'

'Are you angry about that?'

'Nnnaahhh . . . it makes things more interesting. Thing is, I was hoping you'd be together so that you could, y'know – persuade him. Make him see sense. But . . .'

'He no longer listens to me. He is ruled by the demons inside his head.'

'Yeah . . . ' We all have them, thought Steve. Perhaps even you have a darker side that I don't yet know about. This . . . thing that binds us together, this feeling I find so hard to control – where will it lead? Will it give us the strength to go all the way to the top – or will it destroy us both?

The coverlet was seductively thin, and whenever their limbs touched it generated a delicious electric current that made his body tingle from head to toe. Time would tell which way they were headed but, if she was to be the death of him, he could not think of a sweeter way to go.

Hey, c'mon! Pull yourself together, Brickman! Concentrate!

He edged away and lay on his stomach, heart and loins beating in unison against the quilted mattress. When he had quelled the rising tide he said: 'Listen. About Cadillac. There's something we have to agree on. If we can't persuade him to leave Ne-Issan of his own accord, then we'll have to make it impossible for him to stay here. D'you understand what I'm getting at?'

Pushing down the coverlet, Clearwater turned towards him and lay against his right shoulder. Steve felt her breasts touch his skin – felt her heart beating against his shoulderblade. She ran her hand across the base of his neck, then down his spine and put her mouth close to his ear. 'Do whatever it is you have to do . . .'

Steve locked his thighs together, pressed his pelvis into the mattress and tried to think straight. 'I have a plan. Well, a few half-baked ideas. Whether they'll work or not depends on what happens in the next few weeks.' He broke off and gasped with a mixture of pleasure and frustration. 'Hey! Come on! Lay off a minute. This is important!'

Clearwater's hand came back to rest innocently on his neck. His right shoulder was still sandwiched somewhat less innocently between her breasts, but as the rest of her body from the ribcage down was still under wraps, Steve was just about able to keep his mind on the *real* reason for his midnight swim.

Pretending not to notice what her tongue and teeth were doing to his ear, he told her about the offer made by the Man in Black: her life in exchange for the death of the Consul-General. The ear nibbling stopped abruptly. And when he got to the details of how Toh-Shiba was to die, she shrank away.

Steve hoisted himself up on to one elbow and looked down at her. During his swim across the lake the moon had been riding high in the night sky, skimming the silvered edges of coal-black, scudding clouds. It had been bright enough to cast a grey shadow in front of him as he moved stealthily towards the house, but inside the room it was too dark to see her face clearly.

'Does the thought of his death upset you?'

Her arms reached out to hold him. 'No. It is your life I fear for. When the time comes, let me kill him for you.'

'No,' said Steve. 'That could put you in danger. If something happens to me, you'll still be able to help Cadillac get away. But if we lose you it'll ruin everything. None of us'll have a chance.'

'But nothing will happen! Was I not born, like you, in the shadow of Talisman? Mr Snow told Cadillac and I that we were his sword and shield. His power runs through me!'

'I know. That's what I'm counting on. But it's vital we use it at the right time.' He kissed the tip of her nose. 'I appreciate the offer, but I'm going to have to do this the way they want.' His voice hardened. 'Besides which, it'll make me feel a whole lot better.'

Clearwater caressed his face. 'Oh, cloud warrior, you have no reason to be jealous of any man. Not even Cadillac has shared what *we* have known! The Iron Master has possessed my body – not my heart and soul. I have been an empty vessel, bereft of all feeling – yet he tells me I am the woman of his dreams. And that is what I am for him, a dream – nothing more. Most of what he does with me takes place inside his head.'

Steve listened keenly as she explained how she had used her powers to warp the mind of the Consul-General. It seemed like the break he was looking for. He returned to his dealings with the Man in Black. 'The trouble is, I don't trust him. That's why, when the time comes, you have to be with us at the Heron Pool. I can't tell you how, or when, but if I manage to do everything that's been asked of me, a truly prodigious amount of shit is gonna hit the fan. And about three seconds later, the Iron Masters are gonna come down on our backs like a landslide. Your earth-magic is the only thing that can get us out from under.'

'I will do whatever you ask, you know that.'

'Sure. But all that's still a long way off. None of us will be going anywhere unless I can get into the Pool to start laying the groundwork. And that brings us to the other problem. The dinks are combing the Ne-Issan for Trackers who know how to fly – and here I am decked out like a Mute!'

'It suits you.'

'Don't get me wrong. I don't have any hang-ups about it. You should know that better than anyone. I brought a bundle of those pink soap-leaves with me, but the Man in Black took them and doesn't seem too keen to hand them back. Do you have any?'

'A few – but not enough to clean your whole body.'

Steve cursed under his breath. Never mind – will you let me have them? You never know, it might just do the trick.'

'Do you want them now?'

'No, later. Listen, I've been thinking. If you're able to put ideas into Toh-Shiba's head, maybe you can get him to transfer me to the Heron Pool.'

'What as – a Tracker?'

'No, that's too tricky. I don't have any ID. They've got me marked down as a Mute, so I'll have to stay that way till I see how things work out, then maybe make the switch later.'

'So what shall I tell him to do?'

'Tell him to order an inspection of the post-house and

everybody working there – including the roadrunners. When he walks down the line, I want him to pick me out and have me transferred on to Cadillac's household staff. It doesn't matter what as.'

'Are you sure you know what you're doing?'

Steve laughed quietly. 'Don't worry. After three months in the A-Levels up to my knees in sewage I can handle anything Cadillac cares to throw at me. A little humility never did anyone any harm – and being able to order me around is going to make his day.' He took hold of her shoulders. 'I know it's asking a lot, but . . . can you do that for me?'

'I can try.' She reached up and clasped her hands behind his neck.

'Well, it's a lot better than the other ideas you've been putting into his head.'

'How many times do I have to tell you? He means *nothing* to me!' She tried to pull him down but he stayed there, unyielding.

'What about Cadillac?'

'We grew up together – like brother and sister. We shared each other's joys, fought each other's battles. I can never break the ties that bind us. But it is my strength he needs, not my love.'

Steve succumbed to the pull of her arms and lay down close beside her. 'There's so much I have to tell you –'

'Ssshhh . . . ' Clearwater drew the coverlet over them both. 'The touch of your skin on mine tells me all I need to know. Hold me, cloud warrior. There is so little time left for us to share.'

'But there are things I need to explain –'

Clearwater stilled his lips with a kiss. 'Let go of the world, my love,' she whispered. 'We are like two leaves at the Yellowing, borne away on the West Wind. Our lives were shaped long before our spirits were poured into our mothers' womb. The Wheel turns. The Path is drawn. And we must go wherever it leads us . . .'

Her body became one with his.

Hhooohhh! Jeez! Ohhh! Krriss-topher!

It was dangerously close to dawn when Steve clambered ashore at the point where he had left his clothes. Fortunately, he didn't have far to go. Two Island Lake formed the western boundary of the Consul-General's estate, and the main post-house, to which he'd been assigned, was situated close to Toh-Shiba's official residence. With time running out, he was forced to pass under the walls of the barracks where the regiment of government troops was quartered, but he managed to do so without being spotted and was back inside the roadrunners' bunk-house before anyone was up and about.

Roadrunners, like all Mutes in Ne-Issan, were not locked away at night. The punishment meted out to would-be escapees was so severe, only the foolhardy and those who had reached the limits of endurance attempted to run away. As the job of roadrunner brought the holder enviable privileges, it was assumed that no Mute lucky enough to be selected would do anything that might land him back on the dungheap.

The Iron Masters were harsh, demanding taskmasters but they were not totally heartless monsters. The captive Mutes, which they viewed as little better than animals, were allowed the same freedom to copulate at random, and those within the same workforce were permitted to form family groups. A slave-master might lose a few weeks of fieldwork during the latter stages of the pregnancy, but Iron-foot children were a welcome addition to the labour force. Not only were they delivered free of charge, they were a growing asset.

For roadrunners it meant that, in off-duty hours, they were allowed to fraternise with the female Mutes staffing the kitchens, bath-house and laundry, or any others whose services were available in the immediate vicinity of the compound. The lake was some four miles away – which put it definitely off-limits. Had Steve run into a watch patrol he'd have been in big trouble but, once again, his luck had held.

The following night, Steve got the opportunity to transmit his first message to Commander-General Karlstrom, head of AMEXICO. Using the tiny stylus, he ran the diagnostic program to check that the transceiver was fully operational, then keyed in his call-sign and details of his present position. This was followed by a summary of the information he had given to Side-Winder and the news that he had made contact with his two remaining targets. He ended with the three-letter code requesting acknowledgement of his transmission, signed off as he had begun with 'HG-FR', selected the appropriate time-interval, then pressed the Auto-Transmit key.

Knowing that the set would now broadcast his message at regular intervals during the next allotted two-hour transmission time between 2200 and 2400 and again between 0400 and 0600, Steve reassembled the knife, put it back in its hiding place, and went to sleep.

*

Unable to understand how a radio with such a limited range could transmit a message back to the Federation, Steve had concluded that the First Family must have installed secret relay stations inside Ne-Issan. In his ignorance, he had been thinking laterally, instead of vertically. Four times a day, when tracking an undercover operation, one or more aircraft belonging to AMEXICO, and of a type unknown to Steve, flew back and forth on preset flight-paths, with electronic ears tuned to the ground below.

The overflights had begun fifty years ago, but their presence in the sky had remained undetected by the Iron Masters because of their operating altitude. Flying five miles above the surface of the earth, they were virtually invisible from the ground, and they could not be heard because their specially designed slim wings enabled them to glide silently across the width of Ne-Issan from the Appalachians to the sea. Once over the water, they turned on their engines to regain the small amount of height they had lost, then began the return leg, recording messages from agents, fixing their locations, and transmitting instructions from AMEXICO.

*

The next day, Steve's delivery run took him westwards to the place once known as Springfield – a 140-mile round trip that meant spending three nights away from base. On the way back, he put on an extra spurt on his way into and out of Awo-seisa, so that he had almost forty-five minutes in hand when he reached the Heron Pool.

Once again, he was lucky. Cadillac was working in the house and caught sight of him through the open side-screens as he came up the path. As before, the Mute greeted him in a friendly but guarded fashion. Steve decided not to spoil things by mentioning he'd seen Clearwater and had spent a couple of hours in her bed.

Cadillac led him to the drafting table and they spent a short time discussing how best to convert the existing model into a two-seater. Their conversation was interrupted when Cadillac was called away to sort out some problem in the workshops. Promising to return shortly, he left Steve alone in the study, suggesting that he make himself useful by sketching out his ideas for the conversion.

Steve did so, but he also took the opportunity to remove the radio-knife from its hiding place beneath the lining at the bottom of his mailbag. Checking the memory store, he found a brief congratulatory message from Karlstrom acknowledging receipt of his transmission.

The message also included an offer of assistance and the chilling line: 'DON'T WORRY IF OBLIGED MAINTAIN LONG PERIOD RADIO SILENCE/YOUR KIN-SISTER ROZ IS HELPING US KEEP TRACK OF YOU/MIKE X-RAY ONE' – Karlstrom's call-sign. It was a timely reminder that the lives of Roz and his guard-parents still hung in the balance. And if his kin-sister was still reading him in moments of stress and high emotion as well as she had done before, it also meant that the First Family had him by the short hairs.

Steve hurriedly keyed in another message requesting some background data and scientific formulae he required, selected Auto-Transmit, wrapped up the knife and hid it at the back of one of the floor storage units. It was an optimistic move based on the firm belief that he would soon be working alongside his rival, and also a precautionary measure. The data would be of no use unless he got to the Heron Pool and now that he'd made contact, there was no point in risking his neck by keeping the knife in his possession. AMEXICO knew where he was, and if they wanted to know what he was up to, all they had to do was ask Roz.

How much had she told them? The thought that the First Family were using her to reach into his mind made him feel like a trapped animal. He cursed his stupidity for letting his own, similar power fall into disuse. But it was worse than that; he had deliberately suppressed it. The ability to 'connect' had been part of their unique togetherness. But in growing up, he had tried to grow apart from Roz, had tried to build a wall between them behind which he could plan and scheme in secret. All he had succeeded in doing was to build a cage that his mind could not get out of, while hers was still able to slip in through the bars.

Well done, Brickman. There was a lesson in there somewhere, just as there was something to be learned from being painted up like a Mute while Cadillac and Clearwater passed themselves off as Trackers. The reversal in their roles had struck him forcibly during the brief moment he had spent in her arms. It showed that, in the final analysis, it was not the colour of the skin that mattered, but the person underneath.

On his return to the post-house, Steve found himself caught up in the frenzied preparations for a tour of

305

inspection by the Consul-General. He felt a surge of excitement. Had Clearwater worked her magic – or had all this been planned long ago? He would only know for sure when Toh-Shiba walked down the line and gave him his marching orders.

All the roadrunners were mobilized to help with the cleaning, and extra labour was drafted in to sweep and scrub, scrape and polish. Every speck of loose dirt and rubbish was carefully removed from the post-house yard, hollows and car-ruts were filled, the gate was freshly painted, signs and emblems refurbished. Walls were cleaned – even the tiled roofs were washed down, and in the laundry, the team of Mute women worked through the night preparing spotless sets of uniforms and bedding to be worn and displayed in the roadrunners' bunkhouse.

On the following day, three hours before the Consul-General was due, the post-master and his senior clerks emerged, impeccably dressed in their best clothes, and inspected every inch of the post-house and the other ancillary buildings within its official boundaries. The Chinese and Korean staff who made up the middle and lower echelons of the organisation stood like statues at their usual place of work, moving only to bow from the waist when the party of Japs came upon them.

Satisfied that everything was as it should be, the clerks and roadrunners were ordered to assemble in the yard. The Mute washerwomen, cooks and cleaners were told to stay indoors and keep out of sight until it was all over.

At the appointed hour, the post-master and his six senior clerks positioned themselves facing the gateway. Behind them, the rest of their staff stood in three ranks with their toes touching the rear edge of a line of straw mats. With a sudden flourish of unseen trumpets, Nakane Toh-Shiba swept into the yard on horseback, escorted by ten mounted samurai and a troop of foot-soldiers. The senior staff bowed from the waist, the lower echelons went down on their knees and bowed their heads and the roadrunners put their noses to the ground.

Toh-Shiba dismounted along with five of his samurai

and strode forward to meet the post-master. The other riders stayed watchfully in their saddles while the troop commander deployed the foot-soldiers around the yard and outside the gate. The Consul-General's life was not in danger – as far as anyone knew. All senior government officials travelled with armed escorts, no matter how friendly the local domain-lord might be. With errant bands of *ronin* looking for ransom opportunities, one could never be too careful.

Having bowed the requisite number of times, the post-master greeted Toh-Shiba in the usual effusive manner, but his words were aimed at the samurai who stood between them. Since Toh-Shiba was a high-ranking nobleman *and* related by marriage to the Shogun, it would have been an unthinkable breach of etiquette to have spoken to him directly. The samurai had no need to repeat what was said; he was merely the conduit through which superior and inferior could address each other. Toh-Shiba made a perfunctory reply via the same circuitous route and accepted the offer of refreshments. A tray of cool drinks was produced and offered with great ceremony.

What a way to run a country! thought Steve. If they waste as much time as this when a war is on, it'll be a pushover.

A barked command in Japanese caused the lower ranks to rise and stand with heads bowed. A clerk who was fluent in Basic ordered the roadrunners to sit back on their heels, hands on thighs, chin on chest. Accompanied by the post-master, Toh-Shiba and his escort inspected the two lines of clerks, each one bowing from the waist as the Consul-General reached him.

Nakane Toh-Shiba was above average height for an Iron Master and, while not exactly fat, was quite heavily built. The broad-shouldered, padded kimono he was wearing made it hard to gauge his physique accurately, but he had plump short fingers and a pudgy face. Steve, who had been studying his target out of the corner of his eyes, decided the Consul-General looked pampered and overfed.

Despite his bulk, Toh-Shiba was light on his feet and moved with regal assurance – as well he might. Like all of the high ranking Japs, he wore a wig of Mute hair with the usual samurai top-knot, and he had a small funny-looking hat perched on the front of his head. Since Steve had never seen one like it during his travels he concluded it must signify Toh-Shiba's rank – which it did.

The Consul-General's party turned towards the line of kneeling roadrunners.

This is it! thought Steve. But it wasn't. He waited until the last moment before putting his nose on the mat, but Toh-Shiba strode past followed by his samurai-bodyguard and the post-master.

Shrill, simultaneous commands from the senior clerks sent the staff scurrying away to their posts – a move that had already been rehearsed several times. Steve and the other roadrunners formed their usual line along the veranda to the left of the post-house door. Thanks to his position near the end of the line in the yard, this move put Steve close to the entrance. But once again, in deference to their visitor, they were required to kneel and touch the floor with their noses as the Consul-General's party went inside to view the postal clerks going about their work.

With Toh-Shiba's disappearance, the roadrunners were allowed to sit on the log bench. *Shit*! Steve cursed his luck and vented his frustration by slamming a fist against his open palm. Once again, the fat-fingered dink had walked past without giving the line of Mutes a second glance. So much for Mute magic. If Clearwater had failed to do something as simple as this, she might not be able to deliver when the *real* crunch came. What a pill! And just when he needed to show the Man in Black he could manage without him!

*

Within fifteen minutes of entering the post-house, Toh-Shiba – who had begun to wonder what he was

308

doing there in the first place – had seen and heard more than enough about the receipt and onward transmission of private and official documents. The Consul-General did not believe in cluttering his head with knowledge of procedures that his staff were expected to know about and deal with.

As a nobleman, Toh-Shiba had never once in his life concerned himself with the problems of laundering; he merely expected to find a clean set of clothes laid out for his use whenever they might be required. It was the same with letters: you ordered them written, applied your seal, and they were delivered. What happened to them between leaving your hand and reaching that of the recipient was the concern of lesser mortals – such as the obsequious, tiresome pip-squeak now hovering at his elbow.

Toh-Shiba, who had been languidly fanning himself to alleviate the late summer heat, snapped the fan shut against his left palm; a signal to his aide-de-camp that he wished to leave – without delay. The samurai silenced the post-master with a raised hand and announced that the visit had been most instructive. His master was extremely pleased with the alertness and dedication of the postal-staff. Et cetera, et cetera . . .

The post-master and his clerks hurried on to the veranda, and bowed Toh-Shiba's party out of the post-house. In doing so, they blocked his view of the roadrunners, but, as he descended the steps and moved towards his waiting horse, the Consul-General was aware of something niggling away inside his brain. It was something he had intended to do – connected with his visit to the post-house – but for the life of him he couldn't remember what it was.

The mental pressure to perform some action built up rapidly and was translated into a stabbing pain. Toh-Shiba shook his head in an effort to clear it, then mounted his horse. His samurai guards followed suit, forming up around him with their colleagues.

Steve's heart sank.

Toh-Shiba gathered the reins and wheeled his horse. The pain inside his skull reached a new crescendo, causing one hand to fly to his forehead. An image of a golden-haired Mute appeared before his inner eye and, as he recalled the real reason for his visit, the stabbing pains eased a little. With a cry of exasperation, he pulled his horse's head round and urged it back towards the veranda.

The post-master and his senior clerks wavered uncertainly as they tried to divine the reason for the Consul-General's sudden change of mood and direction. The roadrunners, who'd been on their knees since his exit from the post-house, hurriedly got their heads down as the horse stopped with its nose almost touching the rail.

Toh-Shiba, the pain in his head now fading fast, cast his eyes along the line of Mutes then pointed his baton at Steve and shouted rapidly in Japanese. 'That grass-monkey, third from the door! I want him dismissed from the postal service! Immediately! Is that understood?'

'H-H-H-Has his conduct d-d-displeased my n-n-noble lord in any way?' stammered the trembling post-master. 'If so, I will p-p-per-personally ensure he is s-s-severely punished.'

'Not necessary,' barked Toh-Shiba. 'I just don't like the colour of his hair. Get him out of here.'

Steve didn't have a clue what was going on until he was hauled to his feet and hustled away as the post-master, who was now bowing at two-second intervals, launched into a breast-beating apology for his inexcusable careless-ness in the selection of ancillary staff.

Toh-Shiba surveyed the remaining roadrunners, all of whom had dark brown or black hair. 'That looks much better.' The pain in his head was almost gone. 'The individual you have just removed is to be sent to the Heron Pool as house-slave to the cloud warrior. See to it and send me written confirmation.'

The post-master assured him, via his aide-de-camp, that his order would be complied with instantly.

Toh-Shiba nodded with satisfaction and rode off

towards the gate feeling strangely elated.

The post-master and his senior clerks kept their heads down until the last foot-soldier had disappeared, then broke ranks with sighs of relief. No one could fathom why the Consul-General had acted in such a bizarre fashion. A brainstorm perhaps; theirs was not to reason why. The roadrunner unit could easily be brought back to full strength. Meanwhile, there was a small score to be settled. The post-master instructed a clerk to bring him a whipping-cane. The Consul-General had dismissed his offer to punish severely the yellow-haired Mute. His wishes would be obeyed. The Mute would only be punished *moderately* – for being the cause of such unwarranted anxiety.

Steve contrived to look suitably downcast as he stripped and handed in his uniform, mailbag and roadrunner's gorget. A slave-tag was attached to his arm and a 'yellow card' to cover his move down the road was hung round his neck. The clothes he was given consisted of a worn, loose grey tunic and trousers, an old pair of sandals with wafer-thin soles and a straw hat. The jute poncho and cotton quilt issued to Mute slaves were rolled into a bundle for him to carry under his arm. In terms of status and appearance he had slipped back to the bottom rung of the ladder, but it didn't matter. Clearwater had shown that her skills as a summoner were as potent as ever. And thanks to her, he was on his way.

What he hadn't bargained for was his going-away present from the post-master. As Steve bowed himself out backwards through the door, trying hard not to smile, he was seized by several pairs of hands, held down over the rail of the veranda and given a salutary thrashing that left him shaking and breathless but stopped short of drawing blood.

*

'Rockets,' said Steve.

Cadillac, who was seated at the drafting table, stared down at him with a puzzled frown.

311

Steve, who had been on his hands and knees sweeping the straw-matted floor, laid his brush and pan aside and adopted a cross-legged position. 'You've been to the trading post, haven't you?'

'Yes, last year.'

'Didn't the wheelboats launch any? Mr Snow told me they do it every time they set sail.'

'They sent up burning arrows which burst, and showered down coloured fire,' admitted Cadillac.

'They're called rockets – and they used green ones that didn't burst to signal where you had to land when you flew to Ne-Issan . . .'

'How did you know about that?'

'Clearwater told me. When we were being held by the *ronin*.'

'I still don't see what you're getting at.'

'What you saw was a firework display. Pyrotechnics. Behind those pretty coloured lights is a combination of chemistry and physics. A force exerted in one direction produces an equal and opposite force in the other direction. It's called "thrust".'

'I know about that,' interjected Cadillac. 'It's what the engines of your Skyhawks generate.'

'Exactly,' said Steve. 'Well, the same propellant charge that pushes up those rockets can be used to put your flying-horses into the air. All we need is a bigger rocket that packs more punch.'

'Yeah . . . I see what you mean.' Cadillac mulled the idea over, then eyed Steve. 'How come I didn't think of that?'

'You just did. I only sweep the floors around here.' Steve waited for a more positive reaction. If someone had handed him an idea like that on a plate he'd have been turning cartwheels. But Cadillac just sat there. 'You don't look convinced.'

'No, it's not that. I can see it has possibilities, but . . . won't it be dangerous?'

'Not as dangerous as sitting here on the ground. You said yourself that Min-Orota was showing signs of impatience. If he decides to pull the plug – ' Steve swept a hand round the study – 'you can kiss goodbye to all this.'

'Don't remind me . . .'

'There are risks, obviously. We just have to make sure we get the mixture right. We bench-test small batches of it first, then find a lightweight container that'll hold several pounds of the stuff. Some kind of tube, sealed at one end. And it must be fireproof, otherwise we could find ourselves with flames coming out of our ass.

'We then attach the tube – we'll probably need several – to one of your ground trolleys. We load the trolley with stones to represent the weight of aircraft and pilot, light the blue touch paper and, uhh . . . see what happens. What we want is a fast even burn. But not too fast. We don't want to rip the wings off.'

'No . . .'

'It's an ideal solution. It'll require a little ingenuity on our part, but it uses available materials, basic engineering skills and – best of all – won't require any major alterations to your existing airframe. We can just attach them to the underside of the fuselage pod and use a booster on the launching trolley.'

'Launching trolley?'

'The ground trolley you use for wheeling the planes into the hangar. We just strengthen it a little.'

'But this propellant charge –'

Steve tapped his forehead. COLUMBUS had come up with the data he needed. 'Don't worry, it's all up here. Ingredients, proportions, mixing procedures, binding agents . . . ' He paused as he saw Cadillac's expression. 'I'll need your help, of course.'

The Mute responded with a huffy laugh. 'Looks like you've got it all worked out.' He clearly didn't like being upstaged.

Steve threw in a large dollop of soft-soap. 'Sure. I know what needs to be done. But at the moment, it's just words. Hot air. Nothing can happen unless Min-Orota agrees to provide us with the materials we need. And *you* are the only one who can arrange that.'

'Yes,' said Cadillac. 'And I can also arrange to have you shipped out of here. So watch your step.'

Steve acknowledged this with a mocking bow and went back to sweeping the floor.

*

As Steve had anticipated, Cadillac had been unable to resist this opportunity to cut him down to size. Now that he was clear-skinned he had the upper hand, and he was not going to let Steve forget it. But in any case, the rules concerning the treatment of Mutes were already well established. Steve was obliged to sleep outside the house in a small, low wooden shack and, since he had no means with which to prepare his own food, his meals were placed outside the kitchen door by Cadillac's Thai domestic staff.

Thais, who ranked below Vietnamese and just above the slave population, came perilously close in the eyes of their Japanese overlords to being non-persons themselves. They were, nevertheless, notionally superior to captive Trackers, but, for the eight working in the house, they were at Cadillac's beck and call just as Steve was. The Thais were able to cope with this because, first, they did not have a lot of 'face' to lose and, second, they were not really serving Cadillac but Lord Min-Orota. And Steve didn't mind being treated like dirt, because things were working out just fine. Cadillac had a long way to fall. Oh, yes. When he hit the ground, they'd hear the thud in Houston/GC . . .

Rising at cock-crow – a feathered alarm-system widely used in Ne-Issan to rouse the lower orders – Steve was required to perform several menial tasks before being given breakfast. The list of chores included splitting a set quantity of kindling wood and stacking it neatly by the bath-house, carrying away the previous day's ashes, and disposing of what was politely known as 'night-soil' – buckets containing urine and assorted faeces.

In Ne-Issan, nothing was wasted. All the kitchen

refuse went on to the dung heap along with the crap, to rot down before being dug back into the soil – just as the effluent produced by the Federation was processed and fed into the acres of shallow tanks that the Trackers used to grow soya beans and other vegetables.

After breakfast, and for the rest of the day, Steve became Cadillac's 'go-fer'. Bathed and wearing a clean set of brown clothes, he was obliged to follow the Mute everywhere he went like a dog on a short lead. When they were alone, working together in the study, Cadillac treated Steve as an equal. He was polite, friendly, willing to listen and eager to learn. But when they were with Jodi, Kelso and the other Trackers, or in the presence of Iron Masters, he became haughty and dismissive.

On these occasions, Steve stayed in the background and kept his mouth firmly shut. He knew Cadillac was enjoying every minute of it, but it was also necessary for him to act that way to avoid arousing the suspicions of the thirty-odd dinks who acted as overseers. They did not participate in the production process, they just looked over people's shoulders and generally kept a beady eye on what was going on. A group of clerks took care of the paperwork involved in the procuring of the raw materials – timber, mild steel and woven silk – needed to construct the flying-horses. Some of the accessories, such as trolley wheels and axles and woven cane seats, were built by local craftsmen and delivered complete.

After a week of running errands for Cadillac, Steve became a familiar figure around the Heron Pool. The area in which the Iron Masters were housed was off-limits, but apart from that he was able to move around with almost total freedom. Within days of his arrival he was able to build up a detailed picture of the operation and the overall layout of the site – knowledge that would come in handy when the time came to make their escape.

He also contrived to meet up with Jodi. There was no danger in being seen together in off-duty hours, provided it didn't happen too often and they kept their conversations short and sweet. Steve also had to be careful to keep his distance. Kelso was the only other person who had seen him coloured up as a Mute. As far as the rest of Jodi's male colleagues were concerned he was the real thing. If they observed him getting too friendly, it could lead to trouble.

'You amaze me, Brickman,' said Jodi, when they met. 'You come in as an illegal, row yourself into one of the best jobs going and now here you are working for the head man. How d'you always end up on the inside track?'

'Listen, I start the day emptying shit buckets. Is that what you call being on the inside track?'

'You know what I mean.'

Steve smiled. 'I got friends in high places.' There was no harm in telling her the truth. It was clear she didn't believe him. There were moments when he could hardly believe it himself. 'I had to get here. I meant what I said about escaping. Things are starting to come together. If it works, I'm taking off with those two Mutes I told you about. You still with me?'

'Yeah. Count me in.'

'Have you had a chance to sound out Kelso?'

'Not yet. I've been waiting for the right opportunity.' Jodi gave a quick laugh. 'Seeing you again has ruined his digestion.'

'Maybe I'd better speak to him myself. Put him right about a few things.'

'I wouldn't do that,' said Jodi. 'From the noises he's been making I think he'd still like to get you down a dark alley. But he can't risk it because you're working with the honcho. If he queered things, the other guys would take him apart.'

'Has he told the others I'm one of you?'

'No. And I haven't told him you're an undercover Fed –'

'Jodi! How many times do I have to tell you?! I'm not a –'

316

'Yeah, I know. You were forced into this because they're threatening your kin-sister. Maybe they are, maybe they aren't. It doesn't matter. I'm not stupid, Brickman. You're never going to admit you're an undercover Fed because, officially, there ain't no such thing – right? That's how it works, don't it? Nobody knows for sure, so nobody sticks their neck out. They're too busy looking over their shoulder. But you and I know *exactly* what you are. So from here on in, don't give me any more of the wide-eyed innocent shit.'

Steve studied her as he weighed his reply. 'You're right. I *am* on the payroll. But it's true about Roz. They used her to force me into this.'

Jodi gave a wry smile. 'Don't worry. I won't blow your cover. You were right about me too. I *am* a True Blue. We've flown together and been bunk-mates aboard the Lady. You asked for my help and I agreed to do whatever I can. Try and remember if we ever get out of here.'

'I'm not sure what you mean . . .'

'It's very simple. I'm willing to go back – but not if they're gonna send me to the wall.'

'That's not going to happen.'

'Sure. But if the wrong signals start coming down the line, give me a chance to get away. That's all I'm asking. If I'm gonna die I'd rather do it up here where the sun shines. Okay?'

'You have my word on that.' Steve thrust out his hand but she didn't take it.

'I gotta go,' said Jodi. 'There's a couple of the guys over there who've had their eye on us. Wouldn't want them to get the wrong idea.'

Steve stood up and backed off. 'Sure . . . I understand. One last thing. If you're still not sure about me, deep down, why get involved? Why don't you just turn me in?'

Jodi shrugged. 'Maybe it's because guys who break the rules are more exciting to be with.' She gave a dry laugh. 'Crazy, isn't it? If I wasn't any use to you, you wouldn't

317

give me the time of day. Especially now I've only got half a face.'

'That's not true,' hissed Steve. 'I told you way back. I care what happens to you.'

Jodi treated him to a penetrating, sideways glance and laughed again. 'You wanna know something, Brickman? Not that it makes any difference but – I don't think you've ever really cared about anybody in your whole life.'

Steve watched her walk away. His chest felt like an empty, frozen cave. She's *wrong*! he told himself. He recalled what Donna Monroe Lundkwist had said to him when they'd put the bomb in the barrel after the passing-out parade. Donna, his classmate and rival at the Air Force Academy, who had asked him to kill her as she lay paralysed by a crossbow bolt buried in her spine. She had been wrong about him too. It wasn't true. It wasn't!

And it was not female vanity that caused Jodi to remark upon her disfigurement; she no longer felt whole. The ideal of unblemished physical fitness was inculcated in Trackers from day one. They might vary in size, build and appearance but, seen en masse, they all looked as if they'd come off the same production line. There were no dwarfs or beanpoles. Everybody was strong, healthy, clear-eyed and well proportioned. Heroes like Poppa Jack, Steve's guard-father, dying gracefully from the inside out from radiation-induced cancer, were paraded in their wheel-chairs, but permanent invalidity did not exist. No malformed or brain-damaged infants ever emerged from the delivery rooms of the Life Institute, and it was an accepted fact that Trackers who had the misfortune to be severely disabled or disfigured through an underground accident or while on overground operations never recovered from surgery.

*

The proposal to power the flying-horses using rockets was conveyed to Min-Orota through the usual intermediaries. Two days later, Cadillac received a secret summons to

318

appear before the domain-lord. This was their fifth meeting and, as before, he was conveyed in a sealed carriage-box to the palace at Ba-satana then conducted via the back stairs into a small chamber reserved for private audiences.

From the knowledge he had gained by tapping into the Iron Masters' psyches, Cadillac knew their relationship was without precedent – and unlikely to be repeated. Face-to-face meetings between slaves and domain-lords were just not possible, and these covert assignations had proved to be the most convenient way of circumventing the restrictive protocols. To Cadillac, the fact that Min-Orota had gone to such lengths was a sign of the esteem in which he was held. His desire for 'standing' was so overwhelming, it never occurred to him that this esteem had a built-in time limit and had only been accorded for tactical reasons.

Seated between two of his closest advisers, Min-Orota – who had a good grasp of Basic – listened intently as Cadillac explained his plans with the aid of detailed sketches which Steve had helped him prepare. He then waited with bowed head while the domain-lord discussed the proposal with his advisers in Japanese – unaware that Cadillac had been quietly absorbing the language since his arrival in Ne-Issan and could understand everything they were saying.

When the three Iron Masters had concluded their deliberations, one of the advisers informed 'Brickman' that his proposal had been accepted. The necessary authorisations would be issued and the materials he required would be delivered to the Heron Pool. It was, said the adviser, Lord Min-Orota's desire that he commence work without delay.

Bowing low, Cadillac humbly expressed his deep gratitude – and silently blessed Mo-Town, the Great Sky-Mother.

*

As soon as the materials arrived, Cadillac and Steve set to work with the help of six Trackers who had been assigned to what had been grandly called the 'power unit'. Cadillac had chosen the candidates personally, unaware that Steve had made sure Jodi and Kelso were among those selected. He'd done this by priming Jodi with the basic facts of solid rocketry, and had told her to share the data with Kelso. So when Cadillac lined up his workforce and asked if anyone knew anything about rocket propulsion systems, they were able to raise their arms and step forward with confidence.

And whenever they ran into a problem that couldn't be solved on the spot, Steve promised to think about it overnight. The next morning, he always had the answer. Cadillac, who was able to absorb this new information as fast as Steve acquired it, couldn't figure out how Steve always managed to keep one step ahead.

The reasons were complex but the answer was simple. Cadillac was only able to gain access to certain parts of Steve's brain; he could not read his mind. As with the Iron Masters, the areas he could tap into were concerned with acquired knowledge: specialist education and training, language skills, behavioural patterns, social mores and information about people Steve had met – but not how he felt about them. It meant, for instance, that Cadillac knew about radio-knives but *didn't* know that Steve had one in his possession – and was putting it to good use.

From the moment Steve had begun to keep in regular touch with AMEXICO, Karlstrom had arranged for one of his highflying signals aircraft to orbit the Heron Pool daily, between 2200 and midnight.

Tucked away in his little shack, Steve was able to send a stream of queries to AMEXICO while Cadillac lay dead to the world, wiped out by another skinful of *sake*. After acknowledging the transmission with the instruction 'STAND BY/IMMEDIATE RESPONSE', the pilot automatically relayed Steve's messages at high speed to Rio Lobo, AMEXICO's headquarters in Houston/GC.

From there they were keyed directly into COLUMBUS. A few seconds later, the required information was being bounced off the radio antenna of the orbiting signals aircraft and down into the memory bank of Steve's radio-knife.

The same information was fed simultaneously into Karlstrom's personal video-communications network, and a message announcing its presence was flashed on the screen nearest to wherever he happened to be. This was done solely to keep him informed of what was going on. Karlstrom had no need to vet the questions and answers before they were relayed to Steve. COLUMBUS, whose virtually limitless memory also contained the records of every Tracker from the First Family down to the humblest zed-head, knew exactly what areas and levels of information 8902 Brickman, S.R. was allowed to access.

To Steve – who still knew nothing about the air link – the rapidity and efficiency of the service was a constant source of amazement. It was also a timely reminder of the power possessed by the First Family. There was no escaping them. No matter how far you ran, they would always have some way to reach you.

CHAPTER THIRTEEN

Since the licence to build flying-horses had been granted to the Min-Orota family on the understanding that the Shogun's representatives were to be granted unhindered access to the Heron Pool, the Consul-General was duly informed of the decision to develop a system of rocket propulsion.

Consul-General Nakane Toh-Shiba, whose interests were centred round the pleasures of the field and the flesh, reacted with only perfunctory interest as the news was read out to him, but when his letter reached Yoritomo's summer palace, the young Shogun was quick to spot the military potential of such a device.

Black powder had been manufactured for centuries, but up to now it had only been used for blasting in the mines and quarries, in rifle cartridges, and in the cannon that were employed – mainly by the Shogunate – to reduce the fortresses of rebellious domain-lords.

Designed for use in siege warfare, these large pieces were extremely difficult to manoeuvre, and in the decades of peace under the Toh-Yota, their use had been confined to delivering ceremonial salutes. Smaller cannon, such as those on Lord Yama-Shita's wheelboats, did exist, but in general artillery pieces were not favoured by the Iron Masters because of their limited mobility.

As might be expected of warriors imbued with the samurai ethos, they were temperamentally unsuited to long-range engagements with heavy-calibre weapons. The clash of arms in close-quarter combat was viewed as the ideal type of warfare and, as a result, the outcome of most battles depended on the martial skills of fast-moving formations of mounted swordsmen and archers, and lightly armed foot-soldiers.

Rockets filled with black powder were employed by military formations as signalling devices, but their primary use was as harmless entertainment. Vast quantities of these, along with other types of firework, were used to enliven private and public celebrations and religious festivals, filling the night sky with bursts of coloured rain.

But if a rocket could be made powerful enough to hurl a flying-horse and its rider into the sky, it could also hurl an explosive charge into the heart of enemy formations encamped, say, on a steep hillside – or even beyond it. And if such a rocket could be carried on the back of a foot-soldier, then hundreds could be launched in a single volley, delivering a murderous hammer blow that would leave the enemy dazed and demoralised. At which point . . .

Yes . . . This matter would have to be watched closely.

*

The message summoning the Herald Toshiro to appear before the Shogun reached him in the middle of a jovial dinner with Guard-Captain Kamakura. The good captain's wife and her five daughters had received Toshiro with their customary warmth and hospitality, lavishing their attentions on him from the moment he stepped through the door, and the news that he had to depart without even completing the meal – the best of which was yet to come – threw the women of the family into disarray. Tearful and downcast, they lined up to bend at the knee, bowing over his hand as they bade him farewell. Toshiro responded with the customary expressions of gratitude, then apologised extravagantly for being unable to stay long enough to sample the delicacies they had prepared. Had he known of the nightcap that had been due to follow the dessert he might have felt a genuine twinge of regret. The second youngest and prettiest of the Kamakura girls had been chosen by her ambitious mother to grace the Herald's bed. But once again her attempt to snare him had been frustrated by pressing affairs of state. And time was passing! Another year was on the wane. If the Herald eluded them much longer, the two eldest girls might have to be married off to low-born soldiers like her own well-meaning but slow-brained husband!

*

The news that field tests of the rockets were about to take place reached Toshiro soon after his return, at the Shogun's behest, to the domain of Lord Min-Orota. Because Heralds acted as the confidential link between the Shogun and his regional officials, a suite of rooms in the Consul-General's residence was kept at their disposal. The estate, which to all intents and purposes was government territory, served Toshiro as a base from which he would often emerge in disguise to meet with agents or to mingle with the lower orders. But the residence was also a home in which he had been made welcome by Her Highness, the Lady Mishiko Toh-Shiba, Nakane's long-suffering wife, and her three children.

Despite her husband's outrageous and insulting behaviour, she had never once uttered a word of complaint to her all-powerful brother, and maintained the same discreet, dignified silence amid those who were closest to her, concealing her distress behind a calm, serene manner.

Many took this as a studied indifference to her fate, but over the years Toshiro had discovered this was not so. The Lady Mishiko was desperately unhappy, and the Herald could not understand how anyone – even an insensitive oaf like the Consul-General – could neglect and abuse a woman who, besides being extremely intelligent, artistic and of the highest rank, was also tender-hearted, sweet-natured and beautiful.

It was a pity, reflected Toshiro, that the Consul-General would die without realising how blind he had been. It would have added a bittersweet edge to his fall. No matter. As the saying went: 'One man's loss . . .'

From one of his informants, Toshiro learned of the Consul-General's curious behaviour while inspecting the main post-house. The Herald could not fathom why the odious buffoon should suddenly have taken it into his head to move the 'mexican', but he was relieved the matter had been taken out of his hands. Toshiro was tied into an efficient network of informers but he did not, as he had boasted to Steve, have eyes and ears everywhere, and he was not able to move people around like pawns on a chessboard. He had been able to get Steve registered as a roadrunner because he appeared to all and sundry to be a Mute, and because the registration had taken place in the domain of the Mitsu-Bishi, firm allies of the Shogun.

Things were different here. Masa-chusa and Ro-diren were, in a sense, hostile territory, where the Herald was publicly received with the appropriate pomp and ceremony and privately viewed as a spy-master and *agent provocateur*. This was why he had to exercise extreme caution to avoid compromising himself and, by extension, the Shogun. Switching identities from grass-monkey to long-dog was not quite as simple as Brickman seemed to think. Only one person could have provided forged papers – Ieyasu, the Court Chamberlain: the one person Toshiro dared not turn to. Life was already difficult enough without becoming enmeshed in *that* spider's web.

Without realising it, Nakane Toh-Shiba had saved him a great deal of time and trouble and, unwittingly, had signed and sealed his own death warrant. If rocket power proved to be the answer, then the Consul-General would be among the first Iron Masters to take to the air. The letter ordering him to do so had already been written and was in Toshiro's possession – and he was burning with impatience to hand it over.

Two days later, Samurai-Major Ryoshi – one of the top military men in Min-Orota's household – called at

325

the residence to escort Toshiro to the Heron Pool. The Herald had no qualms about visiting the site in his official capacity. Unless he chose to make contact, there was no way Brickman could recognise him. Even if their paths crossed they were unlikely to come face to face; the mexican would have his nose in the dirt like all the other Mute slaves who worked there. And since Brickman did not speak a word of Japanese, he could not learn of his identity through any conversation he might happen to overhear.

Shigamitsu, the samurai-captain in charge of the Heron Pool, greeted the two men deferentially and, after a brief ceremony of welcome, led them past the workshops to where the first of three weighted launching trolleys stood at the edge of the flying-field.

A fifteen-foot section of wing and a beam carrying a crude tail assembly had been mounted on timber struts to simulate the aircraft the trolley would later hold. The front axle had been widened to give greater stability. The vehicle was driven by four rockets encased in reusable tubes made of rolled brass with soldered and riveted joints. The tubes – about two feet long and three inches in diameter – were arranged in pairs, one above the other, and linked together by a short length of safety-fuse.

Toshiro, Ryoshi and the other Japs from Ba-satana inspected the vehicle closely. Its creator, a dark-haired long-dog who knelt submissively near by, did not rate a second glance. When Shigamitsu had dealt with their questions, the long-dog sought his permission to proceed with the tests. Shigamitsu referred the question to the Herald and Ryoshi with the usual elaborate courtesy, then, upon receiving their assent, invited them to watch the proceedings from a safe distance.

The dark-haired long-dog applied a burning taper to the fuse. Two more slaves seized the sides of the trolley and ran it forward. The first pair of rockets flared into life. *Shwaahh-pa-POWW!* Long searing tongues of flame erupted from the necked ends of the tubes. The

326

stub-winged trolley went racing across the field, leaving two thin plumes of smoke in its wake.

Ppa-ppPOWW! The second pair of rockets ignited. The speed of the trolley increased. A cry went up from the long-dogs gathered at the doors of the workshops as it hit a bump and became momentarily airborne, quickly followed by a groan as it dropped at an awkward angle, tore off the left front wheel, then cartwheeled several times before finally collapsing in a mangled heap.

Toshiro and Ryoshi brushed aside the Heron Pool commander's abject apologies. The demonstration had shown that the propulsion system worked. A second trolley, rigged with the same rudimentary wing and tail, was wheeled out. Several more dressed stones were added to increase the weight, and the test was repeated. This time, the trolley veered wildly from side to side but stayed in contact with the ground. When the rockets burned out, the trolley thundered on across the grass and – to the great delight of the watching Iron Masters – exploded into matchwood as it hit the low stone wall at the far side of the field.

'Was that all?' enquired the Herald.

No. 'Brickman' still had a card to play. A third trolley was produced from the workshops, but this one was manned. In addition to the stub-wing and the tail perched on two struts at the rear, there were more struts at the front; a triangular cage in which a Mute slave was seated on a basket-weave chair. On closer inspection, Toshiro saw it was his co-conspirator – the disguised 'mexican'.

Hhhawww!

Via Shigamitsu, 'Brickman' explained that by means of a simple steering device controlled by the passenger's feet, the tail could be pivoted to the left and right. This third trolley only had one front wheel and this could be turned in the same direction as the tail when the Mute pushed the bar with his feet. The rear edge of the wing could also be pivoted up and down by moving the vertical stick set between the passenger's knees. This deflected the air passing over the wing and kept the vehicle on the ground.

Ahh-so . . !

The Iron Masters retired once more, the fuse was lit and the trolley was sent on its way. Toshiro watched anxiously as the first two rockets ignited. He did not want the 'mexican' to come to an untimely end demonstrating something that had already been shown to work. He had much more important things to do – such as disposing of the Consul-General. His Japanese colleagues, unaware of his private concerns, watched avidly. All Iron Masters were fascinated with the aesthetics of savagery. In peacetime this was expressed through their pursuit of bloodsports – from cock-fighting to hunting with spear and bow. For them, the climactic kill was an essential part of life, and they now waited with gleeful anticipation for the trolley and its rider to self-destruct against the stone wall.

Ppa-ppowww! The speeding trolley accelerated as the second pair of rockets ignited. Steve felt himself pushed back against the seat. The first static tests had not produced an impressive amount of thrust, but with the additives that AMEXICO had advised him to throw into the basic mix the rockets were now delivering a real kick in the pants.

The stone wall was now coming up at a high rate of knots. Time for the party trick. It hadn't been his idea, but he'd been obliged to go along with it in order to worm his way deeper into Cadillac's confidence. And it had better goddam work, he told himself. Otherwise they'd be shipping him out feet first.

The visiting Iron Masters and the motley crowd of unofficial spectators were unaware that, with Shigamitsu's agreement, a low, grass-covered ramp had been secretly constructed on the far side of the field. Situated close to the wall, it could not be seen from where Toshiro and the other Iron Masters stood. Steve applied a touch of left rudder to bring the speeding trolley into line with the ramp. He'd been keeping the stick forward to keep the wheels firmly on the ground but, as he hit the ramp, he pulled it hard back and found himself sailing through the air. This was the bit there hadn't been time to rehearse. Steve and Cadillac had been over the ground and agreed it was feasible. But only just.

A collective gasp of surprise left the throats of the invited guests and watching workers as the stub-winged trolley took off. Rising steeply like a heron from a marsh, it cleared the stone wall by at least twenty feet and continued to climb.

Beyond the wall was a narrow stretch of boggy ground spinkled with tussocks of long grass, and beyond that a large pond whose far end was fringed with trees. As Steve crossed the edge of the pond at a height of fifty feet, the last two rockets cut out. The trolley, whose glide characteristics were only marginally better than those of the humble house-brick, promptly went into a steep dive. Steve stood it on its tail to lose speed, then took a deep breath as it wallowed drunkenly out of the stall and went in more or less ass-first. *Kerr-SPLUNCH*!

The watching Iron Masters burst into great guffaws of thigh-slapping laughter as a huge cloud of spray rose into the air above the wall. Toshiro's enjoyment was tempered by his concern about the fate of his chosen assassin, but even he found himself smiling broadly.

Min-Orota's samurai-major, who had travelled with a ten-strong party from Ba-satana to watch the demonstration, turned to the Herald and gave him a comradely slap on the shoulder. 'Ha! If this long-dog can make carts fly like chickens, then you and I will soon have horses that can fly like eagles!'

'That day cannot come soon enough for me,' replied Toshiro.

Jodi and Kelso, who were up and running as soon as Steve left the ground, were the first over the wall. Jodi, like the Herald, was genuinely worried; with Kelso, it was more a case of wanting to be there when they picked up the pieces. His unforgiving half had been hoping to see that self-satisfied grin wiped off Brickman's face when he hit the wall; the other half had been tinged with grudging concern for a fellow wingman who had drawn the short straw. But the lucky sonofabitch had gotten away with it again and was now wading ashore draped in green slime. Behind him, the crumpled stub-wing floated in the middle of the pond, surrounded by a few broken struts.

They met Brickman as he stepped ashore with a cheerful grin. He had blood running down one side of his face.

'Go back in and wash that gunk off,' said Jodi. 'You smell just awful.'

Steve obeyed meekly.

'You must be crazy pulling a stunt like that.' Neither she nor Kelso had known about the ramp.

'You got it wrong, lady. I didn't volunteer. I was drafted.'

'Nyehh, what the hell, it worked,' growled Kelso. 'These birds are gonna fly.'

'Looks that way . . . ' Steve took hold of Kelso's outstretched hand and clambered back on to firm ground.

Jodi checked his scalp wound. 'You'll live.'

Kelso eyed him keenly. 'Kaz tells me these rockets were your idea.'

'That's just between the three of us. Officially it's all down to Mister "Brickman" – okay?'

'Yeah. I've been meaning to ask you about him. Who the hell is he – and why is he using your name?'

'Dave, I'd like to tell you, but . . . it's a long story and it would only confuse you.'

They picked their way back towards the wall through the tussocks of marsh grass. A handful of Trackers were gathered on the other side. Having seen he was in one piece and on his feet, they hadn't bothered to climb over. As far as they were concerned he was only another stinking Mute – and a nosy one at that.

Steve scrambled over the wall ahead of the two wingmen and skirted round the waiting linemen.

'Hey, Kelso! Make sure you wash that hand o' yours!' said one of them loudly. 'Touchin' lump-shit makes your fingers fall off.'

The others greeted this jibe with raucous laughter and looked expectantly at Steve, but he averted his eyes and ran limping across the field towards the workshops.

*

'Well done,' said Cadillac, as Steve stopped to massage his knee. The visiting Iron Masters had all departed. 'You okay?'

Steve grimaced. 'Yeah. I just twisted this leg a little. How did it go your end?'

'Terrific. They're over the moon. That lift-off put them in a really good mood. Ryoshi – the head of the party that came down from Ba-satana – is one of Min-Orota's top men. He says we can have whatever materials we need. They want to move ahead as fast as possible. All the plans under construction are to be completed. They're talking about putting on some kind of display for the Shogun.'

'Good. Did they say anything about drafting in more people to speed things up?'

'Yes. But they won't be Trackers.'

'Japs.'

'No. They'd lose too much face working alongside us. They'll probably be Koreans or Vietnamese.'

'Gotcha.' Steve tested his wrenched leg by putting his full weight upon it. It was still tender. 'Listen, while we're on the subject of dinks, I saw a horse tied to one of the hitching-posts out front. Had this black cloth on its back, trimmed with red –'

'It's called a "caparison" . . .'

Steve ignored the interruption ' – and there were red doo-dabs –'

'Tassels . . .'

' – hanging from the reins. Did you, by any chance, see who it belonged to?'

'Yeah. Toshiro Hase-Gawa. He's a Herald to the Inner Court.'

'Sounds important . . .'

'He *is* important.' Cadillac gave Steve a concise explanation of the Heralds' role, their position in the government hierarchy and their special relationship with the Shogun.

Steve listened intently. He'd asked because the horse, with its red and black trappings, was identical to the one he'd encountered near Two Island Lake. So the Man in Black was Toshiro Hase-Gawa, Herald to the Inner Court, one of the 'eyes and ears' of the Shogun – the top man in Ne-Issan. He really *was* caught up in a high-level conspiracy.

Once again his gut-feeling and that silent inner voice had enabled him to put it all together. It *was* the Shogun who wanted the Consul-General killed. And by using a lowly long-dog, he made sure no one would ever be able to point the finger at the prime mover. Neat. Steve was prepared to keep his side of the bargain to secure Clearwater's release, but what then? The Shogun, he imagined, merely had to lift his little finger and his people would be falling over themselves to ensure their safe delivery to the border. Except, of course, that, for the same reason they were using him to make the hit, they would not want to be seen doing so.

It would make things a lot easier if they could move under the Shogun's protection, but could he be trusted? How much did he know about what was going on? Had he, for instance, bought the story about the massive air strike that would be delivered if he did not return safely with Cadillac and Clearwater? The Man in Black was a tricky customer. He might be using his position as intermediary to settle a few scores of his own.

Fascinating problem. What was even more fascinating was the intimate knowledge Cadillac had garnered about the Iron Masters. 'Tell me,' said Steve, 'how do you know all this?'

'By listening to what they say.'

Steve looked puzzled. 'Are you telling me you understand their language? How the eff-eff did you learn to do that?'

'The same way I learned to build airplanes.'

'Unbelievable. Can you speak Japanese too?'

'Yes, like a native. And just for the record I can read and write it as well.' Cadillac checked their immediate surroundings, then uttered a fluent stream of gobbledegook.

Steve didn't understand a word, but it certainly sounded like the real thing. He shook his head in amazement. 'Why the hell didn't you tell me about this before?'

'You never asked. But forget I told you. Outlanders aren't allowed to speak Japanese. If they found out, they'd kill me.'

'Don't worry, I won't breathe a word.'

'Good. C'mon, let's go back to the house.'

'What about the ground trolleys?'

'Your friends can pick up the pieces. You and I have got something to celebrate.'

We certainly have, thought Steve. He found it hard to contain his excitement. Christopher! This could be the final break he'd been looking for. Ever since Jodi had told him about the yellow-card system and the arm-stamps, Steve had been trying to find a way round the problem of the paperwork. He had also discovered the small problem that Side-Winder had omitted to mention: slaves weren't allowed to carry money. The only dink who could procure their tickets was the Herald, but Steve was not about to reveal the planned escape route to anyone he was not totally sure of. And now, the Herald would not be needed. Steve pictured the whole thing in his mind. Yeah . . . it was brilliant. Cadillac could do it all.

*

Seated cross-legged at the low table, Cadillac pulled the stopper on a fresh bottle of *sake* and filled their cups to the blue line painted round the rim. He took one and toasted

Steve. 'To the daring young man in his flying machine.'

'Very funny.' Steve raised his cup in response, then took a heart-warming swallow. 'Next time, I want something with real wings on. Otherwise you can get yourself a new assistant.'

'You shall have it,' said Cadillac. He examined the inside of his cup thoughtfully, as if he was trying to work out why it was empty. 'Look, I know you took a tremendous risk, but it worked perfectly. I know how these people's minds work. When they saw that cart take off it really made their day.'

'Glad to hear it. It almost put paid to mine.'

'Yeah. For a minute I thought it was going to flip right over, but . . . ' Cadillac replenished Steve's cup and refilled his own.

Steve couldn't figure out why he didn't just drink it straight from the bottle.

' . . . you got away with it yet again. You're the luckiest man I know. Cheers.'

It sounded more like a reproach than a compliment. 'Don't lose heart,' said Steve. 'After a few more stunts like that it may run out on me.' He downed some more *sake*. He'd put on an air of bravado when he'd waded ashore, but his insides had been shaking like a Seamster working a jackhammer. The *sake* brought almost instant relief. He'd have to watch it. A guy could get to like this stuff. He laid his cup firmly on the table and held it there. 'So . . . what next?'

'That's easy. You helped me design that two-seater. I'm going to teach you to fly it.'

Steve stared at him for a moment, then laughed. 'That should be an interesting experience, but do you really think it's necessary?'

'Absolutely. You're going to take up the rocket-powered prototype. After all, it was your idea.'

'Yes, but –'

'It's very simple. Apart from myself, there are only two other people here with flight experience. Kazan and Kelso. I'm not going to put their lives at risk until the system's been properly tested – in the air.'

'And that's where I come in.'

'Exactly. I hate to say it, but you're the best man for the job. That's why I want you to take it up.'

'Okay, but why the pretence?'

It was Cadillac's turn to laugh. 'You're not usually this slow to catch on. Must be the *sake*.' Cadillac tipped his head back, drained his cup in one gulp, then banged it down on the table. 'You're a grass monkey, Brickman. Endowed with a certain, limited intelligence but basically an unskilled, untutored savage. Never mind. I have decided to take you under my wing – so to speak – and as part of your education I am going to teach you to fly.'

'Smart move,' said Steve. 'How many crack-ups am I allowed?'

'None. You're a fast learner.' Cadillac refilled his cup and toasted Steve for the third time.

'The average at the academy is ten hours. Better make it fifteen.'

'We'll make it twenty. You're not *that* clever.'

Steve raised his cup with a rueful smile and started to empty it a sip at a time. The ground tests had only used a short burn. The rockets they planned to fit to the flying-horses would last twice as long. But, unlike a normal power plant, there was no throttle and no cut-out. Once they ignited that was it. You just had to sit there and ride it out. Provided the acceleration didn't rip the wings off, he did not foresee any insurmountable problems. Not with the aircraft, anyway. 'This is all fine with me, but how about the dinks? Are they going to let you do this?'

'Do what?' Cadillac's voice was starting to slur.

'Teach me to fly. As you just reminded me – I'm a Mute.'

'I don't see what you're getting at.'

'Aren't the Iron Masters going to end up flying these things?'

'That's the general idea. So what?'

335

'Well . . . they don't even let low-ranking dinks ride horses. They're reserved for samurai – like these airplanes you're making. Won't they object to a slave becoming a pilot?'

'I don't see why they should,' replied Cadillac. 'Trackers are slaves too. Okay, they may be better educated and some may possess high-level technical skills, but the Iron Masters don't place any greater value on their lives. That's because there's not enough of you in Ne-Issan to form a useful workforce on their own – on top of which you can't reproduce yourselves. As far as the Japs are concerned, we're all lumped together at the bottom of the heap and we're all expendable.'

'Except you,' said Steve.

Cadillac greeted the proposition with a lopsided grin. 'Yeah, that's what I've been telling myself.' The bottle of *sake* clattered against the rim of the cup as he refilled it. 'But I heard something today which may oblige me to, uhh . . . cut short my stay.'

Steve waved away the offered bottle. 'Oh, yeah?'

'Yeah . . . I overheard Min-Orota's people talking as they were on their way out. If the flight tests using these rockets prove satisfactory they're going to send a group of samurai to Heron Pool for pilot training.'

Steve's mind swiftly grasped the possibilities this move opened up. 'Congratulations.'

Cadillac eyed him sullenly. 'They may be a little premature.'

'I don't understand. Isn't this what you expected?'

'That wasn't all I heard. The Japs who have been looking over our shoulders are all craft-masters.'

'So . . .?'

'Isn't it obvious? They're drafting in their own people to help us complete this first batch. When the samurai earn their wings they'll be in a position to teach others to fly.'

'Yeah, go on . . .'

'And they will also have learnt every detail of the production process. We could find ourselves surplus to requirements.'

336

All this was music to Steve's ears, but he couldn't resist clawing back a few points. 'Me and the other guys, perhaps, but not you, surely – after all you've done?'

Cadillac eyed him but he didn't say anything.

Steve could see the Mute was steadily drinking himself into insensibility, but he was still able to feel that little shaft drive home. Time for another. 'I'm surprised you didn't see it coming. Haven't you been reading the stones?'

'Not since I saw the pain and grief you were going to bring. You're bad news, Brickman.'

Steve kept it light. 'Hey, c'mon! That's past history. What happened wasn't my fault. "The Path is drawn." Isn't that what Mr Snow said? I'm here 'cause I'm trying to help. Why don't you grab a reading-stone and get an update on what's due to happen to us?'

Cadillac shook his head wearily. 'Won't work. I've looked, but I . . . can't find one.'

'But there has to be –'

'Oh, sure, they're here. I just can't see them anymore.' He raised his cup of *sake*. 'This seems to have dulled my perception.'

'Pity,' said Steve. 'Guess we'll just have to work round it.' He would have liked to know if they were going to get away – but on the other hand it meant Cadillac didn't have a clue about what was going to happen. It was better that way. If he was brought in on the escape plan, then had yet another change of heart, it would only complicate matters even further.

Cadillac tried to bolster his morale with another stiff shot of the pale yellow liquor, but he couldn't keep his steely-eyed act together. His voice cracked and his face crumpled. He leaned forward quickly and massaged his cheeks and forehead in an effort to hide his tears. 'Why is it my life always falls apart whenever you appear?'

Steve felt a twinge of remorse. 'You're reading it wrong,' he said softly. 'Your life's not falling apart. It's coming together.'

Cadillac kept his head down. 'Oh, yeah?' he sniffed.

'Yeah! What the eff-eff are you complaining about? Mr Snow's taught you all *he* knows. Add in everything you picked up from me and the other guys here and what you've learned from these hairless wonders, hell – you're like a two-legged version of COLUMBUS!'

'Except I may not be walking around on two legs much longer.'

'Don't even think about it!' cried Steve. 'You gotta stay on top of this thing! Okay. Maybe the Japs *are* planning to take over this operation, but that won't be until after you've shown 'em you can put these birds in the air and keep 'em there.'

'Yeah, but . . . supposing we fail?'

Boy! thought Steve. When this guy hits a downer he goes straight to the bottom of the shaft . . .

He didn't know that alcoholic elation could flip over into manic depression between one swallow and the next. 'It's not *going* to fail! We're going to do the best job we can and we're going to put this place on the map – because when this project finally takes off, so do we.'

Cadillac slowly raised his head and fixed his eyes on Steve. 'Oh, yeah? Just how do we do that?'

Bad move, thought Steve. *Bad move*! 'Leave all that to me,' he said hastily. 'You've got enough to worry about.' He moved the bottle out of reach. 'And go easy on this stuff. Otherwise you'll end up with a headful of boiled rice instead of brains.'

'What about Clearwater?'

'Don't worry. When, and if, the time comes, she'll be right with you.'

'Okay, but promise me one thing.'

'What's that?'

'That you won't make any moves – do anything foolish – without clearing it with me. I want to know what's happening – *before* it happens.'

'Sure.'

'And if it turns out I got it wrong and Min-Orota decides he is not going to re-staff the Heron Pool with his own people, then we forget the whole thing. If you want to take Clearwater back – fine. But I'm staying. Is that understood?'

'Absolutely.'

'Okay. But . . . ' Cadillac jabbed his forefinger at Steve while he searched for the words. He was fading fast. ' . . . if I, uhh – if I find you're trying to shaft me –'

'Christopher Columbus!' hissed Steve. 'What kind of person do you think I am? You saved my life! How many times do I have to tell you? What happened with Clearwater wasn't my fault –'

'I don't care about that!'

'Well I do! And I'm trying to make it up to you! There may be times when you have cause to doubt me, but I'm your *friend*! I told Mr Snow I'd come and find you, but if you want to stay, well – that's tough on him but its okay by me. Clearwater and I will just fade away quietly. You won't even know we've gone.' Steve thrust his right hand across the table and radiated sincerity. 'You have my word on that. Is it a deal?'

Cadillac eyed the offered hand. 'Maybe. I'll sleep on it.'

Steve picked up the bottle of *sake* he'd removed and set it down in front of the Mute. 'Be my guest . . .'

*

Cadillac's reading of the situation turned out to be correct. Permission to take Steve up in the newly modified glider was granted, and after stage-managing a few hesitant approaches and hair-raising landings, he went solo with twenty hours of instruction.

On the ground, Steve was still obliged to act out his public role as a menial subordinate. His newfound ability to fly brought a few belligerent comments about 'uppity Mutes', but Cadillac smoothed the ruffled feelings of the Tracker linemen by stressing the risky nature of the first proving flights. The fair-haired grass-monkey was a sacrificial victim who, if things did not work out, could end up as a burnt offering.

339

The modified glider was powered by five slim rockets attached to the underside of a metal tray mounted beneath the fuselage pod. The trolley was fitted with two short-burn boosters ignited, as before, by means of a length of safety fuse; those under the aircraft were fired in succession by an ingenious trigger system which detonated a wad of the same paper caps used to fire bullets from the rifles which Lord Yama-Shita had supplied to the M'Calls.

The glider was to be launched from a redesigned three-wheeled trolley based on the one used by Steve. This new model had a low, ground-hugging profile to give extra stability during the take-off run and four quick-release shackles that kept the trolley attached to the glider until it was jettisoned by the pilot.

Since the Iron Masters did not possess the precise measuring devices and the computer-modelling techniques employed by the Federation, Cadillac's flying-horse had been constructed using the simplest calculations. The same applied to the rockets. Using the mathematical formulae transmitted by AMEXICO, Steve was able to make a guesstimate of the foot/pounds of thrust generated during the burn. But the figures didn't mean much when your employers didn't measure in feet and inches, or calculate weights in pounds and ounces.

In his guise as errand boy, Steve shadowed Cadillac throughout the assembly process to make sure that everything was done to his own exacting standards. At his suggestion, Jodi and Kelso were picked to work with Cadillac behind closed doors through the night prior to the launch, enabling him to take an active part in the final adjustments. By first light, they had tested and checked every joint and attachment and passed them A-OK. One big question mark remained. The tests with the weighted ground trolleys had shown the rockets were powerful enough to move it through the air – but just how fast was this silk-winged coffin going to travel?

In a few hours Steve was due to get the answer. The

flight, which was to be staged before the same high-ranking delegation of Iron Masters, was scheduled for mid-morning, and it was rumoured that the Consul-General of Ro-diren and Masa-chusa might grace the occasion with his presence. The cadre of Japs who ran the Heron Pool drafted in an extra squad of cleaners and gardeners and hung out some banners and bunting, but they did not work themselves into a frenzy. They were required to treat the Shogun's permanent representative with due deference, but they weren't government employees like the post-master and his quivering clerks. The Consul-General only exercised absolute power within the borders of his estate. The Heron Pool formed part of the domain of Lord Min-Orota, and everyone who worked there was subject to his rule – and under his protection.

Steve didn't return to his shack until four in the morning, but since it was his big day he was allowed to skip the obligatory quota of yard work. Around 0500 he felt like getting up and strangling the cockerel, but he managed to fall asleep again, and did not wake until one of the servants banged on the door three hours later.

As a Mute, Steve wasn't allowed to use the bath-house, only a tub in the yard, but on this occasion Cadillac summoned him into the section reserved for the house-owner and invited him to take the plunge. Steve slipped off his work-stained clothes and jumped in. Since the deep tub was already occupied by Cadillac and two of his body-slaves, things were a little crowded at first, but they eventually managed to disentangle themselves and proceed with the serious business of getting clean.

The two dark-eyed Thais, wearing nothing but polite smiles and headscarves, were somewhat disconcerted to find themselves sharing the same tub as a Mute, but hunting the elusive bar of soap proved a real ice-breaker. After a memorable scrub back and front, Steve attempted to climb out, but the girls, egged on by Cadillac, hauled him back in and started to give him a second going-over just for luck. Ordinarily, Steve would have been more than happy to co-operate, but at that moment he had more on his mind than fun and frolics. As they ducked him playfully he slipped out of their grasp and plunged between their legs to the bottom of the tub. The move caused considerable excitement but their squeals of delight turned to cries of disappointment when he surfaced holding the big wooden plug and hurled it across the room.

*

Besides learning the Iron Masters' tongue-twisting language, Cadillac had picked up their love of ceremony. The communal bath was followed by an invitation to eat breakfast in the house wearing one of Cadillac's wrap-around robes – supplied courtesy of Lord Kiyomori Min-Orota.

'Feel nervous?'

'Haven't given it a thought,' said Steve lightly. It was a lie of course, and he could see Cadillac didn't believe him.

When they had finished eating, one of the body-slaves brought Steve a white cotton outfit: the usual loose square-sleeved jacket and wide, calf-length trousers. On top of the neatly folded garments were a fresh set of underclothes, white cotton socks and rope-soled, lace-up sandals. There was also a white headscarf bearing several blood-red Japanese word-symbols.

Cadillac folded it carefully, laid the portion with the symbols across Steve's forehead, then knotted it on the nape of his neck. 'That too tight?'

'No, just right.' Steve looked at himself in the small, square wall-mirror. 'What does all this junk mean?'

' "We praise the wisdom of Lord Min-Orota and the greatness of all his works." '

'Hmmmph . . . D'you write that?'

'I could have, but that would have been unwise. So I composed the line in Basic and got one of the scribes to translate it for me.'

Steve pushed the headscarf clear of his eyebrows. 'You're turning into a real toady.'

'It's part of the basic survival kit, Brickman. You should know that better than anyone.'

'Just kidding. C'mon, let's go.'

Cadillac escorted Steve over to the Heron Pool. The aircraft they had worked on till dawn stood poised on its launching trolley at the edge of the field, with a short stepladder leading up to the cockpit. Jodi Kazan and Dave Kelso, still red-eyed from their extended nightshift, stood by in fresh worksuits. A long stretch of fishing net had been raised on poles on the far side of the field to snare the speeding trolley, and most of the Tracker workforce were ranged behind it – presumably to pick up the pieces if Steve should fail to get off the ground.

Cadillac and Steve positioned themselves on the straw mats placed by the nose of the aircraft and knelt to pay homage to the assembled Iron Masters, who were seated some fifty yards away on a cloth-covered dais with their aides ranged behind them. Long bamboo poles with narrow banners bearing three different emblems fluttered above their heads.

'The ones on the left are the Min-Orota,' whispered Cadillac. 'Those on the right belong to Yama-Shita, and the group in the middle are the Toh-Yota – the Shogun's house.'

'A neat way of saying we've got you surrounded,' said Steve.

They bowed again, touching the mat with their noses. Behind them, Jodi and Kelso did the same.

'Okay, let's go for it,' said Steve. He checked the movement of the five hammers that would fire the rockets, then settled into the cockpit. After satisfying himself that the control surfaces responded to movements of the stick and rudder bar, he pulled the row of triggers that had been fitted to a rudimentary dashboard.

Cadillac confirmed that all five firing-pins had slammed home.

'Okay. Prime the chambers!'

Jodi and Kelso pushed the wads of percussion caps into the firing chambers fixed to the rear of the rocket tubes.

'Chambers primed, hammers cocked,' cried Cadillac.

Steve closed his right hand firmly round the stick and looped his left forefinger through the ring-pull that would fire the first rocket. 'Light the boosters!'

Cadillac applied the taper. 'Lit and burning!'

Steve settled back firmly in his seat and began the countdown through clenched teeth. *Ten–nine–eight* . . .

Jodi and Kelso put their shoulders to the push-bars on each side of the trolley and heaved. It started to move forward. The black powder safety fuse sputtered and sparked; the flame divided and burnt its way towards the crimped nozzles of the two boosters.

Five–four–three : . . Steve checked the front-wheel steering by moving the rudder bar . . . *two–one–zero—*

SHHHhooowwaAHHH! The boosters ignited with a swishing roar. Jodi and Kelso leaped clear and watched anxiously as the trolley bolted across the field, its rear end wreathed in fire and smoke.

'Go! Go! Go! GO!' they chanted, double-punching the air on each exclamation mark.

Once again Steve felt himself pressed back into his seat as the trolley continued to accelerate. From the rough measurements they had made during the ground tests with the aid of marker poles, he knew that the trolley reached its maximum speed in eight seconds.

. . . *five–four–three–two–one–IGNITION*!

Steve triggered the centre rocket and, as he heard it ignite, he reached outside the cockpit, yanked the toggle that released the aircraft from the trolley, pulled back on the stick and aimed for the clouds.

Whoooossshhh! It was a fantastic feeling. He had never climbed so steeply or so fast before. Glancing down, he saw the ground drop rapidly away. The upturned faces of the spectators became featureless pale dots – like tiny flowers scattered across a meadow.

In less than fifteen seconds he was nearly 2,000 feet

up. The hissing sound ceased abruptly as the rocket reached the end of its burn and the drumming vibration that had threatened to shake his teeth loose was replaced by an eerie silence. Steve rolled out of the climb, going over and down in a descending right-hand turn. Straightening out his line of descent, he fired the second rocket.

Shuwahh-pa-powwW! Another giant kick in the pants.

Steve kept the nose down. With no instruments, he could only gauge his speed by the keening noise of the air as it rushed over the silken wings and the sickening judder generated by the stresses on the airframe. Now! He pulled up into a loop, rolled off the top and went straight into another loop – an aerobatic manoeuvre known as an upward-S.

The rocket cut out as he came off the top of the second loop, but he had enough speed to go into a barrel roll. Steve was forced to admit Cadillac had done a good job – with a little help from his friends. As a glider, its performance had been no more than average, but under power, the aircraft handled well.

Yep, she was a sweet bird . . .

The upward-S had added another thousand feet of altitude, enabling Steve to see Ba-satana, perched on the edge of the Eastern Sea. That was one big stretch of water. Was that the edge of the world – or did something lie beyond? He used up the next two rockets in a variety of aerobatic manoeuvres, working his way closer to the ground as he gave serious thought to buzzing the display stand from behind to give the dinks the fright of their lives. He came to the conclusion that it might not appeal to their warped sense of humour, and settled for a low-level, high-speed pass across the field, scattering the watching Trackers and clearing the stone wall by inches.

Up again he went, during the final seconds of the fifth and last burn, finishing off with three victory rolls before turning back towards the field for an immaculate landing.

The total burn time had been seventy-five seconds, but

by gliding in between firings he had been able to stay aloft for about twenty minutes. He had deliberately kept it short to sustain the Iron Masters' interest, but could have remained airborne for much longer – and flown further. A westward climb using four rockets would have taken him close to 8,000 feet, leaving one in reserve. From that height he would have been able to glide all the way to the Hudson – with a passenger. Yeah. Things were coming together just fine . . .

His spectacular handling of the flying-horse and its faultless performance put the Iron Masters in a convivial mood. Anxious to demonstrate that his flying skills were the equal of Steve's, Cadillac made the next two flights with Jodi, then Kelso, riding in the front passenger seat. To the casual observer his performance was every bit as good as Steve's. Jodi and Kelso, who knew the difference, were impressed but not bowled over. Cadillac's flying lacked that indefinable something that separates the gritted-teeth routine of a competent pilot trying to do his best from the easy brilliance of the born-to-fly aces who simply can't do it any other way.

After an alfresco lunch, the Iron Masters sent a samurai from Min-Orota's party up with Cadillac. He burned off two rockets in a steep eastward climb, circled silently over the port of Ba-satana, then made a swooping dive over Lord Min-Orota's palace. The samurai had maintained a white-knuckled grip on the rim of the cockpit during the climb-out, but as the minutes passed his initial terror eased. And when he saw the field-workers pause in their labours, and the soldiers and servants stream out of the palace to catch a glimpse of them as they flew overhead, he chortled happily and waved with both hands. Cadillac fired the third rocket to regain altitude and expended the remaining pair doing gentle aerobatics in sight of the field.

When Cadillac landed, Shigamitsu, the samurai in command of the Heron Pool, announced that the Shogun's Herald had expressed the wish to be taken into the air by the pilot who had made the first flight of the morning. After a new set of rockets had been fitted to the glider and trolley, Toshiro Hase-Gawa was ushered forward with the usual elaborate courtesies. Once he was settled comfortably in the front seat, Steve was allowed back on the scene. Shigamitsu had overcome the ticklish problem of protocol by ordering up a pair of gloves and a straw mask for Steve to wear. In this way, the Herald would not come face to face with a Mute slave.

Since sheet glass was in short supply and Perspex was unheard of, the windscreens on the glider were pretty basic. Cadillac had managed to get a couple of pairs of goggles made up, and a cotton scarf tied across the nose and chin completed the flying kit. Steve, who could only see the back of his passenger's head, had no inkling of his identity until he heard a muffled voice say: 'Okay, take it away, sport.'

In response to Toshiro's request for a brief scenic tour, Steve followed Cadillac's flight pattern, taking in Basatana and the Min-Orota's family estates. On the way back he circled above the Consul-General's residence and Two Island Lake. Clearwater was down there. Was she in the garden, looking up at the white stiff-winged bird floating lazily overhead? With the power off, the only sounds were a gentle swish of air over the glider's silken skin and the flip-flapping tail-ends of their headscarves.

Toshiro edged round in his seat as far as his safety harness would allow and pulled the scarf clear of his mouth. 'Have you thought about where you're going to make the drop?'

Steve jabbed a finger over the side and shouted into the slipstream. 'I thought the lake would be a good place. Give him something to think about on the way down.'

Toshiro nodded. 'Nice touch! How are you going to do it?'

'By rigging the safety harness! The lap straps are anchored to the floor by pins and the shoulder straps are fixed here – on the bulkhead behind your seat!'

'Got it . . .'

'I'll fix the pins so they'll come loose when I pull a wire, and before he knows what's happening, I turn her over – ' Steve rammed the stick against his right thigh, ' – *like this*!'

Toshiro's mouth flew open in alarm as the plane rolled onto its back. Up to now, the flight had been fairly sedate, and here he was, suddenly hanging upside down 3,000 feet above the ground, supported by four two-inch-wide straps.

'And away he goes!' Steve kept the glider inverted for a couple of minutes, and watched Toshiro's head bob from side to side as he scrabbled around inside the cockpit for something to hold on to. It wouldn't do him any harm to know how the Consul-General would feel in that gut-wrenching moment before he started treading air.

Steve pulled the nose down in a half-loop, then levelled out the right way up. His passenger sank down gratefully into his seat. 'You see? Couldn't be simpler!'

No response.

'Are you okay?'

Toshiro nodded but didn't look round. He had made the flight in order to pave the way for the Consul-General's one-way trip, but this would also be his first and last ride on a flying-horse. Never again! Never!

When the final rocket had been fired and they were gliding back towards the field, Steve reached forward and nudged the Herald's shoulder. 'Can we talk?'

'What about?'

'I need that bundle of pink leaves.'

Toshiro gave him a sideways glance. 'One thing at a time. I got you transferred to the Heron Pool, didn't I?'

'Yeah, that's right . . . Thanks a lot.' I don't believe it, thought Steve. Our lives are in this guy's hands and he's full of shit!

They landed smoothly on the twin bamboo skids. Wheels would have made things a lot easier, but the Iron Masters weren't geared up to produce the kind they needed. It had been a major headache finding cartwheels small and light enough for the launch trollies.

'Don't stay away too long,' said Steve, as the ashen-faced Herald made a shaky exit. 'Things are starting to move pretty fast around here.'

'Don't worry,' replied Toshiro, with feeling. 'We'll meet soon enough, you need have no fear of that.'

What an insolent swine this outlander was! He had endured Brickman's boorish behaviour in order to secure the death of the Consul-General. It was an unsavoury alliance, but his wounded pride had been soothed by the prospect of exacting an exquisite revenge once the fat degenerate had been dispatched. But now the Shogun had decided that the long-dog should be allowed to escape with his two captives, and that made Brickman's brash confidence doubly irksome.

It was almost as if someone had told the mexican that the veiled threats he, Toshiro, had uttered against him were not to be taken seriously. Was it possible that the Chamberlain's office had become involved in this affair? Ieyasu's spidery tentacles were rumoured to extend into the farthest corners of Ne-Issan. It was a chilling thought. The Herald prayed it was not so, and cursed himself for having taken the course he had. But there could be no turning back. Promises had been made, expectations raised. He would have to aid Brickman. It was his duty to do so. But he would keep the painted gutter-hound on tenterhooks for as long as possible.

Steve kept his eyes down as Toshiro squared his shoulders and swaggered back to his friends. It would be courting disaster to rely on any offers made by the Jap to aid their escape. Or to deliver Clearwater. She would have to get to the Heron Pool the same way she had secured his own transfer – by getting inside the Consul-General's head.

*

When the VIPs had been bowed out of the compound, Cadillac told Steve what had been decided. The conversion of the twelve existing and semi-completed

349

airframes into dual-control two-seaters was to be given top priority. Twenty-four samurai would be sent to the Heron Pool for flight-aptitude tests. The twelve best candidates were to be given gliding instruction. After going solo, the top six pupils from this group were to be given advanced training on the rocket-powered version. When they had reached the required level of competence, they would display their flying skills before the domain-lords Min-Orota and Yama-Shita, the chief members of their households and – it was hoped – the Shogun himself.

'Did they give you a date?'

'Yes. A month from now. If they leave it any later, the Shogun won't be around. He spends the summer on a big island off the coast of Ro-diren, then moves south during the Yellowing.'

Steve nodded thoughtfully. Cadillac's use of the Mute term for autumn prompted memories of his brief spell with the M'Calls – and the fact that time was passing. 'The three of you are going to have your work cut out.'

'Yeah, it's all your fault. Mine too in a way. We outsmarted ourselves. The reason the Shogun's Herald went up with you was because he wanted to check you out. He told Min-Orota's people that if I could teach a grass-monkey to fly like that in a week, then their samurai ought to be able to grow wings of their own in four.'

Steve bit back a smile. 'Do you want me to help?'

'As an instructor?' Cadillac shook his head. 'They'd never wear it. They didn't mind me using you as the fall-guy during the trials, but they couldn't cope with a Mute telling them what to do. It goes against everything they've been taught to believe in.'

'That figures, but . . . like you said, Trackers are slaves too. How are you and the other guys going to put the message across?'

'With difficulty,' sighed Cadillac. 'But they've managed to rationalise the situation with the aid of some very convoluted thinking. As outlanders, they regard us as non-persons, but they're prepared to acknowledge the fact that Jodi, Dave and myself possess certain high-grade skills they don't have. While they are acquiring those skills they're prepared to defer to us in those specific areas. But once we're out of the cockpit, away from the flying field or outside the workshops, they expect to see our noses in the dirt.'

'What a bunch of stiff-necked assholes.'

'Yeah, well . . . that's the way it goes.'

'It's a pity I couldn't get cleaned up and re-registered as a Tracker . . . ' Steve let the suggestion hang in the air.

'Well . . . I've got some soap-leaves –'

'You have?'

'Yes, a whole bunch of them. Got a set of body-paints too. Clearwater and I both brought a set – just in case.'

'Good thinking,' mused Steve. 'Yeah . . . I'm glad you told me.'

'But there's no way I could get you a set of papers.'

'Then fake 'em. You can write. Make a copy of Kelso's.'

'It's not as easy as that. Everyone's papers are held in the Records Office. I just can't walk in there. It's not my territory. But even if I could, what about the arm tag? They're stamped out of metal. I don't see how we can fake one of those.'

'Yeah.' Steve grimaced reflectively. It looked as if they'd have to rely on the Herald after all. With his connections, Hase-Whoever should be able to come up with everything they needed, including a route-map and a compass. 'You're right. Forget it.' He mulled things over, then cocked a finger at Cadillac. 'There is one way we can speed things along. You, Jodi and Kelso concentrate on training these dinks and I'll, uhh –'

'Flight-test the planes as they come off the line . . .?'

Steve spread his hands. 'You got there ahead of me.' Soft-soaping this guy really paid off. 'And I'll also see what can be done to improve the performance of those rockets. I'm sure we can boost the power *and* duration

351

without a significant increase in weight. What d'you say?'

Cadillac thought it over. 'Yeah, okay. Good idea.'

Are you kidding? It's not just a good idea, amigo, it's a stroke of pure fucking genius . . .

*

Steve stayed with Cadillac in the study, poring over the constructional drawings of the glider, trying to decide how they could strengthen the airframe to cope with the added stresses of powered flight. Along with Jodi and Kelso, they had both found the vibration slightly unnerving, and what they were looking for was some way of dampening it down without getting into a major rebuild.

Their search for a quick fix went on till after dark. Some of the drawings they needed to look at had been left in the assembly workshop, and when Cadillac broke for supper he sent Steve over to fetch them.

As Steve left the workshop with the drawings and came back up the almost pitch-black alley he heard someone humming a familiar tune.

'Dah-dee da-da-dahh . . . down Mexico way . . . dah-dee dah-dee dee-dee dah-dee dee-dee . . . she knelt to pray . . .'

A bulky figure eased itself off the wall ahead of him. It was Kelso. 'Hi.'

Steve stopped just beyond the reach of the big Tracker. Kelso had treated him with grudging camaraderie ever since his hop over the wall, but Jodi had been with them. Now that they were on their own there was no telling which way it might go. 'Haven't heard anyone sing that song in a long time,' he said.

Kelso responded with a dry laugh. 'Not many people know it. Trouble is, I keep forgetting the words.' He hummed a few bars. 'How does the last bit go?'

'The mission bells told me, I couldn't stay –'

Kelso chimed in, 'South of the border, down Mexico way . . . Yeah, that's it.'

The song, and the exchange of half-remembered lines

was one of the secret signals AMEXICO operatives employed to announce their presence to any fellow mexicans who happened to be around. Steve fingered the back of his ear, pressing on the tiny, implanted transceiver but there was no response to his Morse-coded call-sign. There was always the possibility that Kelso had heard the routine at one time or another but even so . . .

Watch your step, Stevie . . .

Kelso, his arms folded, moved closer to Steve and laid his right shoulder against the wall. 'I hear you're not planning on staying long either . . .'

'Who told you that?'

'Kaz.'

'Oh, yeah?'

'Yeah. I've been reading you wrong, Brickman. I had you figured for a lump-sucker, but you're all right. You did well today.'

'It wasn't any big deal. Any True Blue could've done it.'

'Don't bullshit me, Brickman. Modesty doesn't become you.'

Steve let it pass.

'These crates we're building. If a guy knew which way to head, he could go a long way in one of those things.'

'Depends on where he was aiming for . . .'

'Yeah, well, the first thing is to get the hell out of here – then work out the rest later.'

'You're probably right,' said Steve. 'Just how much did Jodi tell you?'

'Just how much does she know?'

'Come on, Dave. You can do better than that.'

'She told me someone was leaning on your kin-sister, that you been sent to pick up a couple of badhats, and . . . that she's going back in with you.'

'And how d'you feel about that?'

'Life in the Big Open ain't all it's cracked up to be. This deal you promised her. D'you really think you can swing that?'

'Yeah, I'm sure I can. She's already saved my life once. You helped her, remember? That's why you're both here.'

'Don't worry. I hadn't forgotten.' Kelso hesitated, then said: 'Could you get the same deal for me?'

Steve found it hard to read the Tracker's face in the darkness. 'Don't see why not. But are you sure that's what you want?'

'Listen. If Kaz is happy to throw in with you, then I'd like to come along too.'

'Glad to hear it.' Steve wasn't at all sure whether he could really trust Kelso but – as a long-gone American President once said when challenged for giving a troublesome opponent a plum post in the White House – it was better to have him inside the tent pissing out, than have him on the outside, pissing in.

He offered his hand to the renegade. 'Welcome aboard.'

CHAPTER FOURTEEN

As the month neared its end, Cadillac had every reason to feel satisfied. The Tracker workforce, assisted by a newly drafted batch of Vietnamese craftsmen, had put in long hours to convert and complete the first twelve aircraft. Four had sustained varying degrees of damage during the initial training period, but these had been quickly repaired and put back into service.

Of the twelve samurai selected as potential pilots, eight were judged to possess the necessary aptitude to complete the intensive four-week training course that was to culminate in rocket-powered formation aerobatics. By the end of the third week, it became clear that only five of the eight had the degree of co-ordination required to perform as a team. The other three had reached a satisfactory level of competence but lacked that indefinable extra something which, in another age, had been called 'the right stuff'. Thanks to the efforts of Kazan and Kelso, his co-instructors, the five top students had reached a remarkably high standard and were now rehearsing the exhibition routine that he and Steve had worked out.

Dozens of gardeners aided by gangs of Mutes were busy tidying up the landscape. A brand-new access road now linked the highway to the eastern side of the flying field where a hundred Korean craftsmen were building a wooden grandstand with boxes at the front for the two domain-lords and the other top VIPs and several tiers of benches for those of inferior rank.

The euphoria generated by the achievements of all concerned and the preparations for what was obviously going to be a major spectacle – of which he was the principal architect – swept away Cadillac's doubts about his future prospects. If all went well, it could signal the beginning of a new, and even more glorious, stage in his career. Looking back on what had been accomplished in the last few weeks made the notion that his services might be dispensed with seem totally absurd. He should never have revealed his temporary feelings of insecurity. But had he not done so, the fair-haired Tracker would not have been so forthcoming about his plans to escape. Yes. Only one cloud marred an otherwise dazzling horizon: Brickman.

What the stones had foretold was coming true. Sooner or later Brickman would carry Clearwater away to the dark world beneath the deserts of the south. And many would die. Cadillac did not fear for his own life. Mr Snow, who spoke with the Sky Voices, had assured him that he and Clearwater would both live. For he was to be the sword and she the shield of Talisman.

The meaning of Mr Snow's words was unclear, but in any case it referred to some future event. What concerned Cadillac was the here and now. The cloud warrior's presence had disinterred the crushing sense of guilt he had tried so hard to bury. His betrayal of Mr Snow's trust, his indifference to Clearwater's present fate and the abandonment of his duty towards the clan M'Call were the main reasons why he sought nightly oblivion with the aid of *sake*.

Yes, guilt was one element of his present unease but the root cause was envy – generated by his own reaction at having to measure up to and work with his rival. A rival who did not even bother to compete; whose sense of superiority was so crushing he cheerfully accepted the demeaning role of a Mute slave, tackling the menial tasks he was given with the same enthusiasm he brought to solving a knotty problem of aerodynamics. What made it worse was knowing that he could not have got this far without Brickman's shrewd counsel and unflagging co-operation.

The realisation that he was still not the equal of the cloud warrior increased Cadillac's smouldering resentment. But it was worse than that. He needed

Brickman. His presence acted as a spur; made him sharper, helped his own brain to function better. But to be dependent on someone you could not trust was both foolish and dangerous. Cadillac cursed himself for not denouncing Brickman at the very beginning. It was now too late, and he doubted whether he could ever have done it. He already had too many betrayals on his conscience. No . . . escape was the answer. Let him take Clearwater. Provided the manner of their departure did not jeopardise his own situation, he would be happy to be rid of both of them.

He had meant what he had said to Brickman about there being nothing for him to go back to. The will of Talisman might one day bring Clearwater back into his life, but for the foreseeable future he had lost her. The hopes he had nurtured about patching up their relationship had vanished with Brickman's arrival in Ne-Issan. If he went back to the clan, he would be obliged to resume his role as Mr Snow's apprentice; his obedient shadow. He would only acquire proper standing in the eyes of the clan after Mr Snow's death. But the stones had shown him that after the old wordsmith went to the High Ground the M'Calls would cease to exist. So what was the point of returning? He might be without friends here, but without Mr Snow and Clearwater he had no real friends anywhere. His association with the cloud warrior was something else entirely. There were many things they had in common, but it was not friendship that bound them together. It was destiny.

*

Steve had been busy too. Eight pilots flying several rocket-propelled sorties a day, seven days a week, consumed a lot of black powder. Once used, the rocket tubes and launch boosters could be refilled, but the whole operation had to be geared up to meet the demand. At Steve's suggestion, Cadillac put in a call for reinforcements and a mixed bag of Thais and

357

Vietnamese women duly arrived from the local fireworks factory to help out in the packing department.

Cadillac had also taken up another of Steve's suggestions and arranged for Jodi Kazan and Dave Kelso to be moved from their billets in the compound to his own grace-and-favour residence – now flanked by the new access road. The move had been justified by the high-pressure training programme. By living together, all three instructors had more time to review their pupils' progress after flying had finished for the day, and could co-ordinate any changes that needed to be made in the schedule.

The arrangement also fitted in perfectly with Steve's forward planning. With Jodi and Kelso close at hand he could confer with them at length, without falling foul of the other Tracker renegades on the workforce. To them he was still an 'uppity Mute', and the fact that he was able to fly and had been given the task of test-piloting the newly completed aircraft had served to fuel their barely concealed resentment.

In the few moments when he hadn't been run off his feet, Steve had also been considering Cadillac's future prospects. Instead of just keeping an eye on the various processes, the Iron Masters were now lending a hand. At a rough head-count, the Japs and assorted lower-ranking dinks now outnumbered the original Tracker workforce by three to one. Was this another stage of the eventual takeover Cadillac had hinted at before he'd nose-dived into his *sake*? Steve had been waiting for the Mute to say something, but he appeared totally unconcerned, and since their original conversation had not uttered one word about the idea of escaping.

Given Cadillac's character, it was not all that surprising. The Mute preferred to clutch at any straw rather than face up to the possibility that he was merely being used and could shortly become expendable. The forthcoming show – now only days away – was to be his big moment, and he didn't want anyone raining on his parade. Tough. Like it or not, he was going over the wall. And by the time good ol' Stevie had done his number,

Cadillac would be glad someone had booked him a seat on the flight out.

As rumoured, Min-Orota had issued an invitation to the Shogun. Yoritomo had initially indicated his willingness to attend, and a tastefully decorated private box was being prepared for him at the front of the grandstand. The efforts of the craftsmen were in vain for, that very morning, Cadillac had overheard the news that the Shogun had decided to take a raincheck. The Consul-General Nakane Toh-Shiba and the Herald Toshiro Hase-Gawa would be attending the ceremony on his behalf. Wise move.

*

Yoritomo's letter to Lord Min-Orota did not explain the reason for his change of heart – the Shogun was not required to justify any decision he cared to take – but he reaffirmed his continuing support for the project, about which he had received glowing reports. The letter – couched in the warmest terms the official court language allowed – ended with the fervently expressed hope that the day's ceremonies would be crowned with success and that all those concerned would be justly rewarded for their efforts. Lord Kiyo Min-Orota pondered at length over the meaning of that last phrase. In the end he decided what troubled him was not the Shogun's words but the knowledge of his own treacherous intentions.

*

With just under a week to go, Steve still had several major hurdles to clear. He had to see Clearwater again, he still had to solve the problem of their travel stamps and papers, and he had to pick up the last of several surprise packages that had been delivered by AMEXICO over the last four weeks.

The packages had been dropped into the pond behind the Heron Pool on nights when the moon was obscured by cloud. To ensure accurate delivery and avoid detection, the all-black aircraft made a power-off

359

approach, gliding on incredibly slim wings to within a hundred feet of the surface before releasing the waterproof containers. The only sound was a whispering rush of air that built to a swift crescendo, then fell away in a dying sigh like a sudden gust of wind in the tree-tops. Slowed by a drag-chute, the splash made by the containers was no louder than that of a rising fish. Once on the bottom, a float disguised as a stick was released to mark its position. To date, Steve had managed to pinpoint them soon after dawn and then fish them out when everyone was in bed.

*

Shielding the flame of a lighted taper, Steve ducked through the door of his low-roofed shack and pulled it shut behind him. Kneeling on the flattened straw that served both as floor and mattress, he lit the wick of the light-bowl that stood on a small shelf.

As the flame grew and cast its dim orange glow over the dark interior, he saw what he had failed to sense – a figure, dressed in black from head to foot, sitting cross-legged in the far corner of the shack, with a half-drawn short-sword across his lap. His right hand gripped the hilt, his left the scabbard. A cloth was wrapped round his face, leaving a narrow gap across the eyes, but it was so deeply shadowed that even they remained hidden from view.

'How're you doing, sport?' It was the Herald, in his original disguise.

'As well as can be expected. You been here long?'

'Long enough.'

Steve shuffled round to face him and bowed low, trying to forget about the killer blade that lay within striking distance of his neck. It was all part of the Herald's act. 'Your illustrious presence greatly honours my humble abode. May I beg to ask the purpose of your visit?'

'Don't overdo it, Brickman. Bad things happen to

360

people who try to take the rise out of me.'

'Nothing was further from my thoughts, sire.' Steve straightened his back. 'What can I do for you?'

'I want to know what your plans are. We're getting close to the off.'

'I know. Apart from a few minor details, everything's more or less sewn up. The only thing you have to do is make sure that the Consul-General turns up for his big ride.'

The Herald snorted with annoyance. 'He'll *be* there! What about the other half of your assignment?'

'I just told you. It's all sewn up.'

'I want details, Brickman. C'mon! Spell it out. We haven't got all night.'

'The flying demonstration that's been laid on is not going to go too well. In fact, it's going to be a total disaster. I don't know what precautions you plan to take on the day, but I'm relieved to hear your boss is not going to be here. Could have made things very awkward.'

Toshiro's grip on the short-sword tightened. 'My . . . boss?'

'Yes. The Shogun. His Exalted Highness Yoritomo Toh-Yota. He's what . . . twenty-eight years old? Unmarried but two of his four sisters are – correct?'

'Long-dog swine! How dare you utter his name?' It was only by a supreme effort of will that Toshiro managed to restrain his sword arm.

Steve appeared oblivious of the danger. 'C'mon, be reasonable. Have I shown disrespect? If you and I are going to do business, we can't stand on ceremony.'

'Watch your mouth, Brickman. No one is indispensable. Not even you.' Toshiro paused. 'As a man who lacks any sense of honour you probably think that's an empty threat. You'd be wrong. Deal or no deal, I have my limits. Push me too far and I'll be obliged to kill you – regardless of the consequences. And in my case they will be dire, believe me.'

Steve bowed his head. 'Nobody knows that better than I, sire. My masters are as merciless as yours.'

The long-dog's reply served to remind Toshiro of the

terrible risks facing those involved in his own double-game. Regaining his composure, he said, 'How did you come by this information?'

'The same way that I know you are a Herald of the Inner Court and that your name is Toshiro Hase-Gawa.'

The Herald pulled the scarf down to reveal the lower half of his face. 'I won't warn you again, Brickman. Tread carefully.'

'Do you think we met by chance? You were pinpointed from the moment we knew the two runaway Mutes had reached this area.' It was pure bluff, put together from the assorted information Cadillac had garnered from the Iron Masters. But the Herald didn't know that.

'Pinpointed?'

'As the man with his finger on the pulse. Someone we could do business with.' Steve watched the Herald closely. 'Intelligent, imaginative, resourceful . . . ambitious.' The last word had the most impact, but it was quickly erased.

Aware that he had lost the initiative, Toshiro fixed Steve with his expressionless eyes and waited.

Steve stared back, neither challenging nor fearful. 'You don't seem surprised.'

'I try to avoid surprises,' replied Toshiro. 'You are the envoy of a powerful nation. However, I *am* curious to know why you didn't disclose this knowledge before.'

Steve responded with a calculating smile. 'Have you put all *your* cards on the table? Despite the gulf between our two societies you and I are – with all due respect, sire – two of a kind.'

Toshiro conceded the point with a burst of suppressed laughter. 'Brickman, despite your total lack of sensitivity, I'm sure you are aware there have been several occasions when I've been itching to kill you – and I could cheerfully do so now.' He slammed the half-drawn sword back into its scabbard. 'One day, perhaps, I may have that pleasure.'

'Not if I see you first.'

His spirited reply caused the Herald to slap his thigh.

'Well said! Now – ' he lowered his voice again ' – how do you plan to escape?'

'We're going to take three of the flying horses,' whispered Steve.

Toshiro frowned. 'But the western border is nearly 1,000 leagues from here. Can these machines travel that far?'

'One day they will – but not now.' Steve fed him the false lead. 'Once we're across the Hudson, we fly south-west to a rendezvous point near Scranton. The place you call Skara-tana.'

'Ahh, so . . .'

'Our own people are flying in to pick us up from there. We'll be back home before nightfall.'

Toshiro tried hard not to look impressed. 'What about the woman? Where and when do you want her delivered?'

'Don't worry about it. The Consul-General will be bringing her.'

The news took Toshiro's breath away. 'You've arranged this?'

'Not yet. I was planning to do that tonight. The Consul-General is dining with Lord Min-Orota, and won't be back until tomorrow morning.' Steve had learned of this from a conversation Cadillac had overheard. 'But of course, you already know that.'

The Herald did, and had already made plans to take advantage of Toh-Shiba's absence. But how did Brickman know – and what did his words imply? 'You . . . astound me.'

'Don't see why,' replied Steve. 'Just doing my job.'

'But –'

'There is *one* thing you could help me with.' Steve had taken the Herald's warning seriously, but sensed that, for the moment, he had him on the ropes. He cocked a finger at him. 'Did you bring your horse?'

'Yes –'

'Terrific. I'm glad we had this opportunity to talk, but it's put me behind schedule. What are the chances of hitching a ride over to Two Island Lake?'

*

Despite the tempting offer of another round of bodily delights, Steve did not linger in Clearwater's arms once the last crucial details had been ironed out. To return to the Heron Pool meant a long swim to the western side of the lake followed by a three-mile run. With the onset of autumn, the nights had become noticeably chill, and while the water was relatively warm, the surface was shrouded in a thick layer of pale grey mist.

The mist had seeped up the steep sides of the lake, cloaking the tangle of boulders, bushes, fallen branches and rotting vegetation that formed a swamp-like morass at the water's edge. It was difficult to negotiate in daylight; with an almost naked body in almost total darkness, it had been both hazardous and painful.

In swimming towards the island, he had aimed for the pale yellow point of light emanating from the lantern which they had agreed Clearwater would hang in her window if she was alone – and unlikely to be disturbed by her fat friend.

To help guide him back, Steve had hung two lanterns in line with the direction he wanted to go: yellow in front, pink behind. The lake-house was perched among trees on the highest point of the island, so by porpoising out of the water he was able to see the lights through the wraith-like top layer of the mist. As long as he could see only the yellow light, he knew he was on the correct heading and not swimming round in circles.

Halfway across, Steve encountered a narrow mist-free channel. He turned over and switched to a back stroke. It was noisier than the breast stroke, but just as powerful. And it meant he could swim and keep an eye on the lights at the same time.

Even if he had been facing the right way, it was doubtful if he would have been quick enough to avoid the coarse fishing net that was suddenly drawn out of the water a yard or so beyond the end of the clear channel.

The ends of the net were held by six shadowy figures.

They were standing in two long, low-hulled boats, but these were hidden beneath the surrounding layer of mist. With the swift, practised movements that only came from years of fishing the waters, the net was brought over and under Steve and hauled tight. The boats came together, meeting first at the bows before gently colliding sideways on. One man in each boat mounted the bows and lifted their struggling catch clear of the water. Before Steve was fully able to grasp what was happening, he was dumped in the bottom of the left-hand boat and knocked unconscious with a swift, well-aimed blow on the back of the head.

*

When he returned to his senses, Steve found that he was dry, but still naked. Two figures dressed in black stood over him. As his eyes fluttered open, they hauled him into a kneeling position. It took a few seconds for him to realise what kind of trouble he was in. His arms had been raised to shoulder height and roped to a short pole which went over the back of his neck and under his bent elbows, leaving his fingers brushing his ears.

It was already causing a certain amount of discomfort, and when cramp set in would soon become painful. But not as painful as the thin cord that had been looped around his penis and scrotum and pulled taut before the other end had been tied round his neck. A neat trick. The only way to ease the tension was to lean forward. If he tried to straighten his back he would yank his balls off.

Terrific . . .

Facing him was a third man. He was also dressed in black, but his lined, skull-like face was uncovered. With deep-set slitted eyes, a square jaw, and a mouth like a joint between two steel plates, he looked like bad news.

A lantern hung from the top of a short angled pole stuck into the ground to Steve's right. His brown worksuit, which he had left stashed under a fallen tree, lay neatly folded beside it. The back of his head throbbed painfully. He moved it gingerly from side to side to try and ease the stiffness in his neck, and it was only then that he realised he was inside a black tent.

Skull-Face filled a small cup with *sake* from a leather-covered flask and held it out to the guard on Steve's right. 'Drink up. It may help you collect your thoughts.'

The guard held the cup to Steve's lips. With the cord round his neck and his privates, he had to lean even further forward in order to get his mouth at the right angle.

'Feeling better?'

'Yes. Thank you.'

'Good.' Skull-Face barked a command in Japanese.

The two masked guards picked up whipping-canes and positioned themselves behind Steve's shoulders.

'I won't beat about the bush, Mr Brickman. Neither of us has much time to spare. You will therefore answer any questions I put to you directly and without hesitation. As you will soon discover, I know the score – so do not prevaricate and, above all, don't get smart. My job is to help you escape, and in return you are going to help me. Is that clear?'

'Yes, but . . . what happens if I don't know the answers?'

Skull-Face sighed. 'I warned you not to prevaricate,' he said softly. 'But I see you've forgotten already.' He motioned to the black-clad figures.

ThurWIKK! ThurWOKK! Steve gasped as he received two stinging blows across the shoulderblades in quick succession. Christopher! Those whipping-canes really bit deep. And arching his back under the impact of the blows had tightened the noose round his throat and put a sickening squeeze on his scrotum.

'I hope that will convince you we are not here to play games,' said Skull-Face. 'If you give me any more trouble, I'll cut your prick and balls off and send you home with them in this pickle jar.' Reaching both hands behind him, he produced a curved dagger and a capped glass jar and placed them in front of Steve.

It was the kind of stunt that dear old Uncle Bart might

have pulled, but Steve had a chill feeling that this guy really meant it.

'Okay, Mr Brickman. We know that you're an agent of AMEXICO and that you have been dealing with a representative of the ruling faction. We also know that you have come to an arrangement whereby you are to wreck the Heron Pool project and cause the death of Consul-General Nakane Toh-Shiba. In return, you have been promised unhindered passage out of the country with the two long-dogs who delivered the original flying-horses to Domain-Lord Hiro Yama-Shita. Is that correct?'

There was only one thing to say. 'Yes.'

'Good. These arrangements have our approval. You will proceed as planned. Now – do you know the identity of the man you have been dealing with?'

'He has never divulged it, but I believe him to be a Herald of the Inner Court called Toshiro Hase-Gawa.'

'Excellent. We're making progress. I am now going to ask you what plans you have made for your escape. But before you do so, let me answer a question which I am sure is in your mind. "Am I in the hands of people who are working with Hase-Gawa?" No. You are not. As is already clear, we share certain objectives, but we belong to a . . . rival organisation. Which no doubt leads you to ask: "What proof is there of this?" '

'Let me give you three facts which I am sure you are certain the Herald is unaware of. Facts which will demonstrate the extent of our knowledge and the efficiency of our organisation, and – who knows – may even persuade you to trust us.

'Fact One: we know that it was the female you have just visited who used her influence to persuade the Consul-General to transfer you from the post-house to the Heron Pool.

'Fact Two: we know her male companion, who has assumed your identity, can speak our language fluently.

'Fact Three: we know you have had discussions with a colleague of yours about taking a boat-trip through the canal-system from Ari-bani to Bu-faro. Your colleague is disguised as a Mute. He wears a red bandanna, and his code-name is Side-Winder.'

Steve tried but failed to hide his astonishment.

Skull-Face eyed him with a thin smile. 'We've known about him for a long time. We picked him up a few weeks after he was inserted into Ne-Issan, and we've been doing business with him ever since. In fact, it was through us he got his present job on the wheelboats.'

Already naked, Steve felt as if he was now being stripped bare on the inside as well. Was there anything these people were not aware of? Did they know that his talk of a 'massive intervention' was nothing more than a colossal bluff? In spite of being painfully trussed up and totally defenceless, he did his best to exude an air of calm assurance. Underneath, though, he was more frightened than he'd been in a long time.

And also totally bewildered. His preparations for the big break, and his last session with the Herald, had gone so well he had allowed himself to lapse into a careless, self-congratulatory mood. He was the guy that could do it all. And he'd swum blindly into the net. But even if he'd been alert, he doubted whether he could have evaded his present captors. Steve had packed in a lot of experience – much of it painful – since emerging onto the overground. He knew he was in the hands of hard men who, as his interrogator had revealed, were real professionals. Christo! He'd been beavering away thinking he's gotten himself into the big game, only to discover that there was an even bigger game going on!

Skull-Face, who had been watching him closely, said: 'I can see you find all of this rather difficult to take on board. But then you are still a relative beginner. In time you will discover that those involved in the gathering of intelligence and the maintenance of internal security are often linked by common interests – that are not always shared by their masters.'

Steve nodded gingerly. 'I can understand that.'

'For instance, we know you have been using a concealed radio to keep in contact with AMEXICO. We also have a number of similar devices.' Skull-Face produced a compact but powerful-looking walkie-talkie that could only have come from the Federation.

The Jap pressed the Transmit button and spoke briefly into the mouthpiece. Steve heard someone reply with a burst of gobbledegook.

'That's our man at the Heron Pool,' explained Skull-Face. 'He's keeping an eye on your shack. It might be awkward if someone discovered you weren't there.' He acknowledged the message, then laid the handset on the mat between them.

Steve followed it down with his eyes and stared at it fixedly as he tried to come to grips with what he'd got himself into.

'Let me try and guess what you are thinking,' said Skull-Face. 'You are trying to reconcile your discovery that our organisation is using radios with your knowledge that what we call the Dark Light and any object which contains it is expressly forbidden. In fact, to introduce a device of this kind into Ne-Issan is an act of high treason.'

'It did cross my mind,' admitted Steve.

'Rightly so. The Dark Light is a destructive force that must never again be allowed to fall into the hands of the greedy or the unscrupulous. Never again will the spinners and weavers imprison the world in their evil nets. But *we* do not seek power, we merely exercise the power we are given to maintain the status quo – and we are prepared to use any means to achieve that end.'

Skull-Face picked up the walkie-talkie and bared his teeth in what Steve assumed to be a smile. His gums had shrunk away from his parchment-yellow teeth. A real Dr Death.

'There is a saying that dates from The World Before: "In the country of the blind, the one-eyed man is king." '

'Gotcha. Smart move . . .'

Skull-Face nodded. 'Now tell me about yours. How did you plan to get out of here?'

Steve told the Jap what he wanted to know. There was no point in trying to conceal anything. If Side-Winder was

369

working both sides of the track, the ship-board escape route via Bu-faro was already totally compromised. Steve explained how, after reaching the Hudson River by air, he had planned to use Cadillac's ability to speak Japanese. Dressed in one of Clearwater's silken robes and the white mask she had worn on her travels, the Mute would pose as the courtesan 'Yoko Mi-Shima'. As such, he would be able to purchase the boat-tickets, buy food and answer any questions about the four Mute slaves accompanying 'her'. Apart from the middle finger of his right hand, Steve was already dressed for the part. The two sets of body-paints were to be used to disguise Jodi and Kelso – whom he had recruited to help guard his prisoners. In Clearwater's case, it was not really a disguise but a return to her usual colouring.

Skull-Face mulled things over, then asked: 'Did Hase-Gawa know that the two individuals you sought were grass-monkeys?'

'Yes, I told him and Clearwater confirmed it later on.'

The Jap's slitted eyes seemed to close completely. 'You are absolutely sure about this? There could have been no room for any misunderstanding?'

'No. He questioned her at length. Ask the other samurai who was there. The chief *ronin*. Noburo Naka-Jima.'

It was Skull-Face's turn to look surprised. 'How do you know this man's name?'

'It's a long story. I saved the life of his wife and child. But that's irrelevant. He took me to meet the Herald. He was sat right beside me when I told Hase-Gawa he'd got it wrong.'

'I see. And he was also there when the Herald questioned the female?'

'No. When she was brought in, he stayed in the other room. But the walls were only made of paper. Maybe he listened in.'

'Maybe he did . . . ' mused Skull-Face. 'Describe what happened when you left the pavilion.'

'Noburo's men took Clearwater away first, then he tied

my hands behind my back and Hase-Gawa led me away.'

'It was dark?'

'Pitch-black.'

'Go on . . .'

'After we'd gone a short distance – a hundred yards or so – he suddenly turned around and hit me – hard.' Steve turned his head to one side. 'Just under my left ear. Must have knocked me clean out. When I came to he was kneeling over me, massaging my neck.'

'So you have no idea how long you were unconscious?'

'No.'

'Never mind. What you have said may help us solve a mystery. Now – I wonder if you can explain something else that I find quite baffling – how was the male Mute able to learn to speak our language without being taught – and how was the female able to influence the actions of the Consul-General?'

'They are what the Plainfolk call "gifted" individuals. They have certain powers. I don't know how it works; no one does. But I *do* know they can do extraordinary things. Most people dismiss the stories they hear about "Mute magic". But there *is* such a thing. I've been there when the forces have been released. It's awesome.'

Skull-Face accepted this with a thoughtful nod. 'Are there many of these "gifted" grass-monkeys?'

'No. Fortunately, they are extremely rare. My experience is limited to one Plainfolk clan, but it appears that the only Mutes who possess these . . . special abilities, are smooth-boned and clear-skinned.' It wasn't strictly true, but if challenged he could always plead ignorance. 'What we in the Federation call super-straights.'

'Because they look exactly like you . . .'

'They *resemble* us, but inside they're totally different. Their society, their whole belief system is totally alien to ours. That's what makes them so dangerous.'

'So why not just kill them? Why are these two so important to your masters?'

'Our world is different from yours,' replied Steve. 'We

do not fear the Dark Light. It is the source of our strength. Its power nourishes our world like the blood that runs through our veins. We use it to create special instruments and processes that enable us to examine the smallest particles of matter – the building blocks which, when combined in the correct sequence, create human beings and everything in the world around us.'

Steve was glad he had listened to his kin-sister's account of her Basic Genetics course. 'By examining the constituent parts of these two individuals, we can discover the rogue element that makes them different and find ways to counteract it.'

Skull-Face did not pursue the matter further. 'Let's get back to the escape plan. What was to happen once you had assumed your various disguises?'

'Yeah, well . . . that's where the whole thing fell to pieces. It appears that courtesans only travel in sealed carriage-boxes that are either carried or wheeled by porters. Not Mutes. Clearwater was confident she could get the money we needed from the Consul-General, but not the ID papers, travel passes and neck-tags.'

'I'm glad to hear it,' replied Skull-Face.

'And there was also the problem of the arm-stamps that slaves collect at the various control points they pass through.'

Skull-Face bared his teeth again. 'Now you know it's not just a case of bureaucracy gone mad. It's to help keep tabs on people like you.' He reached into the saddlebags that lay to his left and produced what, when unfolded, turned out to be a beautifully made writing box. Pulling a moistened brush from a tube, he charged it with ink from a solid palette and wrote an indecipherable message with swift, flowing strokes. He then cleaned the brush, and put it back in its container.

'Okay. There's not much time left, but we are going to help you with your travel arrangements – assuming, of course, that you manage to escape from the Heron Pool. A map will be delivered to your shack in the next couple of days. We will put it in the same place you have been hiding your radio-knife. The map will guide you to a point near the east bank of the Uda-sona. The field where you are to land will be marked with a hollow white square. You will be met by one of our people.'

Skull-Face checked the sheet of paper to see if the ink was dry, then folded it into a small square and laid it in front of Steve. 'Give this to your Japanese-speaking friend. It tells him what words our man will use to introduce himself and what he must say in return. Once you've identified yourselves, you can converse in Basic. He will give you the necessary papers and tags for four Mute slaves and the courtesan Yoko Mi-Shima. Plus boat tickets and some money for the voyage.

'The "lady" will be provided with a carriage-box and two serving women. When you are ready to travel, porters will be hired to take the box down to the ferry. Once across the river, they'll deliver it to the dockside. We will alert Side-Winder to expect you to board at Ari-bani – though I imagine you will be in contact with him yourself. Once you're on the wheelboat it should be plain sailing as far as Bu-faro. After that, the ball's in your court.'

It all seemed too good to be true. If his arms and shoulders hadn't been wracked with agonising cramp, he'd have been tempted to loose the Trail-Blazer's rebel yell. He did his best to conceal the pain, but his voice gave him away. 'I – I don't know what to – say!'

'You don't have to say anything,' replied Skull-Face, unmoved by Steve's growing distress. He closed the writing box with slow, deliberate movements and put it away. 'In this case, actions speak louder than words. If you don't deliver your end of the deal, you won't be leaving on a boat – or any other way. Comprendo?'

'Perfectly!' gasped Steve.

'Good.' Skull-Face uncrossed his legs, picked up the curved dagger and moved towards Steve on his knees.

Steve's heart missed a beat. The point of the blade was aimed dangerously low but, at the last minute, Skull-Face lifted it level with his navel and cut through the cord stretched between neck and groin. The Jap then got to his feet and stood back as the two guards untied Steve's arms.

'Now get dressed.'

Steve prised loose the cord that had been biting into his penis and scrotum and gained some much needed relief. Oh, boy! As he started to pull on his clothes he found that his arms were painfully stiff. His fingers wouldn't grip properly. Halfway through he had to stop and massage his arms to restore the circulation. There was nothing he could do about the damage downstairs except hope the pain would go away. Pulling the sash tight round his waist, he stooped down and pocketed the folded piece of paper containing the vital passwords.

Skull-Face doused the lantern and exited from the tent. He was waiting outside as Steve ducked through the flap in between the two guards. Now that he was up on his feet and out of immediate danger, the three Japs looked a lot less daunting. After he'd stretched his spine and filled his lungs with night air, Steve found he was half a head taller than the biggest of the two guards. Skull-Face, his chief tormentor, now looked as if he was standing in a hole. No wonder they'd kept him bent almost double.

'That shelf inside your shack . . .'

'Yes?'

'If you find two small stones on it – one black, one white – it means that everything is in place at the other end.'

'Got it.'

Skull-Face walked with him to the edge of the trail that ran through the pines. Behind and below them, Steve caught a glimpse of the lake as the half-moon found a gap in the clouds and brushed its dark surface with a fleeting coat of silver. They had only gone a few yards, but the black tent was now invisible.

The Jap turned to face him. 'Will you be able to find your way back from here?'

Steve bowed politely. 'Yes, sire. No problem.'

'Good. One last thing. As you've no doubt guessed, in return for services rendered, we have also obtained a number of bugging devices from your people. Just out of interest, was jacking up that female Mute part of your assignment?'

It wasn't a question Steve had been expecting, but he took it in his stride. 'Yes, sire. It's a standard operating procedure which I'm sure even your organisation must use from time to time. We call it "sexual entrapment".'

Skull-Face nodded. 'I see. Well, I suppose that's as good a description as any. Goodnight, Mr Brickman. You are what used to be called "a plausible rogue". If you can manage to keep your balls out of the jar I have a feeling you could go a long way.'

*

On the day before the display, Steve discovered he wasn't the only one who had been making plans. The Iron Masters had also been quietly putting their own act together. Shigamitsu broke the news to Cadillac while making his daily round of the workshops. The Japanese staff of the Heron Pool would be running things on the day, and the newly drafted team of Koreans, Viets and Thais would look after the ground-handling, together with the reloading of the rocket-trays and ground trolleys. All Trackers would be confined to their quarters – the two long bunk-houses inside the walled compound.

In the last month, the strict rules governing the behaviour of slaves had been relaxed. To speed things along, captive Trackers were no longer required to kneel before samurai during working hours. This arrangement only covered the Iron Masters on the permanent staff; all visitors were to be shown the utmost deference.

As Cadillac's constant shadow, Steve was included in this temporary dispensation, but he was still required to bow from the waist when addressed and to keep his eyes averted whilst in the presence of samurai. He did so now and was able to steal a sideways glance at Cadillac.

When in the company of his new masters the Mute tried very hard to keep his face as expressionless as theirs. The Plainfolk called the Japs 'dead-faces' on account of the fearsome metal masks they wore, but their real faces underneath were just as lifeless. They were a strange people. Given an angry dressing-down by a superior, or some really bad news, they became more blank-faced than ever. Laughter was occasionally allowed to break through, but only when among equals or when the top man present gave the cue.

On this particular occasion, Cadillac wasn't doing too well. Steve knew the Mute had been giving a lot of thought to what he was going to wear and how he was going to comport himself when he stood in line to get his share of the praise the domain-lords were bound to hand out. But that wasn't going to happen. When Steve and his two friends were through the only things the dinks would be handing out were neck-trims – if you were lucky – or a meltdown in boiling water if you weren't. But at this point the Mute didn't know that.

After bowing from the waist, Cadillac enquired if, in view of his past and present contribution, he might be allowed to attend as a spectator. Shigamitsu told him he had already raised this point with the palace. The answer was 'No'. From one hour prior to the arrival of their distinguished guests, he and the other two pilots were to remain in the house Lord Min-Orota had graciously provided, and would not emerge until called upon to do so. The same ruling applied to the grass-monkey he had taken on as his assistant.

Cadillac and Steve accepted this with another deep bow and kept their heads down until Shigamitsu and his two aides had moved on. When they both straightened up, Steve found himself looking at a broken man. Cadillac's pride had been dealt a mortal blow, his expectations cruelly shattered.

It was sad to see the new persona he'd stitched together coming apart at the seams, but if he was hoping for sympathy he didn't get it. 'Don't look at me,' said

Steve. 'You were the one who saw this coming, but you preferred to stick your head in the sand.'

The Mute – who was not normally lost for words – didn't say anything. Neither did Steve. Cadillac had always displayed a certain defensive arrogance, but this aspect of his character had been puffed up out of all proportion through the quite exceptional privileges granted to him by Lord Min-Orota and his subordinates. In trying to ape Steve, Cadillac had lost touch with his own inner strengths, his true nature and his heritage as a child of the Plainfolk. In his eagerness to abandon his past life in favour of a new existence, he had blinded himself to the fact that it was totally dependent on the continued patronage of the Iron Masters. Now he was paying the price, and there was nothing Steve could do except stand back and wait until it was time to pick up the pieces.

'What are we going to do?'

'I'd say it was more a question of what *they're* going to do,' replied Steve. 'But, either way, I don't intend to hang around and find out.'

Cadillac was too preoccupied to get the message. 'What?'

'I'm going to take one of these planes we've built and fly out of here with Clearwater. And if you've got any sense you'll do the same.'

The news caused the Mute to look beyond the ruins of a once-promising career. 'You're crazy. You'll never get away with it.'

'You got a better idea?'

'No, but . . . ' Cadillac looked over his shoulder to see who was near by, then dropped his voice even further. 'There'll be eight pilots on parade tomorrow – twelve if you count the glider pilots. Even if we managed to steal a couple of planes they'd be able to follow us.'

'Then we must make sure they don't . . .'

Cadillac's eyes flickered uneasily as he considered the implications of Steve's reply. 'You mean . . . spike the rockets?'

377

'Something like that.' Steve wasn't yet ready to reveal his hand. 'Any objections?'

'I don't know. I'm not sure.' Cadillac took another look round. 'I – I need time to think about it.'

'There *is* no time!' hissed Steve. 'Tomorrow's our one and only chance! We *have* to take it!'

'But how are we –'

'Never mind *how*! Are you willing to go for it? Yes or no?'

Cadillac sighed heavily. 'Since I don't seem to have much choice, I suppose the answer's yes. Satisfied?'

'You don't sound too sure. Once we commit, that's it. You're not going to be able to turn round and say – "Sorry Mr Shigamitsu, I didn't mean it".'

'I know that! I'm not an idiot, Brickman. It's just that this is all happening so fast!' He swept both arms round the busy workshop. 'I worked my buns off to make all this happen.' He dropped his voice again. 'And now you're asking me to help you destroy it!'

'Yes, I am,' said Steve. 'Before it destroys *you*!'

It was true, and Cadillac knew it. His face contorted as his mind twisted around like a fish trying to get off the hook. 'You still haven't explained how we're going to spike the rockets.'

'I don't have to. That's not how it's going to happen.'

'But –'

'Forget it! It's already been taken care of.'

Cadillac may have been robbed of all certainty about his future prospects, but he knew exactly how he felt about Steve. 'You lying sonofabitch! You gave me your word!'

Steve bared his teeth. 'Yeah, that's right, I did! Double-crossing you was the only way to save your ass! If we'd played it *your* way we'd be standing here now wringing our hands. Instead of calling the shots we'd have been totally shafted! This way at least we've got a better than evens chance of making it back to Wyoming. So stop all this name-calling crap and start co-operating!'

*

Lord Hiro Yama-Shita had already begun his journey towards the Heron Pool some days before Cadillac reluctantly decided to terminate his career as a designer of flying machines. Accompanied by his usual entourage of aides and escorted by a hundred samurai and an equal number of foot-soldiers, he boarded his red and gold wheelboat for the trip down the Hudson River. At Na-yuk, the last river port in his domain, his party and their horses transferred to three large ocean-going junks which took them through the straits of Nyo-Yoko into the open sea to the south of Aron-giren, then north around the coast to the port of Ba-satana.

Yama-Shita would have had a much shorter journey if he had crossed the Hudson at Arib-bani and travelled to Ba-satana along the main east–west highway, but in this case distance was no object. He preferred to remain for as long as possible in an environment over which he had total control. Yama-Shita had made a triumphal progress by road through the domain of his close allies, the Se-Iko, but they were a long way from the centre of power. His friends the Min-Orota occupied a more vulnerable piece of real-estate.

It was 170 miles by road from Ari-bani to Ba-satana; a mere four-day journey. The trouble was the first eighty of those miles cut across the original domain of the Shogun's family, the Toh-Yota. From its southernmost point at Nyo-Yoko, it ran northwards between the Uda-sona and Konei-tika rivers to the great ice-river boundary that divided Ne-Issan from the Fog People. While crossing their territory his column would have been exposed to prying eyes every step of the way. No. Yama-Shita preferred the comfort and privacy of his own state-rooms – especially when he was transporting a valuable and highly sensitive piece of cargo.

Packed inside a chest which, when opened, appeared to contain richly woven bolts of silk, was the engine which had powered the long-dog's original flying-horse. Yama-Shita had attempted to fake its destruction some months before, but he had subsequently received several

379

disquieting indications that his ruse had not succeeded. At least two of the Shogun's Heralds had been involved in equally unsuccessful attempts to persuade certain disaffected members of his own household either to confirm its continued existence or to reveal its present hiding place.

The clumsy fools had not had the wit to realise that he would never have involved any envious or untrustworthy relatives in such a sensitive affair. Those selected as potential traitors quickly informed him of the approaches that had been made and of the inducements offered. Whatever their private differences, loyalty to the family took precedence over their obligations to the Shogun. They were also motivated by a strong sense of self-preservation. Yama-Shita had risen to power because he had ruthlessly eliminated anyone foolish enough to oppose his policies or challenge his leadership – either openly or in secret. Friend or relation, mother or child, he had spared no one. And age had not mellowed him.

The only threat to his growing power and influence came from his neighbours the Toh-Yota. Despite his family's role in bringing them to power and the solid support they had given to the Shogunate in the past, Yama-Shita knew that it had become an uneasy alliance tinged with envy and suspicion. The thirty-year-old merger between the Yama-Ha and the Matsu-Shita families had produced a menacing combination of wealth and military power, and it was well known that kings often turned against the kingmakers. All they needed was a convincing pretext that could be used to muster the necessary support. If they held together, a pack of snivelling street-hounds could always overcome a mountain lion, but it rarely happened. Faced with a spirited resistance, the more cowardly mongrels always tended to slink away.

It was the same with the running dogs in the Toh-Yota pack. Some would follow their leader blindly, others would turn tail – or even change sides – if the battle proved too hard and too bloody. Even so, it would be foolish to underestimate the resources of the Shogunate. Yoritomo had somehow got wind of the tentative plan to resurrect the Dark Light. The rumours – for that was all they could be at this stage – had been given substance by his suspected involvement in the transportation of the long-dog bitch the idiot Toh-Shiba had taken into his bed.

If she was to be believed, no charges could be levelled against himself or his colleague, Kiyo Min-Orota – but could she? Yama-Shita had few grounds for complacency. The eleven assassins who had been dispatched to kill her in two teams of three and a final, somewhat desperate, quintet, had all vanished without trace. To a seasoned power-broker like Yama-Shita that did not auger well. He doubted that the Consul-General had either the foresight or the means to protect his outlandish whore against such dedicated professionals. No. Another unseen hand was at work here – and Yama-Shita had a shrewd idea to whom it belonged. If he was correct about the assumptions and intentions of his adversaries, it would be unwise to remain in possession of the engine. It was for this reason he had brought it with him. Kiyo Min-Orota had been eager to share in the fruits of this hazardous enterprise. It was only right and proper that he shared the risks – something which, up to now, he had been noticeably reluctant to do.

The move made good sense. Despite being linked with the Yama-Shita family in the Heron Pool project and the deeper suspicions that surrounded it, the Min-Orota were still regarded as being loyal allies of the Toh-Yota Shogunate – to whom they were tied by marriage. Temporarily wayward allies, perhaps – but a family who, in the end, would realise where their duty and their best interests lay. Excellent. Trusted servants were always best placed to betray their masters.

Kiyo's reaction on being made guardian of the infernal machine that could destroy them both would be a good measure of his resolve. If he was willing to grasp the nettle, then the cloud warrior who had already demonstrated his skills in the building of flying-horses should be given a new project. The rockets he had devised were only a stopgap solution. To have any worthwhile military application, the flying-horses had to be able to alight and take to the air from any suitable terrain and be capable of sustained powered flight. That would require two things: some kind of wheeled carriage *fixed to the body of the craft* and an engine similar to the one he had brought with him. How its component parts could be reproduced was something the cloud warrior would have to solve. But that could come later. The first step was to get him to reveal the secret methods used by the spinners and weavers to capture and manipulate the Dark Light.

As his flotilla of junks sailed parallel with the southern shore of Aron-giren, Yama-Shita paid no heed to the passing watchboats flying the flag of the Toh-Yota. There was not the slightest danger of being stopped and searched; any vessel carrying a domain-lord was deemed to be an extension of his personal fief, and for government sea-soldiers to have boarded it would have been tantamount to an armed invasion of his territory – an act of war which could have the most serious consequences.

No. His voyage past the Shogun's fish-island would be serene and unhindered. Despite the irritating attentions of Yoritomo's agents, he was more than a match for the young occupant of the Summer Palace. It was Ieyasu, the Court Chamberlain, who was his most dangerous adversary, but fortunately he was a man you could do business with. He was a realist, a man's man with a balanced view of the iniquitous side of human nature – not a smooth-faced soft-brained idealist who hardly ever ventured beyond the silken cocoon of the Inner Court.

Yes. Slowly but surely, all the strands would draw together and the noose would tighten round the neck of the Toh-Yota. A costly debilitating war would not be necessary. In a smooth transition of power, the young Shogun would be deposed and disposed of. A wiser, more worldly and more amenable figure would be invited to lead Ne-Issan forward into a new progressive age in which the Yama-Shita would be the standard-bearers. They would set the pace, they would amend the rules, encourage new thoughts and new ideas and, eventually, they would – by popular consent – take over the reins of power.

Rounding the eastern tip of Aron-giren, the three square-sailed junks set course for Kei-pakoda against a freshening breeze that put white crests on the incoming waves. Aided by the steam engine whose sonorous beat could be felt as well as heard on the main deck, the broad bows dipped and rose gently as they ploughed through the light, even swell. Except for white clouds rimming the far horizon, the sky was clear, with a promise of more fair weather to come. Just what was needed for the performance he was to witness on the morrow. The image that met Yama-Shita's eyes as he surveyed the scene around him was one of majestic, unstoppable power. And it pleased him.

*

The Iron Masters and the mixed bag of dink craftsmen who now formed the bulk of the Heron Pool staff put the finishing touches to the twelve aircraft at around 1800 and retired to make their own personal preparations for the big event. The original group of Trackers was left to tidy up, then the two workshops were shut for the night and left in the care of the usual team of night-watchmen. With his constant to-ing and fro-ing on Cadillac's behalf, and their joint midnight oil-burning sessions with Jodi and Kelso, Steve had come to be regarded as part of the furniture, and he had taken the opportunity to familiarise himself with the watchmen's routine.

His original plan had been to bury a fist-sized chunk of plastic explosive into the head of a rocket tube, arm it with a detonator, then pack in the special black powder mix. During the fifteen-second burn, the flame would eat its way down the tube, ignite the detonator and – *blamm*! One flying-horse transformed into singed silken confetti and charcoal chips.

But things hadn't gone as planned. The influx of dinks

had totally upset the work routines, and to meet the increased demand for rockets, the 'power unit' had been almost completely restaffed. Jodi and Kelso – on whom Steve had been counting to help him spike the rockets – had been totally occupied with training the pupil pilots, and he himself had been kept busy checking and flight-testing the completed craft as they came off the production line.

By the end of the month, the Tracker workforce had been eased into subordinate roles in all the processes except flying – a move which limited Steve's precious total freedom of access to every department. To make life more difficult, the Iron Masters kept changing the programme for the big day, and Cadillac had ended up training eight rocket-pilots instead of five. Unaware of Steve's escape plans, Cadillac had come close to wrecking their chances by giving additional gliding instruction to the remaining four of the initial batch of twelve trainees. All four had flown several hours solo and proved themselves reasonably proficient. Which meant that – if the Iron Masters so decided – *all* the available aircraft might now be in use when Steve had been gambling on having half of them on the ground, strategically parked, fuelled and ready to go when H-Hour struck!

He only planned to steal three aircraft, but when he threw the switch it was impossible to predict what the Iron Masters' reaction might be. He was hoping, with Clearwater's help, to throw them into total confusion. But if there was an unexpectedly strong backlash, some of the aircraft might get damaged in the crossfire – so it was important to have at least one in reserve. Fine in theory, but difficult to arrange when the Iron Masters were changing their minds almost daily. Every time Steve took steps to cope with the new situation he found he'd been wrong-footed by yet another switch in the schedule. It was almost as if Min-Orota's people suspected someone was out to ruin things and were trying to keep everybody guessing.

In the end, their indecision proved a blessing in disguise. When it became clear that he was effectively locked out of the powder room, Steve called up AMEXICO and arranged for a fifth and final package to be airmailed into the pond. In the light of the bombshell news that they had been dropped from the team and were not even going to be allowed to watch from the sidelines, it was his smartest move yet.

As night closed in on the eve of the display, Steve pulled the 'forgotten drawings' routine to gain entry to the workshop where the twelve aircraft had been parked in a neat interlocking line. By arriving at precisely the right moment, he was able to lace the nightwatchmen's supper with some specially formulated dope in the few vital minutes between its delivery and distribution. The onset of sleep was gentle, the period of unconsciousness was brief but profound, and the sleeper's breath smelt of *sake*. AMEXICO had come up with the goods yet again.

Steve had two hours to make the last connections. He only needed one. The charge of plastic explosive, disguised as a small wooden reinforcing strut, was already in place. Steve had positioned some of them during the test-flights he'd made; the other aircraft had been primed by Jodi and Kelso. All he had to do now was to insert the ingenious device that AMEXICO had provided. It would not be difficult. Each insertion only took a couple of minutes. The workshops and powder room had already been wired up; the surprise package for the guardhouse inside the compound would be delivered tomorrow morning. Just these gizmos and that was it.

Yep . . . Once they were in place it didn't matter if the Iron Masters changed the programme for the umpteenth time or decided to make it another day. Coming or going, or just standing still, they were going to get it right in the kisser.

CHAPTER FIFTEEN

When the sun had risen clear of the Eastern Sea, Nakane Toh-Shiba, the Consul-General, left Clearwater's bed in the lakehouse and returned to his official residence. A thin, velvety layer of mist still lingered on the surface of the water and it swirled around the hull of the one-oared flatboat that brought him ashore. The five samurai who acted as his personal bodyguard on such visits sat facing him in the bow.

Normally, the Consul-General oozed contentment after coupling with his olive-skinned long-dog, but this morning, despite the joyous delirium produced by his repeated penetration of her body, his mood was sombre. And with good reason. He had received a letter from the Shogun ordering him to take to the air in one of the newly constructed flying-horses.

In the three days since the Herald had delivered the letter, Toh-Shiba had read it over and over again, and each time it had left him disturbed and apprehensive. He might lack some of the bleaker moral principles to which samurai were expected to adhere, but he did not lack courage. He did, however, fear the unknown. In his youth, he had fought to secure the snow-laden northern marches, and was still ready to wield a sword if duty called – provided he had both feet planted firmly on the ground, or in his stirrups.

Since he was the Shogun's official representative, it would have been highly improper to comment upon the wisdom of Yoritomo's decision to support the Heron Pool project but, privately, the whole idea filled Toh-Shiba with deep foreboding. If men had been meant to fly, Ameratsu would have given them wings. The sky was the realm of the *kami*, and only birds had been granted passage through it. Man had been placed on the earth and the waters, and he should not seek to alter the divine plan.

In the ancient world, ruled by the Dark Light, men had sailed across the cloud-world in great sky-boats. They had attempted to conquer the realm of the *kami* and steal the glittering jewels of heaven. But they had been cast down. The shining silver sails that bore them aloft had been torn apart and thunderbolts had turned their proud hulls into funeral pyres. Crews and passengers trapped inside the shattered hulks perished as they crashed down upon the cities of the fools who had built them.

Blinded by vaulting ambition and indifferent to the wrath of the *kami*, humankind had continued its assault on the heavens using the powers given to it by the spinners and weavers of the Dark Light. They had trodden upon the face of the moon-goddess and sent spy-chariots hurtling towards the stars. Finally, Ameratsu-Omikami had purged the world of its madness by casting the sun into the sea.

Those early voyagers who had ventured aloft had been utterly destroyed, and this new attempt was also doomed to fail. It was for this reason, concluded Toh-Shiba, that the Shogun's own family had distanced themselves from the enterprise. The scheme to build flying-horses had been the brainchild of Lord Hiro Yama-Shita, a man whose ambitions could not be ignored. By granting the licence to the Min-Orota, the Shogun had skilfully brought the enterprise within his sphere of influence whilst still keeping it at arm's length.

The Herald Toshiro Hase-Gawa – who had privately confessed to being terrified at the prospect – had mounted one of the flying-horses in order to be able to make a first-hand report on its qualities to the Inner Court. And now that their relative safety had been demonstrated by the training, without any serious incident, of twelve samurai, the Shogun had asked his

Consul-General to make a similar flight before delivering his own opinion of their military potential.

As the highest-ranking representative of the *bakufu* at the ceremony, his flight would be a symbolic seal of approval; an indication of the importance the Shogun attached to the work being carried out at the Heron Pool. That, in essence was the text of the letter.

Framed as a request, it was, in fact, an order to take to the air. The memory of the punishment meted out upon humankind for its past follies in this direction was sufficient to cause him to feel worried by the contents of Yoritomo's letter, but he had been even more disturbed by the way it had been written. Nakane Toh-Shiba was, after all, related by marriage to the writer, and all previous communications from his brother-in-law had been noticeably warmer. Toh-Shiba was not the total buffoon many thought him to be. While it was true he expended a great deal of energy indulging his obsession in forcing open the rose-petalled gates of the secret garden which was to be found cupped between a firm pair of female thighs, it was not his sole interest in life. In his youth, he had received an education befitting the son of a noble house, and he had spent several years at court. He was therefore able to discern the subtle but significant changes in phrasing and choice of words.

Yoritomo's letter was courteous and correct but, if one read between the lines, it was cold and dismissive. Toh-Shiba was astute enough to realise it marked a change in their relationship. Had Lord Min-Orota been correct when he had hinted that news of his present dubious liaison could have reached the wrong ears? The position could only be resolved through a personal encounter with his brother-in-law but, unfortunately, that would have to wait.

Perhaps it was time to deny himself the delights furnished so willingly by the long-dog. The thought of parting company with her serpent-like body was unbearable, but sometimes a man had to sacrifice that which he held most dear in order to prove he was master of his own heart – if not his own destiny. Not yet, perhaps, but soon. He would then travel with his family to Aron-giren to present his report on the flying-horses in person. And when that matter was disposed of, he would draw Yoritomo's attention to the apparent coldness of his letter, secure in the knowledge that the probable cause of the Shogun's displeasure had been dismembered, boiled and boned before being ground into pig-food.

Perhaps it was the Herald Toshiro Hase-Gawa who had passed on some scabrous rumour garnered in the sinks and stews frequented by the soldiers from the government garrison. A handful of them had been present when the long-dog had revealed her true colours. They did not know what had become of her, and the staff of the lake-house where she had been placed like a bird in a gilded cage never left the island. News of her presence could have reached shore through the boatman who ferried supplies across, as well as the Consul-General, but it would have to have been in the form of a letter, because Toh-Shiba had ordered the man's tongue to be removed some years before. It was a simple precaution and a salutary warning to others whose tongues were inclined to wag, but it was unlikely to prove a major stumbling-block to the impudent young Herald. His zealous pursuit of traitors and backsliders had proved so successful he now felt it was his right and duty to stick his nose into everyone's affairs, without regard to whether they were friend or foe.

The nests of vipers to which the Shogun often alluded needed to be rooted out but, like all the Heralds, Toshiro Hase-Gawa was imbued with the same tiresome morality as his master. At the first whiff of wrongdoing, be it high treason or an illicit liaison that posed no threat to anyone, the Herald's nose was aquiver and he was off on the trail like a game-dog. Nakane admired 'upright' men, but he favoured the more earthy interpretation that Ieyasu, the Court Chamberlain, put upon the word.

The blissful state of uprightness he had enjoyed

throughout much of the night caused him to reflect on the third cause for his present sombre mood. Despite his private fears about taking to the air, he had boasted to the long-dog that he was about to do so, and he had scoffed at the Herald's lack of courage. The long-dog – to whom he had given the name Safaiya – Sapphire– because of her wondrous blue eyes – had greeted the news excitedly. Her admiration for him knew no bounds. He was, she said, as adventurous as he was ardent, and her only regret was that she would not be there to witness his bravery on this truly momentous occasion.

Toh-Shiba was unable to recall quite what it was she had said to persuade him, but he had finally agreed to have her conveyed in a sealed carriage-box to the Heron Pool. But he did remember explaining that she could not travel as part of his retinue, and that she would have to watch the proceedings from a discreet distance. These conditions had been accepted without hesitation, and she had kissed his feet and dried her tears of happiness on the hem of his robe.

Oh, what joy his words had brought her! By what undeserved stroke of good fortune had she, a worthless slave, been blessed with so noble, glorious and generous a master? His presence within brought her to a state of ecstasy, but merely to look upon him made her heart leap and her loins tremble. When he addressed her with words of kindness or of love, her enraptured soul felt as if it had entered paradise. To be touched by his shadow, to breathe the same air, was an unparalleled honour, a source of constant delight and exaltation. Et cetera, et cetera . . .

Toh-Shiba would never have expressed his feelings for her in such extravagant terms, but, by and large, they were reciprocated – especially after she had shown her gratitude in ways that sent his mind reeling. But now that he was back in his official residence, his promise to let her attend the ceremony began to look increasingly rash.

Even though his wife, Mishiko, was indisposed and would not be accompanying him, the long-dog's presence at or anywhere near the Heron Pool could be potentially embarrassing. She had sworn to die rather than reveal their liaison, but if by some mischance she was unmasked and traced back through the hire of the vehicle to him –

No. It was sheer folly.

The solution to his predicament was simple. All he had to do was – do nothing. But try as he might, he could not bring himself to reverse his decision. Some mental imperative drove him forward, and he heard his own, disembodied voice ordering his private secretary to secure a wheeled carriage-box and the necessary porters.

The secretary, with his usual discretion, asked for the basic details and timing of the journey, but did not attempt to establish the identity or gender of the passenger. The Consul-General informed him that the party in question was to be collected from his private retreat on Two Island Lake and conveyed to the pavilion situated immediately to the east of the Heron Pool. There would be no servants in attendance, and the porters were to return with the carriage-box as soon as its passenger had alighted.

Toh-Shiba could not quite understand the logic of this arrangement, but it seemed the most sensible thing to do. The grounds of the pavilion – which was occupied by her fellow long-dog – bordered the flying field behind the Heron Pool. If she removed her mask and borrowed a spare set of his clothes, she could watch the proceedings from there without attracting attention.

His secretary bowed himself out of the room, leaving Toh-Shiba feeling enormously relieved that the matter had been disposed of.

*

The private secretary was the Consul-General's man, but one of his office staff was receiving an additional stipend from another quarter. The news that the Consul-General's concubine was on the move was rapidly conveyed to the Herald. Toshiro could scarcely believe his ears when he heard where she was to be taken. How, in heaven's name, had Brickman managed it?

After discovering when this transfer was due to take place, Toshiro hurriedly completed his own preparations, and rode out followed by four mounted standard-bearers from the government garrison. As envoys of the Shogun, Heralds were always escorted when attending ceremonial occasions.

He caught up with the sealed carriage-box on the eastern outskirts of the tiny village of Mara-bara. Motioning his escort to halt, Toshiro went on alone. The sight of the Herald, resplendent in his black and red armour, coming up astern stopped the porters dead in their tracks. They trundled the carriage-box on to the grass verge and knelt with bowed heads, expecting the magnificent horseman to pass by. When he stopped in front of them, they experienced the same sense of dread that had gripped Steve.

Adopting his most arrogant manner, Toshiro dismounted and warned the trembling porters to remain forever deaf, dumb and blind to what was about to take place. After their spokesman had assured him that their memories were already blank, he ordered them to move thirty paces down the road.

As they scurried away, Toshiro hitched the horse to one of the trucking-poles of the carriage-box, untied a bag attached to the pommel of his saddle and rapped his armoured knuckles against the door. After allowing the occupant a brief delay to compose herself, he tried the handle. The door was still fastened on the inside. He put his mouth close to the grille. 'Open up! I've got a present for your friend, Brickman.'

The catch was withdrawn, allowing the door to open outwards. Toshiro peeped inside and saw Clearwater seated on the padded bench, dressed in a brightly coloured embroidered silk kimono. She had shrunk into the far corner like some night-creature who feared the light. Her hair was swept up in the style of the geishas from the 'floating world', spiked with wooden pins and bulked out with lacquered hair-pieces. Her face was concealed behind the same dead white oval mask with its tiny, red-painted lips, its thin enigmatic eye-slits and even thinner brows perched high on the forehead.

Toshiro tossed the bag on to Clearwater's lap and bowed with mock politeness. 'Tell him the Herald hopes that good fortune smiles upon his enterprise. And assure him that, should he fail, I shall do my utmost to make sure my sword is the first to reach him.' He closed the door, remounted and motioned to his escorts to rejoin him. The kneeling porters buried their faces in the grass and kept them there until the hoofbeats died away.

*

Cadillac's house-servants had been in a state of high excitement since early morning, when the advance party of soldiers and officials from Bo-sona had arrived to make sure that all was in order. Lowly domestics living in a rural backwater were seldom accorded such a treat, and here they were with a first-class view of what promised to be a splendid occasion.

It was to begin with a procession. Led by trumpets and drums, flutes, bells, gongs and chanting priests, *two* domain-lords with their richly dressed retinues were due to pass along the new road on the eastern side of the pavilion. Foot-soldiers with tall pikes bearing the pennants of the Min-Orota and Yama-Shita families had already begun to take up their positions along the route. The sun was rising into a blue sky whose vault was thinly veiled with wispy clouds like drawn threads of white silk.

Oh, yes. It promised to be a memorable day.

*

Through the gap in another set of screens, Steve, Cadillac, Jodi and Kelso were also watching the steady influx of people, but in their case it was with mounting

393

tension, not excitement. Steve knew the adrenalin would not start flowing until he went into action – and nothing could happen until Clearwater arrived. They had worked out a plan on his last visit, but how well had it succeeded? Only time would tell and, as usual, it was the waiting and the uncertainty he found hardest to bear. When they struck the first blow they would have the advantage of surprise, but despite the careful planning they were taking a colossal gamble against odds of at least 200 to 1. Only Clearwater had the power to even things up.

Oh, sweet Sky Mother! Get her here, that's all I ask . . .

Cadillac nudged him and pointed to a group of five horsemen passing at a brisk canter. The lead rider was the Herald Toshiro Hase-Gawa. Some help *he'd* turned out to be. No. That was unfair. He had been dumb enough to buy Steve's story and smart enough to get him the job of roadrunner. Without his backing they wouldn't be standing here now with their finger poised on the button. The Herald had ignored his warning to stay away – presumably because he was obliged to put in an appearance. If nobody from the Shogun's team showed up, it wouldn't look too good when the bad guys started raking over the ashes. Yeah, well . . . T.H.G. would just have to take his chances like everybody else. When the guys from Big Blue were through he'd be glad he was wearing a tin hat.

They heard the sound of distant trumpets and the beat of marching drums. Peeking through the screens, Steve saw a mounted samurai canter down the road towards the Heron Pool, shouting to the soldiers stationed at intervals on both sides of the road. The soldiers drew themselves up and adopted an aggressive review stance, left foot out and forward, left fist planted high on the hip, right arm extended level with the shoulder to form a precise right-angle with their pike-shafts. The drums and trumpets grew louder and now Steve could hear other instruments too.

C'mon, Clearwater! Where the eff-eff are you?

From the various conversations Cadillac had listened in on, Steve knew there would be a lot of ceremonial bowing and scraping before the first flight of the day, but he wanted Clearwater to get there to keep Cadillac in line. The Mute had already taken two stiff shots of *sake* to steady his nerves or drown his sorrows – or both. Steve had taken the bottle away from him and threatened that all three of them would beat him over the head with it if he touched another drop.

The previous night, while Steve had been risking his ass putting the gizmos aboard the planes, Cadillac had drunk himself under the table. Just the kind of partner a guy needed at a time like this – 100 per cent unreliable. His rejection by the Iron Masters had hit the Mute hard, but the lesson still hadn't sunk home. Given the chance, he could still renege at the last minute and go crawling back to them. Steve had told Jodi and Kelso not to let him out of their sight. If and when Clearwater arrived, she would put some iron in his soul. That was why Mr Snow had sent her along. Crazy old coot. All this blood, sweat and tears – and what for? A hundred stone-age rifles that were no fucking use to anybody except the Iron Masters who were using them to strengthen their trading position.

The thought of the rifles caused Steve to cross over to the floor storage units where he had hidden the handguns and the remainder of the grenades AMEXICO had dropped into the lake. The units were set along the edge of the raised floor section and were, in effect, boxes with hinged lids that matched the surrounding wood planking. They were covered, like the rest of the floor, with the ubiquitous *tatami*.

Sliding one of the mats aside, Steve opened the centre trapdoor and lifted the corner of the folded quilt that lay inside. Beneath the quilt were four multi-shot air pistols with several spare magazines and pressurised cartridges, fragmentation grenades, smoke, phosphorus and riot-gas. Steve and Jodi hadn't encountered this last type of grenade before but, according to Kelso, one sniff made you feel you'd been hit in the chest by a charging buffalo. It apparently attacked the nerves or muscles or whatever it was that controlled the respiratory system, causing painful contractions of the lungs and throat. By rendering you almost incapable of breathing, it made you incapable of doing anything else. Depending on the degree of dispersion, the victim was immobilised for an hour or more; prolonged inhalation in a confined space could kill.

Smoke grenades didn't damage your health, the other grenades you could at least try and duck away from, but these little horrors could sneak up on you when you weren't looking – which was why AMEXICO had thoughtfully included five face-masks with chemical air filters.

The fanfares and drumbeats grew louder still. Cadillac turned from the window. 'Here they come . . .'

As he spoke, the door to the study slid open. The two house-women who had shared the bathtub padded in with a curious stooping gait. Stilling their fluttering hands, they bowed in Cadillac's direction. 'Ahh, you have, ahh, impah-tan visitah!' they stammered, and fell on their knees as Toshiro Hase-Gawa strode into the room.

The sight of the armed and armoured samurai caused Cadillac, Jodi and Kelso to go down on their knees.

Steve was already on his. He casually eased the trap-door back into place and stood up. 'Nice of you to drop in.' It was asking for trouble, but he was so keyed up he was past caring.

The Herald's hand tightened on the hilt of his sword. 'I hear there's been a change of plan,' he said, through gritted teeth.

'Are we talking about the Consul-General?'

'We are.'

'What's happened? Did someone cancel the trip?'

'No. It's still on. He's even been boasting about it.'

'Then he'll be taken care of.'

'That wasn't the deal, Brickman. You know what my client's wishes were. It was to be in the air. The way you showed me.'

'Yeah, well, due to circumstances beyond our control, it's not going to be quite like that. But don't worry, he's still going off the top board.'

'Do you mind telling me how?'

'I can't explain how. You wouldn't understand. But since your friends won't let me fly, I'm having to use a device powered by the Dark Light. Okay? All I can say is you won't be disappointed. And I won't have to explain how I accidentally lost a very important passenger.' He shrugged. 'So it works out fine for both of us.'

'Oh, Brickman . . .' breathed Toshiro.

'Yeah,' said Steve. 'I know how you feel. But why spoil all the fun?'

The atmosphere became electric as they stared each other out. Cadillac, Jodi and Kelso kept their heads down. The two Trackers had a feeling they'd seen the Jap before, but they didn't know who he was or why Steve was courting death by facing him down at such a crucial moment, or what was going to happen next. Just when the suspense was becoming unbearable there was another timid knock on the door.

A wavering voice addressed the Herald in Japanese. Toshiro responded with a gruff command. The door slid open to reveal the two house-women kneeling outside, then Clearwater – still masked – appeared between them and stepped through into the room.

Steve's heart leapt, but he didn't let it show in case the Herald got the wrong idea. 'What kept you?'

Toshiro, who didn't realise that the question was rhetorical, answered for her. 'I think you'll find her porters had to step aside to let the procession pass.'

Clearwater didn't say anything. The only time she had met the Herald he had been swathed in black from head to toe. Although she had encountered him on the road and his voice was vaguely familiar, she didn't know who this imposing figure was or what he was doing there. But since Steve was on his feet she stayed on hers.

The two house-women, crouched low over bent knees,

397

shuffled in and deposited Clearwater's luggage: a cloth bundle and a bag.

Toshiro issued some kind of order in Japanese. One of the house-women picked up the bag and came forward on her knees to hand it to him. He gave them another order which they both acknowledged with a grovelling bow then backed out of the room, sliding the door shut behind them.

Steve heard their cottoned feet beat a hasty retreat down the corridor as Toshiro turned and tossed him the bag.

'The leaves you've been asking me for. That wraps up my half of the deal. Make sure you deliver yours.'

Steve nodded. 'Nice doing business with you. Better go out the back way. If you were to be –'

Toshiro cut him short. 'Brickman, advice from you is one thing I don't need. I thought it would have been clear by now you weren't dealing with an amateur.'

Steve bowed politely.

Neither are you, gorgeous. Neither are you . . .

*

Seated with their chief lieutenants in the centre of the grandstand and separated from the other spectators by a three-deep wall of their own samurai, Lords Yama-Shita and Min-Orota surveyed their surroundings. Immediately below them, hidden by the canopy erected to shield the Shogun from the view of any potential assassin, sat the Consul-General and the Herald Toshiro Hase-Gawa. Their box was guarded on all four sides by government soldiers from the Mara-bara garrison.

To Yama-Shita's right, the stand was filled with officials and merchants from his own domain; the other half was occupied by a similar group from the Min-Orota family. Ranged on the field before them was a line of eight flying-horses, with a second staggered row of four behind. All twelve were perched on wheeled trolleys. Their gleaming white, silk-covered wings and bodies

398

were marked on both sides with the *hinomaru*, the blood-red disc that was the symbol of Ne-Issan, Land of the Rising Sun. The tails carried two signs: a Tracker numeral and its Japanese equivalent.

The alien markings had been necessary to allow the original workforce of outlanders to identify the individual craft. This explanation came from Shigamitsu, the Heron Pool commander, who was seated behind the two domain-lords to answer any questions they might wish to put to him. He also informed them that the first eight flying-horses were fitted with rocket-trays, whose efficiency would be demonstrated later: those behind were used as gliders for initial training.

Two samurai – a pilot and an observer – stood by the nose of each craft and four ground-handlers were lined up under the high tails. The aircrews were dressed in all-white outfits, with headbands bearing the *hinomaru* flanked by two Japanese ideograms. Seven pilots were from the Min-Orota, five from the Yama-Shita family, and their individual house symbol was emblazoned on the left breast and back of their loose-sleeved tunics.

The show began with a drumbeat parade of the cavalry and foot-soldiers who had accompanied the two domain-lords. Bearing the tall narrow banners of the respective houses, the cavalcade passed between the line of flying-horses and the grandstand in review order, led by a standard-bearer carrying the flag of the Toh-Yota Shogunate and a detachment of government troops. It was only a token presence, but it was customary for them to head any procession at which the Consul-General was present in his official capacity. And since all the spectators were, in theory, loyal subjects of the Shogun, they rose and declaimed the oath of allegiance as Yoritomo's flying-crane banner was carried past.

With the parade over, the troop detachments of the two domain-lords reassembled on either side of the grandstand, with the government soldiers ranged to the left of the Min-Orota and within a stone's throw of the wall separating the flying field from the tree-fringed grounds at the rear of the pavilion occupied by Cadillac.

Following the troops past the grandstand was a group of *shinto* priests of varied rank and importance and their assistants bearing flutes, tubular bells and drums. This group stopped as the soldiers withdrew, bowed en masse to the assembled dignitaries, then moved to the left-hand end of the line-up. In a lengthy ceremony involving the singing of invocations and responses, the waving of burning joss-sticks, the sprinkling of water and the distribution of garlands of paper flowers, the samurai and their flying-horses were blessed on behalf of the Iron Masters' sky-gods and – presumably – awarded the celestial equivalent of an airworthiness certificate.

Returning to the grandstand, the priests formed up into two lines like a guard of honour, bowed to the assembly, then turned to face each other. It was the signal for the two domain-lords to descend with their immediate entourage to inspect the aircrews and their flying-machines.

Watching through a narrow gap in the screens at the rear of the pavilion, Steve saw the Consul-General and Toshiro attach themselves to the group as it left the stand. Shigamitsu and his two chief lieutenants at the Heron Pool followed dutifully behind. Using a 'scope with a zoom lens that had been included in the third airmail package, Steve was able to zero in for head and shoulder shots of individuals in the group. The two guys at the front were obviously the domain-lords but, having never seen either before, he didn't know which was which.

The preliminaries were almost over. In a few minutes the real action would start. He passed the 'scope to Cadillac. 'Keep your eye on the Consul-General. Unless they've changed things around again, he's due to open the flying display.'

'May I look through this magic eye too?' enquired Clearwater.

'Sure . . .' Steve sent her a message with his eyes, then started to pull the hidden weapons out of the floor storage units.

Jodi had already checked the house and found it empty.

Every member of Cadillac's small domestic staff was now lined up along the back wall, totally absorbed in the happenings beyond. It was unlikely they would be disturbed, but there was no point in taking chances. Situations like this were governed by Sod's Law: if something could go wrong, you could bet your last meal-credit it most probably would. That was why she and Kelso had armed themselves with concealed handguns and were now roving silently around the house, keeping an eye on the various entrances in case they had any unexpected callers.

Stripping off his loose jacket, Steve donned the sleeveless padded vest that AMEXICO had supplied. It contained a holster for his air pistol, pockets for the spare mags and pressure cartridges, and clips to hold the grenades under a loose flap that concealed their tell-tale outlines. There was another pocket positioned level with his right elbow to hold the face mask. He filled up the various compartments and selected a lethal cocktail of grenades. By the time he was finished, he was a one-man war machine.

He began to load up the three other vests. 'How're we doing?'

Cadillac told him: 'Min-Orota's finished his inspection of the pilots and planes. The man next to him must be Yama-Shita. The four machines in the second line are being moved back towards the workshops, but the crews have been stood down and have gone to the front of the stand.'

'Good. That's more than enough for us.'

'And they've just started to move five from the first line.'

'Where to?'

'They're pushing them towards the grandstand. Wait a minute.' Cadillac lapsed into silence, then said: 'Ah, yes . . . They've parked them in a V-formation right in front of the stand, with their tails pointing towards the spectators.'

'And the crews?'

'They're positioned front and rear like they were before.'

Steve continued loading the pockets of the combat vests. 'So that leaves three out on the field . . . Can you see their numbers?'

'Yes. Six, Seven and Eight. One to Five are in front of the stand.'

'Good.' The tidy-minded Iron Masters couldn't have made his task easier. Steve looked up and saw that Clearwater had taken over the 'scope. 'Where's lover boy now?'

'He's handing his swords to your friend, the Herald. And now he's taking off his hat and wig and tying a scarf around his head.' Clearwater moved the 'scope on to Min-Orota, then found Yama-Shita's face filling the rectangular frame. She was gripped by a sudden chill as she recognized the slitted eyes and steel-trap mouth. It was her tormentor, the implacable master of the wheelboats who had crushed, drowned and tortured eight Plainfolk Mutes to demonstrate what could happen to her if she did not obey him.

She felt the hatred well up within her. Not reckless and unreasoning, but cold and calculating. The memory of the merciless game played out on the giant paddle-wheel and of the two mutilated heads she had had to share her cabin with was still as fresh and as shocking as ever. She had vowed to avenge the deaths of her fellow Mutes and she would do so today. Yes . . . this soulless monster and his servants would pay the blood-debt. Many times over.

Oh, Talisman, when I call upon you, lend me your strength!

'Now he's taking his seat in the front of the flying-horse. And a samurai is climbing into the seat behind.'

Steve repossessed the 'scope and zeroed in the Consul-General, then panned left on to the tail. Number Seven. Cadillac had told him that one of the gods in the Iron Masters' pantheon was in charge of lucky breaks.

He didn't know whether they viewed the number seven as having any specially favourable significance, but if they did, the fat man was in for a big surprise.

The set-up was becoming clearer by the second. Toh-Shiba was going up with Six and Eight acting as escort. All three aircraft were being pushed back on a diagonal line across the field to the take-off point by the workshops, followed by the other two pilots and their observers. Yama-Shita and Min-Orota were returning to their seats in the stand.

And the Herald? Ah, yes . . . he was walking past Min-Orota's troops towards the government detachment, moving forward on a line that would take him to Steve's right. Steve tracked ahead with the 'scope and caught sight of Toshiro's horse with its distinctive trappings. Another mounted samurai was holding the reins. Steve watched as the Herald was helped up into the saddle. He had obviously decided to improve his chances of survival by staying mobile. Smart move . . .

Steve called Jodi and Kelso back into the study and handed out the combat vests. They put them on under their tunics. Steve helped Cadillac into his. 'I hope you know how to use this stuff . . .'

'If you do I do.'

'Yeah, well, this is the one to watch.' He unclipped a gas grenade and explained its effects to Cadillac and Clearwater, and how they could protect themselves by using the face-mask. He handed the last one to Clearwater and told her to try it on.

Steve saw her eyes widen in alarm through the visor as her muffled voice leaked through the side-filters. 'I feel as if I am drowning!' She pulled the mask off quickly.

He laid a calming hand on her arm. 'There's nothing to be frightened about. You're not going to suffocate. Just breathe deeply. You won't have to wear it for long, but you *must* put it on when you see any of us give this signal –' he brought his hand down over his face. 'Immediately. You understand?'

Clearwater nodded.

'And don't take it off until we remove ours. You got that?'

'Yes.'

'Okay. Time to get changed.' Steve produced a canvas tote-bag and handed it to Clearwater, then placed a faded blue Tracker worksuit on top of it. 'Pack your white mask, robe and whatever you're wearing underneath in the bag. But do it carefully. Did you bring that set of body-paints?'

'Yes. They're bundled up with the clothes I came in. Plus the other things you asked for.'

Steve turned to Cadillac. 'What about your walking skins?'

'I burned them.'

Steve eyed him. 'Trust you. Where're the body-paints you told me about?'

'In one of those cupboards . . .'

'Well, we need 'em.' Steve laid the bag of precious pink cleaning leaves on top of the worksuit. 'Put these in too, plus anything else that might come in useful.' He signalled Jodi and Kelso to precede him through the door. 'Okay. We're just gonna take a look around. You've got five minutes to get changed and packed. Then we'll go over the plan.' Steve stepped quickly outside, then popped his head back into the room. 'And while you're at it, why don't you two patch things up? We've got a long haul ahead of us, and we're gonna need each other every step of the way.'

He slid the door shut and joined Jodi and Kelso at the far side of the adjoining room, whose window screens faced the side wall of the Heron Pool compound.

Kelso eyed him thoughtfully. 'I ain't too happy 'bout that lumphead walking around with all that hardware. S'pose he turns it on us?'

'Yeah,' murmured Jodi. 'I thought we were taking these two guys back as prisoners.'

'That comes later,' said Steve. 'At the moment, we're all supposed to be on the same side. You're a couple of renegades helping us make the break. You want to get back to the Big Open, and they're going back to their own people.'

'And you're going with them . . .'

Steve shrugged. 'Listen. As long as they believe that, it's gonna make our job a whole lot easier – right?'

'I just hope you know what you're doing,' muttered Kelso.

'Trust me,' said Steve.

*

Steve stepped out of the pavilion on to the rear veranda and walked down the steps into the yard. Beyond it was a small vegetable garden, then a short stretch of grass which ended in a line of shrubs and trees and a stone wall. Cadillac's domestic staff were still ranged along it, with their children perched on top.

Even though they had been watching the build-up since early morning, their attention was now riveted on the three planes preparing for take-off. Over the past months, flying machines had become a familiar sight but today's events were special because of the importance of the people involved and the surrounding pomp and ceremony. No one noticed Steve cross quickly to the dung-heap where he had left two wooden buckets containing the usual night mix but, as he went to pick them up, the plump, bossy cook turned to pick up a wandering bare-assed infant. Recovering from her surprise, she gave him a suspicious stare. Steve tilted the bucket towards her to reveal its contents then pretended to empty it.

There was a dramatic roll of drums and –

Shwaah-ba-ba-BOOOMMM! The sound of three pairs of launch boosters igniting in quick succession rippled towards the pavilion. The cook hurriedly lifted the small child on to the wall and sought a foothold herself to get a better view. A full-throated roar of approval came from the seated spectators and watching troops as the Consul-General's flying-horse climbed steeply into the sky followed by his two escorts.

Steve took a firm grip on both buckets and hurried out of sight. Entering the bath-house, he stripped off his distinctive brown uniform and donned a set of borrowed clothes: the sleeveless wrap-over top and trousers worn by the Mutes who manned the cookhouse and other services provided for the Tracker workforce. After making sure the load of ordnance that was packed round his ribs didn't show, Steve pulled a battered wide-brimmed straw hat down about his ears, collected his buckets and went down the newly worn path that linked the pavilion to the workshops behind the Heron Pool compound.

The name, which had only come into use at the beginning of the year when the project had begun, came from the pond behind the flying field. The compound itself had been built several decades before and had originally been used to house a detachment of horse-soldiers belonging to the Min-Orota. Years of peace and partial demobilization had left it empty except for a caretaker and his family, and most of the original buildings had been dismantled and transported else-where. It had then been rented by the local landowner as a feed and grain store and as winter quarters for his livestock.

Situated in a quiet rural area, close to the main east–west highway and bordering on a large stretch of grazing land, the site had appealed to Min-Orota's advisers and had been promptly repossessed. The dilapidated lean-to which was still standing in the north-west corner had been allotted to the Mute slaves, and new wooden units had been constructed to house the Trackers, their guards and overseers. Shigamitsu, the Heron Pool commander, his two chief lieutenants and their families had been billeted in the nearby house of the local landowner – who had been obliged to find another roof to sleep under. 'Leaseholder' was a more accurate term, and the duration of the contract depended entirely on the whim of the domain-lord. Like the robber-barons of old, Min-Orota was the ultimate possessor of every square inch of land, everything on it and underneath it.

The only drawback to the compound was its size. Workers and workshops could not both be contained within its walls. This was why the two long-roofed structures had been erected on either side of a wide alleyway leading from the arched gate in the rear wall. There was a six-foot gap between the southern ends of the workshops and the peeling back wall of the compound, and it had become part of the shortcut that Steve and Cadillac used when going to and from work. The alternative would have meant going through the compound, out of the main gate, then left along the road towards Mara-bara.

For some unexplained reason, the rear gate was only intermittently guarded. When the Trackers began and ended work they were counted out and counted back in, but Steve had noticed that people were passing to and fro during the day without being stopped and, perhaps because he'd been seen going backwards and forwards with Cadillac, no one challenged him when he took the shortcut to the pavilion on his own.

It was surprising, given all the hassles he had encountered elsewhere. Maybe it was because the privilege of working there – as with the Mutes who had been selected for the job of roadrunner – meant that security wasn't a problem. As Simons had said to Jodi and Kelso, no Tracker in his right mind would do anything to screw up a sweet little number like this. Whatever the reason, it suited Steve. The sweet little number was due to come to an abrupt end. And that could prove tough on the renegade linemen who made up the original workforce, but Steve found it hard to be sorry for them. Not knowing who he was, they had treated him with the same contempt as they would any other Mute errand-boy. And when they had realized he was smarter than they were and could perform tasks that were beyond them, they had gone out of their way to give him a hard time.

Carrying a loaded bucket in each hand, Steve stepped through the arch and surveyed the interior of the compound. He now had his back against the north wall. To his left lay the quarters of the Japs and other dinks that made up the permanent staff. Ahead of him was an assortment of wooden buildings – cookhouse, laundry, bath-house, clothing and bedding store staffed by Mutes. Set along the wall immediately to his right were the ramshackle remains of the buildings once used by the horse-soldiers and now housing the Mutes. Beyond them, in the north-west corner, was the spot where the compound's collective shit was dumped until it was carted away to neighbouring farms.

The two long bunk-houses in which the Tracker workforce was now confined lay side by side, parallel with the west wall. They were separated from their Mute neighbours by a fifteen-yard strip of raked gravel which contained four cruciform whipping-posts used for minor infractions. On the occasions Steve had seen them in use, the victim had simply been left tied up for a day in a position guaranteed to rack him with excruciating cramps; most defaulters, whose crime was not showing a sufficient degree of respect to a passing Iron Master, were usually made to kneel on the sharp-edged gravel chips with their hands on their heads for an hour or two.

There was one other building of even greater importance; the guard-house. This was the first structure that met a visitor's eye when he entered by the main, southern gate and found himself in an open area which was used as a parade ground. The guard-house lay facing the main gate, on the far side of this open space. Running along the wall on the eastern edge of the parade ground was an off-duty *cantina* for the lower ranks, where they could meet wives and relatives, and where itinerant traders were allowed to offer their wares. A similar building, against the west wall, offered another form of relaxation that Steve had never encountered in an institutionalized form. Cadillac had told him it was a *bordello* staffed by half a dozen self-employed females.

The whole business of money and the commercial activity which underpinned Iron Master society was a totally new concept, which Steve had found difficult to grasp. The idea of having to work to earn units of currency which you then handed to the person you wanted to jack up seemed quite bizarre.

The *cantina* and the *bordello* were of no concern to Steve. His target was the guard-house, but he could not see it from his present position alongside the archway at the back of the compound. He was also unable to see the double entrance gates, but guessed they would probably be open. A handful of the thirty soldiers who manned the guard-house at any one time would be stationed at the gate, gossiping with passing farm-girls and bargaining with pedlars anxious to sell their wares to the patrons of the *cantina*.

The buckets, with their aromatic contents, were part of his disguise. Many Mutes in Ne-Issan were permanently employed on what captive Trackers termed 'the shit detail'. With a full load, he was unlikely to arouse the suspicions of any guards, but even if he was stopped he would only be subjected to the most cursory examination. That was what he was counting on. During one of the earlier nightshifts, before they had been outnumbered by the present crowd of dinks, Steve had fashioned two planked circles that fitted inside the buckets, creating a false bottom. Hidden underneath, wrapped in transparent plasfilm, was a hefty charge of plastic explosive plus two gas grenades. Both packages were primed with one of AMEXICO's special detonators, and they were guaranteed to spoil the day of anyone unlucky enough to be crapping into either bucket when it exploded.

Steve had reckoned that most of the resident Iron Masters would be on the field in front of the hangars at the far end of the workshops, or seated in the grandstand, leaving only a skeleton staff inside the compound. Apart from a handful of Mutes working on various chores, the place looked deserted. But Steve knew the guard-house would still be fully manned. In order to stand a chance of seizing the three aircraft needed to make their getaway, they had to eliminate as much of the opposition as possible. That meant taking out those who were closest to the action first, and using that blast to draw in others to where they could be caught in the second strike.

Approaching the rotting dungheap, he emptied both buckets and rinsed them out in the stone trough. The false bottoms had now been in place for a week and were indistinguishable from the real thing. Provided nobody compared their weight with the genuine article, no one would guess they'd been rigged.

Okay. Here goes . . .

Steve skirted the gravel punishment area and carried the buckets up the path fronting the Tracker bunk-houses, then turned left along the edge of the parade ground. As expected, some of the guards were loitering by the gate, and he saw some others on the veranda of the *cantina*. They were all dressed up for the big day but, like all soldiers throughout the age, they knew precisely when they could relax and just how far they could go.

It wasn't hard to imagine what they were laughing and joking about. On a day like this, when the top brass were busy enjoying themselves, those who had been relegated to guard duty could afford to take it easy. Unlike those poor fools from the palace who had had to march all the way from Ba-satana in parade order and now had to stand in line, under the gaze of their officers, watching a bunch of even bigger fools shoot across the sky in all directions like dragonflies with their tails on fire.

At the rear of the guard-house, under an overhang of the roof, was a screened four-hole privy. The Iron Masters had a relaxed approach to bodily functions. On his journeys as a roadrunner, Steve had often passed people of both sexes cheerfully urinating in public – sometimes without interrupting their conversation. Faeces, on the other hand, be they horse droppings, cattle turds or the human variety, were a collector's item, and this, again according to Cadillac, had led to the communal bench and bucket system. Higher-ranking Iron Masters made use of private indoor closets in which the wooden bucket was replaced by a similar container made of glazed porcelain. Besides its more elegant shape, it had the added advantage of not smelling after it had been washed. Fortunately, this luxury had not percolated down to the lower ranks – otherwise Steve would have been well and truly shafted.

Having made sure that the privy was empty, Steve entered and replaced the buckets at each end with those he was carrying. He then emptied and rinsed the middle pair, picked up his load and left. As he started to walk away, someone behind him shouted out the Japanese command to halt – a sound all slaves soon learned to react to. Instantly.

Steve froze, then turned back, a bucket gripped in each hand. Two soldiers, with a plump, giggling farm-girl between them, had just turned the corner of the guard-house and were walking towards him. As far as Steve could tell they were unarmed. He was packing enough ordnance to kill them ten times over, but he could not risk cutting them down. The girl hung back as the two soldiers approached. Their cheeks were flushed and they were bright-eyed – a sign they'd knocked back a cup or two of *sake*. Steve put down the buckets and knelt between them, head bowed. He couldn't understand what the dinks were saying to each other or the girl, but they were clearly having a joke at his expense. And so it proved. After swaggering round him, both soldiers stuck a fumbling hand into their trousers, pulled out their hairless dongs and proceeded to pee into the buckets. The real joke came halfway through when they changed aim and widdled over him.

Terrific. There was nothing Steve could do but play the part of the abject slave. *Enjoy it while you can, fellas, 'cause, believe me, in a short while you ain't gonna find much to laugh about . . .*

When Steve had been well watered, the two soldiers

411

waved him away and strutted back to the giggling farm-girl. Steve got to his feet and stood with his head bowed until the trio had disappeared through the back door of the guard-house.

Time for Phase Two. Steve hurried back down the path past the Tracker bunk-houses towards the arch in the rear wall. He kept his head down, hiding his face under the brim of the straw hat. If any of the Trackers inside happened to look out of one of the windows and recognise him, the more sharp-witted amongst them would know he was up to something. Given the way they felt about him, they might try to summon the attention of the guard. And that would really throw a spanner in the works.

CHAPTER SIXTEEN

To a burst of applause from the dignitaries in the stand and the cheers of the lesser spectators, five flying-horses rose clear of their launching trolleys and thundered skywards, one after the other, trailing blue ribbons of smoke. Levelling off at 1,000 feet, the five craft drew together into an arrowhead formation as they circled the field, then dived to build up speed before pulling up into a loop. Rolling upright as they came down off the top – a manoeuvre once known, after its creator, as an Immelman turn – they hauled their noses up and round for a second loop.

Their formation flying was not immaculate, but it was still impressive. It had been made possible by the fitting of a crude retro-thrust device which could be cranked down over the business end of the rocket tubes. A row of curved metal plates like miniature double ploughshares deflected the exhaust gases sideways and downwards, reducing the forward thrust. It was primitive, but it gave each pilot a measure of control over his forward speed – all-important when they were trying to keep their place in the formation.

There was a gasp from the watching crowd when the lines of blue smoke were suddenly severed from the aircraft as they hung upside down. The first rocket had reached the end of its brief life. Time for the second burn. Amid growing apprehension, the five flying-horses continued their downward plunge, then, with a reassuring explosion of sound, a stabbing, white-hot finger of flame appeared beneath the fuselage pod of the lead aircraft. Two, three, four – five!

The watching Iron Masters responded with a deep-throated roar of approval.

Cadillac heard their reaction as he stood on the rear veranda of the pavilion and watched the machines he had created weave smoke trails across the sky. Clearwater, now dressed in one of his white worksuits, came and stood by his side, her dark, sun-streaked hair hanging loose about her neck and shoulders.

The Iron Masters had banned him from the display, but they could not rob him of his moment of triumph. *He* had made this happen and he felt happy that Clearwater was here to witness it. If in the past he had been less in her eyes than he felt he should have been, here – at last – was proof of his abilities, his vision. His eyes met hers and she answered the unspoken question by hugging his arm tightly. He would have preferred a more wholehearted embrace, but her gestures had always been restrained in public or – as in this case – under the watchful gaze of Kazan and Kelso.

Cadillac knew from his penetration of the Iron Masters' minds that his flying machines appealed to their aesthetic sensibilities. Like the proud horses of the samurai, they were lithe and graceful, and the echoing thunder that marked their passage through the sky conveyed the same feeling of irresistible power as the hoofbeats of their galloping steeds.

He was not ungrateful for the few, paltry privileges they had granted him, but he had earned them. He merited even better treatment, should have been given greater power, more responsibility. Today was to have been just the beginning: the best was yet to come. But no. The short-sighted fools had allowed themselves to be blinded by their mistrust of outlanders – no matter how gifted they were. Trusting their honeyed words, he had placed his future in their hands and they had shattered his bright hopes. But the failure was not his. *They* had failed him. So be it. This goose would fly away and lay his golden eggs elsewhere.

After burning up the second rocket with a couple more variations on the basic loop, the five samurai pilots used the third to execute individual slow, flick and hesitation rolls, corkscrewing upwards to gain height for the manoeuvre that had proved the most difficult to master in the time available: a formation barrel-roll.

Whereas ordinary rolls are rotations round an imaginary line drawn between the nose and tail of an aircraft, a barrel-roll, as its name suggests, requires the same 360-degree rotation whilst tracing a spiralling line around the surface of an imaginary barrel. A competent trainee pilot can quickly master the basic control movements required, but to perform the same manoeuvre as one of a group of five aircraft requires a much higher degree of co-ordination.

After several hair-raising near-collisions, Jodi and Kelso had urged Cadillac to drop it from the programme. Not wanting the display to be anything less than a triumphant success, he had been tempted to do so, but their five star pupils had insisted on its inclusion. Their socially inferior instructors were in no position to argue, but managed to persuade the glory-seekers to keep well apart going in, and on the upward half of the roll, then draw closer together on the round-out. The final practice sessions had still been heart-in-the-mouth experiences, but they had managed to avoid sliding into one another. With luck, they would do as well today.

Gliding across the sky, the five machines reassembled into an arrowhead formation like white geese heading south for the winter. They were now high in the air beyond the pond on the north side of the field, and to the right of Lord Yama-Shita's troops, ready to begin the manoeuvre which would carry them in a left-hand spiral round an invisible barrel hanging in the sky in front of the grandstand.

From a height of some 2,000 feet, they dropped their right wingtips as the fourth rocket flamed into life, flew down the curve of the 'barrel', then rolled over on to their left wingtips as they climbed up the other side. The arrowhead formation was now almost completely upside-down, approaching the high-point of the roll directly in front of the seated domain-lords. Both men gazed up with rapt attention as the five machines curved towards them.

*

Hidden in a clump of bushes to the west of the workshops where he had a clear view of the field, Steve pressed the first five buttons on a powerful hand-held transmitter that AMEXICO had sent him. The signals, each on a precisely defined wavelength, triggered the radio-controlled detonators now attached to the plastic explosive he had concealed aboard the aircraft in the formation.

BooOOMM! Boo-boo-BOOMMM! BooOOOMMM!

Lords Yama-Shita and Min-Orota froze in their seats with speechless horror as each of the five flying-horses was engulfed in a ball of flame. The slender silk-covered wings and bodies, crumpled, were ripped to pieces then rapidly consumed by orange tongues of fire. High-ranking guests and assembled troops were thrown into confusion as the shower of burning debris spiralled down towards the packed stand preceded by the rag-doll bodies of the pilots and observers.

*

As the first machine exploded, Kelso rushed out onto the veranda and tossed the tote-bag and cloth bundle into the arms of Cadillac and Clearwater. 'Okay! Go-Go-GO!'

Jodi was already in position by the bath-house on the west side of the yard. She pulled the pin on a gas grenade and hurled it towards the servants lined up along the wall. A gush of white smoke mushroomed out as the

416

grenade detonated, filling the air with disabling nerve gas. Kelso followed it up with another as he raced across the yard behind Cadillac and Clearwater.

Like everybody else, the servants had been temporarily stunned by the aerial conflagration, but the dull report of the first gas grenade coincided with the protective reaction of two of the female servants. As they gathered up their children and turned to flee from the scene, they saw the burst of white smoke, saw their ex-master running across the yard, and watched as the red-haired slave behind him threw what looked like a stone in their direction.

Running along the path towards the workshops, Jodi and Kelso heard the women scream shrilly as they gave the alarm. It didn't matter. A lot of other people were screaming and shouting too. By the time the nearest soldiers reached the garden wall, none of the servants would be in a fit state to tell them anything – and the soldiers would soon find they were short of breath too.

*

As Steve was about to press the first of the buttons that would destroy the aerobatic formation, the plane carrying Consul-General Nakane Toh-Shiba returned from its overflight of Ba-satana and began to circle above his official residence and the government-owned estate which surrounded it. The Consul had not changed his views about flying but, having overcome his initial terror, he had become fascinated by this new view of the world, and his eyes were fixed on the larger of the two islands in the lake which now lay almost directly below.

Everything looked so small! But it was down there, in the summerhouse surrounded by trees and a rock garden, that he had spent the most memorable hours of his life in the arms of his secret paramour; the beautiful alien creature who possessed that rarest of gifts – lustrous, sweet-smelling body hair. The thought of his next visit to her filled him with pleasurable anticipation;

the realisation that it would probably be their last moment together made the feeling bitter-sweet. He had no inkling that it was not *her* death that was drawing ever closer, but his own.

His craft, gliding silently in a V-formation with its two escorts, was banking round in the direction of the Heron Pool when Steve blew the first five planes out of the air. The Consul's pilot saw the fireballs blossom and fall. Signalling frantically with both arms, he managed to attract the attention of his wingmen. They drifted in until their wingtips were almost touching. The lead pilot shouted vainly to his colleagues, pointing repeatedly over the nose. The flaming debris had plunged earthwards, but the drifting trail of smoke that marked the formation's fall was still visible. Both wingmen indicated that they understood. The Consul's pilot gave the signal to fire the last of their five rockets and led them back towards the field.

*

On the ground, beyond the lines of horse- and foot-soldiers of the Min-Orota stationed to the left of the grandstand, the Herald Toshiro Hase-Gawa struggled to control his restive horse. He too had been stunned by the sudden disintegration of the five flying-horses, but since the blow had been delivered against known enemies of the state, he was not gripped by the general sense of horror. What *had* shaken him was Brickman's ruthless efficiency and the power at his command. Beyond that, it was hard to think of anything except how to stay in the saddle and comport himself with the necessary degree of dignity in the midst of the almost total pandemonium that had engulfed the spectators in the stand and the troops on either side.

In the absence of any orders from above, line-officers and squad-leaders were simultaneously screaming at the other ranks to stay in line and watching the sky to avoid being hit by falling debris. The legless body of one of the

418

pilots spiralled out of the sky and hit the ground with a sickening thud only yards away from the Herald's rearing horse. As he hauled savagely on the reins and laid his whip across its neck, one of the sheet-metal rocket-trays planed down like a roof-tile torn loose in a storm and scythed into the wavering ranks of the Min-Orota, decapitating a foot-soldier and flattening a dozen more. Those around the point of impact scattered in all directions.

In the same few seconds, Clearwater, Cadillac, Jodi and Kelso reached the rear of the compound and paused to catch their breath in the passageway between the wall and the first workshop. Jodi glanced through the arch into the compound, then dashed across the alley and crouched down in the gap on the other side.

She and Kelso were linked to Steve by pocket-sized radios fitted with a plug-in earpiece and throat mike. 'Steve! We're at the back gate. No problem so far!'

His voice came back in her ear. 'Okay. Get ready to move. I'm gonna hit it on three. One! And –'

Three Jap guards who must have been patrolling the compound when the formation blew to pieces burst through the arch and ran down the alleyway. They went several yards before their minds reacted to what their eyes had seen: four Trackers hiding between the back wall and the workshops. As they turned back, their eyes met Jodi's raised pistol. Kelso was facing the other way, covering the arch.

'Two – and –'

Chu-wittt-chu-witt-chuwitt! All three went down.

Kelso motioned Clearwater and Cadillac to join Jodi across the alleyway, then sent a gas grenade rolling through the arch into the compound.

'Three!' Steve detonated the buckets in the privy at the back of the guard-house.

Baa-BLAMMM! The blast shattered the walls and brought the roof down. It also pulverised the four gas-grenades taped to the explosive, mixing their toxic fumes with the rolling clouds of dust and causing would-be rescuers to collapse among the debris alongside the few stunned survivors.

*

Steve had engineered the guard-house blast for two reasons: to eliminate a possible armed intervention from that quarter and to create a diversion that would draw the workshop staff and ground-handlers up the alleyway and into the compound – away from the four aircraft now parked along the western boundary of the field.

The troops and spectators in the grandstand on the eastern side were still in a state of confusion. Before they could regroup and grasp what was happening, he intended to throw them into further disarray. He couldn't do that until the crowd of Japs milling around on the field in front of the workshops had been cut down to size. Apart from some fifty ground-handlers, there were sixty-odd workshop staff and the twenty women packers from the 'powder room'. Plus some friends and relatives who had sneaked in to get a better view.

They were now seeing more than they had bargained for. When the ground shook under their feet and they saw the smoke and dust rise above the back wall of the compound, some of the crowd had already started across the field towards the grandstand to help pick up the pieces. A few kept on going; the majority turned back towards their friends, who reacted as Steve hoped they would. Apart from a panicky handful who hung back uncertainly, they streamed up the alleyway towards the smoking compound.

Clearwater, Cadillac, Jodi and Kelso threw themselves down beside Steve as he hit another button, triggering the six charges spaced alongside the inside of the flanking walls.

B-B-B-B-BA-BAMM!

The double-sided blast tore through the walls and through the Japs trapped between them, and the six incendiary grenades that Steve had taped to the plastic spewed out a glutinous rain of fire in all directions.

Seconds later, racks of timber, wooden workbenches and the rafters of the collapsing roofs were ablaze.

'Shee-itt,' breathed Kelso. 'This escape plan of yours had better work. I'd hate to be here when they start figuring on just who's gonna pay for the damage!'

Jodi pointed to the south-east corner of the sky. 'Three on their way in! See 'em?!'

'Yeah, they're next,' said Steve. 'C'mon!'

Grabbing Clearwater's bundle, he motioned to her and Cadillac to follow him in a crouching run. They left the cover of the bushes and leaped into the ditch that ran behind the low grassy earth bank made from the outfill. The bank divided the western edge of the field from the smaller adjoining pasture. The ditch was calf-deep in water, but by moving along it they were able to remain hidden. So far, the only people who had seen them were dead, or too ill to talk about it.

When they drew level with the four planes perched on their launching trolleys, they flopped against the bank and peered over the top. Drawn up behind the four planes were two carts containing racks of the plump launch boosters and the thinner rocket tubes carried by the planes.

Steve drew Kelso's attention to the handful of dinks who hadn't been sucked into the alley and were now running around like headless chickens on the edge of the raging inferno. 'Think you can frag them from here?'

Kelso weighed up the yardage involved. 'Be easier to pitch it from behind that end cart.'

Steve patted him over the shoulder. Kelso slithered sideways over the bank and ran for cover.

'I think we've been spotted,' said Cadillac.

Steve looked up to his left. The approaching three-plane formation had broken up. Two were now descending in line astern along the northern edge of the field where he had taken his flying leap over the stone wall into the pond. The third aircraft had stayed high and out of trouble.

That would be the Consul-General. Yeah . . . Had to be.

The two planes made a wide sweeping turn behind them just as Kelso stood up and winged the first of two fragmentation grenades at the panicky dinks. Now only 500 feet up, the two-man crews could not miss seeing them crouched in the ditch.

*

The Herald saw the two flying-horses pass over the burning workshops and dip towards the grandstand just as the commander of the Min-Orota troops dispatched half his force across the field to tackle the blaze. Toshiro ordered the government troop detachment to stand fast. It was Min-Orota property that was going up in flames. Until called upon to help, he was not required to do so.

*

Grasping the radio transmitter in both hands, Steve used his thumbs to press buttons six and eight.

Baa-bamm!

Both aircraft disintegrated as they angled across the path of the advancing troops – the first at a height of some two hundred feet, the second at barely a hundred. Their forward momentum caused the debris to arc down like a salvo of air-to-ground missiles upon the already jittery formation. The commander was swept from his horse by a charred, half-naked body. Discipline cracked; the soldiers turned tail and fled to the comparative safety of the access road beyond the eastern edge of the field.

Shouting above the tumult, Toshiro Hase-Gawa called upon the garrison commander to pull back his own small force. By the convoluted laws of protocol, he himself could not leave the field before the Consul-General, and he was thus obliged to remain astride his terrified horse. It was a parade animal, unused to being subjected to a rain of fiery projectiles, and was now circling restlessly, pitting its strength against his. Eyes rolling, teeth bared, neck arched, it tried its utmost to grasp the bit between its teeth, but Toshiro held the reins in a vice-like grip, drawing the horse's foaming jaws against its chest. His own eyes were fixed on a more tranquil animal; the flying-horse now circling high overhead.

Come on, Brickman! What are you waiting for?

*

Steve had already handed the transmitter to Clearwater and the tip of her finger was, at that very instant, exerting a downward pressure on the appropriate button.

*

Having just witnessed the inexplicable destruction of his escort, the Consul-General's initial terror returned. His fears had *not* been groundless. The *kami* had held back their anger, choosing to strike at a moment when they could inflict the greatest possible humiliation on the vain and foolish men who had dared, once again, to flout the divine plan!

They had been taught a richly deserved lesson. But *he* was an innocent passenger; his only error that of blind obedience to his sovereign liege-lord. And here he was in mortal danger of being consumed by a fiery thunderbolt from heaven!

Oh, Ameratsu-Omikami! Have pity on this unwilling trespasser who was driven by duty alone to set foot in your cloudy domain! If I must forfeit my life for this foolish act, then let me die an honourable death with a sword in my hand! I will face it unflinchingly this very day! This very hour! But let it be among men, with the ground beneath my feet!

Forcing his bulky body round in his seat, the Consul shouted to the samurai pilot. 'I wish to alight! Go down! Go down!'

As the wind tore the words from his mouth, the pilot and the centre-section of the flying-horse was suddenly engulfed in an orange-white sheet of flame. The smooth forward motion ended with a sickening lurch and the Consul-General, the right side of his face now hideously seared and blistered, his sightless eye steaming in its socket and with the back of his robe on fire, found himself projected into a world where sky and earth revolved and became one.

He clutched desperately at the sides of the cockpit in an effort to steady himself, but the wooden structure around him came apart in his hands. The straps that held him to his seat slipped from his shoulders and he found himself floating on a cushion of air. Below him lay a patchwork quilt of red, brown and orange fields. The world had stopped spinning; had separated once more into earth and sky.

The shock of what was happening, the suffocating rush of air, numbed the shrieking pain and drove the terror from his mind. His education had not included the chilling fact that bodies in free fall accelerate at a rate of 32 feet per second until they reach a speed of 120 m.p.h. A velocity that is terminal in every sense of the word.

At 2,000 feet, with arms and legs outstretched, you still have a few moments left in which to feel you could fly for ever and that – if you only knew the secret – you could skim down like a bird in a graceful curve to alight gently on your feet. It is only when you pass through the 1,000-foot mark that you suddenly realise the ground is rising to meet you at a frightening speed and that it is all going to end quite differently.

Cowering under the canopy of their box and surrounded protectively by their bodyguards, Yama-Shita and Min-Orota watched with appalled fascination as the Consul-General plummeted to earth, arms and legs flailing like a deranged mechanical doll.

Whumm-ff!

Toshiro had long awaited this moment, but he still flinched as the Consul-General punched a six-inch-deep outline of his body into the ground and split open like an over-ripe melon. *And so it ends . . .* Seized by a sudden feeling of exhilaration, he forced his skittering horse to wheel, then galloped off the field as the remaining debris fluttered to earth around the smouldering corpse.

*

Incredible, thought Jodi. She glanced at her digital watch – one of three AMEXICO had thoughtfully provided to help co-ordinate their getaway. So much death and destruction, but less than eight minutes had elapsed since Brickman had blown up the first plane and they had begun their run from the pavilion. She saw Cadillac rubbing his eyes with the back of his hand. His face was streaked with tears.

Steve waved them forward over the bank. 'Okay, c'mon! Let's go for it!'

The four of them scrambled on to the field and ran towards the parked aircraft. They joined Kelso under the tail of number twelve. He was holding the end-plate – a safety device the dinks had begun fitting over the nozzles of the five rocket tubes to prevent accidental ignition or damage whilst aircraft were being manhandled – and he was ashen-faced. 'This one's not tubed up!'

Steve stared at him, thunderstruck. 'Not –'

'The rocket tray's empty! LOOK!'

It was true. Steve's stomach turned over. 'Shit, shit, SHIT!' He seized Jodi and Cadillac by the shoulder. 'Check these next two! I'll do Nine!'

The boosters were fitted to the launching trolley, but the tray was empty. They all were. Some idiot dink had stuck end-plates on all the trays – presumably because he thought they looked better that way. Jodi and Cadillac joined up with him as he raced back to Kelso. 'What a jackass!' He punched his thigh angrily. 'And they were there, right in front of us all the time! *Jeez!*'

'At least we've got a cartload of rockets,' said Cadillac.

'Yeah. And you can thank Mo-Town they're already primed! Start emptying your pockets!' Steve hurriedly divested himself of most of his grenades and spare magazines. Cadillac did the same, passing them to Jodi and Kelso.

'We'll load, you two cover us!'

'We'll never make it,' said Kelso.

'We're gonna have a damned good try! But maybe we'll have to go with three tubes instead of a full –' Steve suddenly realised that Clearwater wasn't with them.

*

Clearwater had left the others as soon as she realised they needed more time to put right whatever it was that had gone wrong. She did not understand the workings of the flying-horses, but she knew that only she had the power to hold back the warriors on the far side of the field. She could sense their mounting wrath and knew they would soon rally. They must not be allowed to strike at the cloud warrior. If he and Cadillac were overwhelmed, all would be lost. But she also had another task: to avenge the Plainfolk.

*

Steve and the others paused for an instant and watched her run towards the middle of the field.

'What the eff-eff does she think she's doing?' cried Kelso.

'She's going to buy us some time,' murmured Steve. He moved towards the rocket cart.

'But she's not even armed!'

'Armed?' Cadillac gave a contemptuous laugh as the sense of belonging welled up within him. It was like meeting a long-lost friend. 'Watch and take heed, sand-burrower! You are about to witness the *real* power of the Plainfolk!'

*

When the first five flying-horses had been inexplicably blown out of the sky, the two domain-lords had assumed the catastrophe was either an accident or the work of some malevolent deity. But when an explosion in the compound had been followed by several more which had reduced the workshops to a blazing heap of rubble, both realised the Heron Pool was under systematic attack.

But from whom? Before anyone could begin to search for an answer, two more flying-horses had disintegrated dangerously close to where they stood and the Consul-General had been hurled from the skies – half-digging his own grave in the process. Where was this invisible enemy? Lord Yama-Shita feared the divine wrath of the *kami* like all Iron Masters, but the Heron Pool had not been struck by sky thunderbolts. This was the handiwork of ruthless men!

It was at this point that the first glimmerings of an answer came. The observer from the second escort plane which, with its sister craft, had been attempting an emergency landing when they were destroyed, had not been killed outright. The wreckage in which he was trapped had hit the ground at a shallow angle, splintering and tearing apart as it slithered towards the grandstand. Although almost every bone in his body was broken, the dying samurai had somehow found the strength to gasp a few strangled words to the nearest of those who knelt over him.

His reported sighting of five people dressed in the colours of slaves lurking near the four remaining flying-horses was rapidly conveyed to Lord Min-Orota. He and Yama-Shita shared the sense of shock and bewilderment that gripped those around them, but while fear might have loosened their bowels, their brains had not turned to jelly. Both men reached the same conclusion at almost the same instant. What had happened was the result of a revolt by the slave-workers at the Heron Pool! It was a stupendous act of folly for which they, and countless others, would pay dearly.

Since his own men were, at that moment, falling back

in disarray, he called upon Lord Yama-Shita to dispatch some of his mounted samurai to investigate. The domain-lord had just passed this order down the chain of command when a single white-clad figure was sighted advancing across the field towards them. Neither man could fathom what this slim solitary figure hoped to achieve, but the slave's appearance was an intolerable act of defiance that had to be crushed. Immediately!

Rising to his feet, Yama-Shita aimed his lacquered staff at the offending slave and screamed an order to his samurai bodyguard. Lord Min-Orota promptly followed suit. Leaving ten of their number to shield their masters, both sets of samurai – some sixty in all – left their positions around the canopied box and ran down on to the field. Some drew their long-swords, the others pulled arrows from the quivers on their back. Fitting them to their bows, they began a slow, deliberate advance upon the intruders.

Yama-Shita sent a second hurried order to the troop of horsemen who were preparing to move off. They were to ignore this white-clad individual and proceed along the northern stone-walled edge of the field before cutting across to the four flying horses.

As he spoke, his brain was chilled by an unearthly cry – the piercing ululation of a Mute summoner.

*

Kelso, who had been roped in to help load the trays, almost dropped the two rockets he was carrying. 'What the fu –?'

'Keep going, keep going!' shouted Steve. He and Cadillac had already got two rockets fitted in the ring clamps under all four machines. But two were not enough. He had talked about going on three, but what they really needed was a full load. They didn't need four planes, but with their escape now hanging in the balance they had to keep all options open.

Jodi, who had been crouching by the grass-covered

bank to guard against a sneak attack from the rear, decided to lend a hand. Holstering her pistol, she ran towards the cart. Halfway across, the ground shuddered violently, throwing her against one of the wheels. Looking up, she saw that the tremor had caused several of the rockets to slide partly out of the racks. She hauled herself up and caught one just before it toppled to the ground. Clearwater, her feet now planted firmly astride and with her arms raised to form the letter X, felt Talisman's power flow into her from the earth and sky. To those watching in the crowded grandstand, her body seemed to be surrounded by a shimmering veil of light. With a swift movement she brought her arms down and her fingertips together, sighting at Yama-Shita through the V made by her thumbs.

There was another sudden rumble of earth-thunder. A jet of smoke burst from the ground in front of her, then it split apart, becoming a ragged fissure that raced away across the field towards the centre of the grandstand. The earth heaved, throwing the advancing samurai to the ground, then, an instant later, the quake struck the packed stand, causing the tiers to fall in on each other as the supporting structure collapsed.

The detachment of mounted samurai who had started to gallop along the northern edge of the field hauled on their reins and milled about in confusion. Drawing his sword, their leader wheeled his horse around on its rear legs, shouting at his men to rally and attack the white-clad figure.

Clearwater flung her left arm out sideways towards the stone wall, then slowly swept her outstretched fingers upwards. The wall shivered as it responded to her call. It rippled along its length like a grey-brown snake stirring from sleep. It cracked and rattled as the stones worked themselves loose and then flew into the air like fallen leaves swept up in a whirlwind. And with her right hand, she summoned the wall behind the pavilion to come to her aid.

> *. . . The eagles shall be his golden arrows,*
> *the stones of the earth his hammer*
> *and a nation shall be forged from the fires of War.*
> *The Plainfolk shall be as a bright sword*
> *in the hands of Talisman, their Saviour!*

Man and horse were utterly overwhelmed by the airborne avalanche. But the stones continued to fly, further and faster and in ever greater numbers, raining down from both sides upon the rest of Yama-Shita's troops, into the wreckage of the grandstand, and on to the access road beyond where Min-Orota's line-officers were making another attempt to marshal their demoralised troops.

On the field in front of the stand, the shaken samurai rose on unsteady feet and summoned up their courage. Several warriors had been felled by stones from the wall. More were flying in their direction. Men were going down on all sides, but they could not retreat. Drawing their bows, the surviving archers loosed several flights of arrows at the she-devil – for they were now close enough to see her long hair flowing in the wind like dark wings on either side of her chalk-white face.

Once again Clearwater brought her outstretched hands together level with her shoulders, drawing the shifting vaporous planes of light around her into a vertical wedge whose point lay beyond her fingertips.

As the speeding arrows reached her, they were deflected to either side of her body. *Hhawww*! The archers fired another volley. And again they bounced off in all directions! It was as if she was protected by an invisible wall! Throwing aside their bows, the samurai – now reduced by the hail of stones to a third of their number – pressed forward cautiously, brandishing their swords and calling on Ameratsu-Omikami to aid them.

Clearwater turned her outstretched palms towards the ground and splayed her fingers as the tips of her thumbs came together. A second chilling cry burst from her lips, more frightening than the first. The advancing samurai found themselves rooted to the spot. The ground under their feet trembled, making their bodies quiver and their teeth rattle. Their swords fell from their twitching fingers. Their stomachs churned, their hearts pounded faster and faster and their heads felt as if they were about to burst. The weak-walled blood vessels – the fatal legacy of their defective gene structure – gave way as they were struck down by massive multiple haemorrhages. Veins split open, causing their faces and hands to turn greyish purple. Blood oozed from their eyes and noses as major arteries ruptured, flooding their brains and plunging them into a dark bottomless pit.

All were dead before they hit the ground.

Lord Yama-Shita, his rich clothes bloodied and torn, stumbled from the wrecked grandstand in time to see the white-faced figure step over the bodies of his fallen samurai. With a sudden flash of awareness he realised whose face lay behind the mask.

The Consul-General's long-dog whore! The gutter-bitch whose hairy body he had secretly observed with a mixture of loathing and fascination. The non-person he had so cruelly mocked had defied his power, wreaked havoc on his family and brought him to the edge of ruin! It was beyond belief, but the proof lay all around him. A curse on her! A curse on *all* women!

Drawing his sword, he tossed the scabbard aside and looked around for support. About a dozen members of his own family had clawed their way out of the wreckage; others were still struggling to free themselves. He called upon those who could to come to his aid. With his sword held out in front of him, both hands gripping the hilt, he limped towards Clearwater. No one followed. So be it. He would show them the kind of courage it took to become the most powerful domain-lord in Ne-Issan.

Clearwater waited silently as he approached, her arms still outstretched, fingertips together, pointing at Yama-Shita's face. The domain-lord stopped a blade's length away and assumed the splay-footed stance that preceded the killing stroke. His eyes met hers, saw them glow like ice crystals pierced by the sun. The ground trembled under his feet. His leg muscles quivered. His brain urged him to strike before it was too late, but his arms did not respond and he could no longer deflect his gaze from her eyes.

Clearwater slowly interlocked finger and thumb and clenched her hands together. Those watching with bated breath saw Yama-Shita reverse his grip on the sword hilt then slowly raise his arms to bring the angled tip of the blade in line with his belly. And they saw the white-faced witch – for that was what she must be – flex her arms, then thrust her clenched hands towards the domain-lord.

Yama-Shita knew the power that flooded through his arms and drove the point of his sword through his body was not his own, but it was impossible to resist. Nor could he resist the silent command to withdraw the sword and plunge it in again. And again! The first two thrusts had numbed his brain and frozen his tongue, but now the accumulated pain swiftly took hold and he screamed with agony as the sword made its third passage through his body.

The weaker members of his family who had lacked the courage to follow him watched in horrified disbelief as he thrust the sword through his body for a fourth time. And again he screamed. But did not fall. A fifth thrust reduced him to a gibbering wretch, swaying unsteadily on blood-soaked feet, alternately shrieking and sobbing as he begged for mercy. But the white witch was unmoved.

Only when he had pierced his body for the eighth time did Clearwater let Yama-Shita sink to his knees in a pool of his own blood. And she did not move until he toppled forward, still clutching the hilt of his buried sword, and came to rest with his lifeless face kissing the grass at her feet.

Clearwater stretched her arms upwards in triumph and the earth responded with a dying peal of earth-thunder. Those before her who were still on their feet backed away, then turned and ran for their lives.

Steve, who had managed to catch the reins of one of several runaway horses, rode up behind her. When their eyes met, he saw in her gaze a look that sent a chill down his spine. If the eyes, as Mr Snow had said, were the window of the soul, then there was a stranger lurking in the room beyond.

'So perish all enemies of the Plainfolk . . .' Her hushed voice was drained of all emotion.

Steve helped her up on to the horse. Her body seemed incredibly light and fragile, like a dry corn husk. She clasped her arms round his waist. 'Hold tight,' he said. He held on to her wrists as he turned the horse and galloped towards the waiting planes.

Three were now lined up with their noses into wind. Cadillac was already aboard the first. He reached over and helped lift Clearwater into the front seat. The Mute was bright-eyed and raring to go. Steve eyed him. Yeah. Of course. That was his hang-up: what made him run. Cadillac always wanted to be on the winning side.

Steve blew a kiss to Clearwater, then slapped the outside of the cockpit. 'Okay, move it! We'll be right behind you!' He stepped back as Cadillac fired the booster and watched the machine speed away from the grass. Six seconds into the burn, Cadillac fired two tubes instead of one, then jettisoned the trolley.

Kelso watched over Steve's shoulder as the plane went up in an almost vertical climb. 'Should you have let them go together?'

'Did you want to ride with her?'

'Not after what I just saw, but –'

'Don't worry. These four planes are wired to blow just like the others. And I've still got the transmitter.'

Kelso gave a quick laugh. 'In that case I'd better watch my step.'

'Hey! Cut the jokes!' cried Jodi. 'I think there's some guys coming round back of us!'

Steve heard the tell-tale drumming of hoofbeats as he followed her pointing finger. 'You're right! Go on two – like Cadillac did!' He pushed Jodi and Kelso towards the

433

nearest plane and ran to the next in line. Jodi still had one leg outside the cockpit when Kelso fired the boosters. Steve reached out and yanked the firing handle as the first wave of horsemen crashed through the bushes and galloped on to the field.

Shwaa-paa-POWW! The plane started to roll forward. *C'mon, c'mon, c'mon*!

The trolley rapidly picked up speed, but not fast enough to out-distance the leading horseman. The samurai galloped out to the right to avoid the smoke trail from the booster rockets and drew level with the wing, his bow arched. At that distance he couldn't miss, but Mo-Town must have been rooting for Steve. The arrow hit one of the upright spruce struts, splitting it as it punched through, and buried its point in Steve's thigh. Ahhghh, Christo!

The samurai didn't get a chance for a second shot. As he reached over his shoulder for another arrow, Steve aimed his arm over the side and blew him out of the saddle with a triple volley.

As Kelso and Jodi soared into the air ahead of him, Steve saw why Cadillac had fired two tubes and fired them early. The field ahead was littered with stones and bodies. Gritting his teeth against the pain that lanced through his right leg, he triggered one and five and followed the two Trackers up into the sky in a steep climbing turn to the west.

Beyond the line of crimson forested hills lay the Hudson. And if Skull-Face had meant what he had said, there'd be a field like the one marked on the map that had been left in his shack, with a white hollow square in it. But first, there was one last piece of business to attend to.

Steve dropped his left wing and looked down at the tiny figures swarming around the plane they'd left behind. With the help of Jodi, Kelso and Cadillac, he had hauled the two rocket carts close in on either side of the plane, then tossed nearly all their remaining grenades into the cockpit. He took out the transmitter and selected the appropriate button. 'Adios, amigos.'

434

There were two, almost simultaneous flashes. First the plastic explosive aboard the plane with its extra topping of grenades, then the two rocket carts. The smoke ballooned onwards, then rolled back in on itself and rose into the sky, leaving the ground beneath ablaze. Most of the tiny figures had stopped moving.

Steve let his gaze roam further afield. There was little sign of movement anywhere. The Heron Pool had been devastated, the swaggering Iron Masters had been dealt a blow they would long remember. But what of the cost? How many had died in the crossfire while he, Clearwater, the Shogun – and maybe his Herald – had been settling their personal accounts? How many more would suffer for what he had done? He quickly killed the rising feelings of remorse. These things had to be done.

Best not to think about it too much . . .

At 3,000 feet the air was noticeably colder. But no doubt things would soon start to warm up. He joined the others, slipping between them to take the lead as they drifted westwards, rising on a gentle updraft. Clearwater waved, Cadillac gave him a thumbs-up sign. Jodi and Kelso punched the air with their fists; the exultant victory sign used by Trail-Blazers.

Steve responded instinctively. YO!

They'd been lucky. Everyone had pulled their weight, but it was Clearwater who had saved the day. He'd been lucky too. If the arrow hadn't hit the strut first it could have gone right through his thigh. Sweet Mother! It was really hurting. Still, there wasn't too much blood. He would survive. And getting it out wouldn't be as bad as when Cadillac had pulled that crossbow bolt through his arm.

But apart from that – all in all – quite a reasonable start to the day . . .

CHAPTER SEVENTEEN

Clearwater's revenge upon Lord Yama-Shita and his companions was, in a sense, a hollow victory. Despite being buried in the wreckage, Lord Kiyo Min-Orota was found to be alive when his body was uncovered. His escape, with only minor injuries, was viewed by his rescuers as miraculous. Shigamitsu, the Heron Pool commander, who was only inches away when the freak earthquake had hit the stand, had been crushed to death.

The samurai was fortunate to have been granted so swift a demise; had he lived, Lord Min-Orota would have had him cruelly tortured. Despite his rank, he would not have been allowed to commit *seppuku*. He would, instead, have been treated like a common criminal, forced to endure in public the grossest indignities that could have been devised.

Even in death he did not escape Min-Orota's vengeful wrath. His mangled body was beheaded and then quartered. The pieces were hung from the tiled lintel above the gates to the Heron Pool and his head impaled on a wooden pole by the entrance, with a placard denouncing his criminal incompetence. His wife, whose sole crime was her marital status, was ordered to kill their two children and then herself, and their bodies were hung alongside his.

In Min-Orota's eyes, the blame for what had happened lay entirely with the staff of the Heron Pool. Had they been more vigilant, the long-dogs and their Mute accomplice could not have staged this unprecedented revolt. He preferred to ignore his own involvement in the affair, and refused to face the implications of the terrifying display of demonic powers that had climaxed the long-dogs' assault.

All surviving members of the Heron Pool staff, the Tracker renegades who had spent the day confined to their quarters, and the Mute slaves who had done their cleaning and cooking, were assembled in the compound under heavy guard. Lined up with them were the soldiers from the parade detachment. In Min-Orota's eyes they were as guilty as the rest. It was their cowardly behaviour which had allowed the perpetrators of this outrage to escape.

When their wrists and feet had been shackled, they were marched out on to the road by their whip-toting escort and led in single file towards Bo-sona. Ahead of them, several parties of Mutes were digging post-holes by the roadside. The holes were set 100 paces apart. Each time a hole was reached, the column was halted. The leading man or woman was then forced to take a post from the loaded cart ahead of them and help plant it firmly in the ground before being tied to it and left to die an agonising death.

The process, which Lord Min-Orota watched from the comfort of his carriage, was doubly sadistic, for the remainder of the column was obliged to march on past the succession of tortured victims – leaving them in no illusion as to their eventual fate.

This macabre procession continued all the way to Ba-satana, and when the original column was exhausted, Mute slaves working on the lands north and south of the road were rounded up and put to death, followed by those who had laboured to dig the post-holes.

By the time Min-Orota reached his palace, his immediate thirst for blood had been satisfied but, when he sat down to a sombre dinner with the chief members of his own family and the principal survivors of Yama-Shita's party, he had little to feel happy about.

His friend's body had been conveyed in a hastily prepared coffin from the Heron Pool to his ship in the harbour but the issues raised by his death were not so easily disposed of. Although it was Lord Yama-Shita who had brought the flying-horse and its two riders to

Masa-chusa, and persuaded the Shogun to allow more to be built, it was already clear that he, Kiyo Min-Orota, was going to be held responsible for the domain-lord's death.

The charge was patently unfair, but with a powerful family like the Yama-Shita, justice lay in the eye of the beholder. They would demand reparations: goods, money – and perhaps blood. It could place a crippling burden on his domain, but if he were to reject their claims, the alternative could be even more unpleasant.

Lord Min-Orota also faced the prospect of trouble from another quarter. The Consul-General had been killed whilst flying in one of the machines for whose manufacture he, Min-Orota, was once again ultimately responsible. Worse still, the revolt – due entirely to lack of proper surveillance of the slave-workers – had not been a simple escape attempt. There had been a murderous attack on those of high rank and noble birth. The grandstand had been totally destroyed, including the viewing box that had been built to house the Shogun! If he had been present and had suffered insult and injury to his person . . . Min-Orota put the thought from his mind. The consequences were too awful to contemplate.

When he retired to his private quarters – now guarded by three times the usual number of samurai – the domain-lord found a sealed letter by his bedside. It informed him that a courier from the Lord Chamberlain's office had arrived in Ba-satana with a verbal dispatch of the utmost importance. The letter urged Min-Orota to receive the courier without delay. The meeting was to take place in the greatest secrecy, the provenance of the courier was not to be disclosed to anyone, and no aides were to be present when he presented his dispatch.

Min-Orota had not the faintest idea what the man had to tell him, but the temptation to find out was irresistible. Any approach by Ieyasu could not be lightly dismissed. After destroying the letter as instructed, he dispatched his most trusted servant to the address given, with orders to bring the courier into the palace by the secret stairways that led directly to his own private quarters.

Ieyasu's courier appeared before him shortly after midnight and, after exchanging the arranged passwords, presented his seals of office. The man's face, when revealed, was like a living skull. It was Steve's diminutive interrogator. The name he gave was Fuji-Wara, but it was probably not his own.

Lord Chamberlain Ieyasu's message was essentially this: news of the catastrophic events at the Heron Pool had reached his office and had also been conveyed directly to the Shogun. His Exalted Highness was – as Min-Orota might imagine – deeply concerned by his narrow escape from what could have been a serious threat upon his life.

The Shogun had also been stricken by the loss of his brother-in-law, the highly regarded Consul-General Nakane Toh-Shiba. His death had not only caused him personal anguish; it had disturbed him in his official capacity as ruler of Ne-Issan. It was as Min-Orota had feared: an attack upon the Consul-General – and the Herald Toshiro Hase-Gawa – was an attack upon the Shogunate itself. If he, as a domain-lord, could not suppress dissident elements and ensure the personal safety and unmolested passage of government appointees, then the Shogunate would have to protect its rights by all lawful means.

The courier, Fuji-Wara, did not need to spell out what that meant. Compensation would have to be paid to the Consul-General's widow, of course. An official of his rank didn't come cheap – and since his wife was the Shogun's sister, the going rate would probably be multiplied by ten. The wider consequences of the Heron Pool incident could also prove expensive. Extra taxes could be imposed, commercial licences could be withdrawn, assets could be seized. The lives of senior aides who were involved with the Heron Pool project but had gone unpunished could be forfeit, and there could also be a dramatic increase in the number of government officials and troop garrisons – to whose upkeep he would be obliged to contribute.

If a domain-lord chose to resist such measures his lands could be proclaimed a 'dissident fief'. That gave the Shogunate the right to place his domain under military occupation. His own family could, if the situation worsened, be deposed, or subjected to much harsher terms of vassalage. Not a pleasant prospect – especially when he was already under threat of unspecified reprisals by the Yama-Shita family.

Fuji-Wara, a man clearly experienced in delicate, high-level negotiations of this kind, revealed that his master was aware of the precarious nature of the relationship between the Min-Orota and the Yama-Shita following the death of their domain-lord. The Lord Chamberlain wished to come to the aid of the house of Min-Orota – who were, after all, friends and allies of the Toh-Yota. Both houses were, in their different ways, threatened by the Yama-Shita. If some way could be found for them to act together to eliminate or reduce that threat then, said the courier, he was sure that Ieyasu could persuade the Shogun to take a more lenient view of what had occurred and to demand only nominal reparation for the death of the Consul-General.

It was, basically, an offer he couldn't refuse.

Min-Orota was in need of help, but even though he was backed into a corner he was shrewd enough to realise that the courier's visit was merely the tip of a political iceberg. That sly old fox, Ieyasu, had been up to his tricks again, just when his critics and enemies were confidently expecting to be called upon to sit through his funeral oration. The domain-lord considered the options and then assured his visitor that he was, as might be expected, constantly ready to be of service to the Shogun – but what action was he being called upon to perform?

Skull-Face, a.k.a. Fuji-Wara, proceeded to tell him.

*

The three ocean-going junks which had brought Lord Yama-Shita, his armed entourage and his escort to Ba-satana were still moored in the harbour, and the survivors – including those who had dined with Lord Min-Orota – had spent the night on board. The ships' crews, who had not ventured beyond the docks counted themselves fortunate to have been spared the terrible ordeal their compatriots had undergone.

When captains and crews awoke, they saw that another large junk, flying the house-flags of the Hase-Gawa, had arrived during the night and now lay at anchor to starboard, on the north side of the harbour. Over breakfast, the temporary heads of the delegation discussed their next move. Should they set sail immediately – or should they wait until additional men – mainly soldiers – arrived via the overland route to make up their depleted numbers?

News of Yama-Shita's death had been dispatched by horse to the palace at Sara-kusa, but its speedy arrival was not guaranteed, since the rider was obliged to traverse the Toh-Yota's northern domain.

The carrier pigeons used to convey top-secret messages from the domain-lord to the palace had gone with him to the Heron Pool. It was customary for several baskets to accompany Yama-Shita on any journey he undertook so that urgent dispatches could be sent at a moment's notice. Unfortunately, the earthquake had overturned and wrecked the cart. The driver and pigeon-keeper had been found with their skulls crushed – presumably by flying stones – and those birds who had not been killed had escaped when their baskets had broken open.

Whilst they were in the middle of these deliberations, a boat-man brought a message from Lord Min-Orota. The domain-lord, who had descended from his palace to the quayside, requested permission to come aboard with four *shinto* priests in order to pay his last respects to his friend and ally. Two senior members of the delegation went ashore to escort him back to the vessel.

Lord Yama-Shita's open coffin lay atop a catafalque draped in white silk. When the traditional mourning rites had been performed, Min-Orota spent an hour in silent contemplation of his colleague's body, then asked to speak privately with the closest of the dead man's aides. Only two were still on their feet. Four had been badly injured, another was expected to die before reaching home, and the corpses of several more lay in the hold.

When he had assured himself that they could not be overheard, Min-Orota broached the subject of a 'chestful of rich silk cloth' that Lord Yama-Shita had brought with him as an intended gift to the principal ladies of the house of Min-Orota. The domain-lord had stressed the uniquely special nature of the materials and workmanship involved but, alas, he had not lived long enough to make the presentation himself. Did the aides, asked Min-Orota, know of their lord's intentions in this matter and, if so, where was the chest?

Min-Orota was fortunate that the two men facing him were among the four people, outside of himself and the dead domain-lord, who knew the precise nature of the object concealed beneath the bolts of cloth. After exchanging thoughtful glances, the senior of the two aides replied. Yes, they were aware of the intended gift, but since their lord had not lived long enough to offer it himself, they did not feel they had the necessary authority to make the gift on his behalf. That decision could only be made by his successor.

Min-Orota praised their infinite tact and caution. They had misunderstood him. He did not wish to receive that which could not be freely given. What he had come to suggest was that the chest and its contents be placed in his safekeeping until its eventual fate could be decided. He was suggesting this because his spies in the late Consul-General's residence had, that very morning, hastened to bring him some most disquieting news. The Shogun had learned of the junk's sensitive cargo and planned to intercept the flotilla during their return journey on the pretext of according the honours due to the dead domain-lord.

This revelation caused the two aides to exchange wary glances.

Min-Orota expressed his concern. The Shogun's men could easily find some excuse to seize the chest's valuable contents on behalf of their master. If faced with this danger, they could always save themselves by having the chest thrown overboard – but would that not be a woeful betrayal of their dead master's wishes?

The alternative was to transport the chest's contents overland but, once again, the carriers could be intercepted by the Toh-Yota. Only the house of Min-Orota, the chief partner in the enterprise which their dead lord had once described to him as 'the *spinning* and *weaving* of dreams', could be trusted to guard the chest and its contents until Yama-Shita's successor had been chosen.

Min-Orota's choice of words and the emphasis he placed upon them left the two aides in no doubt that he had been fully apprised of Lord Yama-Shita's future plans. After retiring to the far end of the room for a whispered conversation, they returned and knelt before Min-Orota. He signalled them to sit and speak. They bowed respectfully from the waist and adopted a cross-legged position.

They were grateful, said the senior aide, for his warning about the possible interception of their vessels. The chest would be left in his care – but was he aware of the dangers he faced in becoming its guardian?

Min-Orota declared himself ready to accept them. Lord Yama-Shita had made the ultimate sacrifice in his bid to lead Ne-Issan into a new age. He, Kiyo Min-Orota, shared his lofty vision of the future and was happy to risk his own life to help make that vision a reality. It would prove to the man who would soon adopt their dead lord's mantle that he was a worthy ally. Someone who could be trusted with the deepest and *darkest* secrets of all.

Once again, Min-Orota's choice of words made it clear that he understood the real nature of the enterprise: the recapture of the Dark Light. A time and place was arranged: noon at a secluded manor house far removed from the palace and the press of the bustling sea-port. The unloading of the chest in broad daylight would not attract the attention of the watch, and an official from the palace would be on hand to ensure it passed out of the docks without being subjected to the tiresome attentions of customs officials.

On the appointed day and hour, an ox-cart carrying a driver, the chest and four porters made its way towards the rendezvous. It was preceded by the two aides and four other mounted samurai and followed by a second cart containing twelve soldiers in civilian clothes. The three groups varied their pace and distance between each other, merging at times with other traffic on the road. To the casual observer, the carts and riders had no connection with each other, and this was precisely the impression they wished to create.

When the mounted samurai had reconnoitred the area around the manor house to ensure that there were no forces lying in ambush, the two aides ordered the cart bearing the chest to enter the grounds. The second vehicle, carrying the disguised soldiers, whose weapons were concealed beneath the straw on which they lay, stopped on the road outside. To any passer-by they were nothing more than a group of patient peasants stretching their legs whilst the driver and ox-boy fed and watered their animals.

The manor-house – a rambling stone and timber structure with a tiled roof dating from the middle of the previous century – was an uninhabited, dusty, echoing shell. Two of Min-Orota's lieutenants, whom the aides had already met, conducted them and the chest into Min-Orota's presence, then retired with the four porters. This quartet was also disguised soldiers, drawn from the forty or so who had survived the débâcle at the Heron Pool.

Lord Kiyo Min-Orota was seated on a single straw mat, placed in the centre of a dais which ran across the far end of the room. He called upon them to approach and remove the four straw mats covering the section of the main floor in front of where he sat. The aides pulled the mats aside. A trap-door lay beneath. Opening it, they found steps leading down to a deep cellar.

This, explained Lord Min-Orota, was where the chest would be hidden. Once it was safely below, the trap-door would be replaced by planking which would merge with the surrounding floor, and there it would remain until the Yama-Shita came to recover it. But first, he said, he would like the opportunity to look upon the priceless gift he had come so close to receiving and which had coloured their late master's dreams of the future.

The two aides asked him to recall his two lieutenants.

After removing the rolls of silken cloth, the four men lifted a large, heavy object wrapped in linen from the chest. When Min-Orota's men had left the room, the two aides removed part of the wrappings to reveal the engine from a Skyhawk – the basic aircraft carried aboard the Federation's wagon-trains. The engine, with its laminated wooden propeller placed alongside it, was seated securely inside a timber frame.

Min-Orota examined the engine at close quarters without touching it. Was this, he enquired, the strange device that had powered the original flying-horse – and which was believed to have been destroyed?

The aides assured him that it was.

Min-Orota praised Yama-Shita's cleverness. On top of all his other attributes he was also the master of illusion! Was it not true that the Shogun's representatives had been present when the device had been consumed by fire? By what cunning means had such worthies been bamboozled?

Little by little, Min-Orota drew out the full story and – by conceding his own complicity – persuaded them to reveal that Lord Hiro Yama-Shita had been the prime mover in the plan to recapture the Dark Light.

The two aides did not know that the long-dog who was

to help bring the plan to fruition had escaped. None of the Yama-Shita knew. And Lord Min-Orota did not propose to tell them. He did, however, have another proposition. Let us drink, he said, to the success of your master's plan and to his memory!

He struck a small gong to summon his lieutenants, who entered bearing a tray of refreshments. Cups of *sake* were poured out and handed to Min-Orota and the two aides.

'To the Yama-Shita,' proposed Min-Orota. 'Lords of the Dark Light!'

'May the enemies of progress perish!' chorused the aides.

Since Min-Orota had already drunk from the same flask, the two samurai had no hesitation in joining him. The rims of the porcelain cups they raised to their lips had been coated with a potent, transparent poison which caused almost instantaneous paralysis of their motor functions, leaving them unable to move their limbs or cry out, but fully conscious and aware of their predicament.

As the cups fell from their fingers, their arms were pinioned by Min-Orota's lieutenants and quickly bound with ropes. The paralysis was only temporary but had been necessary to prevent the two aides from sounding the alarm or killing themselves. For they would have done so without hesitation at the sight that now met their eyes.

The screens behind the dais were drawn aside, revealing the young Shogun seated between six domain-lords and their field-marshals. Min-Orota knelt to pay homage to Yoritomo. His two lieutenants followed suit, forcing the stricken aides down with them.

It was Ieyasu, the Lord Chamberlain, who had organised this assembly on a variety of pretexts and in conditions of unprecedented secrecy. Seated with the Shogun, as judge and jury, were the domain-lords of the Ko-Nikka, Se-Iko and Mitsu-Bishi, whose lands lay along the southern border of Yama-Shita's domain, and their own immediate neighbours, the Dai-Hatsu, Da-Tsuni and Su-Zuki.

The Ko-Nikka were allied by marriage to the Yama-

Shita; the Se-Iko were regarded as being predisposed to take their side in any serious dispute with the Shogunate. The other four were in the Toh-Yota camp. In terms of power, the Ko-Nikka and Se-Iko outweighed the four other members of the jury, but Ieyasu had done some shrewd wheeling and dealing behind the scenes.

The verdict was unanimous. The house of Yama-Shita was guilty of high treason and must be called to account. Lords Ko-Nikka, Se-Iko and Mitsu-Bishi agreed to journey to Sara-kusa to inform the family of the charge and the evidence on which they had been found guilty by a council of peers. They would also take with them a list of those held to be responsible. Those named could either take the appropriate action – suicide – or throw themselves upon the mercy of the Shogun.

It was a stark choice. Either way they would wind up dead. The only alternative was an armed invasion, seizure of all assets and the possible break-up of the domain.

Ordinarily, the Shogunate would not have dared to make such a move against the Yama-Shita, but with the Ko-Nikka and Se-Iko now firmly on the fence, resistance to the Shogun's demands was not a viable option. No. Yoritomo was confident that those judged guilty of complicity would take their own lives or be quietly disposed of. Any family entering the power game had to be prepared to make sacrifices.

The disguised companions of Yama-Shita's aides, who had been keeping guard outside the manor, had been surprised and overwhelmed when the gong had been struck to summon the *sake*. Their attackers had also been disguised as peasants, some with women and children, aboard three farm carts which had paused to exchange gossip and offer some of their produce for sale. All were executed on the spot.

When the two paralysed aides had been hustled away to meet the same fate, Yoritomo warmly congratulated Min-Orota for the part he had played in exposing the treachery of the Yama-Shita.

No mention was made of his own involvement, or his complaisant support of the Consul-General's affair with the outlandish whore. Matters such as these could wait. The rumoured love-match between Min-Orota's second son and one of Yama-Shita's daughters would die a quiet death. As would the daughter in question and the rest of the domain-lord's immediate family. Parents, wife, sons, daughters, even their newborn child.

It was regrettable but necessary. The past history of Ne-Issan had been shaped on more than one occasion by orphaned children of deposed domain-lords who had grown to become avenging generals of armies and had swept away those who had unwisely spared them.

Lord Yama-Shita had eliminated all serious rivals, but with the disappearance of his own direct line, a worthy – and, it was hoped, a more amenable – successor would appear. All great families, including the Toh-Yota, had strong and weak branches. They were like trees; when a strong branch which took the greater share of the light was lopped off because it shadowed its owner's house, the weaker branches prospered.

The measures taken against the house of Yama-Shita would be punishing but not crippling. Their commercial activities were inextricably linked to the general economic well-being of Ne-Issan. If they were forced to pay too high a price, it would create a source of continuing disaffection.

A balance had to be struck. Firmness had to be tempered with magnanimity. But they would no longer have the monopoly on trade with the Mutes. Their former allies the Ko-Nikka would henceforth be able to build and operate wheelboats across the Western seas, and the Se-Iko would become the land-agents for the slave trade. The Yama-Shita could still bring them ashore, but they could only be sold through the Se-Iko. It was through these two crucial deals, masterminded by Ieyasu, that their loyalty had been purchased – leaving the Yama-Shita to pay the price.

448

The ship flying the house-flags of the Hase-Gawa was, in fact, part of the Shogun's battle fleet. It was this heavily disguised vessel which had brought Yoritomo and the six domain-lords into the port of Ba-satana during the night. On the command of Lord Min-Orota, a salvo of cannon was fired from the island fort which guarded the entrance to the outer bay. It was the signal for the other five warships from the same flotilla to enter harbour. When they hove into sight and their identity became clear, their sister ship hauled down the Hase-Gawa flags and revealed her true colours.

As troops of the Min-Orota flooded on to the dockside, it was clear to the astonished captains of Yama-Shita's vessels that there had been a sea-change in the political fortunes of their dead master's family. With six Toh-Yota ships, barring the only exit, there was little chance of breaking out into the open sea. They were left with two choices: go down fighting, scuttling their junks when defeat seemed certain, or surrender.

Two deck officers from each of the three boats went to the dockside to parley under a flag of truce with representatives of the Toh-Yota, Min-Orota and the six visiting domain-lords. They informed the deck-officers of the charge of high treason against their house. Their vessels were now forfeit. If they surrendered by the next tide, their crews would be returned unharmed to their native domain. Resistance was pointless, but if the captains chose to scuttle their boats, not one man would escape alive. All would be judged to be as guilty as their late master.

The deck-officers returned to their respective ships. An hour later, the house-flags of the Yama-Shita were hauled down and laid reverently over the corpses of the three captains and their senior officers. It was all over without a shot being fired.

*

449

Lord Yama-Shita's death at the hands of the mysterious white witch had not been anticipated by Ieyasu, but if he had lived, the result would have been the same. The pike and not the minnows would have fallen into the trap laid with the help of Kiyo Min-Orota.

The chastened domain-lord, shaken by his own narrow escape from a similar charge of high treason, was now pathetically eager to work his way back into favour. He had actually gone as far as to broach the subject of a marriage between one of his children and one of the Shogun's many nephews or nieces when escorting Yoritomo to the gangway of his vessel.

Yoritomo agreed that the proposal merited serious consideration, but reminded Min-Orota that he still awaited his proposals for compensating Her Highness the Lady Mishiko for the loss of her husband. The veiled threat robbed the domain-lord of the relief he might otherwise have felt at watching the Shogun's fleet sail out of his harbour.

*

The Shogun had been advised by Ieyasu to keep his parting words cool and ambiguous, but political necessity required that there be a marriage, whatever his own personal feelings. And that saddened him. He had thought Kiyo Min-Orota strong, even if he was not totally trustworthy, but he was spineless and treacherous. Perhaps a grandson, who would carry the blood of the Toh-Yota in his veins, would prove to be made of sterner stuff.

On the journey back to his palace on Aron-giren, Yoritomo reflected on the ferment of intrigues that had first been uncovered by Toshiro, his most trusted Herald. It had been Ieyasu who had pressed him to award the licence to build flying-horses to Kiyo Min-Orota. With the discovery of the conspiratorial axis between his house and the Yama-Shita, the Shogun had been convinced that his wily old opponent had finally

450

made the serious error of judgement that could be used to secure his removal from office.

He had secretly hoped Toshiro would produce evidence that would prove Ieyasu was directly implicated in the conspiracy, but it was now evident that he could not have been more wrong. Kiyo Min-Orota had been chosen because the Lord Chamberlain knew *exactly* what he was doing. He knew Min-Orota's strengths and weaknesses and had used him to ensnare and finally betray the Yama-Shita. The sly old fox was still as fast on his feet as ever, and Yoritomo could only count himself fortunate that Ieyasu's allegiance was unshakeable. They might disagree about ways and means, but they both served a common end – the maintenance of the Toh-Yota Shogunate.

*

The Herald, Toshiro Hase-Gawa, took no part in the judgement proceedings. In fact, the secrecy surrounding the event was so complete, he was not even aware that the Shogun and Ieyasu were in Ba-satana. When the action moved into the public domain with the seizure of Yama-Shita's three ocean-going junks, the Herald was already on his way south to Nyo-poro with the Consul-General's grieving wife and her three tear-stained children.

The Lady Mishiko had expressed her wish to return to her brother's palace at Yedo on Aron-giren, and it was his duty to escort her carriage and baggage-train which, among other things, included the casket containing the grossly distorted body of her late husband.

Toshiro had, in any case, to make his personal report to the Shogun on the successful outcome of his assignment. The mexican had escaped with his prisoners; the Consul-General had met his death in the prescribed manner. But he was less certain about how to explain what had occurred after the female Mute had intervened in the struggle. He had left the field immediately after

Nakane Toh-Shiba had crashed to earth, so he had not personally witnessed what some of the Min-Orota line-officers claimed had taken place.

If it was true that Clearwater had employed the demonic powers that witches were reputed to possess then it placed him in a rather delicate position. Better by far to attribute the highly selective earthquake to a wayward Mother Nature and the stories of flying stones to shock, hysteria or over-heated imaginations.

Travelling by the longer but considerably faster sea-route, the Shogun returned to Aron-giren before the Herald arrived with the newly widowed Lady Mishiko. After she had been welcomed in private by the Shogun and had received his brotherly condolences, the Herald was summoned to give his account of what had taken place at the Heron Pool.

When Toshiro entered the Shogun's study, he was surprised to find that Yoritomo was not alone. His uncle, Ieyasu, was with him and had apparently been invited to sit in on the meeting. The Herald paid homage to both men, then sat back cautiously when given permission to do so. It was the first time that the Lord Chamberlain had been present at a debriefing, and Toshiro found his grey, spider-like presence unsettling. What, he wondered, did it presage for the College of Heralds – the end of their privileged access to the Shogun? Had Ieyasu finally managed to outmanoeuvre Yoritomo in their thinly concealed struggle for control of the Inner Court?

Yoritomo and Ieyasu listened in silence as Toshiro presented his carefully edited version of the catastrophic outcome to the flying display. Since he was unsure just how far the Shogun had taken Ieyasu into his confidence, he avoided any reference to the part he had played in the escape of Brickman and his friends and the Consul-General's downfall. Or to the fact that Yoritomo had ordered both.

When he fell silent, the gaunt, ageing Chamberlain said: 'Your tact is highly commendable. But let me put your mind at ease. I have been made fully aware of your central role in this affair and, especially, your negotiations on behalf of this court with the so-called "mexican". The *real* Brickman, as opposed to the individual who – for reasons we have yet to discover – assumed his identity.'

'There is another aspect of this affair which fascinates us. His Exalted Highness and I would like to know if you have had any thoughts on the role of the female who . . .' Ieyasu chose his words carefully '. . . was the object of the Consul-General's fatal fascination.'

Toshiro had a sudden presentiment that he was standing on quicksand, but he had talked his way out of tight corners before. This time, however, he had no glib reply. 'I am not sure I understand you, sire.'

'Perhaps I can explain.' Yoritomo leafed through the wad of papers that lay beside him and selected three handwritten sheets. 'These are recorded eye-witness accounts of the disaster at the Heron Pool – some of which cover incidents that occurred after you led the troops from the Mara-bara garrison from the field.'

Toshiro bowed. 'I did explain my reason for doing so.'

'You did – and it was a wise decision. I am, by the way, extremely pleased at the way you handled this assignment. It has turned out much better than any of us could have hoped.'

Ieyasu nodded. 'I agree. Most satisfactory.'

Yoritomo perused the top sheet, then let it fall back on top of the others in his lap. 'What puzzles me are these accounts – all confirmed by independent witnesses – about the actions of a female long-dog. Am I right in assuming that this is the same individual who occupied the lake-house?'

'I cannot state that with absolute certainty, sire. But I have been given to understand that the female you are referring to *was* wearing a white mask.'

'Of a courtesan.'

'Again, I did not see it myself, but that may be so.'

'You seem to be avoiding my question,' said Yoritomo. 'My brother-in-law's harlot wore a white mask when you met her on the way back from Kari-varan. She was part of the escape package, and you arranged her transfer to the Heron Pool. I think we can safely assume that it was she who performed the actions described by these eye-witnesses – don't you?'

The Shogun consulted the papers on his lap, picking out various lines: '. . . splitting the earth with a shout . . . causing stones to rain down from the sky . . . turning aside arrows with a wall of light . . . killing up to a dozen samurai by pointing her fingers at them and . . . forcing Lord Yama-Shita to kill himself several times over and – it would seem – keeping him alive and on his feet while he did so.'

He shuffled the papers together and passed them to Ieyasu. 'Even if only *half* of these are true, it is clear that Lord Yama-Shita was confronted by someone endowed with quite extraordinary power. Do you have any explanation for what happened?'

'None, sire. People who spoke to me afterwards called her a witch. They said she called upon the dark forces of earth magic. But as you know, little credence is given to such ideas nowadays.'

'True,' replied Yoritomo. 'But if it was not by some form of magic – how were these deeds accomplished?'

Toshiro bowed. 'I cannot say, sire.'

Yoritomo looked thoughtfully at the Herald, then turned to his uncle. 'Didn't Lord Yama-Shita regale us some years ago with tales about grass-monkeys with so-called magic powers?'

'He did,' said Ieyasu. 'But he didn't believe them either.'

Yoritomo laughed drily. 'A big mistake.' He turned his attention back to Toshiro. 'It was only natural he should underrate their abilities, but it's now clear he knew far less about them than a man in his position, and with his experience, should have done.

'For instance, the Lord Chamberlain had recently discovered that not all Mutes have deformed, multi-coloured skins and lumps on their skulls. Some of them are smooth-skinned – like Trackers. I thought the two individuals the "mexican" was sent to recapture were long-dogs but I was wrong. They were Mutes!'

The Shogun threw up his hands. 'What a strange state of affairs! On the one hand we have this "mexican" who claims to be a long-dog – but comes here disguised as a grass-monkey – and on the other, we have two grass-monkeys pretending to be long-dogs!'

Toshiro said nothing. The bottom seemed to have dropped out of his stomach.

'Were you aware of this deception?' asked Ieyasu, the spider, slowly weaving his silken net.

The Herald bowed. 'Yes, sire. I did finally discover their identities a few weeks ago, but I said nothing because –'

'You thought it might confuse me,' suggested Yoritomo.

'No, sire – because it did not change the overall situation. Lord Yama-Shita *was* engaged in a conspiracy with Lord Min-Orota to recapture the Dark Light, and the threat of an attack by the Federation if these individuals were not returned still hung over us.'

'And my dear brother-in-law *was* coupling with a grass-monkey. But you sought to protect my feelings and the honour of my sister by not telling me the whole truth . . .'

'I did take that into consideration, sire, yes.'

'I respect you for that. And that is no doubt one of the reasons why the Lady Mishiko holds you in such high regard.'

Once again, Toshiro said nothing.

Yoritomo turned to the Lord Chamberlain. 'I have something of a personal nature to discuss with this Herald who has rendered us such sterling service. If there are no further matters you wish to raise . . .?'

Toshiro uncrossed his legs and knelt with his forehead almost touching the floor as the Lord Chamberlain took formal leave of the Shogun and then rose and silently backed out of the study. The only sound was the swish of the door screen sliding shut behind him.

Now only the five blank-faced bodyguards remained. Unable to speak or understand a word of Basic, they were regarded as being part of the furniture. For all practical purposes, he and the Shogun were alone.

Yoritomo motioned the Herald to sit as before.

Toshiro placed the palms of his hands on his knees and held his back erect. The day could end well or badly. He would accept whatever lay in store in the same calm fashion.

The Shogun gave him a long, thoughtful look. The sigh that followed was tinged with regret. 'I understand why you acted as you did. And had I been in your . . . situation, I would have probably done the same. But there is a greater issue at stake. You knew what my aims were when I got rid of the riff-raff who were working hand in glove with Ieyasu and set up a new College – with direct access to me.

'The bond that exists between the Shogun and his Heralds is one based on *absolute trust*. You are my eyes and ears. The senses we possess are not infallible. Our eyes sometimes see less clearly than they should, but when the true nature of an object becomes apparent, the eye instantly corrects the faulty information it has fed to the brain. For reasons best known to yourself, you failed to do that.'

Toshiro hung his head. Protest was useless.

'I'm sure you can appreciate the difficulty this places me in. If I am unable to rely on the information my eyes and ears are sending to my brain, then I can no longer feel secure. The world suddenly becomes a dangerous place – full of strange sounds and lurking shadows.'

'Sire, you have nothing to fear from any man in this realm. My loyalty and devotion to your person, and your house, remains undimmed. I cannot, therefore, do other than confess to having kept the truth from you. Through my ignorance of the ways of the Plainfolk, I allowed myself to be misled. By saying nothing I compounded my original error. In that sense I am doubly guilty. I fell victim to false pride.' Toshiro hesitated for a moment, then added: 'I did not wish to appear foolish in your eyes.'

'A fool can be forgiven, but not someone who betrays a trust.'

It was at that moment Toshiro realised that everything was slipping away from him. The Shogun was playing a cat-and-mouse game from which there was no escape. He assumed a kneeling position and bowed again, this time from the waist. 'Sire, I did everything in my power to ensure your objectives were achieved.'

'Everything and more,' replied Yoritomo. 'But in doing so you kept vital information from me. Look at it from my point of view. From now on I can never be sure, can I?'

Toshiro straightened his back, but kept looking at the floor.

'On the other hand there is *someone* – whose word I'm prepared to accept without question – who trusts you absolutely. With her life even.'

Toshiro raised his eyes to meet Yoritomo's.

'My sister, the Lady Mishiko – whose tiresome husband you so obligingly removed. In fact, I believe you were the one who suggested the idea.'

The Herald gazed steadily at the Shogun. Bowing wouldn't make any difference now.

'It came as something of a surprise to learn that Ieyasu has had several of his own men working on this case. And it appears they crossed your path on more than one occasion . . .'

Toshiro waited for the next blow to fall.

'I don't know how true it is, but he claims that my sister was your principal informant regarding the extramural activities of her husband. In particular, his relations with the female long-dog. Or Mute, as the case may be.'

When no reply was forthcoming, Yoritomo said: 'And *she* has informed me of her wish to marry you.' He raised his eyebrows – perhaps in the hope of eliciting a reply.

Once again, Toshiro said nothing.

457

'I know just what you're thinking and I agree,' said Yoritomo. 'It *was* rather impetuous of her. But then you know what women are like. Please – don't misunderstand me. You come from a good family. I don't need to enumerate your qualities. From the moment you joined the College I've looked upon you as one of the family. And now my sister wants to make it official.'

'S-sire,' stammered Toshiro. 'I – I never once entertained the idea that –'

Yoritomo silenced him. 'My dear friend, I can't think of anyone I would rather have as a brother-in-law. I really mean that. I can overlook that mix-up over the Mute. But your pride led you to commit an even greater act of folly.' Opening a small lacquered cabinet that stood beside him, the Shogun drew out a neatly folded piece of paper and tossed it on to the mat between them.

'If only you hadn't sent that letter . . .'

Toshiro recognised it from the way it had been folded and the watermark on the paper. It was the letter he had written to the military commander of the southern district of Lord Se-Iko's domain, informing him of the location of the *ronin* camp and the means by which he could gain entry. The letter he had paid a shopkeeper to post for him at Ari-dina.

His throat tightened, forcing him to speak in a harsh whisper. 'I also killed Noburo Naka-Jima and his two companions.'

Yoritomo nodded. 'Ieyasu told me.' He shook his head wearily. 'Why? What on earth made you, of all people, do such a thing?'

Toshiro sighed. 'The one serious flaw in my character. I can't bear to be wrong.' He hung his head. There were other reasons, but it was unnecessary to go into them now.

'You realise, of course, that this was a particularly scabrous crime – for which you should be flayed, disembowelled, then boiled alive?'

'Yes, sire.'

'But you have done something even worse. You have

458

forced me back into the hands of corrupt, licentious men. And *that* is unforgivable. However, because of the feelings I once had for you, and for the sake of my sister, I will spare you the humiliating death you so richly deserve. I hope you won't display any weakness tomorrow morning.'

Toshiro fell forward on his hands to kiss the mat in abject gratitude. His lips met the fatal letter.

When he sat back, Yoritomo said: 'Who will attend you?'

'Captain Kamakura.'

'Ah, yes – the good captain with the five pretty daughters . . .'

CHAPTER EIGHTEEN

Having informed Guard-Captain Kamakura of the service he was to render shortly after sunrise, Toshiro retired to his quarters in the palace and slept peacefully for several hours before being roused by a servant. After a ritual cleansing of his body, he offered prayers at the small shrine in his room, then penned a short but eloquent letter to the Lady Mishiko. Giving the letter to the servant with a sum of money that would guarantee its discreet delivery, he put on a cloak and made his way down into the stone garden.

As a mark of his personal feelings towards his Herald, the Shogun had given him permission to commit *seppuku* on his own special section of the veranda. Wrapped in his cloak, Toshiro spent two silent hours in contemplation of the darkened, mist-shrouded garden. At first he could see hardly anything, but as night gave way to twilight and the mist began to fade, the shapes and patterns slowly emerged, until at last all became clear.

At the moment of death, he would be plunged back into that darkness; a darkness more profound than he had ever known. If he died badly, he would be cast into the nether regions for ever; if he died well, his soul would rise towards the light that shone from the face of Ameratsu-Omikami.

When the sun rose, Captain Kamakura appeared, followed by four attendants bearing the items that Toshiro would require. He rose and stood aside while they lay down straw mats of the required measurement and edged with white silk. They then positioned the large white cushion on which the Herald would kneel. In front of this was placed the lacquered tray holding the short, razor-sharp dagger.

460

Once everything was in place, Toshiro handed his cloak to one of the servants, who then withdrew. After embracing Captain Kamakura and thanking him for agreeing to act as his *kaishaku-nin*, the Herald knelt on the white cushion and took several slow deep breaths while he concentrated his thoughts on the final act he was required to perform without exhibiting the slightest hesitation or fear. To the true samurai, death was 'as light as a feather' and he awoke each day ready to meet it.

Captain Kamakura now knelt in the prescribed place, behind the Herald, some three and a half feet to his left, the long killing-sword held ready in both hands. Watching from either side of the garden were the Shogun and several members of the Inner Court. Toshiro glimpsed Ieyasu's grey, angular face amongst them.

The Chamberlain had every reason to feel satisfied. He had shaken the Shogun's faith in his Heralds and had demonstrated that his own power to influence events remained undimmed. It would not be long before his private office reinserted itself between the Shogun and his Heralds. They were intelligent, well-intentioned young men, like their master, but they did not know the ways of the world. His nephew Yoritomo needed further guidance before he could be safely left to take Ne-Issan into the next century. He, Ieyasu, would provide that guidance in the few years left to him.

There were difficult times ahead. Yoritomo had all the qualities required to surmount those difficulties, but he needed to introduce a certain flexibility into his moral judgements. In the ancient world, it had been termed 'double standards'; the mental suppleness that allowed a man to bend with the winds of change without being uprooted.

Toshiro reached out and picked up the knife, gazed at it for a moment as if admiring its lethal grace and then, after adjusting his grip so as to hold it firmly with both hands, he drove the full length of the blade into the left side of his belly. The impact caused him to breathe out sharply. He inhaled deeply without relaxing his grip and, with a slow, deliberate sawing motion, he began to draw the blade across to the right hand side of his body.

Beads of sweat gathered on his forehead, but apart from his eyes which stared with frightening intensity at the stone and pebble landscape before him, his face showed no sign of the excruciating pain he was inflicting upon himself. At the end of the lateral cut, he turned the blade of the dagger in his body and made a short, upward cut. The *jumonji*; the final ghastly flourish.

The Herald had gone much further in the act of self-mutilation than was normally deemed necessary, but he had instructed Kamakura not to act before he had pulled the knife from his body. The end to the perfect act of *seppuku*. But his hands had become slippery with blood, and he no longer had the strength to remove the dagger.

Kamakura leaped to his feet. As the *kaishaku-nin*, his duty was to spare the principal actor unnecessary agony. He was empowered to intervene at a pre-arranged moment – which could even be during the act of reaching out for the knife – or at the slightest sign of irresolution. As the Herald bent forward in one last effort to pull out the blade, Kamakura raised his sword high in the air and cut off the young man's head with one swift blow.

It had been a good death, but it gave Kamakura scant cause for satisfaction. As Toshiro's swordmaster he had spent countless hours instructing and counselling the young man, and now Fate had forced him to give the *coup de grâce* to his most promising pupil.

The same blow had put paid to his wife's cherished dreams of having a Herald for a son-in-law. How she had schemed and laboured over the years! And now her plans had come to naught. Kamakura did not relish having to break the news to her. She would understand why he had been obliged to perform this doleful task, but she would never forgive him. And neither would his daughters.

He looked down at the bloodied head with its half-closed eyes. Eyes that had followed him so attentively over the years as he had revealed his unrivalled skill with the sword. What a waste! Kamakura cleaned and sheathed his sword, then turned away. His eyes brimmed with bitter tears, but he held them in check. There would be tears enough. The sound of weeping would fill his house for many months to come.

*

Skull-Face was as good as his word. There *was* a field near the east bank of the Hudson marked with a hollow white square, just as the map had indicated. And they were met on landing by a Jap agent who identified himself to Cadillac in the prescribed manner. Steve came in last, and although he tried to make it as smooth as he could, the skid landing caused agonising jolts of pain to shoot through his wounded thigh.

Kelso had spotted the feathered end of the arrow sticking out through the cockpit side during the flight, and had guessed from Steve's signals what had happened. When his machine slid to a halt, Kelso was there with a borrowed saw to cut him loose. The others helped lift him out, then Clearwater and Cadillac removed the arrowhead. The wound wasn't all that deep, and it hadn't severed any tendons or arteries, but it still hurt. The Jap agent promised him he would get some medication and a bandage later.

Hauling himself upright, Steve discovered that if he didn't put his whole weight on his right leg he was able to hobble around without support. *Haww! Jack me . . .*

Leaves and branches from a number of felled trees around the edge of the field had been gathered to make several bonfires. It explained how Kelso had got hold of a saw. The reason for the lumberjacking now became clear. As soon as they had removed their baggage, the Jap told them to pile bales of straw and branches around the machines and set them alight. Anyone who had seen the planes pass over this forested area could not be certain where, or if, they had landed, and three more columns of smoke would not arouse anyone's curiosity.

While the others were fetching the bales and branches, Steve gritted his teeth and hung head first inside the rear cockpits of each plane. After removing the radio-controlled detonators, he ripped out the explosive struts and stowed everything away in the tote-bag.

They stood back and watched the Jap torch the three planes. It was depressing how quickly weeks of painstaking handiwork were consumed. When all the unburnt pieces around the edge of the fires had been tossed into the centre of the flames, the Jap herded them aboard a closed ox-cart for the next stage of their journey.

Instead of crossing the river and boarding ship straight away, they were obliged to spend the next two nights in a house overlooking the Hudson. The east bank, which they were now on, belonged to the Shogun's family, the Toh-Yota. The west bank, and the land beyond, all the way to what Kelso called the Great Lakes, belonged to the Yama-Shita. The boats of both families plied the navigable stretch of the river from Nyo-Yoko in the south to as far north as you could go, but the canal system that linked the Hudson with Lake Erie was reserved for vessels owned by the Yama-Shita family.

The Jap, who spoke Basic reasonably well, told Steve he had received word that Side-Winder's boat was running late because of some unspecified mechanical failure. 'Buh pleez nah toh wah-ree.' Shortly after their arrival at the house, he had seen it heading downriver, so – barring any further breakdowns – it should return to Ari-bani in the early evening of 'day-arf tah toh-marah'.

The delay proved a blessing in disguise. It allowed the time for Clearwater to produce four top-notch paint-jobs and for Cadillac to get used to wearing women's clothes. Once the wig pieces and combs had been pinned into position, and his coppery skin had been paled by sweet-smelling powder, he was halfway there. When he put on the white mask and gloves he looked totally authentic. And thanks to his uncanny grasp of the Iron Masters' language and mores, he soon adopted the necessary *hauteur*.

Since their Jap contact man had not been present during the dress rehearsals, Steve decided to put the disguise to the test. After setting up Cadillac in another room, he engaged the Jap in conversation as he was returning from one of his frequent sorties. A few minutes later, a shrill Japanese voice emanated from the adjoining room, demanding some service. When the unsuspecting Jap rushed to the door and found Cadillac sitting in solitary splendour, he was so taken aback by the masked figure's imperious bearing and immaculate diction, he instinctively bowed and started to apologise before he cottoned on.

Fortunately, he had a sense of humour. What was even better, it meant they were in with a chance.

Steve already had a Mute identity, but it was exchanged for a new one. Sets of worn clothes, slave-tags and 'yellow cards' were distributed to Jodi, Kelso and Clearwater; travel papers and money were provided for 'Yoko Mi-Shima'. Their slave papers and toll-gate stamps purported to show they had been purchased on behalf of the courtesan at Firi, where there were regular small-scale auctions as well as the big one in late spring following the annual western expedition of the wheelboats.

Slaves were a disposable asset; a medium of exchange that was more secure than carrying cash or banknotes which could be stolen by the thieves and vagabonds who preyed on unwary travellers. Indeed, some enterprising merchants who had made a close study of the seasonal and regional fluctuations in the labour market had amassed considerable fortunes by buying up slaves and slipping them to wherever there was a quick profit to be made. Why feed slaves through the winter in Mah-ina and Nofo-skosha, where the ground could not be worked, when they could labour fruitfully on plantations in the warmer climes of Fyah-jina and Karo-rina?

Side-Winder took charge of Steve and the other 'Mutes' as they came aboard the wheelboat, and shepherded them down into the gloomy bow section of the lower through-deck reserved for the transport of slaves. Cadillac's carriage-box was taken to the door of the cabin that had been booked in the name of Yoko Mi-Shima and he did not meet up with the others until they all disembarked at Bu-faro.

The big mexican remained his usual taciturn self, and only related to them in his official capacity as Mute overseer. He did not treat them any differently from any of the other slaves on board, and because of the lumps on his forehead, Jodi and Kelso assumed he was a genuine Mute. Clearwater appeared to share their opinion, but Steve was not sure what she really thought. Maybe the Plainfolk had other, more subtle, ways of recognising their own kind.

With her help, Steve had concocted Mute names and brief cover-stories for Jodi and Kelso to use in case any of their fellow-travellers wanted to know where they came from. He himself had adopted Cadillac's identity. Why not? It was a fair swap and, best of all, he didn't have to make anything up. Small parties of Plainfolk Mutes came and went, but they were the only ones riding the water all the way to Bu-faro. As it happened, there was very little interchange between groups even when the deck was crowded. Most Mutes became sullen and withdrawn when being transported over water, so their own silence was not viewed as suspicious.

Steve had daily contact with the big mexican, but did not tell the others what the real connection was, and he did not tell Side-Winder what he had learned about AMEXICO's links with the anonymous undercover organisation that Skull-Face worked for. Or that he had been named as one of the intermediaries.

In the short time that had elapsed since joining AMEXICO, Steve had learned that operatives did not probe into the details of each other's missions. You didn't ask questions and you didn't give anything away without clearance from the Operations Control Centre at Rio Lobo. Side-Winder did not even enquire how he and his friends had reached Ari-bani. As far as he was concerned, that was Steve's business – as he had made clear when Steve had attempted to speak about their escape from the Heron Pool. His job, said the big mex, was to oversee their safe passage to Bu-faro – and from there to the Big Open. Apart from that, he didn't want to know.

Unable to see anything but sky through a small latticed hatch-cover in the deck above, Steve spent the greater part of the trip sitting close to Clearwater. Jodi and Kelso had found themselves a niche between some bales a few yards away. It must be a strange experience for them, thought Steve. Both had previously been openly contemptuous of Mutes. Now here they were, clothed in the coloured skin that was the mark of their mortal enemies, and, for the moment at least, their lives depended on how well they could act the part.

From the looks they had given him during the colouring of their skins, it was clear they were aware of the irony of the situation. It had forced them to reconsider their own comforting beliefs and prejudices. Not an easy thing to do after a lifetime of relentless indoctrination – as Steve had discovered for himself.

The existence of clear-skinned Mutes had been their first big surprise. The fact that someone with Cadillac's skills was actually a Mute had been even more unsettling – and Clearwater had knocked them sideways. The power she had unleashed against the Iron Masters had left them bewildered and more than a little uneasy – a reaction that led to the awkward silences between them.

Steve understood this problem too. He had felt the same way when he had witnessed her powers as a summoner for the first time. Jodi and Kelso found it hard to reconcile the vengeful, almost superhuman figure who had held the Iron Masters at bay while they worked frantically to load the rocket trays, with the young, slim-bodied, blue-eyed girl who nestled against Steve's shoulder.

But they did not know her as he did. They did not know the depth of feeling she could inspire, nor the warmth of her response. They saw only a death-machine who, for the moment, had dropped into neutral gear. They did not know she was merely a channel through which the power of Talisman entered the world.

Clearwater had been drained, physically and emotionally, by the ferocious nature of the forces that had poured through her. The enforced delay before boarding the wheelboat had given her a chance to rest and recoup her energies, but she remained quiet and subdued.

Steve put an arm round her shoulder and drew her close. 'You pleased to be going home?'

She settled against him, her forehead touching his cheek. 'I am happy to be with you.'

'That's not a real answer. What about your clan sisters and brothers? And Mr Snow.'

'They are not forgotten. But it is hard to think beyond this moment. When we are together, the world ends with you and I.'

'Yeah,' murmured Steve. 'I've felt that too.'

But not now. Decision time was coming up fast . . .

'When will this journey end?'

'All I can tell you is that it takes about a day and a half to reach Bu-faro. That's on one of the lakes your people call "the Great River". Once we get across that, we'll be in Plainfolk territory – with a long walk ahead of us.' The prospect caused him to knead the wound in his thigh.

Well done, Stevie. What a brilliant piece of timing that was.

Clearwater straightened up a little, so that she could see the whole of his face. 'The man who met us on landing, the others who brought us to the wheelboat. What do you know of them? Who are they?'

'Friends,' said Steve.

'How can that be? They are Iron Masters.'

468

'So?'

'And the Mute, who watches over us, but who is not of the Plainfolk. Is he a friend too?'

Steve took hold of her hands and gripped them tightly. 'Now listen! It doesn't matter who *he* is, or who *they* are! I'm the only friend you need!' He dropped his voice. 'I promised Mr Snow I would bring you both back safe and sound. To get this far I've had to lie and cheat and kill – and I'm ready to do it all over again!'

'And I have killed for you,' she whispered. 'Many times over. Why will you not tell me the –'

'Don't ask me what the truth is! I don't know what the word means any more! This world is a mirage conjured out of shifting sand! The only thing that is *real* for me is the power, the feeling – or whatever it is that binds us together. Maybe it's called "love", or maybe there's another word for it that you and I don't know about. What I *do* know is, it will never change.'

Clearwater gave him a long, searching look and then, with a wistful sigh that seemed to imply she knew something he didn't, she said: 'That is true, cloud warrior. The power of love cannot be destroyed. But perhaps the world will change *us* . . .'

*

It was fortunate that they chose to journey disguised as Mutes and not as captive Trackers. At the frequent cargo and passenger halts along the canal, Side-Winder saw soldiers on the quayside and heard their officers demanding to know from the captain if he was transporting any long-dogs. On several occasions, the wheelboat was boarded by port officials and soldiers who examined the cargo manifest and passenger list, then proceeded to inspect the contents of the through-decks.

Steve and the others had their slave-tags and "yellow cards" examined, and lanterns were used to pry into dark corners where a stowaway might be lurking. Even Cadillac's cabin was entered. No one had warned him this might happen, but the Mute did not lose his cool. He had begun to enjoy the respectful treatment accorded to 'Yoko Mi-Shima' and was playing the part to perfection – right down to the fluttering fan. The officer's polite enquiries brought equally polite replies in the courtly language and accents of the nobility. No one suspected that the person behind the mask was not the genuine article, and his papers were never examined.

The first contact man had told them they would be met at the dockside and, once again, Skull-Face's organisation delivered the goods. A sealed carriage-box was sent aboard for 'Yoko Mi-Shima' and, after they had been shackled, two Korean clerks steered the 'Mutes' through the various layers of officialdom and out of the dock gates.

Steve and the others had no idea who anyone was or what they were saying until they met up with Cadillac later. It then transpired that the clerks were employed by a rich slave-dealer, none other than the man whose name Side-Winder had given Steve during their chance meeting on the dockside at Ari-bani. It was yet further proof of the mexican's tie-in with the Japs. Just how far did this deal between the Federation and the Iron Masters go?

Chivvied along by flicks from the clerk's whipping-canes, Steve, Jodi, Kelso and Clearwater followed the carriage-box through the bustling streets to the slave-dealer's imposing residence. Only Cadillac was invited to go in through the front door; the others were shunted into a stockade at the rear and locked in a pen.

It was one of several, housing varying numbers of Mutes. Raised off the ground, under a lean-to roof, was a slatted wooden floor covered with a thin layer of filthy straw. There was a bucket of water to drink or wash with – assuming anyone wanted to – and another bucket to crap in. A big step down from the plush accommodation units Steve had discovered in Santanna Deep.

From the bawdy exchanges Cadillac had overheard whilst being carried out of the docks it appeared that his services – or rather those of the masked lady in the box – had also been acquired by the slave-master. Amid the laughter and muttered asides, a garrulous tongue revealed that the gentleman in question was a social-climber who had spared no expense to acquire a well-connected, high-class 'entertainer'.

To Cadillac's relief, his new owner did not make any attempt during the night to get value for money. The next morning, when he was congratulating himself on his good fortune at being comfortably housed while the others were freezing their butts off out in the yard, his pampered, perfumed existence came to an abrupt end. One of the Korean clerks who had greeted 'Yoko Mi-Shima' on the dockside entered the bedchamber and ordered the Mute to pick up the canvas tote-bag that had travelled with him. The clerk then opened a concealed door and ushered Cadillac down a narrow, enclosed staircase into a cellar illuminated by several lanterns.

Clearwater was waiting for him. The clerk told Cadillac to remove his mask, wig and clothes. When he had done so, the clerk took everything back upstairs. Clearwater knelt down and searched through the contents of the bag.

Cadillac knelt down obediently beside her as she produced one of the sets of body-paints. 'Will there be enough?'

'Yes.' Using her fingertips, she began to draw the familiar lines on his back and fill in the areas with the different coloured pigments. It was something they had done for each other since she had been chosen by the council of clan elders to be his soul-mate. Reverting to his true colours was the final step in accepting that his destiny lay with the Plainfolk.

Clearwater sang softly to herself as she worked the waterproof dye into Cadillac's skin. It was one of the M'Call fire-songs they both knew well. 'Are you sad?'

'No. What has happened is the will of Talisman.' Cadillac sighed. 'It is our present situation that concerns me.'

'Do you fear something will happen to prevent our escape?'

Cadillac shrugged. 'If we are meant to, we will. What worries me is that Brickman is no longer alone. Why are these Iron Masters helping him? He tells me nothing. Has he spoken to you?'

How strange, thought Clearwater. As the dyes cover more and more of his body, he speaks less and less with the voice of the cloud warrior. 'He says we must trust him.'

Cadillac gave a bitter laugh. 'What else – apart from the truth – could he say?'

'You have read his mind.'

'Yes. But not his thoughts. You are closer to him than I will ever be. You can read his heart and see into his soul.'

'Sometimes . . .'

'And what do you see?'

Clearwater moved round on her knees and began to colour his face. 'Love. Death. Betrayal. A new beginning . . .'

'Are you to be taken from me?'

She traced a gentle line down his cheekbone and on to his neck. 'I cannot tell. It is you who read the stones. But whatever happens, part of me will always remain with you.'

'But you won't.'

Clearwater took hold of his chin. 'If you are to be the sword of Talisman, your strength must not come from me but from within yourself.' She pressed a finger against his heart.

Easier said than done, thought Cadillac. Oh, Sweet Mother! Why did life have to be so hard, and full of pain?

*

Dressed and tagged as a Mute, Cadillac was taken back with Clearwater to join the others in the stockade. It was his first experience of life in Ne-Issan as a grass-monkey. The place stank with the odour of unemptied slop-buckets, and what little food there was was tasteless and unappetising. Worst of all, there was no *sake*.

Later in the day, Side-Winder appeared outside the stockade. Steve walked across and spoke to him through one of the gaps in the vertical planking. 'How come they let you off the boat?'

'Another breakdown. Everybody got shore-leave except the engineers.'

'You come to say goodbye?'

'No. I'm coming with you.' The mexican's hard mouth split open in a happy grin. 'How about that!'

Steve smiled back. 'You're going to miss those lumps.'

'You kidding? Can't wait!'

'I can believe it. Listen. As you're here, and since you'll be travelling back with us, there's something I've been dying to ask you.'

'Oh, yeah, what's that?'

'Well, I can't help noticing you've got a lot of slant-eyed friends. How about filling me in on that?'

Side-Winder's sunny smile turned into a sly grin. 'No can do, amigo. Try asking Mother when you get back to Rio Lobo.'

'Do you think he'll tell me?' The idea of Karlstrom spilling the beans on anything seemed an unlikely prospect.

'Can't say . . .'

'But you *are* going to tell me how we're getting out of here.'

'Yeah. We leave tonight on a fishing-smack, then we transfer on to a couple of power inflatables and cross over to a place called Long Point on the other side of Lake Erie.'

'Is Mother going to hook us up?'

Side-Winder nodded. 'A couple of Sky-Riders are comin' in at first light. They'll take one of us up front and two in the cargo bay. If we don't power-down on the way home, you'll be tucked up safe and sound in one of the Deeps by midnight.'

It suddenly seemed a daunting prospect. Steve

grimaced. 'I promised Jodi and Kelso they'd get a square deal. Y'know – for helping out.' He paused, his eyes searching the mexican's face. 'I couldn't have pulled this off without them.'

'Then they've got nothing to worry about,' said Side-Winder. 'The Federation looks after its own.' He glanced towards Cadillac and Clearwater. 'What about the grass-monkeys?'

'Could be a problem. Once they see those Sky-Riders . . .'

'Yeah, well, there'll be you, me and the two pilots. But there's no reason for things to get heavy. I believe one of your friends has developed a liking for the ol' joy-juice.'

'The other one doesn't drink.'

'There's always a first time, amigo. Hell, when we reach the other side, we're gonna have something to celebrate – right?'

'Right.'

'So we have a little drink, maybe smoke a little grass. *Then* we call in the air force.'

'Gotcha.'

Side-Winder wrinkled his nose. 'Boy, this place really stinks, doesn't it?'

'A little.'

'How's that leg of yours holding up?'

Steve shrugged. 'It's better than no leg at all.'

'Okay.' Side-Winder winked. 'Check you later.'

Steve rejoined Jodi and Kelso. Clearwater and Cadillac were sitting cross-legged on the straw at the other end of the lean-to.

Kelso stared thoughtfully at the place where Side-Winder had been standing. 'There's something about that guy that worries me.'

Steve sat down alongside him. 'It shouldn't. He's one of us.'

'Jack me,' breathed Kelso. 'A Fed.'

Jodi looked at them both but didn't say anything.

'In cahoots with these dinks . . .'

Steve nodded. 'Came as a surprise to me, too. Just shows that, no matter how far you go, you can never get away from the First Family.'

Kelso nodded soberly. 'Do they know how we risked our necks helping you?'

'They will. I told him what the score was.'

'And what'd he say?'

' "The Federation always looks after its own" . . .'

Kelso looked at Jodi and raised his eyebrows.

*

It was still dark when Side-Winder handed out the lifejackets. They followed him over the side of the fishing-smack and down the scaling net into the two power inflatables. Cadillac and Clearwater joined him; Jodi and Kelso went into the second boat with Steve. They cast off, fired up the outboard motors – water-jets, powered by a cylinder of liquid methane – and sped westwards. Behind them, Steve saw the smack's square-cut sails silhouetted against a sky which had already begun to turn grey.

Their destination was a strange, needle-like spit of land some twenty miles long, running almost due east into the middle of the lake. Both inflatables were equipped with compasses, but Steve had been keeping his eyes on the mex's small blue stern light, about fifty yards ahead. He passed the tiller to Jodi and sat in the bows with Kelso.

'What's up with Jodi?'

Kelso gave him an odd look. 'She's had a change of heart.'

'How d'you mean?'

'She doesn't want to go back in.'

Steve kept it casual, turning his back to avoid looking at Jodi. 'Oh, yeah? When did this happen?'

'I think it started soon after touchdown. All those dinks, then your friend, Side-Winder . . .' Kelso shrugged.

Steve laughed and shook his head. 'Did she think we could make it on our own? Where the hell does she think all that explosive and the rest of the hardware came from?'

'Sure. She's not that dumb. She knew what she was getting into. It's just that, well – all this back-up has suddenly brought home what's waiting at the end of the line. Let's not kid around. This is a big deal – right? It's spooked her.'

Steve sighed. 'Take over the tiller.'

Jodi joined him in the bows. They eyed each other for a moment, then she looked straight ahead.

'Kelso tells me you don't want to go back in.'

She didn't answer.

'What's the matter – don't you trust me?'

Again no answer.

'Come on, Jodi. I played it straight with you. Level with me.'

The seconds ticked away. Finally she swung her eyes back on to his and held them there. Defiantly. 'Did Dave tell you he doesn't want to go back either?'

They both turned to look at Kelso. He read Steve's face in the half-light and spread his hands apologetically. Steve greeted the news with a nod then looked away, as Jodi had done, over the bows. Ahead of them to starboard was the foaming wake from Side-Winder's boat. He wondered how the big mex was making out with Cadillac and Clearwater. And whether he realised they knew he wasn't a real lumphead. He began to think of Mr Snow. And how Mr Snow had made him think – really *think* about the world around him and his part in the great scheme of things.

What a mess! So many promises to so many people. Whichever way it went, someone was bound to end up getting shafted. The face of Roz, his kin-sister, appeared before his inner eye. He drove everything else from his mind and concentrated on the image in an effort to make contact. Despite the barriers he had erected, her voice had sometimes found a way through. Like on the shuttle

476

to Grand Central when he'd been under escort and on trial for his life.

Come on, brain! TRY! If it hadn't been for Roz, you and I wouldn't be in this jam!

A delicious coolness filled his skull as he and Roz broke through to each other. He was conscious of weightless, formless, wraith-like bodies embracing, merging. His and hers. He was both observer and participant. The contact had never been as strong as this before. Her voice whispered directly into his brain. Not a single word was spoken, but as he listened, he understood what he had to do. A deep, soothing calm replaced his mental anguish.

He straightened up and found Jodi shaking his shoulder. 'Hey! Are you okay?'

'What? Oh, yeah, sure.'

'You had me worried.'

Steve grimaced. 'Just thinking things over.'

'And . . .?'

'Would it come as a big surprise if I told you I felt the same way?'

Jodi stared at him in disbelief. 'You playing some kind of game with me?'

'Nope. I'm serious. Where were you planning on heading?'

'Wyoming,' she said, cautiously. 'We, uhh – we want to try and get back with Malone and the other guys.'

'Couldn't be better. I'm going the same way.'

Jodi scrambled back to Kelso and broke the news. He beckoned to Steve to join them and raised his voice above the noise of the motor. 'How're we gonna do it?'

'There's five of us and three of them. Shouldn't be too difficult.'

'How about asking your friend Clearwater to help?'

Steve shook his head. 'Mute magic can't be turned on and off like a tap. Besides which, it's too risky. You saw what happened at the Heron Pool. Those planes nearly jumped off their trolleys. We don't want her shaking all the wires loose in those Sky-Riders.'

'So what d'you have in mind?'

Steve laid a hand on the canvas tote-bag. 'Don't ask me why I didn't throw 'em away. It must be Fate. But in here are five face-masks and . . .' he reached inside his tunic and pulled out a grey canister '. . . I've also got one gas grenade.'

Kelso lifted it neatly out of his hand as Jodi screamed with delight and threw her arms round Steve's neck. They both ended up in the bottom of the boat. She hugged him cheek to cheek, then planted a couple of robust kisses on his mouth.

'Jodi! Your face is like a block of ice!'

'So's yours. Never mind. You're a really great guy. Y'know that?'

'Listen, it's nothing. I owe you – remember?'

*

Long Point turned out to be an inhospitable strip made up almost entirely of windswept sand dunes whose crowns were held together by ragged tufts of long grass. Following Side-Winder's directions, they dragged the inflatables up on to the beach. He then paused to get his bearings and concluded they were some 400 yards east of where they should be.

As he grasped one of the carrying handles of his boat, Jodi and Kelso stepped in and gave him a hand, leaving Steve, Cadillac and Clearwater to shift the other. Steve briefed them on what was going to happen as they proceeded down the beach behind the others. They each took a face-mask from the bag, stowed it inside their tunics and did their best to look as downcast as they'd been before.

Side-Winder found what he was looking for: a large watertight compartment whose lid was concealed beneath a cunningly arranged mat of pebbles and small rocks which matched this particular area of the beach. This was no temporary set-up: it was a transit point for people going in and out of Ne-Issan.

After removing the power units and fuel tanks, they

let the air out of the inflatables and stowed everything inside the cache. Side-Winder pulled out a hand-set, a fire-can, a mess-pot, an ice-pack to melt down for hot drinks, a six-pack of moulded foam cups containing sachets of Java and Sweet 'n' White and a flask – which he passed directly to Cadillac. They replaced the lid, kicked a few loose pebbles back round the edges, then carried their baggage and breakfast up over the dunes.

A little way in from the beach they found an area of gently undulating grassland. At some time in the recent past, a visitor had obligingly mowed a wide strip down the middle of it. Side-Winder set up the fire-can, pulled the ignition strip, then put the ice cubes in the mess-pot. A few minutes later, he and the three other Trackers were warming their hands on hot cups of Java.

Side-Winder, who had now dropped all pretence of being a Mute, inhaled the aroma contentedly. 'Ahh, yes. This is the real stuff, all right. Reminds you of all the things you've been missing!'

'Sure does,' said Kelso, busily thinking of all the goodies he would plunder from the beach store before leaving.

Side-Winder turned to Cadillac and Clearwater. Both Mutes were crouched over the fire-can. Clearwater was warming her hands, Cadillac was fondling the open flask of *sake*. 'Good stuff, eh? Just like I said – right?'

Cadillac nodded and took another swallow.

'Get your friend to try some,' urged Side-Winder. 'Go on!' he said to Clearwater. 'It'll warm you up faster than that fire-can will!'

Clearwater took a trial sip and clutched her throat as she was seized by a fit of coughing.

'It's okay, it's okay!' said Side-Winder. 'Always happens. Keep going. The second one will make you feel a whole lot better.' He watched her tip the flask up again and take another swallow. Then another. 'That's it. Y'see? Practice makes perfect.'

Clearwater lowered the flask and put a hand over her face as she started to giggle. She swayed against Cadillac and almost lost her balance. 'Oops!'

Side-Winder reached over and grabbed the flask. 'Careful! Don't want to spill any of this.' He offered up the flask to the others. Nobody responded. 'No takers?' He raised the flask to Cadillac. 'All the more for you and me!' He knocked some back and held the flask out to the two Mutes. 'Okay, who wants it?'

Clearwater made an ineffectual grab, but Cadillac got in first. He put the flask to his lips, tipped his head back and started to pour it down his throat.

'Hey, Hey! Easy, easy!' cried the mex. 'Leave some for blue eyes and me!'

Cadillac sagged forward drunkenly and let Clearwater take the flask from his hands. She drank a little more and giggled again. 'It makes the ground move!'

'No,' said Side-Winder. 'It's not the *sake*. We were a long time on the water. It's the motion of the boat that makes it seem as if the ground's moving. You have some more of that and you won't feel a thing.'

Three minutes later, both Mutes were out cold.

Side-Winder emptied the last few drops of *sake* down his throat, then looked up at Steve. 'See? Told you it wouldn't be a problem.' He capped the empty flask. 'These monkeys can't take this stuff.' The mexican rose and switched on his hand-set. 'This is Farm-Boy. Come in Sky-Bucket. Tell me how you read. Over.'

There was a slight crackle of static, then: 'Five by five, Farm-Boy. Sky-Bucket One and Two standing by. Over.'

'Roger, Sky-Bucket, you are clear to land. Tell Mother we have a full load.'

'Wilco, Farm-Boy. We're on our way . . .'

Jodi was the first to spot them. She pointed out across the lake. Steve and Kelso turned, searching for the two winged dots that quickly became two charcoal-grey Sky-Riders. Behind them, Side-Winder continued to exchange brief messages with the pilots.

The incoming planes flew a cautionary circuit of the headland, then turned across wind and made their final approach from the west, touching down within seconds of each other. The sky to the west was still a deep purple, but to the east a soft-edged wash of burnt orange was spreading along the horizon.

The two fat-bodied Sky-Riders taxied back down the mown grass strip towards them and parked alongside each other. To Steve, they were a familiar sight: he had had two flights as a passenger. First with Donna Lundkwist from the Pueblo way-station, and then with an anonymous MX pilot who had put him down in Nebraska.

The planes were second-generation aircraft built with totally new materials. They were equipped with enclosed cockpits, augmented instrumentation, and all kinds of creature comforts. They had been a big surprise to Steve, making the Skyhawk – the long-serving workhorse of the Federation – look like something out of the stone age, and Cadillac's silken flying-horses look like a joke.

Yep. You had to hand it to the First Family. They were always one step ahead. Always had the answers . . .

Steve had briefed Jodi and Kelso on what to expect, but now that the aircraft were here, the urge to take a closer look was irresistible. He ran over with them, leaving Side-Winder by the fire with the two semi-conscious Mutes.

The mexican dropped some more ice into the mess pot. Cadillac was snoring drunkenly. Clearwater was making feeble efforts to rouse herself, but did not seem to be able to get her head off the ground for more than a few seconds at a time.

The two pilots removed their black-visored crash-helmets, stowed them on top of the instrumental panel, then opened up their front-hinged perspex canopies and climbed out. The tight-lipped guy who had flown Steve to Nebraska had remained hidden and anonymous. This pair even had woven name-tags. BLACKWELL, B. and RITCHIE, K. – the human face of AMEXICO.

The three Trackers exchanged greetings with the two pilots. Both men ran a jaundiced eye over their painted faces as they shook hands.

'Protective colouring,' explained Steve.

481

'Glad to hear it,' said BLACKWELL, B. He glanced towards the three figures over by the fire-can. 'For a minute there, I thought we'd dropped in on a Mute convention.'

Jodi checked out the cockpit. 'Hey, Dave! Take a look at this set up! This is amazing!'

'Is it okay if I sit in the driving seat?' asked Steve. 'Just to see how it feels?'

'Sure. Go ahead.'

As Steve climbed into the cockpit of the nearest plane, Kelso held his handshake with RITCHIE, K. and introduced himself. 'Kelso, Class of '77. Don't I know you from somewhere?'

Baby-faced RITCHIE, K. smiled. 'I doubt it. That was before my time.' He disengaged and turned away as Side-Winder came forward to greet them.

'Got some hot Java for you guys.'

'Great,' said BLACKWELL, B. 'We haven't had anything since we left GC.'

Steve exchanged looks with Jodi and Kelso and closed the cockpit canopy. The pilot had left a pair of black leather gloves inside his crash-helmet. Steve pulled them on. He looked up and saw the two Trackers walk round the nose towards the second plane, a move which took them out of sight of anyone standing by the fire.

The two pilots stood over Side-Winder as he broke open the sachets, poured boiling water into two cups, then handed them over. The foam cups came complete with a plastic swizzle.

BLACKWELL, B. stirred slowly as he gazed down at Clearwater and Cadillac. 'They look happy.'

'Happiest they'll ever be,' said Side-Winder.

RITCHIE, K. snapped his swizzle in half and swallowed some hot Java. 'Is it okay to leave 'em there while we refuel?'

'Sure.'

'How about the two breakers?'

'No problem. Hang-Fire's told 'em they're gonna be heroes.' Side-Winder glanced towards the Sky-Riders and leapt to his feet. *'What the fuck?'*

The two pilots spun round and swore savagely at the sight that met their eyes. The cockpit canopy of the first Sky-Rider was closed – and filled with white smoke. They threw their cups of Java down and raced across the grass. When they reached the aircraft, they saw a figure inside hammering against the canopy, trying to get out.

RITCHIE, K. grasped the starboard release handle and pulled. 'Shit! It's jammed! Grab the one on the other side!'

BLACKWELL, B. sprinted round the nose of the aircraft as Jodi and Kelso appeared from the far side of the second aircraft.

'Christo!' screamed Jodi. 'It's on fire!'

'Stay out of the way!' yelled BLACKWELL, B. He seized hold of the release handle. 'Okay, Ritchie, I got it! *Heave!'*

The canopy flew open and the smoke billowed out, revealing a figure wearing a face-mask. Both pilots staggered backwards as the gas hit them, clutching their chest and throat. Steve threw himself out of the cockpit and disarmed RITCHIE, K. Kelso, who now wore a face-mask, took care of BLACKWELL, B.

Side-Winder, who was a yard or two behind RITCHIE, K. understood what was happening a split second earlier. Spinning round in an effort to escape, he found the masked figure of Clearwater behind him. As he attempted to hurl her aside, he fell full length over the crouching body of Cadillac.

Jodi, who had masked up after her scream, then ducked underneath the aircraft, fell on the big mexican and helped Clearwater hold him down till he started to choke. When they let go, Side-Winder rolled over on to his back and just lay there, convulsed with pain and gasping for breath.

Steve limped over and helped Kelso drag him across to the fire then went back for the two pilots. Jodi was trying to get Cadillac back on his feet. When the pilots had been laid alongside Side-Winder, Kelso pulled out the heavy air pistol he'd taken from BLACKWELL, B. and aimed it at the pilot's head.

Jodi pushed the pistol aside. 'No, Dave! Please. Don't do it!' Her voice, through the mask, sounded full of cotton wool.

'Okay.' Kelso relieved both men of their shoulder-holsters, then checked Side-Winder for hidden weapons.

Nope. Just the hand-set . . .

Clearwater picked up the empty flask of *sake*, slipped it inside the mexican's tunic and gave him a farewell pat on the forehead. Picking up the canvas tote-bag, she walked over to the aircraft with Jodi and Kelso. Cadillac had fallen over again.

'Leave him to me,' said Clearwater.

'How come *you're* still on your feet?' asked Kelso.

'I drank a lot less than you thought,' she said.

Jodi and Kelso helped Steve manhandle the second plane round so that its rear-mounted propeller faced the port side of its sister craft. Steve hauled himself painfully aboard, locked the brakes, hit the starter-button, then pushed the throttle wide open, using the slipstream to clear the gas-filled cockpit.

He allowed a good ten minutes for the toxic fumes to disperse, then eased the throttle right back and climbed out, leaving the prop ticking over. 'Okay. Who's gonna take the first sniff?'

'Cadillac.' Clearwater marched the glassy-eyed Mute forward. 'Don't worry. He won't feel a thing.'

Steve pulled Cadillac's mask off, patted his face to gain his attention, and shouted in his ear. 'Breathe! Deeply!'

Cadillac did his best and showed no ill-effects. Steve tore his own mask off and tossed it away. Everyone else followed suit.

'Okay! Let's make tracks!' Steve pushed Cadillac into Kelso's arms. 'Stow him in the cargo bay. By the time he wakes up, we'll be halfway to Wyoming.'

Kelso hesitated. 'What about that store of goodies on the beach?'

Steve grabbed the tote-bag and backed away towards the second aircraft with Clearwater. 'Forget it, Dave! We can't afford to hang around!'

'Are you crazy? By the time we find Malone we're gonna be up to our asses in snow! We *need* some of that stuff! Look! Give us fifteen minutes to pick up as much as we can carry!'

'All right. But move it!'

Jodi and Kelso stowed Cadillac in the small cargo hold and ran off towards the beach leaving the hatch open. Steve helped Clearwater up into her seat in the cockpit, stowed the tote-bag, then limped over to Kelso's plane and started up the motor so they'd be ready to make an instant getaway. Where AMEXICO was concerned it was best not to take any chances.

*

Down on the beach, Kelso had jumped down into the waterproofed Aladdin's cave and was tossing out as many goodies as he could lay hands on. Medicaid kits, ration packs, filtration packs. There was enough to keep a bunch of guys alive this winter *and* the next.

Jodi knelt down, and gathered them up as fast as she could, stuffing them into a couple of zipper bags Kelso had found in the store. 'Dave! You've had eleven minutes. C'mon! Jack it in!'

Kelso threw out some more packs. 'Are the bags full?'

'Yeah! C'mon! Stop fuggin' around! We gotta get outa here!'

'Okay! You go ahead. If he sees you, he'll know I'm right behind!'

Jodi hauled the bag off the ground and looked down at Kelso. 'You got precisely three minutes and nineteen seconds! If you're not there, I'm leaving without you!'

'For chrissakes! I'm *comin*'!' Kelso started to clamber out of the underground store.

Jodi began a stumbling run up the track that led up through the dunes and on to the strip. Kelso knelt down with his back to her and raked a few more packs into the second zipper bag. When Jodi had disappeared from view, he reached down into the waistband of his tunic and pulled out Side-Winder's handset.

'Mayday, Mayday, Mayday. This is Rat-Catcher. Rat-Catcher to all Mother stations. Does anyone read me? Over.'

A crackle of static. 'Rat-Catcher. This is Sky-Bucket Three. We have your Mayday five by five. Activate your Find and Fix channel for Search and Rescue or state nature of emergency. Over.'

*

Kelso ran back across the grass with the bulging zipper bag perched on his shoulder. Steve and Clearwater sat beneath the closed canopy, helmeted, strapped in and ready to go. Kelso gave them the thumbs-up sign, then threw his bag of goodies into the cargo hold alongside the sleeping Cadillac and slammed the hatch shut. Jodi was in the pilot's seat. 'Move over!'

Jodi gritted her teeth and changed places. 'Where the hell've you been?'

'I'm here, aren't I? Gimme a break!' Kelso gunned the motor and ran quickly through the take-off checks as Jodi read them off the idiot board. They saw Steve turn his aircraft and taxi to the end of the grass strip. Kelso followed, drawing up at an angle beside him. He pulled on the helmet that BLACKWELL, B. had left in the cockpit. The pilots had left the plane-to-plane channel switched on.

Steve's voice came through the earphones. 'This is Big Open Airways, Flight One, ready to roll. How about you?'

'A-OK,' said Kelso. 'Let's burn the hay.'

*

Steve looked across at Clearwater and gave her hand a

486

reassuring squeeze. 'Frightened?'

'No,' her smile was composed, enigmatic. 'I always knew that one day we would fly away together.'

Steve selected fifteen degrees of flap, opened the throttle wide and released the brakes. The Sky-Rider dipped down on its nosewheel as it surged forward, then settled back and was soon skimming over the grass and out across the water. The eastern horizon had now turned golden yellow. Steve looked over his shoulder and saw the second Sky-Rider following him in a climbing turn to the west. For the first time in a long time he felt truly happy.

*

Some thirty minutes after the two Sky-Riders had left the strip at Long Point, a second pair came skimming in over the water from the south. They landed without making a circuit of the strip, and rolled to a stop close by the three immobilised mexicans.

The first pilot to reach them was carrying a special MX first-aid case. Opening it up, he took out a pack of pre-filled hypodermic syringes and gave each man an injection. It was the antidote to the crippling effects of the nerve gas and enabled a victim to recover fully within half an hour.

Eventually, Side-Winder and the two men tagged as BLACKWELL, B. and RITCHIE, K. were helped to their feet and, after a lot of coughing and spitting, took in healing draughts of fresh air.

'Boy,' breathed Side-Winder. 'That stuff's a real killer.' He reached inside his tunic and found the empty *sake* flask. *Ho, ho . . . Big joke*. He tossed it away. What the runaways didn't know was that AMEXICO would have the last laugh.

The second pilot returned to his machine and spoke over an open UHF link to an orbiting signals aircraft. 'Sky-Bucket Three to Cloud-Cover. Message for Mother. Hang-Fire airborne with Rat-Catcher and three targets, zero-six-fifteen. Acknowledge. Over.'

Commander Karlstrom left the central communications room and set off towards the White House to break the news personally to the President-General. So far so good. With a little help, Brickman had performed brilliantly. He had left the Iron Masters in no doubt that the Federation was a force to be reckoned with, and he had brought Cadillac and Clearwater back into play on the main board. He had even rescued a fellow mexican – Rat-Catcher – the 'renegade' he knew as Kelso.

Despite the years of programming, it was not possible to predict which way Brickman was going to jump but Kelso could be relied upon to make sure he didn't jeopardise the overall game-plan. And more subtle pressures could be applied through Roz. In their haste to get away Brickman's party had taken off without realising that Long Point held a store of fuel as well as food. The two Sky-Riders had already flown several hundred miles – which meant they would be forced down long before they reached Wyoming.

They would be landing in hostile territory but Kelso, a.k.a. Rat-Catcher had been told exactly where to aim for. After giving them a chance to get their bearings, they would find themselves surrounded by old friends. At which point, with or without Brickman's assistance, the next stage of the operation would begin . . .